A SCHOLAR'S
CONSCIENCE

ca. 1950, courtesy of the estate of J. Saunders Redding

A SCHOLAR'S CONSCIENCE

Selected Writings of
J. SAUNDERS REDDING
1942–1977

Edited with an Introduction by
FAITH BERRY

THE UNIVERSITY PRESS OF KENTUCKY

Unless otherwise specified, the material in this volume is reprinted by permission of J. Saunders Redding and his literary agent.

Copyright © 1992 by Faith Berry

Published by The University Press of Kentucky
Scholarly publisher for the Commonwealth,
serving Bellarmine College, Berea College, Centre
College of Kentucky, Eastern Kentucky University,
The Filson Club, Georgetown College, Kentucky
Historical Society, Kentucky State University,
Morehead State University, Murray State University,
Northern Kentucky University, Transylvania University,
University of Kentucky, University of Louisville,
and Western Kentucky University.

Editorial and Sales Offices: Lexington, Kentucky 40508-4008

Library of Congress Cataloging-in-Publication Data

Redding, J. Saunders (Jay Saunders), 1906-
    A scholar's conscience : selected writings of J. Saunders Redding,
1942-1977 / edited with an introduction by Faith Berry.
        p.   cm.
    Includes bibliographical references and index.
    ISBN 0-8131-1770-4 (alk. paper)—ISBN 0-8131-0806-3
(pbk. : alk. paper)
    1. Afro-Americans. 2. Afro-Americans—Fiction. 3. Redding, J.
Saunders (Jay Saunders), 1906-   . 4. Afro-Americans—Biography.
I. Berry, Faith. II. Title.
E185.R39   1991
973'.0496073—dc20   91-23200

This book is printed on acid-free paper meeting
the requirements of the American National Standard
for Permanence of Paper for Printed Library Materials.
                            ∞

To the family of the late

J. SAUNDERS REDDING

If modern scholars are to deserve the name of scholar—of moralist, of humanist, of philosopher—they must begin to show a vital concern with what happens to knowledge, with how it is used and why. The essence of true wisdom is distilled in the conscience. It is time that the scholars' conscience spoke out to the world.

J. Saunders Redding
American Scholar, 1953

CONTENTS

Books by Faith Berry

Good Morning Revolution: Uncollected Social Protest Writings by Langston Hughes (edited with introduction)

Langston Hughes: Before and Beyond Harlem, a biography

ACKNOWLEDGMENTS

Grateful acknowledgment is extended to the staff of the Library of Congress, where I began research for this manuscript. At the Strozier Library of Florida State University, where I completed my research, special thanks to the administrators and to the following staff members who made my task easier in numerous helpful ways: Elizabeth Fairley, Carolyn Reynolds, Tom Kupcek, and Chris Schappels, all of the Interlibrary Loan department, and Joseph Evans and Chester Wright of the Microfilms section.

For manuscript materials by and about J. Saunders Redding at Brown University and for gracious assistance in documenting information, I thank Martha Mitchell, university archivist of the John Hay Library.

I am grateful to Professor Charles Nichols of Brown University and Professors Elisabeth Muhlenfeld and Bertram Davis of Florida State University for reading portions of the manuscript and making helpful editorial comments.

At my institution, Florida Atlantic University, I was aided by the willing and efficient staff of the S.E. Wimberly Library. I am also indebted to Dean Sandra Norton of the College of Arts and Humanities and Mary Faraci, chairperson of the Department of English and Comparative Literature, for encouragement and cooperation during the production stage of the manuscript. An able and efficient graduate student, Jeannette Lawson, provided invaluable clerical assistance.

The project began as a labor of commitment without financial aid, although midway through I was the fortunate recipient of a fellowship from the McKnight Foundation/Florida Endowment Fund, which permitted additional research time and access to archives.

My thanks to Elizabeth McKee of Harold Matson Co. for her help during early stages of the manuscript.

I am indebted to J. Saunders Redding for his concurrence with my editorial selections, for making unpublished material available to me, and for permission to reprint "My Most Humiliating Jim Crow Experience," "The Negro Author: His Publisher, His Public and His Purse," "Richard Wright: An Evaluation," "The Negro Writer as Artist," "Of Men and the Writing of Books," "W.E.B. Du Bois: A Mind Matched with Spirit," "American Foreign Policy and the Third World" [Statement before Senate Foreign Relations Committee], an excerpt from "Some Remarks: On Humanism, the Humanities and Human Beings," "Absorption with Blackness Recalls Movement of the '20s," and excerpts from *No Day of Triumph*,

They Came in Chains, Stranger and Alone, On Being Negro in America, An American in India, and *The Lonesome Road.* Permission was also obtained from *Afro-American* newspapers for columns and book reviews; *American Scholar* for excerpts from "The Wonder and the Fear," "Report from India," "The Meaning of Bandung," and "Home to Africa"; *American Studies International* (formerly *American Studies: An International Newsletter*) for "The Black Revolution in American Studies"; *Crisis* for "The Black Arts Movement: A Modest Dissent"; Dodd, Mead and Co. and Jay Martin for a selection from *A Singer in the Dawn: Reinterpretations of Paul Laurence Dunbar,* edited by Jay Martin; *Mississippi Quarterly* for an excerpt of "James Weldon Johnson and the Pastoral Tradition"; and Morrow and Co., Stanton L. Wormley, and the Estate of the late Lewis H. Fenderson for "A Writer's Heritage."

My respectful appreciation to Mrs. Esther Redding for beneficial information at various stages of the manuscript and kind hospitality when I visited Ithaca, New York; my enduring homage to J. Saunders Redding, whose full cooperation and wise counsel gave me added incentive to complete this anthology, which he read but did not live to see in print.

To my parents, and family—thanks, as always, for being an inspiration.

INTRODUCTION

If black America can be said to have its modern Renaissance man, J. Saunders Redding clearly deserved that distinction. Though he wrote no drama or poetry, his work as novelist, essayist, biographer, historian, and critic was filled with both. One might say of him, as Dryden said of Shakespeare, that "when he describes anything, you more than see it, you feel it too." A Shakespearean scholar himself, Redding was, however, best known as one of the first great scholars of Afro-American literature.

He resisted the term "black scholar," in the conviction that humanists should not be defined by a color line. His own study of literature, far from being confined to race, covered instead a wide literary map in which national literatures, events, and authors do not exist in isolation. In practice, this means that as a critic he judged the poetry of Phillis Wheatley with an awareness of Alexander Pope, the novels of William Wells Brown with a knowledge of Charles Brockden Brown, and the speeches of Frederick Douglass with a recognition of William Lloyd Garrison. Redding traced the importance of literary development among a host of Afro-American writers in that same way, from the earliest known works of Jupiter Hammon in the eighteenth century to those of contemporary authors in the twentieth.

As social historian he examined American culture across racial and national boundaries, knowing that its meaning is most likely to be found in influences and confluences, both black and white, past and present. His writings probed the influence of the spirituals and blues on American culture, the relationship of Afro-American history to Afro-American literature, and the frequent exploitation and misrepresentation of racial material by Euro-American artists and writers. His conception of Afro-American culture was, above all else, an affirmation of its link to the American experience. Hence, his unyielding belief that it must be studied and assessed in that context.

He was born October 13, 1906, in Wilmington, Delaware, and christened James Thomas Saunders Redding, the third of seven children. His parents, Lewis Alfred and Mary Ann Holmes Redding, both graduates of Howard University, instilled in their children early the value of education.

Lewis Redding, a postal service worker, and Mary Ann Redding, a school-teacher turned housewife, would appear as unforgettable figures in two of their son's books. He wrote of his father with abiding reverence and devotion, and his mother with an adoration and sorrow that he had not known her longer. After her death when he was sixteen, Redding entered Lincoln University in Pennsylvania, spending one year there before trans-ferring to Brown, where he earned his Ph.B degree in 1928. At Brown, his academic standing made him eligible for the honorary society, Phi Beta Kappa. However, for racial reasons, the honor was not awarded him by the university until 1943—after he had achieved a national reputation as a writer. Paradoxically, the night before he went East to college, his father had told him: "Son . . . remember you're a Negro. You'll have to do twice as much twice better than your classmates." Redding later acknowledged that advice in *On Being Negro in America,* though it was perhaps too painful to unlock the truth that, for "twice as much twice better," it would take him fifteen years to receive his Phi Beta Kappa key.

To appreciate the complete Redding canon, it is necessary to place him and his work in historical perspective. He belongs to the turn-of-the-century generation that, give or take a few years, gave us the poet-critic Sterling Brown and the literary historians Arthur P. Davis and Ulysses Lee, three scholars who in 1941 produced the first comprehensive anthology of Afro-American literature, *The Negro Caravan.* They in turn were contem-poraries of such diverse and talented black writers as Arna Bontemps, Countee Cullen, Rudolph Fisher, Langston Hughes, Jean Toomer, and others whom an older scholar, Alain Locke, called "The New Negro Generation." Redding would become more an interpreter than a product of that literary movement known as the Harlem Renaissance. To some, however, he was considered part of the Renaissance as a young graduate student in New York during the early 1930s. Yet, he said later of that era in *On Being Negro in America,* "I had written and published professionally only one short story at that time. But the Negro art and literary 'renaissance' had not waned enough for those close to it to see that it was fading, and now and then, a completely unknown student, I basked in that artificial light like a homeless beggar keeping himself warm over a sidewalk grating" (72).

The one short story which he had published professionally was "Delaware Coon," a vignette full of modernist tropes about black gigolos and prostitutes. Its appearance in June 1930 in Eugene Jolas's Paris-based avant-garde journal, *transition: An International Quarterly of Creative Experi-ment,* put Redding in the table of contents with a coterie of European writers whose voices were already to be reckoned with: Tristan Tzara, Samuel Beckett, and Rainer Maria Rilke (by then deceased). "Delaware

Coon," however, was a story that, in subject matter, Redding's hardworking and conservative father thought traduced the race. Nearly a decade later the son made him proud by writing *To Make a Poet Black* and dedicating it "To my Father and the memory of my Mother."

To Make a Poet Black (1939), his first published book, was a pioneering critical work devoted exclusively to Afro-American literature at a time when few critics, black or white, were giving it much attention. In four chapters of commentary on selected authors and works from 1760 through the Harlem Renaissance, *To Make a Poet Black* offered the first historical and critical overview by an Afro-American. Going in a different direction than Benjamin Brawley's *The Negro in Literature and Art in the United States* (1918, 1929) or *The Negro Genius* (1937) or Vernon Loggins's *The Negro Author: His Development in America to 1900* (1931) or Nick Aaron Ford's *The Contemporary Negro Novel* (1936) or Sterling Brown's *The Negro in American Fiction* (1937), Redding made the first attempt to place not only authors but also genres and periods in a compendium of Afro-American literary history. As stated in his Preface, the book's objective was "to bring together certain factual material and critical opinion on American Negro literature in a sort of history of Negro thought in America" (vii). Toward that end, he provided a careful analysis and a seven-page bibliography. His emphasis was not on literature as art but as "literature either of purpose or necessity" (vii). With "a mind for the problems of students," he acknowledged a hope that " 'the odor of scholarship' attaches to [the book] so slightly as to give it some appeal to popular taste" (viii). Hence, by modern critical standards, *To Make a Poet Black* is not an extensive or comprehensive study but a valuable reference work that remains a classic in its field. Because its commentary is best read in its full context, the book is not excerpted in this anthology.

His first book, and aforementioned first story, would bear his name preceded by the initial "J." for the name Jay, which he often was called by relatives during his youth. He never signed his prenames James or Thomas to his writings or professional documents. Except for his novel, all his subsequent books and many of his writings for nearly three decades were printed under the middle name he personally preferred as a nom de plume: Saunders Redding. Around 1968, at the urging of family members, he restored "J." to his by-line. The title of this anthology includes it at his request.

Of the Afro-American scholar-critics of his generation—almost all of them also academics—Redding is the only one who, to date, has published an autobiographical work. In doing so, he chronicled not only his family history but a personal odyssey in an America coming of age. Few black intellectuals, before or since, have shared as much of their own heart or mind through the printed word, or written in as many different genres.

Redding wrote of his family in the first chapter of his second book, *No Day of Triumph* (1942). Those autobiographical reminiscences, as skillfully and sensitively written as a bildungsroman, are included in Part I of this anthology. The remainder of *No Day of Triumph* relates his journey through the South and the conditions he found there among black residents on the eve of World War II. The book, commissioned by the University of North Carolina and written on a fellowship from the Rockefeller Foundation, won the North Carolina Historical Society's 1944 Mayflower Award for "Distinguished Writing" by a resident of the state. It was widely acclaimed by critics and also praised by the novelist Richard Wright, who wrote the Introduction. Then famous for his 1940 novel, *Native Son*, Wright said of *No Day of Triumph*: "Redding is the first middle-class Negro to break with the ideology of the 'Talented Tenth' in a complete and final manner. Some may feel that he tears down more than he builds, but that is beside the point. Redding's main task is to expose, exhibit, declare, and he does this job in a dramatic and unforgettable manner, offering his own life as evidence."

By "Talented Tenth," Wright referred to a term first introduced in 1903 by W.E.B. Du Bois, meaning "the educated and intelligent of the Negro people that have led and educated the mass."[1] Wright's postulate that Redding broke with "the ideology of the 'Talented Tenth,'" was not quite true, for Redding agreed with Du Bois. What Redding did not agree with was "the unimaginative, predatory, pretentious" atmosphere in some black institutions of higher learning, whose "Negro schoolmen" he did not hesitate to label the "true bourgeoisie" (*No Day of Triumph*, 42). With few notable exceptions, during his early career he found black college administrators "a bulwark against positive action, liberal or even independent thought, and spiritual and economic freedom" (119-20). That theme runs deep elsewhere in his writings, notably in his novel *Stranger and Alone* and his memoir, *On Being Negro in America*. In the latter, he asserts in no uncertain terms that "Negro colleges have tended to breed fascism" and that some Negro college presidents "play the strongman and the dictator role" (91).

Such views led to dismissal from his first faculty position, at Morehouse College in Atlanta, after three years of teaching, later vividly described in *No Day of Triumph*. Following his stint at Morehouse, he returned to Brown and completed his M.A. in English and American Literature in 1932. Further graduate study followed at Columbia University between 1932 and 1934 with the help of a scholarship and the earnings of his wife,

Esther James Redding, whom he married in 1929. At the height of the economic depression, he reentered academia as an instructor of English.

For most of the next thirty-one years his academic career was spent in black colleges in the South: Louisville Municipal College, as instructor from 1934 to 1936; Southern University, in Baton Rouge, from 1936 to 1938, as chairman of the English department; Elizabeth City State College in North Carolina, as chairman until 1943, when he joined the faculty at Hampton Institute. He remained at Hampton for twenty-two years, the last nine as James Weldon Johnson Professor of Creative Writing.

His early academic employment opportunities were not unlike those of most Afro-American college educators of his generation. Trained in prestigious white colleges and universities, distinguished black academicians were rarely invited to teach in those institutions until the late 1960s, except as "visiting professors." Among rare exceptions were the late and eminent sociologist Ira De A. Reid, who was professor and chairman of the Department of Sociology at Haverford College from 1947 to 1968, and the late W. Allison Davis, the pioneering social anthropologist and author who served on the graduate faculty at the University of Chicago from 1939 until his death in 1983. But on the whole, in the American racial climate of that era, white educators largely ignored black scholars, even if a scholar happened to be a Phi Beta Kappa, a Rhodes Scholar, or a Ph.D. As Redding's experience shows, one could attain Phi Beta Kappa and receive it only belatedly. He never undertook a doctorate, preferring to concentrate on his writing. Ultimately, for his achievement as author and educator, he was the recipient of eight honorary doctoral degrees, including one from his alma mater. From 1970 until his retirement in 1975, he held the endowed Ernest I. White Chair of American Studies and Humane Letters at Cornell University.

Had he been offered the choice, he would have devoted his literary career more to writing fiction than scholarly books. In his informed historical study, *They Came in Chains: Americans from Africa* (1950, 1973), he used his considerable literary gifts to make history as compelling as a novel. Tracing the evolution of Afro-Americans from slaves to citizens in that book, he brought events and people into dramatic conflict through the economic and social forces that shaped their destiny. The twenty Africans who came in chains to Jamestown, Virginia, in 1619 came to life through Redding's interpretation of their legacy. Although the critic-historian Oscar Handlin commented in the *New York Times Review* that the "nature of the tragedy is not made clear," other critics acknowledged the book's scholarly merits, and the *New York Herald Tribune Books* found in it "the motivation, conflict, suspense and inevitability of the best adventure fiction." [2]

In 1950, Redding also published his first novel, *Stranger and Alone*, written with the help of a Guggenheim Fellowship. Originally intended as the first in a trilogy, *Stranger and Alone* has as its protagonist Shelton Howden, a "half-white nigger bastard" (14), who allows himself to be manipulated by southern politicians to exploit his own people. Obliquely, this central character was intended to reveal certain characteristics of Booker T. Washington, a figure whose social philosophy and duplicitous modus operandi Redding loathed with a passion, as is clearly revealed in his nonfiction writings about Washington. Howden is shown with few redeeming qualities, from his earliest student days at southern, "Christian" New Hope College, whose mission, according to its founding white president, is to "devote itself to the education of mulattos who in turn, imbued with the true Christian spirit, will go out and serve the degraded blacks to whom they are brothers in Christ." The book's color-conscious thesis carries Howden to Arcadia State College for Negroes, where, under the tutelage of the authoritarian President Wimbush, a blue-eyed mulatto contemptuous of "darkies," Howden is molded into "the first full-time supervisor of Niggra schools in the state" and finally to a betrayal of his race. The book, on the whole, was less widely appreciated by the reading public than by critics. Ralph Ellison, then two years away from publication of his acclaimed novel *Invisible Man*, praised *Stranger and Alone* in the *New York Times Book Review*, calling it "a vastly important job of reporting the little known role of those Negro 'leaders' who by collaborating with the despoilers of the South do insidious damage to us all." [3] Two decades later, however, Redding's literary colleague and friend, Arthur P. Davis, in *From the Dark Tower: Afro-American Writers 1900 to 1960*, called Redding's *Stranger and Alone* "perhaps his most glaring mistake in judgment." [4]

His 1950 novel—which is excerpted in this volume—should not be evaluated by modernist or postmodernist abstract theories of whether the narrative is crafted as mythic or symbolic fiction or motivated by semiotic codes. He was attempting no new literary experiments in *Stranger and Alone*. The novel is written as literary realism; its theory is mimetic and its verisimilitude is within the text. The novel is not autobiographical, although readers may find the protagonist's conflicts with race and class similar to conflicts Redding himself acknowledges in other writings.

In 1951 he published a still more controversial book, *On Being Negro in America*, his most personal commentary on race relations. It included a poignant though unfulfilled pronouncement, which those who read it are unlikely to forget: "I hope this piece will stand as the epilogue to whatever contribution I have made to the 'literature of race.' I want to get on to other things. I do not know whether I can make this clear, but the obligations

imposed by race on the average educated or talented Negro . . . are vast
and become at last onerous. I am tired of giving up my creative initiative to
these demands. I think I am not alone" (26).

In spite of this valedictory, *On Being Negro in America* was hardly his
epilogue on race. Shortly after the book was published, he was invited as an
exchange lecturer to India by the State Department. The trip resulted in
his sixth book, *An American in India* (1954). The three-month journey gave
him his first view of the Third World, a term not then in use, though it was
soon to find political expression at the 1955 Asian-African Conference in
Bandung—about which he wrote an essay, which is excerpted in this
anthology. The Bandung Conference gave added meaning to what he
discovered about racialism and colonialism in India, as well as new cre-
dence to the W.E.B. Du Bois prophecy that "the problem of the twentieth
century is the problem of the color line." [5]

Events in the United States, in the aftermath of the 1954 Supreme
Court desegregation decision, caused him to concentrate on his seventh
book, *The Lonesome Road*, subtitled *The Story of the Negro's Part in America*.
Commissioned for the Doubleday Mainstream of America Series and published in 1958, it narrated the saga of race relations through biographical
portraits of little-known and well-known Afro-Americans: abolitionists,
soldiers, clergy, labor leaders, doctors, lawyers, journalists, civil rights
leaders, and sports figures. Excerpts are in Part III of this volume.

In 1962, Redding spent six months on a lecture tour in Africa and wrote
a series of weekly articles in the *Afro-American*. His articles offered black
Americans a firsthand glimpse of newly independent African nations, and
his lectures gave Africans an interpretation of black America. He spoke at
universities in West and East Africa and traveled in Southern Africa, under
the auspices of the American Society of African Culture (AMSAC). Five
years later, he and other AMSAC members would learn, to their con-
sternation, that the organization was one of numerous organizations secretly funded as a conduit by the Central Intelligence Agency (CIA)—a
fact that signaled AMSAC's end after less than a decade of existence.

Redding's sojourn in Africa showed him that the continent never was
what it was depicted to be in most American movies and books, as he
acknowledges in essays in Part VI of this volume. His travel experience,
however, did not transform him into a Pan Africanist. The decade of the
1960s, with its many social changes, brought him closer to his American
past then to his African roots. He reflected that attitude in many of his
lectures and articles, some of which are included in Part VII.

His last book appeared in 1967, under the title *Negro*, a 101-page treatise
covering historical events leading up to the civil rights demonstrations and

legislation of the 1960s. Commissioned by Potomac Books for "The U.S.A. Survey Series," the slim volume coincidentally appeared in a year during which fires raged through black urban ghettos in acts of civil disobedience covered widely by the media. At the time, Redding's *They Came in Chains* and *The Lonesome Road* were both out of print, as were many other historical, biographical, and sociological studies that would have shed light on those dark days. Not until a few years later, in the wake of militant nationwide demonstrations by black college students for courses and books relevant to their culture identity, did a host of ethnic publications, including new and reprinted titles, become available.

Redding's essays of the 1970s on such issues as "black studies" do not establish a link between those studies and his own career. But there was an inevitable link. In early 1968 in Washington, D.C., while director of the Division of Publication and Research at the National Endowment for the Humanities (NEH), he gave little attention to an incident that most of the nation's capital also ignored at the time. That spring, some 1,000 under-graduates at Howard University seized control of the institution for four days, occupying the administration building and every campus facility from the parking lot to the switchboard, demanding that the school address certain political grievances and be renamed "Black University" or, as some hoped, "Sterling Brown University." The unprecedented action gained little national attention until the tactic of occupying buildings spread like wildfire to Columbia University. Nevertheless, the strategy of "occupation," first by Howard students, then by black Bowie State College students in nearby Maryland, and within weeks by both black and white students at Columbia, soon hit other campuses with a momentum that shook the foundations of American academia. Saunders Redding, then widely considered the "Dean of Afro-American Scholars," was among the immediate beneficiaries of that momentum. As publishers scurried to add titles on the black experience to their lists, three of Redding's books were rushed back into print. And as college administrators looked for a black presence to add to their faculty, he was among those they hastened to hire. For the academic year 1968-69, he served on the faculty of George Washington University and lectured widely at other institutions. In 1970 he joined the English department at Cornell, the first Afro-American to be appointed to the rank of professor in the College of Arts and Sciences and the first to hold an endowed chair. Earlier, during the mid-1960s, he had served one year as a fellow in the humanities at Duke University, and over a decade earlier as a visiting lecturer at Brown, but it was, more directly than not, the student protests of the late 1960s that finally brought him more invitations from white institutions than he could ever accept. He accepted an appointment to the Cornell faculty, aware that the university faced a crisis when, in April 1969, a group of armed black collegians forcibly occupied a campus center for thirty-six hours.

In an era when slogans such as "Black Power," "Black Revolution," the "Black Aesthetic," and "Black is Beautiful" were being heard throughout the land, Redding had his own interpretation of what they meant—and it was often at odds with that of a younger, more militant generation. Like his older colleague, the late historian Rayford Logan, and their younger colleague, Ralph Ellison, Redding held on to the word "Negro" when it was quickly being displaced by "black." If he remembered when the connotation of the latter word held less dignity than scorn, he was unable to convince some members of a younger generation that blackness did not mean only semantics, name changes, dashikis, Afro hairdos, and an Afrocentric approach to literature and history. Redding heard a different drummer, and he had no intention of changing his message or cultural convictions to fit the trends of the times or the notions of his students.

In certain ways he has been a solitary figure in the black and white academic literary worlds, and it is not insignificant that his books bear such titles as *Stranger and Alone* and *The Lonesome Road*. Few American writers have fought as lonely a battle on two racial fronts. Yet, during a time of increased Afro-American awareness and cultural identity, Redding's voluminous writings have received little serious attention from contemporary students and scholars. Significantly, however, two of his books—*To Make A Poet Black* and *Stranger and Alone*—have been reprinted posthumously with critical introductions. But he has been the subject of no full-scale critical book or biography.

The lack of critical interest in his work is no mystery. His open opposition to the "black aesthetic" movement, which began in the late 1960s and gained momentum in the 1970s, alienated him from some of its defenders and disciples. To them he was too conservative, and to him they were racial chauvinists. In various pieces, including two represented in this collection—"The Black Revolution in American Studies" and "The Black Arts Movement: A Modest Dissent"—he clearly dissociated himself from the black aesthetic philosophy.

He respected but disagreed intellectually with several younger Afro-American critics and editors, such as the late Larry Neal, poet and early theoretician of the black aesthetic movement; the late Hoyt Fuller, influential editor of *Negro Digest* (renamed *Black World*) and *First World;* and the late novelist Julian Mayfield, briefly writer-in-residence at the Cornell University Africana Studies and Research Center (where Redding had no official affiliation as a Cornell professor).

A staunch integrationist, he refused an "imperium in imperio"—
"nation within a nation"—in his vision of ethnic studies, at Cornell and
elsewhere. During two decades as a professor at traditionally black
Hampton Institute, he did not offer classes on "Negro Literature," preferring instead to integrate black authors into the curriculum. That outlook
was apparent as early as 1939 in his pioneering interpretive study, *To Make a
Poet Black*. In the Preface to that work, he notes the importance of literary
development among Negroes in the context of "the general tide of American life." He believed then, and later, that "the profound influence of the
spirituals and other folk matter upon native culture was not fully realized"
(vii). He considered it his duty to show the extent of that influence.
However, his insistence that Afro-American writing and culture be studied
in the context of American life and literature continues to cause controversy. Amiri Baraka angrily penned "A Reply to Saunders Redding's 'The
Black Revolution in American Studies.' " [6] If some of Redding's ideas made
him unpopular, he preferred to remain unpopular rather than to change
them. The teacher who was too "radical" for Morehouse College in the late
1920s seemed almost anachronistically conservative to a new literary generation after the 1960s.

His writings were at the pinnacle of their success in the early 1950s—an
era of pre-civil rights demonstrations and sit-ins—when Afro-American
writers and intellectuals encountered only token recognition from white
editors and publishers. With answers to the "Negro problem" then solic-
ited mostly from white liberals (including foreigners such as the Swedish
economist-sociologist Gunnar Myrdal, author of the 1944 race relations
study, *The American Dilemma*), Redding emerged at a propitious hour as a
writer and critic on racial issues. In manner, education, intellect, and attire,
he fit none of the prevailing stereotypes that most white Americans had of
blacks as second-class citizens. He often wrote as if he were on a mission
to reeducate a nation about the lives and literature and history of a people
who had been erased from standard Americana and often caricatured on
stage and screen. His works were timely, and many of his best paralleled
and illuminated the rise of the civil rights movement. His hopes and
aspirations for equal opportunity and justice, however, always meant assim-
ilation, and he could not understand or accept the call of more radical black
voices who retreated from that position.

The development of his thought and aesthetic was pluralistic and
assimilationist, a pattern that was neither Eurocentric nor Afrocentric but
Americentric. The process was linear, moving in a straight direction,
throughout his four decades as a writer. Literary and political Garveyism—
call it "black nationalism"—had no place in his credo, either at the begin-

ning or the end of his career. His mission, both in fiction and in non-fiction, was shaped by an American ethos. Yet he resisted being hierarchical or patriarchal or gender-biased in his values. Atypical of most male critics—black or white—he respected women writers as his equals; as book editor of the *Afro-American*, he frequently reviewed books by and about them. He proved himself a male feminist at a time when many men expected women to use typewriters to be secretaries, not authors.

He took pride in being a detached, dispassionate critic—as aloof as a clinician in a laboratory. But he could not remain detached and aloof from the rapid political and cultural change in American society during the last two decades of his life. He opposed the Vietnam War, though there is nothing in his late literary canon to show it. Even in a public political statement in 1976 on Afro-American attitudes toward United States foreign policy, he attempted the posture of a disassociated political observer. Having witnessed the establishment outcry toward prominent black opponents of American policy in Vietnam—and the earlier persona non grata status of W.E.B. DuBois and Paul Robeson for their international politics—Redding was careful never to venture too far left of center in print. Some of his early and late political pieces carry the tone of the 1950s Cold War rhetoric of Allen and John Foster Dulles. Nothing he wrote subjected him to the inquisitions of the United States House or Senate anticommunist witch-hunts.

Although politically more liberal than conservative, he never really made the transition from the 1950s into the more turbulent 1960s. His early writings about racial and political issues, compared to some of his later ones, appear like good wine turned to vinegar. His failure was in not recognizing that some of his work had turned sour.

Most contemporary book publishers, content to follow popular trends, have either forgotten or chosen to ignore him, as if his literary sun had faded on the horizon. However, it is an irony that this major partisan of racial integration is largely absent from standard American anthologies integrated for classroom use. Instead, he is represented in several significant volumes of Afro-American literature (see the selected bibliography in this volume). One is *Cavalcade: Negro American Writing from 1760 to the Present*, a college text, which he edited with Arthur P. Davis for publication in 1971 out of a demand for a collection for Afro-American studies.

If one had asked Redding which author he most admired in literature, the answer undoubtedly would have been the writer he also considered a cultural hero: W.E.B. Du Bois. He wrote several pieces about the elder writer, including a final reminiscence that is reproduced in this anthology. Literary history, especially Afro-American literary history, is replete with examples of authors who received more cheers from posterity than they did in their own lifetime. Du Bois, in some ways, is one of them, and Redding may yet be another. It is not unrealistic to suggest that perhaps his most appreciative readers may be in the future, whose who will weigh his entire canon on its merit and judge the conditions that produced it.

If his contribution remains to be assessed, his literary achievement and reputation cannot be denied. He remains one of the few Afro-American authors ever listed in *Who's Who in the World,* even if only two of his eight book titles are currently listed in *Books in Print.*

A survey of twentieth-century Afro-American literary criticism reveals that most black critics have reflected whatever literary theories are popular. Redding did not. As man of letters he ignored those theoretical schools, some of which last only a little longer than an academic semester. He never tried to keep step with the New Criticism of the 1940s and 1950s, and he paid little attention to the linguistic terminology of Structuralism and Post-Structuralism. For twenty years, from 1946 to 1966, he wrote a weekly book review column for the *Afro-American,* setting his own style for the function of criticism. He did likewise as contributor to *American Mercury, American Scholar, Atlantic Monthly, New York Herald Tribune Books, New York Times Book Review, Phylon, Saturday Review of Literature,* and other periodicals. He may properly be called a literary critic but not a literary theorist. If one places him in the tradition of the English classical education that shaped him, he comes closer to being a practical critic such as Samuel Johnson than a theorist such as Samuel Taylor Coleridge. Raised hearing his father read from the Bible and *The Crisis,* his grandmother recite from *The Book of Common Prayer,* his mother quote the poetry of Whittier and Whitman, and his college teachers demonstrate Hugh Blair's *Lectures on Rhetoric and Belles Lettres,* Redding as a critic was intent on communicating an understanding and appreciation of literature to his readers. Contemporary linguistic theories were not part of his vocabulary or his literary style.

One of his ideological adversaries, black author Harold Cruse, wrote in *Rebellion or Revolution* (1968) that "Redding is Negro literature's only claim to any lustre in literary criticism *qua* criticism. That he doesn't shine brilliantly like Edmund Wilson is nobody's fault but his own—he apparently is simply afraid to shine."[7] Perhaps the one thing Redding was least afraid to do was to shine. When his career was at its height, one might say that it shone brightly. For other writers and academicians, and most of all for himself, he insisted on the highest standards of literary and scholarly excellence. Few Afro-American authors have had as many accolades from as many sources: two Guggenheim Fellowships; two terms on the editorial board of the *American Scholar*; a Fulbright Fellowship; an advisory appointment to the Center for Advanced Studies at the University of Virginia; membership on the Board of the Center for Advanced Studies of the American Council of Learned Societies and on the fiction committee of the National Book Awards; selection as honorary consultant on American culture to the Library of Congress and on the Scholarly Worth Editorial Committee of the Howard University Press; service from 1961 to 1981 as a Fellow of the Brown University Corporation, on which he served as Emeritus Fellow until his death. In 1986, Cornell University established in his honor the J. Saunders Redding Fellowship for minority students.

As author, critic, educator and humanist, he served education and the humanities with what F.R. Leavis would call the "central humanity." His belief in the strength of the humanities to heal, nourish and enrich, is manifested in his essay "Some Remarks on Humanism, the Humanities and Human Beings," which is included in these pages. His own experience as a human being included what W.E.B. Du Bois in *The Souls of Black Folk* called the "double consciousness": "his twoness,—an American, a Negro; two souls, two thoughts, two unreconciled strivings."[8]

The writings gathered here attempt to give recognition to his significant contribution to American letters. To become familiar with his canon is to discover not only his "twoness" but the meaning of his heritage, the lesson of his experience, and the richness and beauty of his language.

He is perhaps the writer of his generation who best represents, and comes closest to explaining, the hopes and conflicts of American democracy in a multiracial society, through a legacy of books and articles penned in some of the most memorable and lasting prose of our time.

Following a lingering illness that resulted in loss of memory, Redding died of heart failure at his home in Ithaca, New York, on March 2, 1988, with his wife Esther and a hospice nurse at his bedside. He was eighty-one years old.

—Faith Berry

---

1. W.E.B. Du Bois, "The Talented Tenth, " in *The Negro Problem: A Series of Articles by Representative Negroes of Today*, ed. Booker T. Washington. (New York: Pott, 1903; New York: Arno, 1969).

2. Oscar Handlin, Review of *They Came in Chains*, by [J.] Saunders Redding, *New York Times Book Review*, July 30, 1950, 7; and W. T. Hedden, Review of *They Came in Chains*, by [J.] Saunders Redding, *New York Herald Tribune Books*, July 16, 1950, 6.

3. Ralph Ellison, Review of *Stranger and Alone*, by J. Saunders Redding, *New York Times Book Review*, Feb. 19, 1950, 4.

4. Arthur P. Davis, *From the Dark Tower: Afro-American Writers 1900 to 1960*. (Washington, D.C.: Howard Univ. Press, 1974) 160.

5. W.E.B. Du Bois, "Of the Dawn of Freedom," in *The Souls of Black Folk* (Chicago: McClurg, 1903), 23, 41.

6. Amiri Baraka, "A Reply to Saunders Redding's 'The Black Revolution in American Studies,'" in *Sources for American Studies*, ed. Jefferson B. Kellog and Robert H. Walker (Westport: Greenwood, 1983), 15-24.

7. Harold Cruse, *Rebellion or Revolution* (New York: Morrow, 1968), 24.

8. W.E.B. Du Bois, "Of Our Spiritual Strivings," in *The Souls of Black Folk*, 17.

I

AUTOBIOGRAPHICAL SELECTIONS

Through the four autobiographical reminiscences in Part I, including excerpts from *No Day of Triumph* and *On Being Negro in America*, Redding pens a personal and racial manifesto of the compelling influences, values, and experiences that shaped him as a writer and as an American.

A WRITER'S HERITAGE

I did not set out to be a writer. I doubt that anyone sets out to be what he eventually becomes—a lawyer, politician, priest, or pimp; a good person or a bad; cruel or compassionate; strong or weak. We become what we are by a complex of conditioned instincts first, then by circumstance and chance, and then—but always last, and only sometimes—by taking thought. Circumscribed by natural inheritance, one has almost no choice as to the *kind* of person he will be, free will notwithstanding, and really damned little choice as to *what* he will be. Fitting together the disparate elements of model-image, talent, opportunity, training, motivation, and desire, and getting an answer as to what to be is not easy, and most people never attempt it. Most never "set out" on a predetermined direction. Most drift.

One might be lucky and have some wise, deeply interested person (parent, teacher), who is also patient and commanding, discover what his bent or hidden talent is, and then proceed to motivate, train, cajole, and whip him toward what he can best be. But how many youngsters are that lucky? And what one can best be is not necessarily what he wants to be. He's more than lucky—he's some kind god's favored child—if what he can best be is also what he wants to be. Besides, students of adolescent psychology and high school counselors tell us that the time when youngsters should begin preparing to be what they have greatest aptitude for and can best be is the very time also when they want to be so many things that if they had a real choice they couldn't make it.

I wanted to be a lot of things before I wanted to be a writer. I wanted to be a detective, a traveling evangelist, a hobo, a prizefighter, and a merchant. I had a model-image for each of these, and even now could describe the circumstances under which each one inspired me to emulation. The wish to be a merchant stayed with me longest. A merchant was an acquaintance of my father's, intimately known as a frequent caller at our house. "Merchant" was my maternal grandmother's word, and the household adopted it. Anyone who sold anything was a "merchant," who might also be defined by what he sold and where. There were, for instance, street merchants (whom everyone else called hucksters) and commission merchants, fish merchants, candy merchants, coal merchants, and dry goods merchants. (My maternal grandmother had a lot of language, and all of it was elegant and precious. My paternal grandmother had little language, but all of it was earthy, strong. One spoke of her *limbs;* the other of her *legs* and *shanks*. One spoke of *passing;* the other spoke of *death*. We did not see much of Grandma Redding, but Grandma Conway-Holmes we saw for a month at a stretch every year and at least two weeks every summer.)

Anyway, my model-image merchant, Mr. Raikes, had an establishment called an "emporium," and he dealt in every conceivable second-hand thing—including, my mother used to say, soap. But how my mother would have known this I can't imagine, since Raikes' Emporium was way down on the east side in the "Bridge District," where, so far as I know, my mother and my sisters never went. Mr. Raikes sold clothing and footwear, furniture, beds and bedding, stoves and cooking utensils, sporting goods, and hairpieces—all second hand, but, his monthly handbill said, "guaranteed like new." "Mr. Raikes," my father explained, "sells what colored people can afford to buy."

But Mr. Raikes himself seemed to buy—or at least to acquire—things even few white people could afford. In winter he wore an overcoat collared and lined with luxurious fur. His suits, my father said, were made by Delgrano Brothers, the custom tailors, where the lowest prices were sky-high; his shoes were hand-sewn. He bought the first Peerless Six automobile—a dark green beauty—I ever knew a colored man to own. I thought he was matchlessly wealthy, in a class with the DuPonts; and I thought, too, that the admonitions that rolled off his tongue were matchless gems of wisdom. "Perseverance, that's the winning ticket," he would say, and tapping me on the forehead with a long finger, "Early to bed, early to rise makes a man healthy, wealthy and wise." For weeks I nearly killed myself getting up before dawn.

One day—and for several days—there was dinner-table talk between my mother and father about things which I did not understand—"creditors," "litigation," "collateral," "mortgages overdue"—except that they somehow pertained to Mr. Raikes. It was at about this time that the emporium was boarded up, and Mr. Raikes himself disappeared, and I stopped wanting to be a merchant.

It did not occur to me to want to be a writer even after an essay of mine won a prize given by the short-lived Negro weekly, the Wilmington *Advocate*, for the "best essay written by a high school student." Since the contest was closed to whites, there couldn't have been much competition. I was a high school junior then—one of fourteen classmates—and there were only fifty-one students in all four-year high school classes, and even if all these had entered the competition, which of course they hadn't, it couldn't have been called tough.

I can't remember what my essay was all about. Indeed, I can't now imagine what subject could have moved and interested me so much as to make me write on it. I remember that my father had just bought an Oliver typewriter for us, and a likely explanation is that my interest was less in *writing* than in *typewriting*. It is more than likely, too, that a good bit that went into that essay was simply a crude reflection of my reading—was, in short, cribbed. But if it was, Alice Dunbar Nelson, who judged the contest, did not discover it.

Mrs. Nelson was my high school English teacher and a family friend. (Lest it be thought that friendship had a bearing on her literary judgment in the essay competition, let me hasten to say that the writers' names did not appear on the essays. Each was identified by a number designating a name known only to the contest director.) A flaming redhead of statuesque figure, she was quite a woman. She might have been my model-image of a writer, had I been perceptive enough to have wanted one or to have felt the need for one (and if I could have disregarded the fact that she was a woman). She was a writer—a poet, and, although not widely known as such even locally, a published poet. A slim, autographed copy of her poems graced the bookcase in our back parlor, along with most of the volumes of her late first husband, Paul Laurence Dunbar. One other writer who could be identified as Negro was represented in our bookcase, and to this day I treasure first editions of *The Souls of Black Folk* (which my father owned before I was born), *The Quest of the Silver Fleece*, and *Dark Princess*.

My mother was also something of a poet—though "rhymester" was the word she used. She would compose rhymes for special family occasions, such as birthdays and holidays, and she would make up new lines to go with old tunes, and many a dinner time was made gaily raucous with all of us singing—each in a different key—"Gimme some old time molasses, gimme some old time molasses, it's bound to cure me. It was good for Uncle Rastus," etc., to the tune of "That Old Time Religion." My mother hated sad songs and solemn words. Her wit ran to the satirical, the amusing, and only rarely to the reverent.

When I fell irrevocably in love every fifth or sixth day in my fourteenth year, I tried writing poetry. (Doesn't every boy?) And of course I wrote letters by the ream of my heart's ephemeral liege, pledging undying love. Love was sweet, but love was very painful, and I suppose I realized in some subconscious way that writing about love to my love modified the pain and made it bearable. Also, I enjoyed the responses my letters drew, when they drew them, which was seldom. It seemed that none of the girls I loved cared a thing about me. The quest was fun. Conquest, I'm sure, would have troubled me.

Nothing troubled me until I went to college in New England. I turned seventeen that fall. There were three other Negroes. Two of them were seniors, and one a sophomore, who did not return after Christmas and who killed himself a few months later. We Negroes were aliens, and we knew it, and the knowledge forced us to assume postures of defense and to take on a sort of double-consciousness. It was not a matter of real ambivalence, or a question of identity: we knew who we were. But we feared to act ourselves, feared to "act the nigger," whatever that meant. Where the knowledge that induced this fear came from—for certainly it was a knowledge unconsciously learned—we did not know. All we knew was that it was deeply troubling, and that neither the cramming for high marks (for a sense of competition with the whites was fierce, psychotic), nor the ritualistic excesses of our race-brotherhood, nor the hysterical bouts of party-going in New Haven, Springfield, and Boston was exorcism. It was then that I began to write out of what I have since called my "Negroness." It was all I had, and all I still have, and all any colored person born and reared and schooled in America has to write out of if he pretends to honesty; and all any colored person so born and reared and schooled has to act out of too. To think otherwise is a delusion; to feel otherwise is fakery.

"A Writer's Heritage" appeared in Stanton Wormley and Lewis Fenderson, eds., *Many Shades of Black* (New York: Morrow, 1969), 87-91.

FROM *NO DAY OF TRIUMPH*

As far back as I can remember, it was necessary for my father to eke out his small government salary by doing all sorts of odd jobs after his regular hours and in his vacations. He belonged to a waiters' association, and frequently he served at dinners, banquets, and parties from early evening until dawn. On these occasions he wore the swallow-tailed coat in which he had been married and the black broadcloth trousers which he had picked up at a secondhand shop. This outfit always amused us, for the trousers did not cover his ankles and his big feet spread beneath them in a truly monumental fashion. The coat had a greenish tinge and fitted across his thick shoulders like a harness. My mother had to sew up the shoulder seams after every use. My father cared little about the appearance of his clothes. "So long as they're clean, children," he used to say, when for reasons of pride we used to fidget with his tie, fold down his collars, and see to it that he was wearing a proper belt in his trousers. Our attentions amused him, and he would wink at our mother and say, "Girl, they've all got your side's pride."

Sometimes he would bring from these parties a satchel bulging with steaks, chicken, butter, rolls, and ice cream; and then we feasted—not because we ever went hungry, but because all this was extra and had to be eaten before it spoiled.

My father always took his annual vacation in the late summer or early fall, for then he could find employment among the farmers a few miles outside the city. He would contract to cut corn or harvest potatoes. Sometimes he stayed in the country, but when he did not, he was always back long after we were in bed and gone again before dawn. Often my brother and I, in the room next the bathroom, would wake up in the night and hear my father thrashing about in the tub and murmuring wearily to my mother, who always waited for him late in the night.

As I look back upon it now, I know that my father was driven by more than the necessity to provide a living for his family. Surrounded by whites both at home and at work, he was driven by an intangible something, a merciless, argus-eyed spiritual enemy that stalked his every movement and lurked in every corner. It goaded him every waking hour, but he could not get at it, though he felt it to be embodied in almost every white man he met. Because of this, he moved with defensive caution, calculating the effect of every action and every utterance upon his unseen enemy. Every day he won defensive victories, but every day the final victory seemed more impossible. He was up at dawn, painting the trim, repairing the roof, putting out ashes, shoveling snow from the sidewalk. In fifteen years he was never late for his work, and only once did he allow an illness to keep him home. His endurance was a thing of the spirit.

But the other necessity was there too, the physical need to provide for a family that soon increased to seven. We were a problem. We helled through our clothes, and especially our shoes. My father mended our shoes with thick leather patches that balled clumsily on the soles. He trimmed our hair. When it seemed safe, he avoided doctor's bills by purging us with castor oil, plastering us with goose grease, and swathing us in flannel. I myself was often sick with ruinous colds that threatened a serious illness. I was almost constantly under the care of Dr. Elbert, who spent his time thumping my chest and giving me nauseating medicines. But no saving was too trifling, no economy too stringent for my father to make. Sometimes it was a joking matter. Our garbage pail seldom contained anything but vegetable parings and bones, for my mother, too, knew the value of a penny. Indeed, her thrift was generally more effective and yet less severe than my father's. She had a reasonableness in the matter which he lacked. Sometimes she raised objections— futilely, for instance, to my father's spending his vacation harvesting potatoes or cutting corn. She argued the point of his health, but my father's answer was always the same: "Work wouldn't hurt a man."

When I was fourteen or fifteen, I spent a Saturday on one of these corn-cutting expeditions with him. It was the last week end of his two-weeks vacation, and he had been working on a farm eight miles out of the city. We left home before daylight and reached the farm just at dawn. It was a large farm, and only a part of it was under cultivation. Before we set to work, the farmer joined us. He was a buck-toothed post of a man, with a skin raw and peeled-looking by the sun. The corn field lay some distance from the house and the land sloped away gently to a flat, rocky strip beyond which the corn field rose abruptly. The brown corn stood in marching rows on the side of the hill. The field had not been cared for. High weeds tangled the rows.

"Well, you overstretched yourself, looks like," the farmer said, looking at the uncut corn on the hill.

My father took off his coat and drew his corn knife from the ground, where he had left it the evening before. I saw his jaw tighten like a fist.

"I'll need a knife for my boy here," he said. "We'll get it done. The weeds will hamper us some, but we'll get it done."

"Maybe you will at that," the farmer said, kicking in a mat of weeds. "Didn' have no time to do nothin' with this crop out here myself. Had another colored feller workin' for me, but he ups an' quits 'bout the time I needed him most. Wasn' much of a loss to me, I don't reckon. He sure was a lazy one. This your boy, hunh?"

"Yes," my father said. He looked past the man. "We'll get it done all right."

"I'm from Missouri," the farmer said.

When he came back with the long-bladed corn knife, he stood for a while and watched us work. I had never cut corn before, but it was simply a matter of bending one's back and swinging one's blade as close to the roots as one could. When an armful of stalks was cut, we bound them together and stood them up to finish drying for fodder. The weeds were already giving us trouble. They were wet and tough with dew and they tied themselves around our ankles. But for a while the work did not seem hard to me. My father worked easily, making of bending, swinging, grasping one flowing, rhythmic action.

"The other colored feller sure was a lazy one," the farmer said after a while.

My father did not look up, but I watched the farmer spraddle down the hill and across the rocky gully.

"Damn him," my father said. "Damn him!" It was the only time I ever heard him curse. "Sure. That other colored fellow was lazy. Come on, son. Do you want him to think we're lazy too?"

It began to be hard work cutting uphill, and pretty soon the sun was at us. The weeds grabbed at our blades and we had to hack through them to get at the corn. My father cut very fast and determinedly, paying no attention to me. By nine o'clock my legs were rubbery with fatigue. I could hear my father working the dry, screeching corn somewhere ahead and to the left of me. He made an aspirant sound every time he swung his blade, and this came to me quite distinctly. "Hac. Hac. Hac." I seemed to be floating. My head felt enormously swollen. Bending to the corn, I could feel myself falling, but I had no strength to prevent it. I fell face down in the weeds, struggled up. Then suddenly the earth exploded in my face with blackening, sickening force.

When I came around again, my father was kneeling beside me. His face was gray and hard and his eyes and mouth were like Grandma Redding's. My nose was still bleeding a little and blood was on my shirt and smeared on the damp rag with which my father was stroking my face. He had stuck a twig under my upper lip.

"What's the matter, son?" my father asked. "Feel all right now?"

I spit out the twig. "I can't keep up."

"That's all right. I shouldn't have brought you." He was still stroking my face with the wet, blood-smeared rag. It was unpleasant. I smelled and tasted the blood. He looked across the gully toward the house that stood naked and ugly in the broad stroke of the sun. "I'll give that farmer a piece of my mind yet," he said.

"When he said, 'I'm from Missouri,' that's slang," I said. "People say I'm from Missouri when they don't believe you can do something. They say, 'Show me.'"

"I'll show him," my father said.

After lunch I felt strong enough to work again, but my father made me lie under the lip of the hill out of the sun, and all afternoon I listened to the sound of his working moving farther and farther away from me. He finished the field just before dark.

My mother was tall, with a smooth, rutilant skin and a handsome figure. Her hair began to whiten in her late twenties and whitened very rapidly. I especially liked to be on the street with her, for I enjoyed the compliment of staring which was paid to her. I think she was not aware of these stares. There was pride in her, a kind of glowing consciousness that showed in her carriage in exactly the same way that good blood shows in a horse. But she had no vanity. Her pride gave to everything she did a certain ritualistic élan.

It is surprising to me now how little I learned about my mother in the sixteen years she lived after my birth. It was not that I lacked opportunity, but insight. She was never withdrawn or restrained, purposefully shading out her personality from us. And her speech and actions seemed to have the simple directness and the sharp impact of thrown stones. But she was a woman of many humors, as if, knowing her time to be short, she would live many lives in one. Gaiety and soberness, anger and benignity, joy and woe possessed her with equal force. In all her moods there was an intensity as in a spinning top.

I vividly recall the day when in rage and tears she stormed because another Negro family moved into our neighborhood. When her rage had passed and she had dropped into that stilly tautness that sometimes kept her strained for days, she said to my father:

"That's all it takes, Fellow. Today our house is worth one-third of what it was last night. When those people . . ." She shrugged her wide shoulders and stared at my father.

"Oh, Girl! Girl!" my father said gently. "You mustn't be so hard on them. They may be respectable people."

"Hard! Hard! And respectable people!" She laughed brittlely. "What has respectability got to do with it?"

Then she tried to find the words for what she felt and thought, for we children were present and she did not wish to appear unreasonable before us. The subject of race was for her a narrow bridge over a chasmal sea, and the walking of it was not a part of her daily living. Only when she felt she must save herself from the abyss did she venture to walk. At other times she ignored it, not only in word, but I think in thought as well. She knew the speeches of John Brown and Wendell Phillips, the poetry of Whittier and Whitman, but not as my father knew them; not as battering stones hurled against the strong walls of a prison. She was not imprisoned. Stones, perhaps, but dropped into a dark sea whose tides licked only at the farthest shores of her life. She took this for reasonableness.

I remember she laughed a brittle laugh and said, "The first thing they moved in was one of those pianola things. Oh, we shall have music," she said bitterly, "morning, noon, and midnight. And they're not buying. They're renting. Why can't they stay where they belong!"

"Belong?" my father said.

"Yes. Over the bridge."

"They are our people, Girl," my father said.

My mother looked at him, tears of vexation dewing her eyes. She blinked back the tears and looked fixedly at my father's dark face shining dully under the chandelier, his bald head jutting back from his forehead like a brown rock. As if the words were a bad taste to be rid of, she said;

"Yours maybe. But not mine."

"Oh, Girl. Girl!"

But Mother had already swept from the dining room.

It is strange how little my deep affection for my mother (and hers for all of us) taught me about her while she lived. I have learned much more about her since her death. It is as if the significance of remembered speech and action unfolded to me gradually a long time after. My mother was the most complex personality I have ever known.

But no will of my mother's could abate the heave of the social tide just then beginning to swell. Our new neighbors were the first that we saw of that leaderless mass of blacks that poured up from the South during and after the war years. It was a trickle first, and then a dark flood that soon inundated the east side and burbled restively at our street. Within five months of the time my mother had raged, the whites were gone. But rents and prices in our street were too high for the laborers in morocco and jute mills, shipyards and foundries, the ditch-diggers, coal-heavers, and the parasites. They crowded sometimes as many as eight to a room in the houses below us, and I knew of at least one house of six small rooms in which fifty-one people lived.

Our street and the diagonal street above it were a more exclusive preserve. A few middle-class Jews, a clannish community of Germans clustered about their Turn Hall, and some Catholic Irish lived there. But they were nudged out. The Germans first, for they became the victims of mass hatred during the war, and the last German home was stoned just before the day of the Armistice. Landlords and realtors inflated prices to profit by Negro buyers who clamored for houses as if for heaven. Into our street moved the prosperous class of mulattoes, a physician and a dentist, a minister, an insurance agent, a customs clerk, a well-paid domestic, and several school teachers. Nearly all of these were buying at prices three times normal.

The atmosphere of our street became purely defensive. No neighborhood in the city was so conscious of its position and none, trapped in a raw materialistic struggle between the well-being of the west side and the grinding poverty of the east, fought harder to maintain itself. This struggle was the satanic bond, the blood-pact that held our street together.

But there was also the spiritual side to this struggle. It remained for me for a long time undefined but real. It was not clear and cold in the brain as religion was and taxes and food to eat and paint to buy. It was in the throat like a warm clot of phlegm or blood that no expectorant could dislodge. It was in the bowels and bone. It was memory and history, the pound of the heart, the pump of the lungs. It was Weeping Joe making bursting flares of words on the Court House wall and murmuring like a priest in funeral mass on our back steps of summer evenings. It was east side, west side, the white and the black, the word nigger, the cry of exultation, of shame, of fear when black Lemuel Price shot and killed a white policeman. It was Paul Dunbar, whose great brooding eyes spirit-flowed from his drawn face in a photograph over our mantle. It was sleeping and waking. It was Wilson and Hughes in 1917, Harding and Cox in 1921. It was a science teacher saying sarcastically, "Yes. I know. They won't hire you because you're colored," and, "Moreover, the dog licked Lazarus' wounds," and getting very drunk occasionally and reeling about, his yellow face gone purple, blubbering, "A good chemist, God damn it. A Goddamn good chemist! And here I am teaching a school full of niggers. Oh, damn my unwhite skin! And God damn it!" It was the music of pianolas played from dusk to dawn. And it was books read and recited and hated and loved: fairy tales, *Up From Slavery*, *Leaves of Grass*, *Scaramouche*, *Othello*, *The Yoke*, *Uncle Tom's Cabin*, *The Heroic Story of the Negro in the Spanish-American War*, *The Leopard's Spots*, *Door of the Night*, *Sentimental Tommy*, *The Negro, Man or Beast?*, and the rolling apostrophes of the *World's Best Orations*.

And on this plane allegiances were confused, divided. There was absolute cleavage between those spiritual values represented by Grandma Conway, who thought and lived according to ideas and ideals inherited from a long line of free ancestors and intimates (her father had been white, her mother part Irish, Indian,

Negro. Her first husband was a mulatto carriage maker with a tradition of freedom three generations old) and those ill-defined, uncertain values represented by Grandma Redding and which, somehow, seemed to be close to whatever values our neighbors on the east held. What these were I never knew, nor, I suspect, did Grandma Redding. Certainly she would have cast equal scorn on the east side's black Lizzie Gunnar, who ran a whore house and who two days before every Christmas gathered up all the Negro children she could find and led them to the Court House for the city's party to the poor, because, "Niggahs is jus' about de poores' folks dere is," and white and foreign-born Weeping Joe, who spoke of linking the spirits of men together in the solvent bond of Christ. Her closeness to them was more a sympathetic prepossession than an alliance. They were her people, whether their values were the same as hers or not. Blood was stronger than ideal, and the thing that was between them sprang from emotion rather than mind. It was unreasoning, and as ineluctable as the flight of time. Grandma Redding was the outright inheritor of a historical situation.

But not so Grandma Conway. She had assumed—not to say usurped—both the privileges and the penalties of a tradition that was hers only disingenuously, and therefore all the more fiercely held. The privileges gave her power; the penalties strength. She was certain of her values and she held them to be inviolate. She believed in a personal God and that He was in His heaven and all was right with the world. She believed in a rigid code of morality, but in a double standard, because she believed that there was something in the male animal that made him naturally incontinent, and that some women, always of a class she scornfully pitied, had no other purpose in life than to save good women from men's incontinence. In her notion, such women were not loose any more than rutting bitches were loose. A loose woman was a woman of her own class who had wilfully assumed the privileges and shunned the penalties of her birth. Such women she hated with face-purpling hatred. She believed in banks and schools and prisons. She believed that the world was so ordered that in the end his just desserts came to every man. This latter belief was very comprehensive, for she thought in terms of reciprocal responsibility of man and his class—that man did not live for himself alone and that he could not escape the general defections (she called it "sin") of the group into which he was born.

These beliefs must have been conspicuous to Grandma Conway's most casual acquaintance, but to me—and I have no doubt, to the rest of us long familiar with them—they were past both realizing and remarking, like the skin of one's body.

But realization of her most occult belief must have come quite early. Perhaps it came to me in 1917, when, on one of her visits, she first found the lower boundary of our neighborhood roiling with strange black folk and brazen with conspicuous life. It may have come to me imperceptibly, along with the consciousness of the stigma attaching to blackness of skin. But this stigma was a blemish, not a taint. A black skin was uncomely, but not inferior. My father was less beautiful than my mother, but he was not inferior to her. There were soot-black boys whom I knew in school who could outrun, outplay, and outthink me, but they were less personable than I. And certainly we did not think in any conscious way that Grandma Redding was a lesser person than Grandma Conway. The very core of awareness was this distinction.

But gradually, subtly, depressingly and without shock there entered into my consciousness the knowledge that Grandma Conway believed that a black skin was more than a blemish. In her notion it was a taint of flesh and bone and blood, varying in degree with the color of the skin, overcome sometimes by certain material distinctions and the grace of God, but otherwise fixed in the blood.

To Grandma Conway, as to my mother, our new neighbors on the east were a threat.

In our house a compromise was struck. No one ever talked about it. In the careless flow of our talk, it was the one subject avoided with meticulous concern. My parents were stern disciplinarians, and this subject was so fraught with punishable possibilities and yet so conscious a part of our living that by the time the three older ones of us were in grammar and high school our care for the avoidance of it took on at times an almost hysterical intensity. Many a time, as we heard schoolmates do and as we often did ourselves outside, one or the other of us wished to hurl the epithet "black" or "nigger," or a combination, and dared only sputter, "You, you . . . monkey!" For being called a monkey was not considered half so grave an insult as being called the other; and it was at least as grave a sin to avoid as using the Lord's name in vain. My parents, of course, never used either black or nigger, and avoided mentioning color in describing a person. One was either dark or light, never black or yellow—and between these two was that indeterminate group of browns of which our family was largely composed. We grew up in the very center of a complex.

I think my older brother and sister escaped most of the adolescent emotional conflict and vague melancholy (it came later to them, and especially to my brother, and in decidedly greater force) which were the winds of my course through teenhood. For me it was a matter of choices, secret choices really. For them there was no choice. And yet I had less freedom than they. They went off to a New England college in 1919. Up to then their associates had been first the white and then the mulatto children on our street. Even the children whom they met in high school were largely of the mulatto group, for the dark tide of migration had not then swept the schools. Going to school was distinctly an upper-class pursuit, and the public school was almost as exclusive as the summer playground which Miss Grinnage conducted along stubbornly select lines for "children of the best blood" (it was her favorite phrase), almost as exclusive as the Ethical Culture lectures we attended once each month, or the basement chapel of St. Andrews Episcopal church, where Father Tatnall held segregated services for us twice a month. For my older brother and sister, the road through childhood was straight, without sideroads or crossings.

But by the time I reached high school in the fall of 1919, life was undergoing a tumultuous change. It was as if a placid river had suddenly broken its banks and in blind and senseless rage was destroying old landmarks, leveling the face of the country farther and farther beyond the shore line.

The migrants not only discovered our neighborhood, they discovered the church where we went to Sunday school and where my father was superintendent. They discovered the vast, beautiful reaches of the Brandywine where we used to walk on fair Sundays. They discovered the school. I remember the sickening thrill with which I heard a long-headed black boy arraign the mulatto teachers for always giving the choice parts in plays, the choice chores, the cleanest books to mulatto children. He called the teachers "color-struck," a phrase that was new to me, and "sons-of-bitches," a phrase that was not. He was put out of school. Many black children were put out of school, or not encouraged to continue. Two incidents stand out in my mind.

In my first oratorical competition, I knew—as everyone else knew—that the contestant to beat was a gangling dark fellow named Tom Cephus. He had a fervor that I did not have and for which I was taught to substitute craft. His voice, already changed, boomed with a vibrant quality that was impressive to hear. Moreover, he was controlled, self-possessed, and I was not. For days before the competition I was unable to rest, and when I did finally face the audience, I uttered a sentence or two and from sheer fright and nervous exhaustion burst into uncontrollable tears. Somehow, bawling like a baby, I got through. I was certain that I had lost.

Cephus in his turn was superb. The greater part of the audience was with him. Beyond the first rows of benches, which were friendly to me, stretched row after increasingly dark row of black faces and beaming eyes. It was more than an oratorical contest to them. It was a class and caste struggle as intense as any they would ever know, for it was immediate and possible of compromise and assuagement, if not of victory. Mouths open, strained forward, they vibrated against that booming voice, transfixed in ecstasy. The applause was deafening and vindicative. In the back of the crowded hall someone led three cheers for Cephus (a wholly unheard-of thing) and while the teacher-judges were conferring, cheer after cheer swelled from the audience like the approaching, humming, booming bursting of ocean waves.

A pulsing hush fell on them when the judges returned. They watched the announcer as leashed and hungry dogs watch the approach of food. But the judge was shrewd. She wanted that excitement to simmer down. Flicking a smile at the first rows, she calmly announced the singing of a lullaby and waited, a set smile on her face, until three verses had been sung. Then icily, in sprung-steel Bostonian accents, she announced to an audience whose soft-skinned faces gradually froze in spastic bewilderment, "Third place, Edith Miller. Second place, Thomas Cephus. First place . . ." My name was lost in a void of silence. "Assembly dismissed!"

Stunned beyond expression and feeling, the back rows filed out. The front rows cheered. Cephus's lips worked and he looked at me. I could not look at him. I wanted to fall on my knees.

I was truant from school for a week. When my parents discovered it, I took my punishment without a word. A little later that year, Cephus dropped out of school.

But I was stubborn in my resistance to these lessons. My stubbornness was not a rational thing arrived at through intellection. It was not as simple and as hard as that. I was not a conscious rebel. I liked people, and, for all the straitening effects of environment, I was only lightly color-struck. A dark skin was perhaps not as comely as a brown or yellow, but it was sometimes attractive. In matters of class morality and custom and thought I was perhaps too young to make distinctions. I liked people. When I was sixteen and a senior in high school, I liked a doe-soft black girl named Viny. After school hours, Viny was a servant girl to kindly, dumpy, near-white Miss Kruse, the school principal, who lived across the street from us. I saw a good bit of Viny, for I ran Miss Kruse's confidential errands and did innumerable small things for her. There was nothing clandestine about my relations with her servant girl. We talked and joked in the kitchen. We sometimes walked together from school. We were frequently alone in the house.

But one day Miss Kruse called me to the front porch, where in fine, warm weather she ensconced herself in a rocker especially braced to support her flabby weight. She sat with her back turned squarely to the street. She was very fair, and because she ate heavily of rich, heavy foods, at forty-five she was heavy-jowled, with a broad, pleasant, doughy face. A sack of flesh swelled beneath her chin and seemed to hold her mouth open in a tiny O. She was reading.

"Sit down," she said.

I sat in the chair next to hers, but facing the street, so that we could look directly at each other. Both sides of the street were still lined with trees at that time, and it was June. Hedges were green. Miss Kruse read for a while longer, then she crumpled the paper against herself and folded her fingers over it.

"You like Viny, don't you?" she asked, looking at me with a heavy frown.

"Yes, ma'am," I said.

"Well, you be careful. She'll get you in trouble," she said.

"Trouble?"

"How would you like to marry her?"

I did not answer, for I did not know what to say.

"How?"

"I don't know'm."

This provoked her. She threw the newspaper on the floor. The network of fine pink veins on the lobes of her nose turned purple.

"Well, let her alone! Or she'll trap you to marry her. And what would you look like married to a girl like that?" she said bitingly. "No friends, no future. You might as well be dead! How would you like to spend the rest of your life delivering ice or cleaning outdoor privies? Don't you know girls like her haven't any shame, haven't any decency? She'll get you in trouble."

I stared stupidly at her. I do not know what my reaction was. I remember being confused and hotly embarrassed, and after that a kind of soggy lethargy settled in my stomach, like indigestible food. I distinctly remember that I felt no resentment and no shock, and that my confusion was due less to this first frank indictment of blackness than to the blunt reference to sex. Boys talked about sex in giggly whispers among themselves, but between male and female talk of sex was taboo. In the midst of my embarrassment, I heard Miss Kruse's voice again, calm and gentle now, persuasive, admonitory.

"You're going to college. You're going to get a fine education. You're going to be somebody. You'll be ashamed you ever knew Viny. There'll be fine girls for you to know, to marry."

She sighed, making a round sound of it through her O-shaped mouth, and rubbing her hands hard together as if they were cold.

"Viny. Well, Viny won't ever be anything but what she is already."

And what is she? And what and where are the others? One, who wore the flashy clothes and made loud laughter in the halls, is now a man of God, a solemn, earnest pulpiteer. Cephus, the boy who won and lost, is dead. And Pogie Walker's dead. It is remarkable how many of those I came to know in 1919 are dead. Birdie, Sweetie Pie, and Oliver. Viny? After she quit and moved away, she used to write me once a year on cheap, lined paper. "I'm doing alrite." (She never learned to spell.) "I'm living alrite. I gess I'm geting along alrite. How do these few lines fine you?" And Brunson, the smartest of that migrant lot, who outran, outfought, outthought all of us. He was expelled for writing a letter and passing it among the students. Most of the things he said were true—the exclusion of the very black from the first yearbook, the way one teacher had of referring to the black-skinned kids as "You, Cloudy, there," and never remem-

bering their names. Well, Brunson is a week-end drunk. At other
times he's very bitter. Not long ago I saw him. I spoke to him.
"You don't remember me," I said. "Yeah. I remember you all
right. So what?" He lives down on the east side, way down,
where in the spring the river comes.

  Miss Kruse was right in this: I did go to college.
  My mother was recently dead, and a temporary sentimental
weakness settled on my father. He did not wish me to go far
from home. He considered me too young in 1923 to go off alone
to the college in New England from which my brother had
just been graduated. I had first to spend a year at Lincoln University, a Negro college run by a white Presbyterian church
board in Pennsylvania, only twenty-odd miles from home. That I
should go to college was a matter of course. I was just seventeen,
and I felt no compelling drive. There was nothing in particular
that I wanted to learn, and I had given no thought to a career.
The driven, sharp ambition of some of the chaps (and especially
those from the South) I met there surprised and bewildered me.
They seemed to me to have a brazen, articulating cunning.
They thought of education exclusively in terms of prestige
value. They wanted to be doctors and lawyers—doctors mostly
—professions to which they referred as "rackets." There was
money in them, and they were motivated by the desire to possess,
as indeed they put it, yellow money, yellow cars, and yellow
women. They studied textbooks to that end. Almost none of
them did any reading beyond the requirements of courses. Each
had a singleness of purpose that seemed to me even then as
ruthless and as uninspired as the flame of an acetylene torch.
It was deadly. It was unmixed with either cynicism or idealism.
All their instincts, all their forces were channelized to flow in
one swift, hard, straight stream, to settle at last in a kind of dull
gray lake of fulfillment.
  Perhaps this would have been better for me. But I could not
see life with such baneful certainty. There stirred sluggishly

in me a consciousness of certain incommensurables that could not be measured out in the scales of personal ambition, a certain imponderability that could not be weighed in terms of biology, chemistry, civics, and Greek—or in any other terms of which I knew. I could not spin in a whirring cosmos of my own creation, as the others did. I could not create a cosmos; I haunted others. I could not even spin; I wobbled.

I was lonely a good deal. I studied enough, but with no other purpose than to put a face on things, to make a pretense of ambition that I did not have, for I was ashamed of my groping uncertainty. I read with indiscriminate avidity. The library was open only two hours a day, but I got special permission and a key and spent greedy hours there. Most of the books were old, and three-fourths of them on theology, but in a tumulus of dust I found Stendhal, Meredith, Thackeray, Trevelyan, Bierce, Miller, William James, Dreiser, Henry George, and a half-dozen paper-bound plays by Sedley, Wycherley, and Congreve, which, I am certain, Professor Labaree did not know were there. On Sunday nights I walked four miles to a mission church and listened to the singing of such starkly primitive and beautiful music as I had never heard. At the end of my first year, I transferred to Brown, in Providence, and no one at Lincoln missed me.

There were two other Negroes at Brown, both seniors at the time, and Clyde Bastrop came in my second year. Bastrop and I could have roomed together at a saving, but we did not, for we took elaborate precautions against even the appearance of clannishness. I had found this peculiar behavior in the two seniors, and apparently it had come down to them from a long, thin line of Negro students. Yet among them there must have been a terrific consciousness of kind, just as there was between Bastrop and me. Our denials of this consciousness sometimes took the most exaggerated forms. We made a great show of not seeking each other's companionship, meeting always apparently by accident, and never in the Union or the Commons or the library, and only in each other's rooms at night with the shades drawn.

We never ate together. We recognized no snubs or slights from white associates. We did not even talk of them to each other in the secret of our rooms at night with the shades down. Once in a biology class, the instructor, a man from Tennessee, referred to "niggers" in a humorous, insulting way, but I said nothing. Once a professor committed an act of discrimination so flagrant that even one of his assistants rebelled, but I pretended not to notice. Bastrop and I underwent a kind of purge, but we denied any sense of martyrdom. We were lost in the sacrificial, foreordained, pitilessly wretched way in which the not-quite-saved are lost. But we were not alone. Negro boys in colleges all over New England were also lost; and on occasional very rowdy, very unrestrained parties in Boston we cemented with them a desperate bond of frustration.

These parties were the measure of our tense neurosis, our desperation. I see that now. With an abiding strain of puritanism, I was inclined in those years to put an undue weight of moral significance upon the sins we committed. For days after a week end saved from utter beastliness only by a certain controlling melancholy cynicism, a sort of soul-sickness, I suffered an agony of remorse. I reviled and despised myself. I hated the housemaids, the elevator girls, the hairdressers, and the occasional college girls who shared our unrestraint. But I went again. I always went, as a sick dog returns to his vomit. That shameless bitchery! Those shoddy, temporarily freeing, hysterical bacchanalia!

We thought we had the strained, fine courage of strong men who are doomed and know they are doomed. In reality we carried on a sort of blind quest for disaster, for demotic and moral suicide outside the harbors of sanity.

It was following one of these parties in the late winter of 1926 that Bastrop left. Still red-eyed with sleeplessness, he came to my room in Hope College. He was a round-faced boy, extroverted, I thought, and with a capacity for playing practical jokes of a complicated nature. But this day he was subdued, looking inward upon himself and not liking what he saw.

"I'm leaving," he said, without preliminaries.

"Leaving school, you mean?"

"Yes," he said, and fell silent. He sat on the bed and leaned backward on his elbows. Then he turned over and lay with his chin on his fist, staring at the wall. Around his eyes the skin was almost white, as if he had worn dark glasses in the hot sun for a long time. He raised his head and said, "Yes. I'm leaving."

"But why?" I asked. "What's eating you?"

With a sudden twisting movement he was up and sitting on the edge of the bed, hunched over, hard-drawn. I knew he was not joking.

"There must be some place better than this. God damn it, there must be! I can find a place somewhere. This isn't the place for me. I feel like everybody's staring at me, all these white guys, waiting for me to make a bad break. Things I'd do without thinking about them, I do now like they were the most important things in the whole damned world. How the hell do you stand it? We're always talking about being casual. All right. But what do we do?" He got up nervously, but sat down again almost at once. "I'll tell you good and damn well what we do! We put on the damnedest airs in the world. We're showing off. Casually, casually, by Christ! And yet everything comes so hard you can hear us breathing way over on George Street. I'm sick of being casual! I want to be honest and sincere about something. I want to stop feeling like I'll fall apart if I unclench my teeth. Oh Christ!"

He looked wretched. He sat there on the edge of the bed with his hands in his pockets and his shoulders drawn in a hard curve, as if he were out in the cold without an overcoat. The religious medallion which he wore on a silver chain around his neck had worked through his shirt and he seemed to be staring at it.

"Listen, Bastrop," I said.

He looked up. "Listen, hell! I'm tired of listening," he said angrily.

It was just as well, for I do not know what I would have said. There is no answer to truth. I do not know what I thought or

felt other than the need to retreat from the truth against which
all my defenses had toppled. Suddenly all my resiliency was gone.
I started to make some tea, but even as I made it, I knew that
tea-making was another bluff, a flimsy protective device, like our
careful speech, our careful avoidance of clannishness, and I
knew at the same time that these things were necessary to us in
the same way a sheath is necessary to a sword. I did not want to
lose my hard, fine edge, as Bastrop was doing, I thought cynically.

"That was a hell of a party in Springfield," I said.

Bastrop looked up with angry eagerness. "Did you see Jerry?"
Jerry was a girl we knew from Philadelphia who was a student
in Boston.

"Yes. Sure."

"Listen. Do you enjoy those breakdowns? Do you really
have fun?"

"Sure. Yes," I said.

"All that hog-wallowing?"

"It's something to do. You got to do something."

He looked at me with strange aversion, I thought. But his
thoughts were not on me, for he said:

"Jerry enjoyed it. She actually got a kick out of it," he said,
as if he could not believe it. "And when a girl like that enjoys
that . . . Well, we were dancing," he said, as if he were
wretchedly eager to get something off his mind. "We were
dancing and she said she was enjoying it, said she was going to
be herself. She wasn't drunk then either. She didn't get drunk
until later. You saw how drunk she got. She got pie-eyed."

"Why did you take her in the first place?" I said. "You knew
what kind of party it was going to be."

"I don't know," he said miserably.

"Did you . . . ?"

He looked at me for a wild, frightened, shamefaced moment
and dropped his head. I diverted myself in sham anger.

"So that's the real reason you're leaving. You're afraid," I
said.

He stood up. "Afraid? Afraid? Yes, God damn it! I'm afraid.

But I'm not afraid of what you think. I'm afraid of getting like the rest of the guys. I'm afraid of not having anything inside, of getting so that if anybody touches me I'll fall apart. I've still got enough left to know that there's something wrong with this, and I'm leaving before that goes too!"

That night Bastrop left on the night boat. I never saw him again, for in the late spring he killed himself in the bathroom of his parents' home in Cleveland. He was the first of five suicides in a half-dozen years from that group I knew in New England. Two of them were girls. By any reckoning, this is a high percentage. Excluding that numerous crowd of fourflushers who took an evening course here and there in the various colleges in Boston, there were not more than fifteen of us who knew each other intimately as fellow collegians.

In my senior year I met Lebman. For several lonely months I had been the only Negro in the college, and the sense of competitive enmity, which began to develop slowly in me in my second year, was now at its height. It was more than a sense of competition. It was a perverted feeling of fighting alone against the whole white world. I raged with secret hatred and fear. I hated and feared the whites. I hated and feared and was ashamed of Negroes. (The memory of it even now is painful to me.) I shunned contacts with the general run of the latter, confining myself to the tight little college group centered around Boston. But even this group was no longer as satisfying as once it had been, and I gradually withdrew from it, though the bond of frustration was strong. But my own desperation was stronger. I wished to be alone. My room in University Hall had almost no visitors, but it was peopled by a thousand nameless fears.

Furtively trying to burn out the dark, knotted core of emotion, I wrote acidulous verse and sent bitter essays and stories to various Negro magazines. One editor wrote, "You must be crazy!" Perhaps I was. I was obsessed by nihilistic doctrine. Democracy? It was a failure. Religion? A springe to catch woodcocks. Truth? There was no objective ground of truth, nothing outside myself that made morality a principle. Destroy and destroy, and perhaps, I remember writing cynically, "from the ashes of nothingness will spring a phoenix not altogether devoid of beauty." All my thoughts and feelings were but symptomatic of a withering, grave sickness of doubt.

And then I met Lebman.

He was a Jew. He had lived across the hall from me since the fall, and I had seen him once or twice in only the most casual way. Then late one night he knocked at my door. When I opened it, he was standing there pale and smiling, a lock of damp, dark hair falling across his wide, knotty forehead.

"I saw your light. Do you mind if I ask you something?" he said diffidently.

"Come in," I said automatically; but all my defenses immediately went up.

Still smiling shyly, he came into the room and stood in the center of the floor. He carried a book in his hand, his longer fingers marking the place. He was wearing pajamas and a robe. I remember I did not close the door nor sit down at first, but stood awkwardly waiting, trying to exorcise my suspicion and fear. He looked around the room with quiet, friendly curiosity.

"I've been reading your stuff in the *Quarterly*," he said. "It's good." *

"Thanks," I said. And I remember thinking, 'Don't try to flatter me, damn you. I don't fall for that stuff.' Then I tried to get ahold of myself, groping at my tangled feelings with clumsy fingers of thought in an action almost physical. "Thanks."

"I think you're after something," he said. It was a cliché, and I did not like talking about my writing. It was always like undressing before strangers. But Lebman was sincere, and now unembarrassed.

"You do?" I said, trying to say it in a tone that would end it.

"Yes."

"Why?"

"Oh, it's plain in your writing. You know, I correct papers

in philosophy too. Your paper on Unamuno, it was plain there. That paper was all right too."

"I wish I knew what I was after, or that I was after something," I said defensively, cynically. I closed the door. Then in the still, sharp silence that followed, I moved to the desk and turned the chair to face the other chair in the corner. Lebman sat down.

"What I came in to see you about was this," he said, holding the book up. And in another moment, without really asking me anything, he had plunged into a brilliant, brooding discussion of Rudolph Fisher's *Walls of Jericho*, the book he held in his hand, and of men and books. I listened captiously at first. He did not speak in the rhapsodic way of one who merely loves books and life. He spoke as one who understands and both loves and hates. He sat in the chair in the corner, where the light from the reading lamp fell upon his pale face, his narrow, angular shoulders. Through the window at his elbow we could see the mist-shrouded lights outlining the walks of the middle campus. Lebman talked and talked. I listened.

I do not remember all he said between that midnight and dawn, but one thing I do remember.

"I'm a Jew. I tried denying it, but it was no use. I suppose everyone at some time or other tries to deny some part or all of himself. Suicides, some crazy people go all the way. But spiritual schizophrenes aren't so lucky as suicides and the hopelessly insane. I used to think that only certain Jews suffered from this —the Jews who turn Christian and marry Christian and change their names from Lowenstein to Lowe and Goldberg to Goldsborough and still aren't happy. But they're not the only ones. Fisher makes a point of that. I thought so until I read him. You ought to read him, if you haven't."

"I've read him," I said, trying to remember the point.

"Schizophrenia in the mind, that's the curse of God; but in the spirit, it's man's curse upon himself. It took me a long time —all through college, through three years of reading manuscripts for a publisher, through another two years of graduate school—it took me years to realize what a thing it is. I'm a thirty-six-year-old bird, and I've only just found my roost.

"That's what you want, a roost, a home. And not just a place to hang your hat, but someplace where your spirit's free, where you belong. That's what everybody wants. Not a place in space, you understand. Not a marked place, geographically bounded. Not a place at all, in fact. It's hard to tell to others," he said. "But it's a million things and people, a kind of life and thought that your spirit touches, absorbed and absorbing, understood and understanding, and feels completely free and whole and one."

That midnight conversation—though it was scarcely that— recurred to me many times in the years immediately following.

When I came up for graduation in 1928, it still had not occurred to me to think of finding work to do that would turn my education to some account. My brother had been graduated from Harvard Law, and I thought randomly of earning money to follow him there. My credits were transferred. But I earned very little and I could discover in myself no absorbing interest, no recognition of a purpose. The summer blazed along to August. Then, out of the blue, John Hope offered me a job at Morehouse College in Atlanta. I took it. I was twenty-one in October of that fall, a lonely, random-brooding youth, uncertain, purposeless, lost, and yet so tightly wound that every day I lived big-eyed as death in sharp expectancy of a mortal blow or a vitalizing fulfillment of the unnamable aching emptiness within me.

But Morehouse College and the southern environment disappointed me. The college tottered with spiritual decay. Its students were unimaginative, predatory, pretentious. Theirs was a naked, metal-hard world, stripped of all but its material values, and these glittered like artificial gems in the sun of their ambition. An unwholesome proportion of the faculty was effete, innocuous, and pretentious also, with a flabby softness of intellectual and spiritual fiber and even a lack of personal force. They clustered together like sheared sheep in a storm. They were a sort of mass-man, conscious of no spiritual status even as men, much less as a people. They were a futile, hamstrung group, who took a liberal education (they despised mechanical and technical learning) to be a process of devitalization and to be significant in extrinsics only. They awarded a lot of medallions and watch charms. Try as I might, I could feel no kinship with them. Obviously my home was not among them.

I thought often of Lebman in the pre-dawn quiet of my room, saying, "Not a place in geography, but a million things and people your spirit touches, absorbed and absorbing." I did not want sanctuary, a soft nest protected from the hard, strengthening winds that blew hot and cold through the world's teeming, turbulent valley. I wanted to face the wind. I wanted the strength to face it to come from some inexpressibly deep well of feeling of oneness with the wind, of belonging to something, some soul-force outside myself, bigger than myself, but yet a part of me. Not family merely, or institution, or race; but a people and all their topless strivings; a nation and its million destinies. I did not think in concrete terms at first. Indeed, I had but the shadow of this thought and feeling. But slowly the shadow grew, taking form and outline, until at last I felt and knew that my estrangement from my fellows and theirs from me was but a failure to realize that we were all estranged from something fundamentally ours. We were all withdrawn from the heady, brawling, lusty stream of culture which had nourished us and which was the stream by whose turbid waters all of America fed. We were spiritually homeless, dying and alone, each on his separate hammock of memory and experience.

This was emotional awareness. Intellectual comprehension came slowly, painfully, as an abscess comes. I laid no blame beyond immediate experience. Through hurt and pride and fear, they of this class (and of what others I did not know) had deliberately cut themselves off not only from their historical past but also from their historical future. Life had become a matter of asylum in some extra time-sphere whose hard limits were the rising and the setting sun. Each day was another and a different unrelated epoch in which they had to learn again the

forgetting of ancestral memory, to learn again to bar the senses
from the sights and sounds and tastes of a way of life that they
denied, to close the mind to the incessant close roar of a world
to which they felt unrelated. This vitiated them, wilted them,
dwarfed their spirits, and they slunk about their gray astringent
world like ghosts from the shores of Lethe.

I tried fumblingly to tell them something of this, for my
desire for spiritual wholeness was great. I yearned for some
closer association with these men and women, some bond that
was not knit of frustration and despair. In impersonal terms I
tried to tell them something of this. They snubbed me. They
looked upon me as a pariah who would destroy their societal
bond, their asylum. They called me fool—and perhaps I was.
Certainly I was presumptuous. Their whispers and their sterile
laughter mocked me. They were at pains to ridicule me before
the students. They called me radical, and it was an expletive
the way they used it, said in the same way that one calls another
a snake. For three years I held on, and then I was fired.

But my seeking grew in intensity and the need to find became
an ache almost physical. For seven, eight years after that I
sought with the same frantic insatiability with which one lives
through a brutal, lustful dream. It was planless seeking, for I felt
then that I would not know the thing I sought until I found it.
It was both something within and something without myself.
Within, it was like the buried memory of a name that will not
come to the tongue for utterance. Without, it was the muffled
roll of drums receding through a darkling wood. And so, restricted in ways I had no comprehension of, I sought, and everywhere—because I sought among the things and folk I knew—
I went unfinding.

IN 1940, with funds provided by the Rockefeller Foundation,
the University of North Carolina invited me to do a job.
The assignment was so simple and direct that Mr. Couch and I

had to talk it over a half-dozen times. Sitting in his cool office in Chapel Hill, Mr. Couch said, "Go out into Negro life in the South. Go anywhere you like." It was as simple as that.

"All right," I said. "But I can't promise you what I'll find." I was still questing, still lost.

"If you could, there'd be no need to send you," Mr. Couch said.

I knew what they wanted and I thought I knew vaguely what I wanted, and the two things were not the same. Their wants were simple and direct. Mine seemed neither. I had no trouble getting a leave from teaching. "Good luck," Mr. Couch said, and I went up into Delaware to take leave of my family.

"Be careful," my father warned. My brother said, "Watch those crackers down there." My son put his five-year-old hand in mine, gave me a wet kiss, and went scooting off. My wife held me close for a moment and whispered, rather tensely, as if she were charging me, I thought, "It's all right. This time you're going to find it."

I was not so sure. I think I was frowning and disturbed as I meshed the gears and headed south through Maryland—Elkton, Havre de Grace, and Baltimore. Once through Washington, I thought, I would not care what road I took, so long as it led south. I did not even consult the maps. I was looking for people, for things, for *something*.

Who were these people? What were these things, this some-thing? I did not know. My mind was uneasy, bedeviled by vague doubts. It seemed to me that I was looking for stability in a world that had been slowly disintegrating for a dozen years, and now, half of it at war, was breaking up very fast. No one seemed to know the values that would be preserved, or even those worth preserving. The depression seemed a final paralysis before the death of a way of life that men had thought enduring. The first rantings of a national political campaign were like a monstrous death rattle. Perhaps, I thought, what you will find in this already dying world will not be valid for the world that comes after. The world *I* know, I thought. So? Well and good.

But even as I thought this defiance, I felt my courage dwindle and the long fingers of my memory reach for a saving straw in the dark sea of the past. I had long since forgotten nihilism. Destruction there was and would be. But always there was building, too, however inept, and always something better, finer. This was platitudinous thinking, pretentious thinking, and I did not like it; but it was my thinking all the same, and there was nothing I could do about it.

The world is dying, I thought; think back over the values you were taught and see if there are any worth saving. Think! I thought. There were the bread-and-butter values, the Rocke-feller and Morgan values. There were the intellectual values, about which my notions were hobbled with certain irritating inconsistencies. There were the Christian values, all turned into formulas for material success. And there were those uncertain values memorably represented for me in the brilliantly colored stereopticon slides of famous paintings that were the delight of my childhood. As one who held these things valid, I was an atom of humanity, a man, a public-schooled American, conscious of having in these things a common bond with other Americans. But if the disturbed days of my youth had taught me any lesson it was that I was also a Negro, that as such, there were other values, other validities (no one ever told me what these were), and that these must be, had of necessity to be, I was taught, prescinded from the consideration of my manhood, my common heritage, my Americanism. One was never told, "You are a man." It was always, "You are a Negro." I knew no more now what these values were than when I was a wide-eyed child. Everyone spoke of them and I had seen men weep over them, but no one seemed to know what they were. I was doubtful of ever discovering.

What validity? What reality for this dying world of men and Negroes? It was the old question, but asked myself with the impatient urgency of necessity, for if there were such values, then the discovery of them seemed the very core of the job I had to do. . . .

It was in this direction—in the direction of knowledge and understanding and love—that I felt I had come a little way. I do not boast of this. Under the circumstances it was almost inevitable. I had set out in nearly hopeless desperation to find both as Negro and as American certain values and validities that would hold for me as man. It is not enough in America to be Negro. It is not enough to be Negro American, or brown American, or colored American. There is an easily comprehensible mind-set, a psychosis, indeed, born of more than two centuries of slavery and inbred for dozens of generations. It was the point to Mike Chowan's bitter gibe, "There's a combine you can't beat—American, middle class, Negro." It was the burden of the bitter mouthings of innumerable men (and women) who had exhorted countless Negro audiences: "Be a man!" It is a phrase that has always meant more to a Negro American than non-Negro Americans can imagine. And so, in a bewilderment that years of planless seeking had increased, I had set out as Negro and American to find among my people those validities that proclaimed them and me men.

And I think I found them. Among all that was hollow and false and trifling (and there was much) I think I found those values and validities as quietly alive and solid, as deep-rooted as vigorous trees. They have simple names, and they have been called before. Other peoples have been said to have them, but that makes them no less good. Indeed, that they are the attributes of other peoples, men, makes them of the highest importance to me. That Negroes hold these values in common with others is America's fortune and, in a very immediate sense, the Negro American's salvation. For these things they hold valid and valuable are the highest common denominator of mankind. They are the bane of those who would destroy freedom, and they need no other justification than this. They are the intangibles in the scale of human values. They are, unmistakably, integrity of spirit, love of freedom, courage, patience, hope.

This selection is from *No Day of Triumph* (New York: Harper, 1942), 19-44, 45-47, 339-40.

Editor's Note: *Reference is to the *Brown Literary Quarterly*, which was published from November 1928 until May 1930. Redding published two short stories in the literary journal. (See his short story titles included in the selected bibliography in this volume.)

FROM *ON BEING NEGRO IN AMERICA*

Although I am not a very religious person, I do not see how I can leave God out of consideration in these matters. God has been made to play a very conspicuous part in race relations in America. At one time or another, and often at the same time, He has been the protagonist for both sides. He has damned and blessed first one side and then the other with truly godlike impartiality. His ultimate intentions, revealed to inspired sages, are pre-served in a thousand volumes. Anyone who reads the literature of race cannot but be struck by the immoderate frequency with which God is invoked, and by the painstaking consideration that is given, even by social scientists, to race relations as a problem of Christian ethics.

God, of course, is an implicit assumption in the thought of our age. He is one of those beliefs so spontaneous and ineluctable and taken so much as a matter of course that they operate with great effectiveness (though generally on a level of subconsciousness) in our society. He is a belief that operates just by being, like a boulder met in the path which must be dealt with before one can proceed on his journey. God is a complex composed entirely of simple elements—mediator, father, judge, jury, executioner, and also love, virtue, charity—each of which generates a very motley collection of often contradictory ideas. God is a catalyst, and He is also a formulated doctrine inertly symbolized in the ritual and the dogma of churches called Christian. God is the Absolute Reality, but this does not prevent His being ostentatiously offered as the excuse for our society's failure to come to grips with big but relative realities. God and the Christian religion must be reckoned with.

I do not know how long I have held both God and the Christian religion in some doubt, though it must have been since my teens. Nor do I know exactly how this came about. My father was (and is) very religious, of great and clear unbending faith. My mother was less so, but the family went regularly to church, where we were all active, and I used occasionally to see my mother so deeply touched by a religious feeling that she could not keep back the tears. What inspired it in that chill atmosphere it is impossible to say. I can only think that it came as a result of some very personal communion with God, established perhaps by a random thought, a word, or a certain slant of light through the yellow and rose and purple windows. There was never any shouting or "getting happy" among us, or in our church; none of that ecstatic abandon that set men and women jumping and dancing and screaming in the aisles. After the northward migration follow-ing the First World War, a few people who may have had a natural tendency to such transports found their way to our church, but they were frustrated by the mechanical expertness of the uninspired sermons, the formalized prayers, and by the choirmaster's preference for hymns translated from fifteenth-century Latin. Never did I hear a spiritual sung in our church, and only rarely a common-meter Calvinist hymn.

Sometime during my teens I became aware that for most Negroes God was a great deal more than a spirit to be worshiped on Sundays. He had a terrifying immediacy as material provider and protector. Once a group of us teen-agers went on a Sunday evening (our own church worshiped only in the morning) to a mission church deep in the Bridge District where the Negro population was concentrated. We went to mock, as some of us had heard our parents do, at the malapropisms of the illiterate minister and his ignorant flock, the crazy singing and shouting, and the uninhibited behavior of members in religious ecstasy. We did not remain to pray, but I was struck by what I saw and heard, and afterward my natural curiosity led me to go occasionally alone. The service did not resemble, either in ritual or content (both of which were created spontaneously), the service to which I was used. Any member of the church could stand up and pray. A whole evening might be given over to these impulsive outbursts. The prayers impressed me with their concreteness, their concern for the everyday. I heard one distraught mother, whose daughter evidently was sitting beside her, beseech God: "Now here's Idabelle, an' she's gone and got herself bigged, an' I'm askin' you, God, to make the young rascal who done it marry her. His name's Herbie Washington, an' he stays on the street nex' to me." They prayed for bread, not in a general, symbolic "give us this day our daily bread" sense, but for specific bread and meat for specific occasions. "Aunt Callie Black's laying up there sick, Lord, an' when I seen her, she tol' me her mouth was watering for some hot biscuit, an' that's the reason I'm asking You to give her some hot biscuit 'fore I go to see her again nex' Tuesday." They wanted clothes and they asked for them. They wanted pitiful but specific sums of money. They wanted protection from their real enemies. "Lord Jesus, don't let that mean nigger, Joe Fisher, stick me with no knife."

Negroes made irrational claims on God which they expected Him to fulfill without any help from them and without any regard for the conditions under which they could be fulfilled, and I suppose that when their claims failed, there was some sort of psychological mechanism that produced satisfactory excuses. It was all very simple and direct, but God just did not work that way—not the white folk's God I was taught to worship.

I do not believe that this incongruity set me thinking until at the small and rather exclusive (though public) high school I attended, a science teacher pointed it up. He was a bitter, frustrated man, full of self-hatred and of contempt for his race. Often staggering drunk outside the classroom, he was said to spend his week ends in an alcoholic fog of hatred writing scurrilous anti-Negro letters to the "people's opinion" column of the local paper. (Such letters did appear there with persistent regularity.) Our science teacher was certainly no good for us. Monday mornings were invariably void of science instruction.

"How many of you went hat-in-hand to God yesterday and asked him to get your chemistry for you this week?" he would begin. "He won't, and you can take my word for that. The trouble with niggers—" what malevolent contempt he put into the word!— "is that they look to God to do for them. That's why they're like they are—not only ignorant, but stupid; not only inferior, but debased. 'You can take all this world, but give me Jesus,' the song says, and that's just what the white people have been doing— taking the world and giving you Jesus. God, if there is a God, which I doubt, helps those who help themselves. Now study your chemistry!"

(How he managed to stay on with his drunkenness and his fundamental corruption, of which everyone was aware, is not beyond my comprehension so much as it is beyond my belief. He was one of the "big," upper-class mulatto families with members thriving in the professions up and down the Eastern seaboard. They were not a powerful family, having neither money, nor political influence, nor potent white patrons; but they had social prestige because of their antiquity, their relatively long tradition of freedom, their education, and their considerable infusion of white blood. In those days the feeling was that such a family must not be disgraced by the derelictions of one of its members. The black sheep must be protected, if he could not be hidden, and pitied because he could not be punished.)

Such assertions were almost daily fare. It was not hard to find support for them. I could see that most Negroes were poor and ignorant and inferior. Every year on the last Sunday in August one of the Negro religious denominations held a "quarterly meeting" in my home town. People from a half dozen states poured in the day before and roamed the streets all night, or slept anywhere they could—on the courthouse lawn, in the wagons and trucks that brought them, in alleys and doorways. But on the Sunday, what excitement! What noisy exuberance! Six city blocks, just below the main street, were inundated with the germinal tide of their living. Preachers exhorted; food vendors shouted; choirs sang; bands played; lost children bawled; city prostitutes pushed brazenly for trade among the young men from the country; people prayed and went into transports.

I do not know when I began to notice the white people. I suppose they had always been there. But along in my fourteenth or fifteenth year, I suddenly seemed to see them. Small phalanxes of them always seemed to be pushing or imperiously demanding passage through the crowds that fell away before them like grain before a scythe. The white people sneered—or so it seemed to me—and took pictures and made derisive comments. They looked down in laughing contempt from the windows, balconies and roofs of the buildings that lined the street. They came, also from miles around, to watch the show, not to be a part of it. I realized with deep shame that what the Negroes did on this holy day made a clowns' circus for the whites. The Negroes' God made fools of them. Worship and religiosity were things to be mocked and scorned, for they stamped the Negro as inferior.

There must have been many vague progressions of thought and many gradations of emotion between the premise and the conclusion. However little I was aware of them, my nerves, muscles and brain—conditioned by a thousand random and forgotten experiences—must have prepared me to accept the conclusion without outrage and shock. I simply rejected religion. I rejected God. Not my instincts, but my deepest feelings revolted compulsively—not because I was I, a sort of neutral human stuff reaching directly to experience, but because I was Negro. It is hard to make it clear; but there were two people sharing my physical existence and tearing me apart. One, I suppose, was the actual self which I wanted to protect and yet which I seemed to hate with a consuming hatred; and the other was the ideal self which tried compulsively to shape the actual self away from all that Negroes seemed to be. At what emotional and psychic cost this deep emotional conflict went on within me I do not know. It was years before I understood that what I had wanted then was to be white.

It was also years before I made a sort of armed truce with religion and with God. I stepped around God determinedly, gingerly, gloating that I was free of Him and that He could not touch me. Indeed, I had to step around Him, for He was always there. He was there, foursquare and solid, at the very center of my father's life. (My father habitually ends his letters, "May the spirit of the Almighty God, whose interest is always manifest, be with you!") At Brown University He was in Dr. Washburn's sermons, and President Faunce's chapel talks, and Professor Ducasse's philosophy course. He was in various people I met and felt affection for. He was in the ineffable, tremulous sweetness of the first love I felt; in the drowning ecstasy of the first sexual experience; in the joy of imaginative creation. But I moved around Him warily, laughing, mocking His pretensions, determined that He would not betray me into Negroness. If there lingered still in the deep recesses of my real self some consciousness of a religious spirit, then the ideal self—the Negro-hating me—did all it could do exorcise it.

How unmitigating and long-lasting this conflict was is proved for me in the fact that only in the last ten years have I been able to go to church without a feeling of indulging in some senseless necromantic ritual, and without feeling that my wanting to go—and I did many times *want* to go; if this seems contradictory, I cannot help it—was a mark of inferiority, the foolish expression of a weak and senseless wish to attain an impossible realm of being differing in its essential nature—that is, in its reality—from anything my experience has taught me can be attained. I do not believe in an afterlife; in otherworldliness. The experiences of this world are too potent and too much with me. I do not see how any Negro can believe in another world, and the religion which has inspired him to that belief, if it has saved him, has done so by making him content with the very degradation of his humanity that is so abhorrent to the principles of Christianity.

But it is not alone for the reasons outlined above that I have held religion suspect. Let us concede that the God of the Negroes has been largely a pagan god and largely stripped of the divinest attributes, interceding intimately and directly for man without man's help. They have fashioned a god to their need. But the whites also have fashioned a god to their need, and have believed in him, and have professed to follow him. He is a moral God, a God of truth and justice and love. I do not wish to carry this too far, for I have no capacity for philosophic speculation; but it seems to me that if the qualities attributed to God represent man's acknowledged needs, and if the principles of Christianity represent the universal source of man's social genius, then he has sacrificed the fulfillment of his basic needs (or "the good life") to the fulfillment of desires that run counter to the purpose of living. He has not given his religion a chance to help him effect that far-going social transformation and evolution which should be religion's end. Religion has become a disembodied sort of activity, when, to be effective, it should be a social function intimately linked up with man's fate on earth.

While there is almost no religion operating in race relations, there is plenty of God. I do not say this facetiously, nor with ironic intent; and, anyway, it has at least been implied before. There is an extensive literature on the part God has played in race relations since the fifteenth century. Principally God and the word of God have been used to perpetuate the wicked idea of human inferiority. I need not go into this farther than to point out modern man's subtle modifications of the idea of God and the intellectual gymnastics that have made those modifications possible, even when, it seems to me, the environment has not made them necessary, and even though in the fundamental concept of the Godhead is the idea of immutability. But God has changed, and though man himself has wrought these changes, he has declared them God's own changes and therefore factors, equations, and of a piece with the mysterious and unknowable nature of God. Indeed, God's very supernaturalness, His mysteriousness and inscrutability ("God moves in mysterious ways His wonders to perform," *ergo* "we cannot know God's purpose in making the black race inferior to the white," and we cannot "fathom the repulsion which God has given one race for another, or one people for another") are largely modern attributions which confound the ancient knowledge and excuse modern sin. God was not always so.

And before the ancient concepts crashed under the onslaught of sophistication, of scientific materialism and the new philosophies it brought into being, Christianity had become a way of life. It had become a way of life to be striven for because it seemed to satisfy the needs of ordinary men. There is nothing mysterious about Christianity. Granted that mystery reposes in the life of Christ (as, let it be said, it did not originally repose in God)—but Christ's life and what he is reported to have done are one thing: what he is reported to have taught is another. What he taught is as clear and concrete and literal as the lead story in a good newspaper. He taught that the kingdom of heaven is here on earth. He preached that men should love one another. He said that all men are brothers. He sought to bind men together in one mighty neighborhood. He was, for all the mystery surrounding him, a social engineer with a far and cosmic vision. The present age has not denied that he was right. Though there are those (and I among them) who reject the traditionally perpetuated events of his life as a factual record, his ministry remains the source of Christian religion. What has happened is that the age, while acknowledging Christianity as the highest way of life that man has thus far conceived, has denied the authority of God to make man live up to Christ's teachings. The dream of God and the reality of Christ have become separated.

If all this seems oversimplified, then I must again plead my lack of resources for such speculation. I do not wish to give an appearance of simplicity to problems that have taxed the best religious philosophers of the past six hundred years. Theology quite aside, it seems to me that the bearing which the Christian religion should have on human relations throughout the world and on race relations in the Western world is simple enough and direct enough. Perhaps it sounds somewhat effete to say now, as William James said at the turn of the century, that life becomes tiresome and meaningless unless it is constantly refreshed by "communion with a wider self through which saving experiences come," but this seems to me to be true. The Christian religion offers that communion with "a wider self." It offers a mature approach to experience. Modern man's incredible good luck in escaping the direst consequences of conduct unlighted by luminous beliefs and uncontrolled by moral principles is fast running out. A third world war may destroy man altogether—if, that is, he does not destroy himself in more subtle and tortuous ways without war. It would be foolish optimism not to assume the possibility of this.

It is not the nobility of Christ's life that I would urge; it is the practicality of his injunctions. It is more a matter of being sensible than of being "good." What I would see joined is the battle between reason and superstition, progress and prejudice, order and chaos, survival and destruction.

This selection is from *On Being Negro in America* (Indianapolis: Bobbs-Merrill, 1951; Indianapolis: Charter, 1962; New York: Harper & Row, 1969), 137-49.

MY MOST HUMILIATING
JIM CROW EXPERIENCE

When I lived in North Carolina, school principals in my section of the state made much of their commencements, Negro History Week celebrations, and other occasions.

They usually tried to get really big-name speakers, but failing in this, they called on lesser folk to make the address of the day. I had more than one invitation saying in effect, "Since Dr. James Shepard (or some other neon name) cannot be with us on this occasion, we would like to have you make the principal address." I generally accepted such invitations, not, as the saying goes, with alacrity, but certainly in an attitude of I'll-show-'em. Carefully preparing what I wished to say, I usually went forth stiff with challenge and armored in determination.

Under such circumstances as these, I was once invited to deliver the commencement address at a rather large school in a fairly large county seat and market town a hundred miles distant. Only the day before, the invitation had come by wire: "Speaker has failed us. Will you make the commencement speech May 3, 8:15 P.M.?"

I had stayed up all night putting the speech together, and when I arrived at the school it pleased me to no end to find the dilapidated auditorium already well filled. While the fifteen graduates, their excited mothers and fluttery teachers milled about us in the hallways, the principal and I stood talking. "I'm sure glad you could come," he said. "Dr. So-and-So (a great big North Carolina name) let us down." The principal was a little gray-black man with reddish eyes. He had been principal for nearly a quarter of a century.

When we finally marched into the auditorium, we found it crowded. People were standing in the aisles and sitting in the windows. I was elated. The only vacant seats I saw were the fourteen semi-circled chairs for the graduates down in front and the three regal-backed chairs on the rostrum—one for the principal, one for the honor graduate, and one for me.

Finally at 8:45 the program got under way with choral singing, and everybody had settled down to enjoy the festivities when, at the double doors in the back, the crowd broke and three white men marched in.

This, I could see, was an entirely unexpected development. The audience gawked. For a moment the principal moved nervously on the seat of his chair. But only for a moment. Then he got up, smiled graciously—oh, so graciously—at the white men, and said, "Come right up, gentlemen. Come right up."

Clapping, and at the same time indicating with his head, his shoulders, and his hands that the audience was to rise and clap also, he applauded the guests until they reached the rostrum, when he bowed and smiled some more. I had no time to wonder where the guests would sit. I was so fascinated by the unexpected performance that I had not even risen. I must have been the only person in the auditorium who had not gotten up.

But I did get up. The principal shooed me up, as one shoos a chicken off a roost. "Thanks, John," one of the white men said to the principal, and the three guests took the seats that the principal, the honor graduate, and I had previously warmed.

Led like a suspicious blind man off the rostrum, I found myself squeezed into a chair in a corner with a kindly but indignant lady, who patted my arm consolingly, one side, and a pumpkin-colored man on the other.

"You should of walked right on out," the lady said in a sort of exhaled stage-whisper. And I guess I should have, but I didn't. I'm a sucker for seeing things through."

This selection was published in *Negro Digest*, Dec. 1944.

II

FICTION

The following fictional excerpt is Chapter Nine from Part Two of Redding's only published novel *Stranger and Alone*. Titled "Lay the Burden Down," the chapter relates an episode in the university education of the protagonist Shelton Howden, a young man of color whose ambivalence about his race underscores his spiritual and social estrangement from others and from himself.

LAY THE BURDEN DOWN

From the early spring of 1929 until the autumn of 1931, Shelton Howden attended the University in New York. His contracts there were extremely limited. One or two of his white fellow students tried at first to be friendly, but Howden, abashed and suspicious, instinctively retreated. He sat in lectures and slipped almost furtively about the halls of the University, wearing a strained look of acute self-consciousness that was at once a confession and an apology.

Yet he was glad that he was the only Negro in his classes. The fact stimulated his pride in a strange, inexplicable way. It made him feel particularly privileged, the one out of many, an exception to the generality of Negroes. By the beginning of his second year, when the grip of the economic depression became most paralyzing, Howden seldom saw another Negro on the Heights. He did not have to worry about being racially linked to some ignorant burr-head out of nowhere, some poke who would surely have disgraced him.

Quite a fussy civic and social life effervesced around the Harlem Y.M.C.A. where Howden lived, but he took no part in it. He did make the acquaintance of a law student from Fordham and of another student from Cooper Union and of one or two other people who lived at the Y, but these contacts never developed beyond the casual stage. Once he did go to a movie with the law student, who afterwards invited him to the apartment of some friends, but Howden was disappointed by the whole thing. The apartment was a dingy walk-up in 132nd Street, and the law student's friends talked with bated enthusiasm about communism and with astringent bitterness about the race question. Later a mixed company, including a pretty, Jewish-looking white girl, came in, and Marxist dialectic (though Howden did not really recognize it as such) crackled like an electric storm.

The pretty girl tried to draw Howden out, really played up to him, but her conversation and her jaunty self-possession were frightening. And anyway, only white people who were communists—and Jewish, or at least foreign, at that—would go to a nobody Negro's apartment. Communism, it seemed to Howden, was merely a league of the dispossessed, and he did not want to think of himself as belonging to it. He put it in the familiar nutshell: the only communists were people who had no shirts to share. He himself had a dozen shirts. He had money in the bank.

On the race question his thinking—if it could be called that—was more complex, more deeply and intricately involved with his emotions. All he wanted to do, he told himself, was let the race problem take care of itself and live his own life as best he could. He really seemed to have a psychic block, at once cynical, self-assuring, and romantic. People who whined about the race question were simply rationalizing their own failures. He felt confirmed in this notion when he learned that the law student's friends were Wall Street messengers and porters, redcaps, and investigators for the Home Relief Bureau. He never went out with the law student again.

There were quite a few girls in and out of the Y, but Howden made no attempt to meet any. Indeed, he had a strange lack of conceit when it came to girls. He would see them in the lobby when he came down from the Heights late of an evening, and on Sundays he would see them in the Y restaurant—girls alone and with fellows and in pairs, some brown, some yellow, and some who might have been white. Sometimes he grew sick with desire for a woman, and then in shamed secret he would love himself. At the Y he always tried to pretend that the women were not there.

And when he walked the streets of Harlem, no one was there. Head up, gaze fixed on any distant object straight ahead, crippled arm held a little stiffly, slightly inward bent at his side, he strode with an arrogant thrust and purposefulness quite different from the way he moved on the Heights. While he saw the kaleidoscopic shuffle of Harlem's multitudinous life, he ignored it. He knew vaguely that there must be people somewhere there who were secure, comfortable, stable, but he had no access to them. The Harlem that he saw was a crowded nigger slum with which he refused to be identified, which he could emotionally reject.

Thus he lived on two planes, each with a different level of awareness, and for each of which he had a separate and distinct personality.

He fully recognized this one day toward the close of his final semester when one of his professors at the University issued an invitation to the class. He was going to entertain the class at the Faculty Club, he told them, and he wanted them all there to eat sandwiches and drink coffee and exchange ideas in an atmosphere less formal than that of the classroom. He was a youngish, eager man, still an assistant professor, but all sorts of people flocked to his lectures.

After class that day, instead of going immediately to his office, the door of which opened behind the lecture platform, Professor Bradford left his books and notes right where they were and sauntered into the hall. He was standing there when Howden, always the last to leave, came out. He was waiting for Howden it seemed.

"Eh," Professor Bradford said, "eh—do you have a minute?" He looked embarrassed, but he looked determined too. "Step back in here a minute, will you?"

Howden felt himself go tighter and more wary. He followed Professor Bradford back through the classroom into the cluttered office. The professor sat down in the swivel chair before the desk and swung it around at an angle not quite facing Howden. It was obvious that, having got this far, he was now thinking how to proceed. He made a sudden gesture of impatience.

"Eh—I don't know quite how to say this," Professor Bradford said. His angular face took on a lively color from his embarrassment. He ran his fingers through his thinning hair.

Howden waited, tense, in-drawn. He could feel the perspiration start in his armpits.

"Eh, this informal sort of seminar I'm asking the class to participate in—" He paused and swung his head suddenly to look at Howden. "Do you think we try to be democratic here at the University?"

The question took Howden by surprise. He had not thought about it, but he said, "Oh, yes, sir," and managed a weak, uncertain smile. He saw Professor Bradford's lank, strong-lined face take on a different expression.

"Well, damn it, man, we don't!" Professor Bradford said incisively. "And you ought to know it as well as I. Do you mean to say—?" Then he checked himself. "Sorry."

Howden felt an odd sense of hurt, of unnecessary injury. He waited because he did not know what else to do. He did not know what Professor Bradford was thinking. He could not tell what was in his mind. He heard the burred, Western voice go on reflectively.

"I thought of this informal discussion group before. I thought of having it meet once a month as a matter of fact—and that's what I should have done." He grunted, pausing pensively. "I should just have gone ahead and done it. But no, I wanted to make it all regular. You don't know what sticklers we are for regularity around here," he said, his eyes glinting satirically behind the steel-rimmed glasses. "I brought it up in departmental meeting. And do you know what? Some of my precious colleagues, some of my best-known and most important colleagues, some of my democracy-loving, ism-hating colleagues advised against it, objected to it. And do you know why?" he demanded rhetorically, suddenly rising from his chair. His voice dropped a pitch but tautened. One hand beat a rapid tattoo on the desk. "Because they said there were Jews and a Negro in the class and some of the students might object to socializing with them. But that wasn't all. I know that. It was only an excuse. They themselves objected to it."

Staring at Howden, Professor Bradford sat slowly down again. There was a long silence. Howden could hear the professor breathing. Without looking fully at him, Howden was aware of the bleak and baffled expression on the professor's face, of the shape of the knuckly hands as he lifted them both and slowly massaged his chin with the tips of his fingers. Howden felt very alert, very careful, very cold. He was not sure what it all meant, but he did not want it to have anything to do with him.

"For four months now I've let that stop me," Professor Bradford said, his voice weary and then getting strong again. "No one told me not to do it, but for four months I've been a moral coward, fearing the criticism of my colleagues for doing what I know to be right, thinking of everything but the one real point. Howden, it's a matter of principle for me—and for you, isn't it?" He paused and flung his head up and looked at Howden again. "I want you to come to that party."

Howden dropped his eyes. He felt that Professor Bradford was being unfair to him, putting him on a spot, trying to get him unnecessarily involved. Somehow he knew that his major professor, the one who either would or would not recommend him for a degree, was one of those in the department who had objected. Howden felt trapped, defenseless. It was no matter of principle, he thought. It was a matter of practical common sense, of self-interest, and of reality for him. If he failed Professor Bradford's course, that would be bad enough, though he didn't need the credit. But if he went against the wishes of his major professor, he would not get his degree. All at once Howden knew what he would do.

Then it happened. He was totally consicous of another self taking possession of him and yet leaving a part of him free to watch and weigh.

"I was going to tell you, sir," he said, covertly studying Professor Bradford's long, eager face. "It's like this, sir. I have an engagement for that night. I—I might be able to get there late. But it's about—you see, sir, it's about something very important to me." He fumbled with the lie.

"Oh, I see," Professor Bradford said, obviously let down. "Well—" He stood, smiling wearily. "But you understand, don't you, about the principle of the thing?"

"Yes, sir. And I would do it if I could," Howden said with deceptive earnestness.

When, at the end of the summer semester, Shelton Howden was granted his degree, and—thanks to the intercession of his major professor—was shortly thereafter offered a job at Arcadia State College for Negroes, he was glad to be through with the University and the North. He had put many things behind him, he thought—the orphanage, for instance, and the railroad, and the status he had known at New Hope. In two and a half years he had written the Clarksons twice, and they were behind him too.

He had never recovered the ruddy undercast to his skin, and now he was merely nondescriptly yellow, with yellow hair which he wore in pressed-down tiny waves straight back from his forehead. All in all, he had a bleached-out look about him.

This chapter is excerpted from *Stranger and Alone* (New York: Harper, [1950], 1969.)

III

HISTORY

In this excerpt from *They Came in Chains*, Redding describes the effects of slavery on both slaves and slaveholders in the American colonies and the early Republic. In a prose narrative that vividly recreates the past, he reveals the black struggle for freedom from bondage.

THE RATIONALE OF FEAR

SLAVEHOLDERS HAD REASON for packing pistols to bed, as any trader might have told them. Alexander Falconbridge, the surgeon on a slaver, could have pointed out that few of the Negroes brooked "the loss of their liberty" and that they were "ever on the watch to take advantage of the least negligence in their oppressors." Insurrections were "frequently the consequences," [1] and they were seldom put down without much bloodshed.

Almost from the beginning there was bloodshed. In Gloucester County, Virginia, in 1663, Negro slaves joined with white indentured servants in a conspiracy to rebel, but the plot was discovered. The alleged ringleaders were drawn and quartered and their bloody heads were impaled on posts in a public place. A slave plot to wipe out the whites galvanized three Virginia counties into panic in 1687, although the ambitious scale of the conspiracy had betrayed it. Again the leaders were caught and horribly done to death; but again the examples made of them did not deter other slaves from desperate bids for freedom. By 1710 there had been a dozen revolts attempted or accomplished in Virginia, Maryland, New Jersey and Massachusetts.

Arson was the facile tool of rebels and avengers. Many a planter leapt to wakefulness in the dead of night to find the sky lurid with flames from his grain pile, his stable, or even his dwelling. In New York, in 1712, a rabble of slaves set fire to some buildings late one night. When the whites rushed forth to put out the flames, the slaves, armed with guns and knives, fell upon them, killing nine. Still unsatisfied, the rebels prowled the fear-shocked streets for several hours threatening death to the whites and putting buildings to the torch. Nor did they all give up when soldiers converged upon them. "One shot first his wife and then himself and some who had hid themselves in town when they went to apprehend them cut their own throats." But more than twenty were caught and sentenced to die, one by "slow fire," that he might "continue in torment for eight or ten hours."

Ships on the brutal Middle Passage from the West Indies to the mainland were sometimes the rolling stages of rebellion. The American slaver *Kentucky* was one such—but she put it down and forty-seven slaves, among them a woman, were killed for daring to revolt. "They were ironed or chained, two together, and when they were hung, a rope was put around their necks and they were drawn up to the yardarm clear of the sail. This did not kill them, but only choked or strangled them. They were then shot in the breast and the bodies thrown overboard. If only one of two that were ironed together was to be hung, the rope was put around his neck and he was drawn up clear of the deck and his leg laid across the rail and chopped off to save the irons." [2]

How the concept of the patient, docile Negro ever came into being is a minor marvel of historical delusion. It was created against tremendous odds of fact and circumstance. Perhaps it was a psychological necessity of the sort that sometimes prompts people to blind themselves to wish-destroying fact, and little boys, frightened of the dark, to whistle gay, pretentious tunes. Whatever the cause of it, there the delusion was, bigger than life, and, it might be said, as real—a sort of sublimation of guilt, or fear, or both. It was there when all actuality denied it. It was there in complete contradiction to the law, to the Black Codes which said in effect that the Negro was restive, dangerous, murderous under slavery; that the Negro loved freedom enough to hazard his life for it on only the dimmest chance of winning; and that in order to quench the leaping fires of his rebellious nature, the flood of despotism must mount unchecked.

The concept of the Negro as knee-bending, head-bowing slave was there, but the law courts did not act as if they credited it. The policy of the law was to avoid the prosecution of masters whose punishment of slaves was "malicious, cruel, and excessive" even to the point of murder. "The power of the master must be absolute to render the submission of the slave perfect," declared a justice of the North Carolina Supreme Court. And the courts of law went ruthlessly about the business of developing juridical and social means of carrying out an involved but consummate system of controls.

It took a little time, for the frontiersman was highly volatile, highly individual. Personal precedent and privilege yielded only haltingly to communal law. But eventually a creed emerged, for it was a transfer-in-trust from Caribbean new world history, a necessitous condition of modern slavery, and a resource of sanguine expectation in the heart of new American man. And what a man he was! How clear-mettled and how ambiguous, how irresolute and how obstinate, how self-righteous and how self-condemning, how kind and how callous, how simple, complex and altogether contradictory. And these opposing attributes are shown nowhere better than in the way he handled slavery.

Devices for controlling slaves developed with the slave system or sprang man-size from the womb of expediency. An early device was the simple but effective one of separating slaves of the same family or tribe. Often the inhabitants of entire African villages, closely knit by ties of memory and blood, were captured and sold individually into slavery. Thus a mother might be traded off into the West Indies, a father in Virginia, and the children scattered among owners in New York, New Jersey and Massachusetts. Later, cries of indignation arose over this dispersion when it affected families that had known nothing but bondage. Indeed, it was called the "darkest crime" of slavery. Curiously enough, while at the same time men argued that slaves had no family-feeling and no finer instincts, those who wished to earn or keep reputations as good masters counted it a mortal sin to drag mother from child, wife from husband, sister from brother. Much of the opprobrium that was heaped upon slave dealers stemmed from a general feeling of revulsion over this practice. Private owners seldom followed it except to save themselves from great financial embarrassment, or except as punishment for the most unruly slaves. From the beginning however, no horror attached to disrupting the family ties of slaves just brought from Africa, and yet it must have been most cruel for these bewildered strangers in a strange land. All they had—if not family love—was tribal memory and the sense of community they shared with each other. Sundering these bonds of consanguinity, of group experience and identity, was the ultimate ravishment.

Nor did it always produce the desired end. Some slaves of course, cut off from all the things and people they had known, committed suicide. But such cases were exceptional, for even under slavery and given to spells of deep melancholy, the Africans had a robust love of life. Forced because of the separation from their own kind, to learn a strange language, take on an alien mode of life, acquire a foreign culture-pattern, the early slaves knit up ties with white indentured servants. The mixing of these two elements in the population compounded discontent. Indentured servants had grievances too. The legal and customary distinctions between them and slaves were so slight as hardly to be observed. They were, most of these servants, "unruly" and "spirited," and the Oliverians among them had a green knowledge of what group rebellion meant. They made common cause with the slaves.

Indeed, as already mentioned, the first serious servile conspiracy to rebel found servants and slaves allied in 1663. Nine years later the colonial Assembly of Virginia deemed it wise to point up an enactment permitting runaway slaves to be killed with impunity with the following words:

Forasmuch as it hath beene manifested to this grand assembly that many negroes have lately beene, and are now out in rebellion in sundry parts of this country, and that noe means have yet beene found for the apprehension and suppression of them from whom many mischiefes of very dangerous consequences may arise to the country if either other negroes, Indians or *servants* should happen to fly forth and joyne with them.

The threat to slave control that these alliances held was very real in some of the other colonies too. New Jersey was aware of it and took steps to put it down. New York was startled in 1741 by the sworn testimony of Mary Barton and Peggy Kerry, white indentured servants and the confessed love-partners of slaves, who revealed a servile plot in which at least twenty-five white redemptioners were allied with four times that number of Negro slaves. The testimony of these two women brought to punishment more than a hundred persons—among them Peggy Kerry's lover and the father of her child—some of whom were burned at the stake, some hanged, and some banished.

All during the late years of the seventeenth and the early years of the eighteenth centuries servant-slave rebellion flared with frightening persistence. A rumor was enough to throw whole countries into panic and to pull the colonial legislative trigger in alarm. Laws for the control of slaves grew steadily more rigorous, until, in general, the master's right of property in his slave involved absolute control over the slave's person and conduct. Thus a master could whip his slaves at will, cut their rations, crop their ears, brand them, pillory them, or inflict upon them any other punishment that seemed, in his judgment, "right." Slaves could not leave their masters' premises without a pass. They had no right of assembly. They could not own property and therefore could not buy or sell or trade. Arms were forbidden them. Dogs were taboo. Slaves could not sue or be sued, prosecute for a battery, nor enter a civil suit. They could not give evidence against a white person. Not even in self-defense could they lift their hands against a "Christian" white, and in Virginia until 1788 it was legally impossible for a white man to murder a slave. The death of a slave under punishment was either accidental homicide or manslaughter, neither of which made white men liable to prosecution.

For the execution of the distinctive body of "Negro laws" most colonies, and later the states, had distinctive courts and procedures. Virginia early instituted a special court for the "speedy prosecution" of slaves. In most states slaves had no right to trial by jury and got none. They could be, and most often were, tried, usually on the warrant of a commission of oyer and terminer, in "Negro courts." The justices might, and frequently did have only the most casual acquaintance with the technicalities of the law. The slave himself, of course, had no acquaintance whatever. He did not really need any; nor, had he had, would it have done him any good. Putting into words the original and long-prevailing fact, the Constitutional Court of South Carolina ruled:

A slave can invoke neither Magna Charta not common law. . . . In the very nature of things he is subject to despotism. Law to him is only a compact between his rulers, and the questions which concern him are matters agitated between them. The various acts concerning slaves contemplate throughout the subordination of the servile class to every free white person and enforce the stern policy which the relation of master and slave necessarily requires. Any conduct of a slave inconsistent with due subordination contravenes the purpose of these acts.

This was in 1847, when by some accounts the ironhanded repressiveness of customary attitudes and of law had somewhat relaxed and, by these same accounts, slavery in the South was a benevolent paternalism.

But when the Black Codes started generating their blacker progeny, the middle of the nineteenth century was a long way off. Meantime the spirit of their increasing purpose seeped into factors of psychological conditioning so various, so subtle and pervasive as to defy complete analysis. There was propaganda; and yet it was not wholly this, for these prolocutors—politicians, preachers, and professors—believed it. Doctrine and the sincerity with which it was uttered were a hard combination to withstand. That belief came after the substance of the law only proves the influence of matter over mind. The law had said that the Negro was inferior; now pointing to the slave's mudsill status as empirical proof, anthropologists and sociologists declared so too. "The political responsibility for bringing slavery to this continent," said the politicians, "can be wiped from our escutcheon." The professors at first were more restrained and cautious. "We think we are prepared to say that when all the evils of slavery [in the South] are put together . . . the fair conclusion will be that the whole sum is but a small fraction of the same classes of evils that from time immemorial have belonged and still belong to the barbarism of the fatherland of this race. . . . We see, then, that the *evils* of American slavery are blessings as compared with the general fate of the African race in their native continent." But professorial restraint went by the board in the 1830's, when Professor Thomas R. Dew, of the College of William and Mary, advanced a philosophical defense of slavery. It was a defense fashioned after the Positivist social order of Auguste Comte, and it boldly cast aside the principles of brotherhood and equality. Liberty and equality? Mere romantic nonsense. Brotherhood? A snare and a delusion. "And what is the meaning [of equality] in the Charter of our rights? Simply, that royal blood, and noble blood, is no better than any other blood; and therefore, that we will have no king, and no aristocracy. . . . It goes no further than to cut off the hereditary claims of kings and nobles."

Nor was this all by any means.

In the beginning slaveholders generally opposed religious instruction and baptism for slaves. They believed that an understanding of Christianity would create grave disturbances among the black people. It was better that the African priests continue to practice the heathen rights of Obi and perpetuate their outlandish gods of sticks and straw among the slaves. The law of 1667, which declared that baptism did not alter "the condition of a person as to his bondage or his freedom," aroused no proselyting zeal among the master class. "Talk to a planter of the soul of a negro," an English observer said in 1705, "and he'll be apt to tell you (or at least his actions speak loudly) that the body of one of them may be worth twenty Pounds; but the souls of an hundred of them would not yield him one Farthing." An English lady of the West Indies wrote the Reverend Morgan Godwyn, a rector in Virginia, that one "might as well baptize puppies as Negroes." Still later, in 1765, a Quaker missionary was moved to complain that "it is too manifest to be denied, that the life of religion is almost lost where slaves are very numerous."

But the English Society for the Propagation of the Bible in Foreign Parts did not campaign for the religious instruction of slaves entirely to no avail. Before the close of the eighteenth century, many churches had slave galleries and many masters hired carefully chosen ministers to preach to their congregated blacks. There were even some Negro preachers, but they were harried bootleggers of the Gospel, like the Reverend William Moses, of Williamsburg, Virginia. Frequently arrested and whipped for holding meetings, Preacher Moses nevertheless carried on between 1770 and 1790, secretly preparing other Negroes for his high calling. Black congregations presided over by black ministers aroused the quick fear and suspicion of the slaveholders, and for a time after 1800, the year of the slave revolt led by Gabriel Prosser, Negro preachers were rated dangerous criminals, for some of them were suspected of being involved with Gabriel.

Still, in spite of the hindrances to participation in the religious life, about one in twenty-five slaves was a member of a church in 1800. To preach to these, ministers were chosen for their skill at squaring the fact of slavery with the word of God. Apparently it was not a hard skill to acquire, and though the established churches—Episcopal and Catholic—did not actually require it, their bishops and archbishops, some of whom owned slaves themselves, looked upon it with smug approval. The right kind of preaching was a method of slave-control. And, indeed, compelling slaves to go to church, as masters did increasingly, might help save both souls and slavery.

"Cursed be Canaan, a servant of servants shall he be unto his brethren!" The eternal righteousness of God had reduced the blacks to their low estate. That was Gospel. It was expounded nicely, emphasized persistently, promoted fervently. "Masters are taught in the Bible, how they must rule their servants, and servants how they must obey their masters," preached the Reverend Alexander Glennie to the slaves in his South Carolina parish. To make sure of its being heard, he read the biblical passage twice over, and continued with kindly persuasiveness, with gentle exhortation: "Our Heavenly Father commands that you, who are servants, should 'be obedient to your masters according to the flesh'; that is, to your earthly master, the master that you serve here while in the body. Here is a very plain command: 'servants be obedient': be obedient to your masters. . . . As you ought to understand well what is the will of God respecting you, I will read to you again this part of the Bible. 'Servants, be obedient. . . .' " [3]

It is no wonder that Frederick Douglass was to say later that he "learned that 'God, up in the sky,' made everybody: and that he made *white* people to be masters and mistresses, and *black* people to be slaves. This did not satisfy me. . . ."

Nor did it satisfy thousands of others before him and after, for slaves were not always fooled by casuistry and sophistry. Their starved emotions did not leap to the lure. They needed a stronger stimulus, and many of them were regular attendants at secret "brush-arbor" meetings and at clandestine gatherings in some slaves' quarters where in the pitch-black of freighted midnight they could evoke some red-eyed god out of the time of their beginnings. They practiced strange medicine then, brought out perhaps the fetishistic survivals of Obi or of Oxala, and chanted in low voices what they could remember of the white folks' hymns set to the pulsing, melancholy minors of African rhythm.

Yet, somehow they evolved a notion of the Christian God. He was a less temperate, but a kinder, more loving God than their masters'. He understood their troubles and would make things right in the sweet by'n by. Sometimes they grew impatient with the white preachers' notions about God. Sometimes they asked questions. Old Uncle Silas who rose in the middle of a sermon to ask whether "us slaves gonna be free in Heaven" got a sophistic brush-off, but the question was the measure of his misery in bondage on earth.

More immediately effective than propaganda in controlling slaves were the personal punishments and rewards that were practically standard on every large slaveholding plantation. For an offense that violated the rules of propriety, a slave might be severely flogged or branded on one or both cheeks. Acts of impropriety ranged from a certain look in the eye of a slave to open impudence; and impudence itself might mean anything, or, as Frederick Douglass put it, "nothing at all, just according to the caprice of the master overseer, at the moment." It was an offense that could be committed in various ways, "in the tone of an answer; in answering at all; in not answering; in the expression of the countenance; in the motion of the head; in the gait, manner and bearing of the slave." No doubt many a slave was marked for life because of a gesture made in a moment when his customary vigilance was relaxed. No doubt, also, many a master had practical cause to regret his ready recourse to brand and whip. Micajah Ricks, a slaveholder of North Carolina, advertised for a runaway: "A few days ago before she went off, I burnt her with a hot iron on the left side of her face; I tried to make the letter M, and she kept a cloth over her head and face, and a fly bonnet on her head so as to cover the burn."

In the final analysis, though few masters seemed to realize it, rewards paid larger and more certain dividends. The loyalty of the body servant and house slave, of old Black Mammy and Uncle Tom and Zeke, over which the Southern romanticists go into their purplest paeans, would have been much less but for the remainders from festive boards, the cast-off clothes, and the occasional coins that were thrown their way. As for the field hands, gay headcloths and chewing tobacco accomplished what lashing could not. Thomas Ruffin, a chief justice of the North Carolina Supreme Court, said that "trivial matters have exceedingly great effect in improving the slave and uniting him to his owner." He knew one successful planter who had produced this effect simply by putting a cheap looking-glass in his slaves' quarters, and another who had done it by having a fence built around the slaves' burial plot.

For good work and for being tractable, slaves were occasionally rewarded with small amounts of cash. Christmas, a holiday that lasted a week on liberal plantations, was usually the time of this happy dispensation. A woman might get as much as a dollar; a man twice as much. This was great plenty for those who had so little. The slaves could do what they wished with their money. Some got drunk. Indeed, for a slave "not to be drunk during the holidays was disgraceful" and aroused masters' suspicions. But to be drunk at any other time also aroused suspicions. An inebriated and foot-loose Negro was a dangerous thing.

But some slaves had other uses for their money. The North Carolina *Standard,* a paper published at Raleigh, lamented satirically that Negroes too often spent money for "expensive costume, whereby very respectable white dandies are scandalized, being insulted by the successful imitation of the style and manner of exquisite and exclusive gentility." Some of those who were vain and improvident enough to buy expensive clothes were also ungrateful enough to run away in them. A Pennsylvania slave master, for instance, advertised a runaway slave as having "a beaver hat, a green worsted coat, a closebodied coat with a green narrow frieze cape," other clothes and a violin. In 1793, one John Dulin, of Maryland, after describing the absconder's rich haberdashery, declared that his runaway slave also had an ample supply of funds.

From giving slaves Christmas money to do with as they wished, to giving them time which they could hire out was a hesitant step in an uncertain direction. Some masters, liberal beyond common and uncommonly affected by pangs of conscience, took it as a means of lightening the slaves' bondage and went on from there to give slaves their freedom or to allow them a share of the earnings, and trusted slaves who had wangled liberal terms could lay by considerable sums. One Milly Lea, of North Carolina, an expert seamstress, saved more than a thousand dollars in a dozen years. Her case was unusual, not because of the comforting size of the sum but because the court gave her a legal right to it. Generally the courts frowned upon slaves having more than enough coin to jingle in their pockets.

Slaves were hired out to industry. Hezekiah Coffin, a manufacturer of Rhode Island, wrote to Moses Brown in 1763 wishing to know "by the first opportunity what the negroes wages was" that he might settle with the masters. The tobacco factories of Richmond, the warehouses and bustling waterfronts of Norfolk, Charleston and New Orleans, and the labor-hungry lumber plants of the mid-South hired the time of slaves. Slaves were used in foundries as forgemen and blacksmiths. In the process of building America and making it go, these slaves learned many skills. They mined coal and tended the engines that burned it; they felled timber and planed the boards for building; they quarried stone, and wrought iron, and tempered steel, and created tools. They were more free than the "free" Negroes and more secure than the free poor whites.

But the unequal competition between bond labor and free was one of the grosser evils of slavery. Interclass and intra-sectional at first, it came to have an impact on the economic competition between North and South in direct proportion to the dependence of one section upon the other. But this was somewhat later. The interclass impact aroused resentment against the hired-out slave and led to demands for his restraint.

Advertisements such as the following appeared frequently in the latter half of the eighteenth century:

Five hundred laborers wanted. We will employ the above number of laborers to work on the Muscle Shoals Canal, etc., at the rate of fifteen dollars per month, for twenty-six working days, or we will employ negroes by the year, or for a less time, as may suit the convenience of the planters. We will also be responsible to slave holders who hire their negroes to us, for any injury or damage that may hereafter happen in progress of blasting rock or of caving in of banks.

Wanted to hire, a negro wheelwright. Master's interest protected.

The free white mechanics and laborers realized their disadvantage, but there was not much they could do about it. Politics was one weapon, and violence was another, but the first was ineffective, as the second was dangerous. Slaveholders were not going to stand for trifling with the incomes which their hired-out hands brought them; they were not going to have valuable slave artisans and craftsmen molested. Men of the master class had most of the power in the South. The great tobacco plantations and the tobacco factories belonged to them. Later, the land on which the cotton grew, the gins that cleaned it, and the mills that spun it into cloth were theirs. The political interests were nearly all gathered in their hands, and in South Carolina at least they manipulated them to their exclusive advantage by setting up qualifications for office that slammed the door on all but members of their own class. On the expanding

Southern frontier, the planters exercised the raw frontier right of the strong to dominate and even utterly destroy the weak. By their connivance and their naked contempt for the poorer whites, they built solid the tradition of class enmity and they cultivated the resultant hatred between laboring white and laboring black, slave and free.

The residue of power reposed in a sturdy, middle class of whites —Scotch Presbyterians, German Lutherans, and Irish Protestants— who were non-slaveholding, independent farmers, business men and professionals. White labor made its appeal to these and gained some indefatigable friends who abhorred slavery and all its works. These were the men who wrote letters and signed petitions. In Athens, Georgia, they complained that hired-out slaves had so much cheapened white labor that all but a few white masons and carpenters were forced to leave the city. In other places in Georgia they protested against "negro mechanics whose masters reside in other places, and who pay nothing toward the support of the government." Registering their own dissatisfaction, white craftsmen in South Carolina, North Carolina and Tennessee inveighed against the training of slaves in skilled trades and against masters who used their slave mechanics to underbid free workers in contracts, to the great injury of said free workers. Middle class Virginians considered it a "public evil" that the increase of white seamen was discouraged by the use of slaves as pilots, navigators, and sailors, and they did something about it. In 1784 a law was passed which limited the number of Negroes used in river and bay navigation to one third the total of persons so employed. Within ten years restrictive legislation on hiring out slaves was pretty general, and North Carolina had made it a serious offense for a master to allow a slave to hire his time "under any pretense whatever."

2

By the middle of the eighteenth century strange ideas called "humanitarian" were being bruited about. They dealt with such concepts as the dignity of the human personality, the inalienable rights of man, the responsibility of government, and the place of man in a world from which magic and witchcraft and mystical metaphysics had been forever banished by the bright-eyed philosophers who followed after Descartes. Humanitarianism, which was eventually to abolish slavery, bring new spirit to penal codes and institutions, and build refuges for the weak and unfortunate, was disturbing. The notions to which it gave rise had an unsettling effect upon slavery, an institution which, anyway, was not calculated to ease the conscience.

Indeed, the psychology of the average slaveholder was already warped and intorted; his acts were often contrary to his beliefs, his head often in mortal conflict with his heart. His was a split personality, baffled and hypersensitized and infected with an insidious illness. Humanitarianism feezed him. The rationale of slavery was in direct contradiction to the doctrines which, after the 1740's, were getting clearer and clearer statement. It was contrary to the flux of the romantic tide that was beginning to swell and beat against the shores of the western world. The effort to engraft slavery on the whole way of American life and to have its acceptance unquestioned lacked moral conviction. The best minds and the leading minds commenced to probe for more tenable positions, less shaky ground. Thomas Jefferson made known his opposition to slavery. Later his first draft of the Declaration of Independence indicted the King of England for violating the "most sacred rights of life and liberty of a distant people, who never offended him, captivating them into slavery in another hemisphere or to incur miserable death in their transportation thither." Less vocal, Henry Laurens, George Mason and St. George Tucker stood at Jefferson's shoulder.

It is a curious fact that the stirring slogans of the western worldwide revolution, which trumpeted the principles of philanthropy— "Liberty or death!" "Liberty, fraternity, equality!"—seemed to abate the tensions of American slavery. Men took the word for the purging deeds and welcomed it with fervor. But riding furiously on the winds of these slogans came the early abolitionists. They, too, were welcomed—but dubiously and with reservations. They pleaded, coaxed—especially the Quakers, Baptists and Methodists—formed societies, and set examples. Their earnest preachments converted some who, already half convinced of human brotherhood, freed their slaves.

When the war itself came, Negroes fought. Some in New England were freed to fight. Some fought as substitutes for their masters. The first man to die under the guns of the Redcoats was Crispus Attucks, an escaped slave. Peter Salem distinguished himself at Bunker Hill

by killing the British Major Pitcairn, and Salem Poor was cited for
heroic action in the Battle of Charleston. In that first year of war,
there was scarcely a skirmish or a battle that black men did not fight
in. But it did not make sense that slaves should fight to win for
others a freedom they could not enjoy. It travestied the principles of
the Revolution, as James Otis was quick to declare.

If Otis thought that something was wrong in abstract principle
only, he was soon disillusioned. Negroes were going over to the
British, who promised them freedom. Lord Dunmore, the Royal
Governor of Virginia, had issued a proclamation to that effect. He
armed slaves to fight against their masters. This disaffection of
the Negroes made a bad situation worse. At first opposed to the en-
listment of Negroes in the Continental Army, General George
Washington was forced to relent enough to admit free Negroes. But
escaping from slavery to go over to the British—or just escaping—
continued to cause grave concern. If Thomas Jefferson was right,
thirty thousand slaves escaped from Virginia masters in one revolutionary year alone. As the situation grew more desperate, following
the gloomy winter of 'Seventy-eight, the colonies themselves relaxed
General Washington's policy still further. New Hampshire, Massachusetts and Rhode Island enlisted battalions of blacks. Maryland
mustered a troop of seven hundred and fifty, promising them freedom and paying bounty to their masters. New York did the same;
Virginia and North Carolina took similar steps. By the Constitution of 1780, Massachusetts practically abolished slavery. Pennsylvania, New York, Connecticut and New Jersey passed acts for
gradual emancipation. Maryland prohibited the importation of slaves
and made manumission easier.

So Negroes fought all through the war. They were at Ticonderoga,
Bemis Heights and Stony Point. With Lafayette was one James
Armistead, so astute a spy that he completely fooled the British Lord
Cornwallis and saved Lafayette's army from defeat. In desperate
battle against Hessian mercenaries at Point Bridge, New York,
Rhode Island blacks "sacrificed themselves to the last man" in defense
of an important position. The only woman to bear arms in the Continental Army was a Negro, Deborah Gannett, who enlisted as Robert
Shurtliff and discharged "the duties of a faithful, gallant soldier, and
at the same time," read the citation of the state of Massachusetts,
"preserved the virtue and chastity of her sex. . . ." A Negro, Captain

Mark Starlin, commanded the Virginia naval vessel *Patriot,* and Negroes served on the *Royal Louis,* the *Tempest* and the *Diligence.* They were at Red Bank, Princeton and Eutaw Springs. Black Samson of Brandywine, whom the Negro poet Dunbar eulogizes, was not a myth: he did "do great deeds of valor." Negroes crossed the Delaware with Washington, died at Valley Forge, and quartered arms with their white comrades at Yorktown, where, legend has it, one black fellow, forgetting military protocol, yelled out, "Mr. British General, you am Cornwallis, but I'se going now to change your name to Cobwallis, for General Washington, with us colored pussons, has shelled all the corn offen you!"[4] When the war was done at last, many Negro soldiers were reenslaved, but by 1790 there were fifty-nine thousand free blacks, forming, as many came to feel, an ominous cloud on the social horizon.

The convulsive struggle of the Revolution brought to furious boil many simmering problems. There was the war itself to recover from. The Articles of Confederation, strong enough to hold the states together in time of mutual danger, were now pendulous and weak under the unlooked-for burden of victory. That the thin membrane of confederate government threatened to rupture was well recognized by 1787. There was a great deal of jealous ambition on the part of each state, and the "diplomats" in the Congress were each concerned with the particular rights and privileges of his own state. In short, the Confederation could scarcely be called a government; "it was an assemblage of governments."

In the opaqueness of their inexperience, men tried to separate political issues from social and social from economic, but there was no way of separating them. The common people had little left them save political liberty, which was still something of an abstraction, and land, which was largely devastated. Commerce was gone, and money had all but disappeared. The public debt was $170,000,000. In Massachusetts, two thousand men, led by Daniel Shays, rose up with demands that the collection of debts be suspended. It was a spontaneous rebellion that lasted several weeks. The concept of aristocratic rule was challenged. The common people demanded land reforms and guarantees of human rights. Adding their strident voices to the clamor, anti-slavery men called for an end to human bondage.

Though slavery was only one of the issues that faced the Constitutional Convention of 1787, its influence was so pervasive and its resilient fibers had become so entwined about the structure of colonial life that it could not be ignored. Indeed, two questions—the taxation of imports, and proportional representation—dragged the slavery issue out in stark and ominous nakedness. It was an ironic and a mixed-up business. For one thing, the Virginia and Maryland delegates stood with the North, where opposition to slavery had grown steadily through the Revolution.

The North argued largely on moral grounds. As a matter of fact, the Pennsylvania Society for Promoting the Abolition of Slavery, founded in 1775, had prepared a resolution to be presented to the Convention by Benjamin Franklin, president of the Pennsylvania group and a delegate to the Convention. George Mason of Virginia declared that "slavery discourages arts and manufactures. The poor despise labor when performed by slaves. . . . [Slaves] produce the most pernicious effect on manners. Every master of slaves is born a petty tyrant. They bring the judgment of heaven on a Country. As nations can not be rewarded or punished in the next world they must in this. By an inevitable chain of causes and effects providence punishes national sins, by national calamities." The North, where steps had already been taken to end slavery importation, wanted an end put to "the infernal traffic." Counting slaves in the population, Luther Martin, of Maryland, thought, would encourage the traffic, and that it was "inconsistent with the principles of the revolution and dishonorable to the American character to have such a feature [as slavery] in the Constitution."

The South argued largely on economic and political grounds, though Charles Pinckney, a delegate from South Carolina, begged leave to point out that "slavery was justified by the example of the world." John Rutledge, also from South Carolina, declared that "religion and humanity had nothing to do with the slavery question. Interest alone is the governing principle with Nations. . . . If the Northern States consult their interest, they will not oppose the increase of slaves which will increase the commodities of which they will become the carriers." Pinckney echoed this same thinking: the traffic in slaves is "for the interest of the whole Union. The more slaves, the more produce to employ the carrying trade; the more consumption also, and the more of this, the more of revenue for the common treasury." The South thought slavery consistent with the interest of the country, and did not want the traffic stopped by any means. As to the question of proportional representation in Congress, the North which professed to look upon slaves as human beings did not want them counted as part of the population. The South, whose laws had the practical effect of making slaves *things,* wanted slaves counted on an equality with whites.

The great debate dragged on for four months. It ended less in compromise than in the North's capitulation and in a sweeping victory for the South.

"We The People of the United States, in Order to form a more perfect Union, establish Justice, insure domestic Tranquility . . . do ordain and establish . . ." that:

"Representatives and direct Taxes shall be apportioned among the several States which may be included within this Union, according to their respective Numbers, which shall be determined by adding to the whole Number of free Persons, including those bound to Service for a Term of Years, and excluding Indians not taxed, three fifths of all other Persons."

And that:

"The migration or Importation of such Persons as any of the States now existing shall think proper to admit, shall not be prohibited by Congress prior to the Year one thousand eight hundred and eight, but a Tax or duty may be imposed on such Importation, not exceeding ten dollars for each person."

And that:

"No Person held to Service or Labour in one State, under the Laws thereof, escaping into another, shall, in Consequence of any Law or Regulation therein, be discharged from such Service or Labour, but shall be delivered up on Claim of the Party to whom such Service or Labour may be due."

The humanitarian light of the Revolution, blown out in the breath of fearful compromise, was not to come on again for almost three-quarters of a century.

Indeed, what had been a happy if partial and fortuitous exercise of equalitarian principle during the Revolution was become a curse by 1790. The presence of so many escaped slaves was embarrassing to the North, now that the Constitution provided that they should be delivered up on demand. In the South the presence of free Negroes was embarrassing, for such Negroes were a constant threat to the

slaveholders' control. Disaffected Negroes, ran common opinion in
the slavery section, were usually free Negroes. Laws to restrict the
increase of this class were passed. Most Southern states, following a
pattern set by Virginia in 1793, prohibited the immigration of free
blacks. In North Carolina the free Negro could not go beyond the
county adjoining his home county. Arriving at Southern ports, free
colored sailors were not allowed to leave ship, or were beaten and
thrown into jail. Restriction, prohibition, proscription. The free
Negro could not vote, could not own or carry arms, could not sell
certain commodities, could not be employed as a clerk or typesetter,
could not obtain credit without the permission of a guardian, could
not be without a guardian, could not testify against a white man
in court, could not entertain slaves nor be entertained by them.
Smothered under the limitations imposed upon him by law, the free
Negro might almost as well have been enslaved.

What had happened was that several factors and events had made
the South more sensitive about slavery after the Revolutionary War.
First of all, the period was one of economic uncertainty. The war
had brought heavy losses in personal wealth. The British had carried off "thousands of slaves, helped themselves to costly silver
plate . . . and left many plantation homes in flames." Rice and
indigo, with fewer slaves to produce them, were in a state of acute
depression. Transportation was badly disorganized; markets scattered
and uncertain. The price of slaves was way down. A good female
slave advertised as "ripe for child-bearing and strong in wind and
limb" could bring no more than two hundred dollars. A good male
slave, offered for five hundred dollars, was thought to be over-
priced. Tobacco, the great cash crop of Maryland, Virginia and
North Carolina, was a glut on the market. The institution of slavery
seemed to be in a precarious state of health.

Moreover, the abolitionist, a grim, persistent breed, had never
given up. Anti-slavery men like Benjamin Rush and Jeremy Belknap,
John Jay and John Filson, David Rice and Robert Pleasants spoke,
wrote and made schemes against slavery. "A thousand laws," shouted
David Rice, "can never make that innocent which the Divine Law
has made criminal; or give them [slaveholders] a right to that which
the Divine Law forbids them to claim." [5] In 1794 various local abolitionist groups—and there were a dozen such from Massachusetts
down to Delaware—formed a cooperate body, and the direction

and combined force of anti-slavery thought put the South on the moral defensive. It could no longer blame the continuance of American slavery on England. Indeed, aroused by Wilberforce, Sharp and Clarkson, the Mother Country was having anti-slavery troubles of her own.

But also in England something more was happening, and its impact upon the slave economy of the South was to be terrific. Industrialization was happening; coal was happening; steam was happening. The invention of the power loom made the manufacture of great quantities of cloth a matter of throwing an engine switch. All at once the demand for cheap textile fibers rose to a strident pitch. Cotton was the answer, but the preparation of cotton for milling was slow and laborious, by hand. If only a quick way could be found to separate the fiber from seed and stalky trash, cotton would be cheaper than silk or linen and more comfortable and versatile than wool. Just at the right time, wandering down from New England, Eli Whitney built the first cotton gin. Moribund slavery, having a powerful restorative now, took a new lease on life. Cotton meant workers, and workers meant slaves—more and more slaves as new lands were opened up and more people bowed down to cotton as king.

Just as this development was getting under way however, a hundred thousand slaves rose up in revolt on the French island of Haiti. Within a few weeks they destroyed "200 sugar plantations, 600 coffee plantations" and a like number of cotton and indigo plantations. More than two thousand whites were killed without mercy. The island became a fire-drenched waste. Bryan Edwards, visiting Haiti almost a month after the start of the nightmare, wrote: "We arrived in the harbor of Le Cap at evening . . . and the first sight which arrested our attention as we approached was a dreadful scene of devastation by fire. The noble plain adjoining Le Cap was covered with ashes, and the surrounding hills, as far as the eye could reach, everywhere presented to us ruins still smoking and houses and plantations at that moment in flames." But after a month, six months, sixteen months, the terrible destruction was not done. It looked as if the Haitian revolutionaries had set in motion a stupendous chain reaction that would blast slavery from the earth. For two years, under their great leader Toussaint L'Ouverture, they struggled unquelled, defeating the British, the Spaniards and the soldiers of

Napoleon. At last the First Republic granted freedom to all slaves loyal to France.

The bloody vengeance done in Haiti revitalized the South's old fears and gave deep concern to the whole country. Nor did these lessen with the restoration of order in the Caribbean, for that order was of the Negroes' making, and St. Domingo was practically a Black Republic. The potentials in the American situation were plain. Would American slaveholders be driven to the same expediency of granting freedom to the slaves—and that at a time when the economic promise of slavery was just risen like a golden sun? Thomas Jefferson at least thought this, or worse. "I become daily more and more convinced," he wrote in 1793, "that all the West India Islands will remain in the hands of the people of colour, and a total expulsion of these whites sooner or later will take place. It is high time we should foresee the bloody scenes which our children certainly, and possibly ourselves (south of Potomac), have to wade through, and try to avert them."

Rumors flew. Aided by the French, who were intent upon world conquest, the revolt-freed Haitians were going to invade the United States and set American blacks at liberty. Failing this, picked agents, even then filtering through the South from the ports of New Orleans, Charleston and Baltimore, were to spread sedition among the slaves. Thomas Jefferson, more sagacious than most, and then Secretary of State, had some part in giving these wild reports currency. He wrote the Governor of South Carolina:

A French gentleman, one of the refugees from St. Domingo, informs me that two Frenchmen, from St. Domingo also, of the names Castaing and La Chaise, are about setting out from this place for Charleston, with a design to excite an insurrection among the negroes. He says that this is in execution of a general plan, formed by the Brissotine party at Paris, the first branch of which has been carried into execution at St. Domingo. My informant is a person with whom I am well acquainted, of good sense, discretion and truth, and certainly believes this himself. I inquired of him the channel of his information. He told me it was one which had never been found to be mistaken. . . . Castaing is described as a small dark mulatto, and La Chaise as a Quatron of a tall fine figure.

Whether these rumors were true or not, credulity was grandsired by fear and given substance by events. Slave revolts and conspiracies to revolt broke out like an epidemic in the States. Undoubtedly the news of the Haitian insurrection was partly to blame, but it is also likely that the remembered "spirit and philosophy of the American Revolution were important in arousing . . . discontent amongst the Negroes." Louisiana, then owned by Spain—which country was at war with France—was disturbed by slave uprisings in 1791 and 1792, but not much is known about them. Better known are the slave plots devised in South Carolina. Indeed, the Charleston trouble of 1793, during which fires apparently of incendiary origin blackened part of the city, bears out the warning of Jefferson's letter. A correspondent wrote: "It is said that St. Domingo negroes have sown these seeds of revolt, and that a magazine has been attempted to be broken open." When fires again broke out with fiendish regularity three years later, the seditious connivance of St. Domingo Negroes was further suspected. North Carolina and Maryland were kept constantly alarmed throughout the 1790's.

These outbreaks were hardly quieting to the slaveholders. They were already laboring with problems that seemed insoluble. Their economic hopes were not being realized. In the upper South, the soil was impoverished by the cultivation of tobacco, which crop was itself a drug on the market. Bankrupt planters were a dime a dozen. Plantation fields lay idle; fine old colonial mansions stood deserted. Slaves, grown surly from hunger, loafed in their mouldy cabins, or, tired of this, ran away. Poverty clutched the land. Nor were things better in the lower South, where rice rotted in the swamps and indigo was not worth the cost of cultivation. Still, planters looked upon the times as merely an interlude between promise and fulfillment, and, though some of them gave up, selling or abandoning their holdings and selling or freeing their slaves, most held on.

But if there was a bond in poverty, there was a greater bond in terror, and in 1800, when only the intercession of nature saved Richmond and the surrounding country from the fate of St. Domingo, the South fully realized it. No other slave conspiracy was so well planned as that of Gabriel Prosser's; none, either, came nearer to success.

Gabriel Prosser was no ordinary slave, nor, for that matter, was he an ordinary man. Of giant stature, he possessed the kind of magnetic energy that inspires fanatic confidence in the followers of a leader or a prophet. Gabriel himself had no doubt that he was both.

His face was a scarred black rock. Like many a revolutionary before and after him, he believed that he was God-intended to bring "a great deliverance" to his people. If this was mystical nonsense, there was none in the planning that went on for months. Aided by his wife, his brothers, and Jack Bowler, another giant Negro, Gabriel recruited from his own district and from Carolina County, Goochland, and Petersburg upwards of a thousand slaves. Some of these, having been in the Revolutionary War, had an elementary knowledge of military tactics, for which reason they were made group leaders. Gabriel supplied them with crude arms—pikes and bludgeons made of wood, swords made of scythe blades, and a few antiquated guns. Gabriel cautiously sounded out the Catawba Indians, but decided against their help. He planned to steal horses for greater mobility. Finally, satisfied with his planning, he set a time when the fields would be ready for harvest, the cattle fat for slaughter. The insurrectionists would live off the land.

The operation was to begin on the night of August 20. All the whites (save the French and the Quakers) in the neighborhood of the Prosser plantation were to be killed. Picking up hundreds of pledged recruits from the surrounding country and augmented by hundreds—even thousands—from the city, the slaves were to descend on Richmond. Gabriel knew the city as well as he knew his master's barn, for he had made it the object of special study every Sunday for months. Once in Richmond, where it was expected that all bondmen would rally to the cause, the slaves were to set fires as a diversionary tactic, seize the arsenal and the State House, put all whites to the sword, and establish a black monarchy with Gabriel as king. Failing in this, they were to take to the mountains and defend themselves to the end. Their flag was to bear the legend "Liberty or Death."

Everything went well—for a while. No fewer than a thousand slaves kept the rendezvous at Old Brook Swamp, six miles from Richmond. Even the rain that began to fall at dusk was good for the plans of the insurrectionists, for it would keep unsuspecting folk indoors. But the rains came harder, blew a storm, a gale weirdly lit by lightning. Roads turned to goo, bridges were swept away, houses blown down, crops destroyed. Progress toward the city was utterly impossible. Pledged to a later rendezvous, the rebellious slaves scattered.

It was only later that they knew that they had been betrayed by other than the gods. Two of their own kind had betrayed them. Governor Monroe learned of the plot in the late afternoon of the twentieth. When the slaves kept their rendezvous, the city was already mobilized, the arsenal and State House were guarded. Cavalry troops clattered through the streets trying to cover all points at once. But nothing had happened when the storm broke, and after that nothing could happen.

The next day evidence of the epic scope of the conspiracy poured in and threw city and state into panic. Martial law was declared. The militia went to work, and Negroes were arrested indiscriminately. Some, according to Thomas W. Higginson, were hanged the same way, and almost as soon as caught. Gabriel himself had escaped, and for a time it looked as if the $300 offered for his capture was not enough. But within a month, once again betrayed by his own, Gabriel was discovered hiding in the hold of the schooner *Mary* which had sailed from Richmond to Norfolk. The outcome of his trial was a foregone conclusion. With fifteen others, Gabriel Prosser was hanged on October 7, 1800, before a wildly cheering mob.

3

But by 1800 the interlude of mere anxious hope was over and the promise of the industrial revolution was being fulfilled. Cotton was truly golden fleece. The area of its production spread to Georgia and Arkansas, and the purchase of Louisiana in 1803 extended it still further. Despite unlimited cultivation, the price of cotton soared, and with it the price of land and slaves. For slaves were as necessary to cotton—so at least thought the South—as the very earth that produced it. And there were not enough slaves.

The upheaval in St. Domingo had thoroughly frightened the South. To import slaves, particularly "seasoned" slaves from the Caribbean islands, was to run the risk of servile revolt. North Carolina, South Carolina, Virginia and Maryland had already passed laws prohibiting slave import. Presumably to help offset this voluntary cutting off and to round up some of the estimated forty-five thousand Negroes who had run away during the war, Congress enacted a fugitive slave law in 1793. But also in the very next year Congress moved to stop the slave trade to foreign ports and to prevent the fitting out of foreign slave ships in American yards.

But these measures were largely ineffective after 1800. Cotton was a powerful club. Returns promised to outweigh risks, and the slave trade to the United States continued to flourish. Trafficking under foreign flags, New England traders flouted the law. Southern planters and buyers connived with them. Anti-slavery interests undoubtedly would try to push through prohibitive measures the first moment the Constitution allowed, and slavers raced against the deadline. In the year 1802 alone, it was estimated that twenty thousand Negroes were imported into Georgia and South Carolina. "So little respect seems to have been paid to the existing prohibitory statute," said one member of Congress, "that it may almost be considered as disregarded by common consent."

But the sickening dread of slave revolt, of suddenly waking to find his life at the mercy of a vengeful black mob, still held validity for the average slaveholder. This dread was sometimes magnified by conscience and by the green awareness of what a precious thing was freedom. The Quakers kept conscience alive. They memorialized Congress; they tramped from door to door; and now and then they went to the length of helping slaves escape.

That there were men who needed no such goads is proved by the facts. In 1803, a Virginia planter, William Ludwell Green, set up an estate for the education of his slaves and willed them freedom. A fellow Virginian, Samuel Gist, purchased lands in free Ohio and settled his manumitted slaves upon it. Other slaveholders bought areas in Indiana, Illinois and Michigan and transported their ex-slaves thither. "I tremble for my country," Thomas Jefferson said, "when I think that God is just," and freed some of his slaves. Then, in 1806, President Jefferson reminded the Congress that the slave trade could be outlawed. In March of the next year a law was passed to prohibit the African slave trade. But the law was practically useless without the cooperation of those very states in which the pro-slavery forces were most powerful and cotton most precious. The wonder crop incited greed. It promised the abundant life; it promised the ease of wealth. The more slaves the more cotton, the more cotton the more land. It was, it seemed, an immutable round upon which even the landless poor aspired to set their weary feet.

So the law got scant observance. Perhaps, as some have held, it "begot a sort of dare-devil spirit on the part of Southern blood . . .

to overcome any doubts arising in their minds." But certainly this much is true: it had the effect of increasing the profits of the slave traffic two and threefold. And if by 1820 there were two hundred thousand free Negroes, they were vastly outnumbered by more than a million and a half slaves.

A million five hundred thousand slaves, the property of, roughly, three hundred thousand people, more than three-quarters of whom owned less than five slaves each! The great gray, faceless mass of Southerners owned no slaves. Indeed, though most of them did not realize it, the slave institution was their greatest enemy. It intensified their economic struggle. It deprived them of opportunity and atrophied ambition. Its class-structure pattern was as rigid as that of medieval Europe, and it left the masses powerless to resist. In the final analysis, it robbed them even of resisting will and made them party to their own degradation. Yet one pride was allowed them—played up, encouraged: they were white after all, and therefore better than the Negroes free or slave. This blinded the majority to the total domination by the slaveholders who determined the South's political and cultural structure, who wrote her laws, who established her mores, who molded the group mind into that sectional oddity known as the mind of the South. It was the slaveholding element that erected an oligarchical superstructure upon the foundation of democracy, and created the fortress of myths within which, it was hoped, the mind of the South could grind out its dream of life in peace.

The threat to the myths reposed in the slaves themselves. It lay in their day to day and hour to hour disaffection—in their silent, passive, mocking resistance: the dawdling, the pretending to be dumb, the pretending not to see and hear and understand, the pretending to be sick. And in the sudden, explosive leap of violence—a slave alone, or many together daring to be bold, defiant, murderous, daring to die. This was the threat, the South knew, to its entire economy, its way of life. To contain that threat and to maintain that way of life, it was necessary, as has been said, to hammer out the Black Codes and to enforce them with such persistent stringency that even the freedom of the master class was curtailed. Almost no act of the slave's, either of nature or of will, but was watched, guarded, spied upon. "Go to de woods to relieve yo'se'f, oberseer heel you der. Go to de cabin when work all done an' you try to res', pattyrollers li'ble to bust in. Go to meetin' on Sunday, white mens. Cain't even down worshup yo' Gawd. White mens. White mens a-watchin' an' a-lis'nin' all de time."

Declared the highest court of South Carolina in 1818: "The peace of society and the safety of individuals require that slaves should be subjected to the authority and control of all freemen when not under the immediate authority of their masters."

And the slave was subject—to the guilt-swelled abuse of master and overseer, to the tender mercy of patrollers, to the tricky whim of any white man who chanced to meet him away from home. He had no more social status than a mule. One white witness could convict him in a court of law. For sedition, and often on suspicion of sedition he could be hanged or burned alive. For reading or distributing incendiary literature he could also be put to death. Running away was an offense for which, if he did not yield when caught, his captor could shoot him down.

If a slave were lucky—and there were degrees of luck—he might live on a small plantation or farm; or he might be a personal servant in a large household; or he might have a kind master. Sometimes he might have the luck to be in two of these circumstances. If he lived on a small plantation, the chances are that there was no overseer and that he worked side by side with the master and the master's children. Personal contact with his owner was to the slave's advantage. He could prove his value; he could ingratiate himself. Sharing experiences tended to humanize the relationship. The slave worked hard, but so did the master, for on the four- and five-slave places life was an elemental struggle against ruin. On such a place the slave's rations might be short, but "sho't rations wont nothin' to de long cat-o-nine" in the hands of an overseer or a "mean, hard" master.

A body servant had even more intimate contacts with his master, and sometimes these led to deep affection and respect on both sides. The house or body slave had many advantages over the field slave. He was a privileged character, the aristocrat of the slave class, and, more frequently than not, a source of envy to other slaves. Cooking the master's food, serving his table, running his personal errands, laying out his clothes and dressing him, standing always within earshot, the body servant learned many things and met many kinds of people. He grew sophisticated, knowing, arrogant and place-conscious. He generally married on his occupation level, for he despised field hands and "common niggers." He dressed much better, ate better, talked better. Coin clinked in his pockets. Sensing that his personal advantage and, indeed, his fate were tied to that of his master, his loyalty was likely to be profound. Moreover, in the unbalanced equation of the Southern culture, master might equal cousin, half-brother, father. Through house slaves many a servile plot came to light, for masters used even the place-jealousies of slaves as instruments of control.

Luckiest of all was the slave who had a kind master. That there were such masters is clearly a part of the record, though many of the contemporary accounts, written by runaway slaves or biased travelers, or ghosted by abolitionists, tended to slight or overlook them. There were masters who were wisely kind, who kept slave families together, who fed and clothed them decently, who forbade cruel punishment. Thomas Jefferson's remaining slaves were "struck dumb" with misery at their master's death, although he had willed them freedom. Thaddeus Herndon, addressing his slaves for the last time, was reported to have said: "Servants, hear me, we have been brothers and sisters, we have grown up together. We have done the best for you. Besides your freedom, we have spent $2,000 in procuring everything we could think of to make you comfortable—clothing, bedding, implements of husbandry, mechanics' tools, tools for the children, Bibles. . . . And now, may God bless you. I can never forget you."

There were those masters who were kindly wise—for profit. But no matter what the souce, *kindness* was goodness to the slave. If he could escape being sold down the river and ward off the bite of the abasing lash; if he could jump the broomstick with a woman of his choosing, worship God in the way that appealed to him, and be made to feel secure in his old age, he was not likely to examine into reasons. For, anyway, much less than these usually made up the paltry sum of his happiness—a runt shoat at Christmas, a cracked mirror, a broken watch, a dance.

"Ole Marsa stan' off in de corner wid his arms folded jus' a-puffin' on his corn-cob pipe as ef he was a-sayin' 'Look at my niggers! Ain' my niggers havin' a good time!' . . . Den ole Missus say to Marsa, 'I b'lieve you lak dem niggers better'n you do me.' Den Marsa say, "Sho', I lak my niggers. Dey works hard and makes money fo' me. . . . I'se gwine stay an' see dat my niggers has a good time.'

"An' we sho' use to have a good time. Yes, sir. We was walkin' an' talkin' wid de devil both day an' night. Settin' all 'round was dem big demi-jonahs of wiskey what Marsa done give us. An' de smell of roast pig an' chicken comin' fum de quarters made ev'ybody feel good." [6]

Yet the slave system was against even such small indulgences as these. When all is said and done, the system could not afford them, for charitableness was its enemy as surely as hate is the enemy of love. The South was in the position of the police state, creating oppression and terror in order to function at all. Truly it was a police state, and all its citizens were policemen. Fanny Kemble, the English actress who married a slaveholder and lived for a time (1838–1839) on a plantation in Georgia, remarked on the extent and nature of the South's militarism. A governor of South Carolina declared that "a state of military preparation must always be with us a state of perfect domestic security." And Frederick Law Olmsted, as objective an observer as ever took a journey, wrote in *A Journey in the Back Country* that one sees in the South

Police machinery such as you never find in towns under free government: citadels, sentries, passports, grapeshotted cannon, and daily public whippings of the subjects for accidental infractions of police ceremonies. I happened myself to see more direct expression of tyranny in a single day and night in Charleston, than at Naples for a week. . . . There is . . . an armed force, with a military organization, which is invested with more arbitrary and cruel power than any police state in Europe.

So for all the laws, the final control of the subject black population was by arbitrary men. There were the men of the federal military, and men of the states' militias; police and private guards. In emergencies, there were the headlong, skylarking youths and men of the volunteer vigilantes. But most tyrannous of all these public agencies were the men of the local patrols, the dreaded "pattyrollers." Every community in every slave state had its patrol. In some places its members were drawn from the state militia; in others they were drafted from the body of citizenry and any adult white male was liable to service.

Finally, in private capacity were the overseers, bred of the diseases of slavery. As a class they earned the reputation they got. "Passionate, careless, inhuman, generally intemperate, and totally unfit for the duties of the position," not even the masters, whose creatures they were, spoke a good word for them. Yet they were considered indispensable, and the laws of some states made them mandatory. The overseer had over the slave all the rights of control of the master, but none of the master's ultimate responsibility. He ordered, made food and clothing allowances, assigned work and saw to its carrying out, issued passes, punished. He was the gross reflection of the master from whom his authority was derived. The aim of that authority was profit; its means cruelty. "If they [the overseers] made plenty o' cotton, the owners never asked how many niggers they'd killed." [7]

For, of course, sometimes a nigger had to be killed, or maimed, or tortured, or at the very least lashed. The slaves were not inclined to extend themselves for the profit of others. They were lazy and irresponsible, to say which is to point up the way the slave system worked. Every moment of the slaves' day was locked into a routine of almost sidereal precision. The rising horn or bell before day, breakfast in the hushed gloom of morning twilight, the fields at dawn. Plowing, planting, hoeing, chopping, picking. Land to clear, ditches to dig, fences to mend. Noon—sidemeat, blackstrap molasses, hoecake. The fields again. Supper—hoecake, blackstrap molasses, cowpeas. And then at night wood to gather, water to draw. In Mississippi slaves could be legally worked eighteen hours in twenty-four; in Georgia and Alabama nineteen. There was no law that said they could not be worked to death.

The slaves had no initiative, no sense of duty; they were dishonest, thriftless, immoral, the planters said. They were "more brute than human . . . they accepted the white man's civilization only through fear and force of habit; they were mean, restless, and dissatisfied. . . . This class of human brute was subdued only through fear, just as the lion is made to perform in the show through fear." [8] They were also stupid and insensate beyond belief.

But the threat to these concepts, too, reposed in the Negroes themselves, slave and free. Benjamin Banneker, for instance, was free, but his remarkable talents, once they came to light, mocked the accepted beliefs. For the first forty years of his life he was just another farmer, with a little more book learning than he actually seemed to need and not enough money and leisure to follow his interests. One thing he had done however: he had made an excellent clock that attracted attention in his local Maryland community.

Then, in the 1780's a Quaker miller, George Ellicott, took an interest in Banneker, lent him books on mathematics and astronomy, and gave him the use of surveyor's tools. By 1789 Banneker had proved himself so skilled in the engineering sciences that President Washington appointed him to the Commission to survey the District of Columbia and lay out the city of Washington. For two years Banneker engaged in this work. When he returned to Maryland, his interest in astronomy asserted itself, and, beginning in 1791, he issued an annual almanac which for the eleven years that he published it was a household reference in America and won praise abroad.

But if Banneker's accomplishments proved something, they were not enough entirely to eradicate, as he had hoped, the "false ideas and opinions" generally held about Negroes.

Nor were Paul Cuffe's. Born free, like Banneker, but a New Englander, Cuffe went to sea on a whaler at the age of sixteen. Four years later he bought his first vessel, and by 1780 Paul Cuffe's ships were sailing to Europe and Africa. Increasing wealth made him liable to taxes, but these he refused to pay so long as he could not vote. The philosophy of the Revolution was on his side of the argument, and he presented it convincingly. Largely through his efforts, Massachusetts extended the right to vote to free Negroes who paid taxes.

Cuffe was a Quaker. In common with his sect, he had a concern for the plight of Negroes unbounded by selfish interests. Realizing the importance of education, he built a school in New Bedford. Knowing the self-respect that regular employment promotes, he operated a shipyard and employed Negro mechanics when he could find them. Negro seamen shipped on his vessels. But even these things were not enough to narrow the immeasurable distance to Negro self-sufficiency. Too many social and psychological barriers stood in the middle ground. To be free of these, the Negro must go back to Africa. He must have his own land and his own government and himself be subject to himself. In 1811, sailing his own vessel, Paul Cuffe went to Africa, where at Sierra Leone he made arrangements looking to the establishment of a colony of free Negroes. The prospects must have pleased him, for after the War of 1812, he sailed again to Africa, taking with him at his own expense a shipload of Negroes.

But America was home for the vast majority of Negroes. Here many of them were born, though in slavery. Their sweat was going into its building, their blood was spilling in its defense. Here—

since to labor and to die were not enough—they must prove themselves. Here they must confound the concept.

At about the time that Banneker was catching the interest of George Ellicott, a fragilely molded, delicately constituted slave girl in Boston was writing:

> Should you, my lord, while you peruse my song,
> Wonder from whence my love of Freedom sprung,
> Whence flow these wishes for the common good,
> By feeling hearts alone best understood,
> I, young in life, by seeming cruel fate
> Was snatched from Afric's fancied happy seat:
> What pangs excrutiating must molest,
> What sorrows labor in my parent's breast!
> Steeled was that soul, and by no misery moved,
> That from a father seized his babe beloved:
> Such, such my case. And can I then but pray
> Others may never feel tyrannic sway?

This was not Phillis Wheatley's first poem. In 1770, when she was seventeen, she had written one "On the Death of the Reverend George Whitefield," and in 1775, during the British siege of Boston, she had addressed General Washington in heroic couplets:

> Proceed, great chief, with virtue on thy side,
> Thy every action let the goddess guide.
> A crown, a mansion, and a throne that shine,
> With gold unfading, *Washington,* be thine.

And later the General had received her at his headquarters in Cambridge. For Phillis was an oddity, especially to a slaveholder from Virginia. She was a slave who could read and write poetry. She was an artist!

Bought in Boston directly off a slave ship from Senegal, Phillis was reared in the pious and cultured home of the John Wheatleys. She was treated more like a member of the family—which at one time numbered seven—than a slave. She was taught to read from the Bible and given lessons in Latin, history, and geography. Voluminous reading helped to make her at eighteen undoubtedly one of the most cultured women of her day. Manumitted and sent to London for her health at twenty, she was entertained by the Countess of Huntington, and Brook Watson, the Lord Mayor, made her a gift of a handsome edition of *Paradise Lost,* now the property of Harvard College. It was in London also that *Poems on Various Subjects, Religious and Moral,* Phillis' first volume, was published. Later the book had many reprintings in America. It was used as a strong argument against the Negro's inherent inferiority in the anti-slavery campaign of the next century.

Returned to America, Phillis found life much less pleasant than it had been. Freedom was precious, but freedom was hard. Mrs. Wheatley was dead, and Mary, the surviving daughter, married. Mr. Wheatley himself died in 1778. Phillis knew little of the real world. The promises of the facile rascal whom she married proved empty, and bit by bit she was reduced to drudgery for the sake of her three children, two of whom soon died. Her own end is told by the anonymous writer of the *Memoirs of Phillis Wheatley.*

In a filthy apartment, in an obscure part of the metropolis, lay the dying mother and child. The woman who had stood honored and respected by the wise and good in that country which was hers by adoption, or rather compulsion, who had graced the ancient halls of old England, and had rolled about in the splendid equipages of the proud nobles of Britain, was now numbering the last hours of her life in a state of the most abject misery, surrounded by all the elements of squalid poverty.

The Boston *Independent Chronicle* noted simply:

Last Lord's Day, died Mrs. Phillis Peters (formerly Phillis Wheatley), aged thirty-one, known to the world by her celebrated miscellaneous poems. Her funeral is to be held this afternoon, at four o'clock, from the house lately improved by Mr. Todd, nearly opposite Dr. Bulfinch's at West Boston, where her friends and acquaintances are desired to attend.

The date was Thursday, December 9, 1784.

This was the very year in which Richard Allen, who had bought his freedom in 1777 and become an inspiring preacher, began attracting the attention of white Methodism. Moving from Delaware to Philadelphia a decade later, he joined the St. George Church, where he was sometimes called upon to preach. But St. George's was a white congregation and there were those among it who objected to worshipping with Negroes. Once at a service Allen's prayers were interrupted by church officials who were determined to enforce the new policy of segregation. Allen resolved to establish his own church.

In 1794 he opened the doors of Bethel Church—now known as Mother Bethel—in Philadelphia, and within ten years branches of this church were running in North Carolina, Virginia, Maryland, New Jersey and Delaware. By 1816, when they incorporated as the African Methodist Episcopal Church, they had a combined membership of forty-five thousand Negroes.

Negro Protestants in other places, stymied by segregation, also established separate churches during the late 1700's. In New York James Varick, Peter Williams and Christopher Rush were instrumental in setting up the African Methodist Episcopal Zion Church. In the South where, after the Revolutionary War, there was determined opposition to Negro congregations under Negro leaders, who might be refractory, black Baptists set up a church in Savannah, Georgia, and kept it alive even though they were persecuted and Andrew Bryan, their preacher, was jailed. The African Baptist Church of Williamsburg, Virginia, was driven underground, but William Moses and Gowan Pamphlet, free Negroes, continued to serve it until the "black laws," following Nat Turner's bloody rebellion in 1830, stopped the mouths of all Negro preachers in Virginia.

The education of colored people was even harder to accomplish in the South, though, strangely enough perhaps, the first American-born Negro to be thoroughly educated lived most of his life in that section. Born in North Carolina, John Chavis was sent to Princeton (then the college of New Jersey) where he seems to have been taught by the president of the college, Dr. Witherspoon. Returning to North Carolina, Chavis taught for thirty years a school which white boys attended by day and Negro boys at night. He was forced to relinquish his service to Negro boys in 1831, when the education of colored people was generally interdicted in the South.

There was also more than a little opposition to it in the North. It was expensive. It did not seem necessary to a people who were doomed to the lowliest occupations: it could only make them unhappy. Yet, with the aid of some philanthropic whites, Negroes did get a yeasty taste of formal learning. As early as 1777 the Philadelphia Quaker, Anthony Benezet, provided funds for a colored school.

There were off-and-on schools in New Jersey. The African Free School in New York taught hundreds of Negroes between 1787 and 1815. One of its students, Ira Aldridge, won European acclaim by his playing of Othello to Edmund Kean's Iago. Whites in Wilmington, Delaware, New Haven, Connecticut, and Boston, Massachusetts, lent support to Negro schools. By 1826, the year of Thomas Jefferson's death, the race had its first bona-fide graduate of an American college in John Russworm, who finished at Bowdoin, and there were ex-slaves who were practicing medicine, teaching school, and preaching sermons to attentive white audiences.

If these lives and works were no clinching proof of anything, they at least were an earnest, and they at least gave some people pause. Jefferson, whose humanitarian interest in the Negro's welfare did not stop him from holding the usual notions about the race's imperviousness to civilizing influences, was impressed by Banneker's accomplishments. He praised the black man's almanac. Indeed, since he sent it to the Academy of Science in Paris, it is not too much to say that he valued it as the product of an American mind. Washington, who had believed black men unworthy to fight in the country's cause, must have been struck by Phillis Wheatley, by the shaping influence of Anglo-Saxon culture upon her. In the deep South too—in Charleston, Savannah and New Orleans—many must have seen beyond the blinders of the concept. Many must have wondered how a people "so stupid, so bereft of mental endowment" could build with axe and adz and simple facing tools fine mansions for their masters, shape stone to monuments of arresting beauty, and forge and anvil iron with subtle artistry.

And ever and again, "insensible as they were of the high dreams of honor and liberty that inspire white men to grandeur," slaves made bold efforts to assert their human dignity. They ran away to freedom. Between them and it stood all the machinery of control, all the pathological watchfulness of frightened masters. Between them and it sucked the ooze of primordial swamps, prowled the shadows of unknown forests, roared rivers, reared mountains. Between slaves and freedom screamed torture, crept starvation, lurked death—yet they ran away. Many thousands ran away.

This selection is from *They Came in Chains: Americans from Africa* (Philadelphia: Lippincott, [1950], 1973), 28-61.

The following notes appeared in slightly different form for Chapter Three of *They Came In Chains*. They were emended by the editor for this volume; reprint of book titles were also added.

1. Falconbridge, Alexander D. *An Account of the Slave Trade on the Coast of Africa*. (London: J. Phillips, 1788) 30. Reprint. New York: AMS, 1973.

2. Spears, John R. *The American Slave Trade: An Account of Its Origin, Growth and Suppression*. (New York: Charles Scribner's Sons, 1907) 79.

3. Glennie, Alexander. *Sermons Preached on Plantations to Congregations of Negroes*. (Charleston, S.C.: A.E. Miller, 1844) 21. Abridged edition. New York: Ballantine, 1960. Reprint. Salem, N.H.: Ayer/Books for Libraries, 1971.

4. Virginia Writer's Program. *The Negro in Virginia*. (New York: Hastings, 1940) 23.

5. Martin, Asa Earl. *The Anti-Slavery Movement in Kentucky Prior to 1850*. (Louisville: Standard Printing 1918) 14. Reprint. Westport: Negro Universities Press, 1970.

6. *The Negro in Virginia*, 88.

7. Buckmaster, Henrietta [Pseudonym]. *Let My People Go: The Story of the Underground Railroad and the Growth of the Abolition Movement*. (New York: Harper, 1941) 6. Reprint. Boston: Beacon, 1959.

8. Price, J[ohn]. A[mbrose]. *The Negro, Past, Present and Future*. (New York: Neale, 1907) 47.

IV

BIOGRAPHY

The biography section, excerpted from *The Lonesome Road*, portrays Sojourner Truth, self-named and widely-proclaimed as the first black woman anti-slavery speaker.

FAITH

1. Isabella No-Name

She was called Isabella at first, and the language spoken in her family was Dutch. But to speak of her "family" is an irony, for ten of her brothers and sisters had been sold away, and only her father, Baumfree, her mother, Bett, and her brother, Peter, remained. The parents had no surname. "Baumfree" was a moniker for tall-as-a-tree, and the father refused to have another. Though in later years the name would have fitted Isabella, in her youth it would not stick. She was variously called Bell, Bella, and Lil Bett. She belonged successively to the Hardenberghs, the Nealys, the Scrivers, and the Dumonts, and for more than a year she gave her considerable services to the Van Wageners, but she took the name of none of them.

She held John Dumont, a man of gross appetites, in fervent, idolatrous regard and bore him children, but she did not take his name either for herself or for them. When she married, probably in 1820 and probably at the age of twenty-three, her husband had no name to give her. He was called simply Tom, or Black Tom—not because of the color of his skin but because he "worked roots" or voodoo and practiced divination. The son Tom begot was called Peter, nothing more. When Peter was a young man in the city of New York he found the lack of a surname a handicap to such a devil-may-care free Negro as himself and he adopted the name of Williams—Peter Williams. He was twice booked into Tombs prison under this name, and under this name he shipped as a seaman to a foreign port in 1839 and was, save once, heard of no more.

Isabella had not only left him nameless, she had left him motherless. In one way or another she left all of her children—five, or six, or seven—motherless. There was a frigid winter spot in the blazing tropics of her soul.

She dismissed Tom, a freedman, while she was still a slave. He died in a poorhouse in 1830. Peter, the son of Tom, and the children she had by Dumont were left with Dumont when she ran away. It is true that she did not run far, or try to lose herself, but this is scarcely evidence that she missed or wanted her children.

Dumont had promised to set her free in 1826, but when the time came he was reluctant to make his promise good. In the interval since her marriage Isabella had got religion and had founded her faith in God. But she never went to church, and hers was a strange religion, compounded of Tom's weird conjure lore and Old Testament maledictions. She worshiped in secret, in "a circular arched alcove" she had constructed "entirely of willows" on an islet in a stream at the edge of the Dumont estate. Also, according to reports, hers was a terrible God—a master black magician apotheosized from every awful attribute of witchcraft, necromancy, and superstition.

She invoked this God for or against Dumont, and then she ran away. Somehow she knew that Dumont would not try to get her back. She had been an embarrassment to him, to his wife, and finally, as they grew up, to his legitimate children. When she left she did take her second child by Tom, an unnamed infant girl, but within a month or two she abandoned her to be reared by strangers in the neighboring town of New Paltz, New York.

Yet there was one curious episode.

Dumont sold the boy Peter. It was 1826. Slavery in New York State had only fourteen months to go. Peter was five and therefore still useless as a slave, but in some circles it was fashionable to train a Negro child as one would train a monkey or a dog and show off its accomplishments in the parlor. Peter's new master, Dr. James Gedney, apparently tired of this entertainment and transferred title in the boy to his brother, Solomon Gedney. Solomon in turn sold Peter to the husband of a sister, a Deep South planter named Fowler. In defiance of the law forbidding native-born slaves to be taken beyond the borders of the state, Fowler carted Peter off to Alabama.

Isabella exploded, a blazing holocaust—but ignited from what kindling and fed by what fuel it is impossible to tell. She defies analysis. Any of a number of elements in the situation might have sparked a simpler woman to maddened action—the loss of a well-loved child, a blind and twisted jealousy, a passion for fair play, a sense of intolerable humiliation—but Isabella is not explicable in terms of any of these.

She went to Dumont and charged him with perfidy. Then she went to the Gedneys' mother and in broken English screamed, "Oh, I must have my child! I will have my child!" She shrieked out maledictions upon the heads of all concerned, invoked hell and death, and cursed to action the sluggard forces of the law. And she had her child. Under delayed sentence and a bond of six hundred dollars, Solomon Gedney fetched Peter back from Alabama.

But Isabella did not really want the boy. She gave him into the keeping of a family in Wahkendall. Then she herself went to live in New York City.

2. Bathed in Holiness

Perhaps a group of thirty ex-slaves living on Manhattan Island were a little too sanguine when in the early 1830s they addressed a letter to their "Afflicted and Beloved Brothers" in the South: "We get wages for our labor. We have schools for our children. . . . We are happy to say that every year is multiplying the facilities. . . ."

Among these facilities were a theater-hotel called the African Grove, the first Negro newspaper, *Freedom's Journal,* the largest Negro church in the United States, and living space in the Five Points district—where kidnapers prowled in armed gangs and shanghaied any likely Negro, free or not, and sold him south to slavery. But kidnapers could not seriously reduce the Negro population. Negroes kept coming all the time, though a vigorous pro-slavery press thundered against them and against abolition, "this most dangerous species of fanaticism extending itself through our society. . . . Shall we, by promptly and fearlessly crushing this many-headed Hydra in the bud, expose the weakness as well as the folly, madness and mischief of these bold and dangerous men?"

But in New York metaphors were not all that was mixed, often for good but sometimes for ill. Daniel Payne, fleeing Charleston in 1835, would stop there briefly, wander in innocent curiosity into Cow Bay Alley, be "revolted" by the brazen prostitution and open "consortium of white drabs and drunken Negro sailors"; but, finally, through his connection with the Methodist Episcopal Church, meet some white teachers and preachers who would provide him with a scholarship to study at the Gettysburg Seminary and send him on his way. And on a September morning three years later Frederick Douglass would find himself "one more added to the mighty throng which, like the confused waves of the troubled sea, surged to and fro between the lofty walls of Broadway." After a few days "of freedom from slavery, but free from food and shelter as well," he too would meet a mixed group, the Vigilance Committee, find refuge in the home of one of them, and be given steamer fare to New Bedford.

Much of the spirit called humanitarian found focus in New York. Assorted idealists and crackpots, hewing their timbers from the forest of radicalism, were busy building the New Jerusalem. Their hammers rang. The forges of Free Enquirers, Sabbatarians, Emancipationists, Feminists,

Owenites, and evangelical sects of all sorts gave off an incandescent glow. Negroes were frequently suffused in it. Many of them attended white churches. They were welcomed in many movements. Situated in what is now Greenwich Village, a mixed utopian community flourished for a time. The Manumission Society had founded the first African Free School in 1787, and by the early 1830s there were seven such schools taught by teachers of both races and supported by appropriations from the state legislature as well as from the Common Council. "It was due mainly to [these schools] that there was produced in New York City . . . a body of intelligent and well-trained colored men and women."

In New York lived John Russwurm, first Negro graduate* of an American college (Bowdoin, 1826). Dr. James McCune Smith, graduate of the Glasgow University, practiced medicine there "without prejudice to his white patients, who were numerous." Alexander Crummell and J. W. C. Pennington, one a graduate of Cambridge University and the other with an honorary degree from Heidelberg, frequently preached to white congregations.

New York was a haven for Isabella when she arrived in 1829. Almost the first people she met were the Elijah Piersons, a white couple of great wealth and inexhaustible mystic faith. Both were unstable; both had begun a tragic descent into unreality. Their devotion to the organized Church had been reamed out in the revival of anti-clericalism in the 1820s and rendered them neurotic prey to a religious eclecticism that was almost as pagan as it was Christian. They had set out to convert the whole of New York City, after which, in their grandoise imaginings, they would convert the world. They had founded an ascetic church called Five Points House, an esoteric group known as the Retrenchment Society, and a house for fallen women named the Magdalene Society. Their own home on Bowery Hill was known as the Kingdom.

Here Isabella went to live with them. Responsive to their religious influences as well as to their kindness, she was quick to substitute their messianic mysticism for the dark and vengeful spirit of the sorcery she had learned from Black Tom. "Our God is a God of love," Pierson drummed into her time and again, "and you are one of His prophets." She had never known a God like theirs. Soon she was having religious seizures—"I feel so light and so well, I could skim around like a gull!"—and visions of great intensity—"It is Jesus!" She was also making prohecies (a practice which must have continued for some time, for Harriet Beecher Stowe, who did not meet her until the 1850s, called her the "Libyan Sybil").

All this seemed to suit Isabella's temperament, and the Piersons seemed her kind of people. They fasted periodically for days at a time, refusing water as well as bread, but Isabella outdid them. When they went preaching in the streets (a "slight, blond" man; a "small, graceful," and dark-haired woman), Isabella preached more fervently. No one could match her prayers. Her voice was timbred like a man's and guttural with the Dutch accent she never quite unlearned. Tall and gaunt, with a strong, dark, homely face jutting angularly below a white headcloth, she attracted attention by her appearance and held it by the power of a personality that no scoffers could shrink.

Under a regimen of prayer, preaching, and fasting, Sarah Pierson's health gave way, and her husband, now mystically renamed "Elijah the Tishbite," refused to have a doctor for her. He himself would effect her recovery according to St. James. "Is any sick among you? Let him call for the elders of the church; and let them pray over him, anointing him with oil in the name of the Lord: And the prayer of faith shall save the sick, and the Lord shall raise him up."

The elders were called, among them Isabella, and they prayed and anointed, but Sarah Pierson died.

But a stranger who had wandered into the Kingdom some time before and announced himself as Matthias explained to a broke Pierson and a faith-faltering Isabella that they had misunderstood the word of God. He *had* raised Sarah up—up into eternal life. Nor was this the only instance in which God's word had been misunderstood, Matthias explained. He would set them right. He, Matthias, was "the Spirit of Truth" that had disappeared from the earth at the death of Matthew in the New Testament. "The spirit of Jesus Christ entered into that Matthias, and I am the same Matthias. . . . I am he that has come to fulfill the word."

And the word was "all things in common." Matthias, who heretofore had been known simply as Robert Matthews, who had deserted his wife and children in Albany, and who had several times been arrested as a public nuisance, very soon had Isabella, Pierson, whose daughter now joined him, and a well-to-do couple, the Benjamin Folgers, completely under his spell. Pooling their considerable resources and turning them over to Matthias, these five moved with him to Sing Sing, New York, to a country place Matthias called Zion Hill. It began as just another experiment in communal living, a material projection of pure idealism such as blistered the American landscape in the 1830s. It ended after two years in a riotous carnival of licentiousness, adultery, and suspected murder.

For Matthias turned the Pierson fasts to feasts, their prayers to pimping. He was not long in convincing Pierson and the Folgers of the divine origin of his "matched souls" doctrine. According to this, Pierson would meet his wife again in the form of another woman: Matthias saw to it.

Whatever Pierson's trysts with his own daughter signified under the doctrine, Matthias himself made open love to any woman who struck his sybaritic fancy—and Mrs. Folger did. In a ceremony that Pierson performed, Mrs. Folger became Matthias' soul mate, and Benjamin Folger himself gave her away. A few days later Elijah Pierson suffered what was called an epileptic fit, and in succeeding days a series of them, and then he died.

But the death of this once wealthy, reputable man, known down in the city for his charitable though eccentric works, did not go unnoticed by his relatives. They were suspicious. The body was exhumed and traces of arsenic found in it. Matthias was arrested and charged with murder. Isabella was implicated with him, and was also accused by the Folgers of trying to poison them. But the evidence against her in both these matters was insupportable, and she escaped indictment.

For the truth seems to be that Isabella was not aware of what went on at Zion Hill and Matthias did not corrupt her with this knowledge. He kept her hypnotically transfixed in a religious state beyond all comprehension of reality and worked on her the same spell that, for different reasons and with quite contrary results, he worked on the Piersons, the Folgers, and other members of the cult.

And Isabella remained spellbound longer. She saw Zion Hill as "bathed in holiness" even while the Folgers were testifying to its abominations. Her defense of Matthias in court was so spiritually naïve and sincere that only perfect innocence could have produced it.

3. Sojourner

The trial of Matthias was the beginning of a new life for Isabella. Though she was now truly religious, the ecstatic seizures ceased and the visions began to fade. She dropped back into reality like one "once blind but now made to see."

What she saw with mundane clarity was a Negro life sunk to a depth almost beyond recovery. She saw it aswarm in the fetid alleys of Five Points, where Negroes "crawled over each other like flies on a dungpile." It lurked in the shadows of the docks, the stables, and the abattoirs, where, perchance, there might be a day's work free from molestation by immigrant whites who, arriving on every ship, were given first rights in such jobs as offered. She saw Negroes trying to beat back the compacted misery of their days with nights spent in Dickens Place, where assorted whores and their pimps did a brisk trade in flesh and thievery.

For, indeed, this was the life her son became involved in. Peter was now in his teens and his sister had just turned ten, and Isabella, after years of neglecting them, tried to make a home. But Peter was man-size, boisterously genial, already hardened in petty crime. Besides, Isabella had to work.

At first she made her living polishing the brass fixtures that adorned the doors of houses along the east-side avenues. She had regular customers to whom she sometimes talked in an earnest, forthright way about God. The notoriety of the Matthias trial still clung to her, and she was regarded as a strange character. She could be seen any day except Sunday, a can of dampened ashes mixed with sand at her feet, polishing rags hanging from the waist of her kilted skirt, putting a shine on name plates, doorknobs, and hinges. But this work depended upon the weather, and eventually she took a job in domestic service.

Even so, there was little time for her home. She was a prominent member of the African Zion Church, the church militant. Here gathered all the social forces that Negroes could command. There was plenty of the old-time religion still, and there were many prayer meetings and "love feasts" where Isabella exercised her gifts for prayer and testimony, but here the "most dangerous species of fanaticism" permeated the atmosphere. When anti-slavery ministers like John Marrs and Dempsey Kennedy came to preach, what Isabella heard was less of the word of Christ and more of the battle cry of freedom. At African Zion Church she heard discussions of the questions of colonization, education, and abolition. Once in the early 1840s, William Lloyd Garrison spoke there. Through her association with the church Isabella met Charles B. Ray, the Negro abolitionist, and it was in his home that she first saw Frederick Douglass, the white and wealthy Tappan brothers, and Gerrit Smith. Strange contours shaped and deep new furrows plowed her mind. James Sturges, the English abolitionist, told her, "This [abolition] is God's work too." She did what she could, but her appearance was against the clandestine work of the Underground Railroad, in which many of the Church's members were engaged. She was better suited to public agitation, to haranguing the street-corner rabble. She drew crowds wherever she spoke.

Meanwhile her son was going to the dogs. All Isabella's prayers could not save him. He professed an interest in the sea, and Isabella gave him the money to pay for a course in navigation, but he spent it on dancing lessons. She got him a job as coachman, but he sold his livery and the stable gear. Three times he went to jail—twice for theft and once for pandering—and when jail threatened for the fourth time Isabella refused to help him, and he sneaked away to sea. She never saw him again.

She had better luck with her daughter. Aged sixteen, the girl married a man named Banks and with him drifted slowly westward. A son born of their union was to be the only blood kin Isabella was ever known to love.

Once again free of responsibility to a family, Isabella poured her great vigor into "God's work." The steely shards of social reform and anti-slavery magnetized around her faith. Her fanatic tendencies blazed up again, but they were controlled by her developing intelligence and ironic insight. It was almost as if she sported with what Harriet B. Stowe was to call her "strange powers." Gradually her visions returned, but they were not now the apocalyptic visions of heaven's pearl and hell's brimstone. They were hardly visions at all, but sleeping dreams in which voices urged her to "go out into the world, gather in the flock." Sometimes it was the voice of the Reverend Charles Ray, sometimes of the Reverend Henry Garnet, sometimes of Gerrit Smith. Sometimes it seemed the voice of God. She grew impatient with the necessity to earn her living. She felt oppressed by New York, where, she said, "the rich do rob the poor, and the poor rob the poorer," and where the "truth of God is locked away" from sight.

Then one day she felt reborn. "I felt so tall within—I felt as if the power of a nation was with me." It was in the spring of 1843—the year Daniel Payne entered the active ministry of the African Methodist Episcopal Church, the year Frederick Douglass took part in "one hundred conventions." She was working for a Mrs. Whiting, who in answer to a question about her erstwhile maid replied: "She told me that she was going away and that the Lord was going to give her a new name. I thought Bell was crazy. She took a pillowcase and put her things in it, and then she left, saying she must be about her father's business. A new name indeed! And what was her father's business? Poor woman, I thought for a fact she was crazy. She said she was going east."

And she did go east. She renamed herself Sojourner Truth, and hiked slowly through Connecticut and into Massachusetts. She had set out with just enough money for a week's supply of the coarsest food: for the rest of her long life she would allow herself only enough to supply her most stringent needs. Sometimes she earned money by doing a day's work. Often money was given her. In mild weather she slept out of doors. When she needed shelter she asked for it. If she shared a family's meal she paid in coin or labor. She went undaunted everywhere. She was welcomed nearly everywhere. She seemed "sent by God," wrote a Massachusetts man.

"Sister, I send you this living messenger, as I believe her to be one that God loves. Ethiopia is stretching forth her hands unto God. You can see by this sister that God does by his spirit alone teach his own children. . . . Please receive her and she will tell you some things. Let her tell her story without interrupting her, and give close attention, and you will see she has got the love of truth, that God helps her to pray where but few can. She cannot read or write, but the law is in her heart. She is sent by God."

Sojourner Truth had the apostolic manner. In some homes she would announce that she had come to talk about the "angelic elect," but her private conversations differed little from her public preachments. She spoke of the "nation's sins against my people." She carried a white satin banner on which was inscribed, "Proclaim Liberty Throughout All the Land unto All the Inhabitants Thereof." When she had unfurled this on the makeshift rostrum of a camp meeting ground, she would begin: "There is more den one kin' of liberty, an' I come to tell you about all kin' of liberty. . . . "

The first winter caught up with her in Northampton, Massachusetts, where she took up temporary residence. Samuel Hill, Parker Pillsbury, and the brother-in-law of Garrison, George Benson—abolitionists all—received her as one of them. When spring came she was off again, this time journeying west. Her reputation outran her. She was the first Negro woman anti-slavery speaker. Sometimes attempts were made to silence and hinder her. She was beaten with sticks and pelted with stones, and on one occasion received injuries that finally ulcerated her leg. She was beaten many times.

4. God's Pilgrim

Slavery had ceased to be a question of moral debate, though the Garrisonians continued to act as if it were. But Garrison's principle of non-resistance had never been popular outside New England—at least of all in the West, where slavery was a matter both of politics, as in the South, and of economics, as in the urban East. The question was dangerously surcharged with emotion everywhere. The best interest of Western farmers could not be served by alliance with slavery, but there were many farmers who hated anti-slavery. Industrial capitalism and slavery were natural enemies, but capitalists joined with slaveholders to fight abolition. The New York Stock Exchange offered five thousand dollars for the head of Arthur Tappan. Midwestern industrialists hired hoodlums to break up abolition meetings. Some "Gentlemen of Property" in Cincinnati posted a notice throughout the city: "Abolitionists. BEWARE! The citizens of Cincinnati, embracing every class, interested in the prosperity of the city, satisfied that the business of the place is receiving a vital stab from the wicked and misguided operations of the abolitionists, are resolved to arrest to their course."

In Cincinnati, James Birney, converted from Alabama slaveholder to Northern emancipationist, was attacked by a mob under the protection of

Nicholas Longworth, the richest man in the Midwest, Jacob Burnet, formerly a judge of the Ohio Supreme Court, and Oliver Spencer, a Methodist minister. The "spirit of lawless violence" that William Jay had deplored in the East was more evident in the West. Pro-slavery sentiment was better organized, more given to deeds than to debate. The president of the new interracial college, Oberlin, Asa Mahan, was stoned in Indiana. Mobbed in Kansas and hounded out of Missouri, Elijah Lovejoy was at last murdered in Illinois.

But violence triggered by any show of radicalism was only half the story. The resolute, refractory, and gentle Quakers were the other half. Their anti-slavery tradition went back more than a hundred years. It went back to Ralph Sandiford, who wrote, and Benjamin Franklin, who published *A Brief Exposition of the Practice of the Times*—a pamphlet "packed with brimstone." It went back to Benjamin Say, who, "to show his indignation against the practice of slavekeeping, once carried a bladder filled with blood into a meeting; and, in the presence of the whole congregation, thrust a sword . . . into the bladder, exclaiming at the same time, 'Thus shall God shed the blood of those persons who enslave their fellow creatures.' The terror of this extravagant and unexpected act produced swooning in several of the women of the congregation."

The Midwestern Quakers no longer carried blood in bladders—they knew better tricks—and their women were too busy to swoon. They were busy devising stratagems of elusion, such as the one a certain Faith Webster pulled. Caching a group of fleeing slaves on the Kentucky side of the Ohio River one dawn when daylight made further progress impossible, she returned in the evening to find slave hunters scouring the area. Faith Webster changed into such clothes as a slave woman would wear, burnt-corked her pretty face, and decoyed the posse into chasing her while the slaves escaped across the river.

Miss Webster had unnumbered colleagues—Quakers and Baptists and those of no denomination—and they were all busy operating the mysterious railroad that "ran underground from Cincinnati to Canada." It was not easy to operate. It jeopardized livelihood. It put life and limb at hazard. But it ran. Whole families ran it—the Rankins, the Coffins, the Sloanes—and three hundred thousand slaves escaped.

Sojourner Truth would have joined in this work, but her appearance was just as conspicuous now as it had been ten years before. So she spoke. She spoke for abolition and for women's rights, which, thanks to Lucy Stone and Jane Swisshelm, was a subject practically inseparable from abolition in the Midwest.

"Where dere is so much racket dere mus' be somethin' out o' kilter,"

Sojourner told the heckling males at a women's rights convention in Akron. "I think dat 'twixt de niggers of de South and de womens of de North all a-talkin' 'bout rights, de white mens'll be in a fix pretty soon. Ef de firs' woman God ever made was strong enough to turn de worl' upside down all by her lonesome se'f dese together ought to be able to turn it back an' git it right side up again, an' now dey is askin' to do it de mens better let 'em. Dey talks 'bout dis thing in the head—what dey call it? Intellec'. Dat's it, honeys—intellec'. Now what's dat got to do wid us women's rights or niggers' rights? Ef my cup won't hol' but a pint an' yourn hol's a quart, wouldn' you be mean not to let me have my little half measure full?"

Sojourner's ironic wit and her subtle power dominated that meeting. The woman who chaired it, Mrs. Frances D. Gage, later reported that Sojourner Truth "had taken us up in her strong arms and carried us safely over the slough of difficulty, turning the whole tide in our favor."

But she was not able always to turn the tide.

There was much hostility in Ohio, where she made Salem and the office of Marius Robinson's *Anti-Slavery Bugle* her headquarters for two years. (Robinson tried to teach her to read, but "my brains is too stiff now," Sojourner told him.) It was 1852, when she judged her age to be "gone sixty," but she went from Ohio town to town speaking, soliciting subscriptions for the *Anti-Slavery Bugle,* and occasionally even making sorties into neighboring states. She could not go into Indiana without facing the threat of arrest, or into Illinois without the chance of violence. But she went many times. She said she was "God's pilgrim" and under God's protection, but that protection sometimes wilted in the hot breath blowing in from Missouri and across the plains of Kansas, where John Brown, drunk on the wine of his coming crucifixion, would soon reappear to make good the defiance flung out by Senator William Seward: "Come on, then, gentlemen of the slave states! Since there is no escaping your challenge, I accept it on behalf of freedom. We will engage in competition for the virgin soil of Kansas, and God give the victory to the side that is stronger in numbers as it is in right."

Sojourner Truth was manhandled in Kansas, and ever afterward needed the support of a cane, which, she avowed, also came in "mighty fine for crackin' skulls."

If this was said jocosely, the rumors, the galling jokes, and the downright lies that followed her everywhere were not. Nor could the portrait of her drawn by Harriet B. Stowe modify them. The people who were Sojourner's detractors did not read the *Atlantic Monthly.* If Sojourner was for Mrs. Stowe a "Sybil," she was a "black witch" for many more, and it was said that she worshiped in graveyards. If, as Mrs. Stowe wrote, she had "power and sweetness," there were others more vociferous who said she cast spells.

The unsavory reputation that surrounded her during the exposure and trial of Matthias was revived. Some believed that she was a man masquerading as a woman for reasons that would not bear examination. The St. Louis *Dispatch* reported, "Sojourner Truth is the name of a man now lecturing in Kansas City." Her vigorous, rail-like frame, her scarred, strong face and heavy-timbred voice were deceptive, and there were those who honestly doubted her femininity. But if such doubts persisted (as late as 1877), it was not Sojourner's fault.

In 1858 she had set a Kansas anti-slavery meeting above the usual pitch of turbulence. The meeting had been rigged by the enemies of abolition. As soon as Sojourner began her speech, a man in the audience interrupted her. "Hold on," he said. "Is the speaker man or woman? The majority of persons present believe the speaker to be a man. . . . I demand that if she is a woman, she submit her breast to the inspection of some of the ladies present . . . !"

While the abolitionists gaped in shocked silence, the pro-slavery claque, stamping their feet and clapping their hands, shouted in ribald mockery, "Uncover! Uncover! You are a man!" The dazed abolitionists responded only with cries of, "No, no! For shame!"

The whole auditorium was in confusion, for there were bully boys on both sides, and Sojourner Truth, facing it from the rostrum, whence had fled the chairman and the other platform guests, waited the tumult out. When it had quieted to manageble proportions, she stepped to the edge of the platform and pounded her cane on the floor.

"My breasts," she said, "has suckled many a white baby when dey shoulda been sucklin' my own." Her voice quavered momentarily, and then rose again firmly, tranquilly. "I dar'st show my breasts to de whole cong'agation. It ain't my shame dat I do dis, but yourn. Here den," she said, ripping her clothes from neckline to waist, "see fer yourself!" Her hard gaze sought and found the face of the man who had first attacked her. She thrust her bared breasts forward and said in an angry scorn, "Mought be you'd like to suck?"

5. "Frederick, Is God Dead?"

But Sojourner Truth was beginning to feel the wear and tear, the slow erosion of the years. Traveling with Parker Pillsbury on one of his speaking tours through the Midwest, she suffered occasional spells of faintness. Her wounded leg ulcerated. In Battle Creek, Michigan, where she had found her daughter's son, Sammy Banks, with whom she now lived, a physician was able to arrest the infection, but it broke out again periodically and gave her great pain. Nevertheless, she refused to stop for long. She went back into Illinois, Kansas, Ohio, Indiana. She went out into New England, where she was the guest of the Stowes in Andover, Massachusetts. And there was one brief interlude, more pleasant than strenuous. She went to Tawawa Springs, Ohio, to visit Daniel Payne, who, with his wife and her two children, was making his home there.

Payne was as busy as ever. He presided over the work of the African Methodist Episcopal Church in Ohio, Indiana, and Canada. His duties had forced him to live at one time or another in Troy, New York, Philadelphia, Baltimore, Washington, and Cincinnati. In addition to his churchly work, he had organized in each place adult Negroes into study groups and started schools for their children. He himself had done most of the teaching— reading, writing, and "social and civic morality" to the adults; a more formal curriculum to the children.

Now he was engaged in a more ambitious educational venture. He was the only Negro trustee of the new Wilberforce University. It had been founded by the white Methodist Church for "the benefit of the African race." (The exigencies of the war were to close it down in 1862, but Payne was to reopen it the very next year and become the first president of the first Negro-controlled college.) While Sojourner was his guest in 1858, he took her to visit the college on the outskirts of Xenia. How she reacted to a campus populated exclusively by the illegitimate mulatto offspring of Southern planters is not recorded, but Payne felt moved to remind her that "these also need learning and God as much as any." When he had her speak to the adults of his Moral and Mental Uplift Society, he wished that there had been a thousand "instead of twenty to hear my simple and eloquent friend."

Before the visit ended, Payne read his friend some verses, pieces of his own published in 1850, and from a book of poems by the slave George M. Horton. Sojourner's comment made him laugh wryly. "Dan," she said, "yourn be pretty, but his'n be strong." She regretted that she could not read them for herself, but the bishop made her a gift of his slim volume anyway.

This visit did Sojourner Truth good, and she left Tawawa Springs to go stumping about as usual, attending meetings and speaking.

But all the most eloquent tongues in Christendom could not have modified the momentum or changed the direction of the decade that was now fast drawing to a close. Neither North nor South had been reconciled to the Compromise of 1850. Neither made serious efforts to preserve intersectional peace. If the North's defiance of the Fugitive Slave Law further embittered the South, then the passage of the Kansas-Nebraska Act exacerbated the feelings of the North and brought about a new political alignment of Northern Whigs, Free-Soilers, and Democrats. Professedly anti-slavery, the Republican party pieced out a program attractive to many who cared nothing about the slavery issue. In 1857 the Dred Scott decision did not prove "happily a matter of but little importance," as President Buchanan had said. It was oil thrown on the fire. In 1859, John Brown staged his raid on Harper's Ferry and achieved his martyrdom. In 1860 the Republicans elected the unknown Abraham Lincoln. In that same year Frederick Douglass, deep in despair on his return from England, spoke at an anti-slavery meeting commemorating West Indian emancipation:

"They [Republicans] are men who are brave enough to trip up a man on crutches, push a blind man off the side-walk, or flog a man when his hands are tied, but too base and cowardly to contend with one who has an equal chance of defense with themselves. The black man, excluded alike from the jury box and the ballot box, is at the mercy of his enemies. . . . All know that the election of Lincoln would destroy all the conciliatory power which this new injustice to the Negro might exert. . . . But what will the colored people and their friends do now . . . ?"

Just at this point Sojourner Truth rose slowly in the back of the hall. "Frederick," she cried, "is God dead?"

God was not dead. Eight months later He was "trampling out the vintage where the grapes of wrath" were stored.

This selection is from *The Lonesome Road: The Story of the Negro's Part in America* (Garden City, N.Y.: Doubleday, 1958), 65-82, 127-48, 153-77.

Editor's Note: *John Russwurm, 1826 alumnus of Bowdoin College, was once widely believed to be the first person of African descent to receive a baccalaureate degree from an American college. However, more recently it has been confirmed that the distinction belongs to Alexander Twilight, who graduated from Middlebury College in 1823. See also Blyden Jackson, *A History of Afro-American Literature, The Long Beginning, 1746-1895*. Vol. 1. (Baton Rouge: Louisiana State Univ. Press, 1989), 123.

V

JOURNALISM

In 1943, Redding began writing a newspaper column entitled "A Second Look," devoted to social, cultural, and political issues in the United States and abroad. The column appeared for eight months on the editorial page of the Norfolk *Journal and Guide,* and for over two years in the Baltimore-based *Afro-American* newspapers. He was subsequently appointed Book Editor for the *Afro;* a cross-section of his book reviews from that newspaper appears in Part VII of this volume. His editorial columns directed attention to some of the most important events and personalities of our time. They are indeed deserving of "a second look." Seven from the *Afro-American* are represented in this anthology.

JUSTICE TO JAPANESE AMERICANS

The eviction of more than one hundred thousand people of Japanese ancestry from their homes in California, Oregon, and Washington was a great wrong. It was a great wrong because the action, taken in 1942, was clearly based on race prejudice and other low consideration, among which was jealousy of the skill shown by the yellow people in farming and fishing.

It was a great wrong because it was discrimination of the rankest kind, and it had little to justify it.

The wrong would not have been lessened had other peoples of enemy-alien ancestry been set up in relocation centers, but it would have given to the act of eviction a blush of justification as an act of national defense.

The Italians, who people South Jersey, the Germans who people Yorkville in New York City and large and cohesive sections of Cincinnati and the Twin Cities of Minnesota could have been evicted with as much reason, on the grounds that they were a threat to our national security.

It would have been silly and wrong to do this, but it would have dispelled the stench of pure race prejudice.

Now the War Department, in revoking its order of eviction, seems to think that it has righted this great wrong. After almost thirty months of dealing out injustice, the War Department thinks that it is now being just.

But it cannot right the wrong, nor deal out compensatory justice. It cannot explain to the Japanese-Americans who died at Anzio and who are dying now on the Western Front why their parents and their brothers and sisters were removed in the first place. It is very silly to whisper in a dead man's ear, "I'm sorry."

Nor can the War Department make it up to those who now are free to go back to their homes. Well over half of these are American citizens, but now they are citizens of a third-class sort, and this is a wrong done them that the War Department can never right.

It allowed its policy toward the Japanese-Americans (as in the case of colored Americans) to be governed by the attitudes of a particular region and therefore gave a sort of national sanction to the attitudes of that region.

Anyone who reads the papers knows that anti-Japanese feeling has grown greater in the West. The home-coming of the evictees will, as the War Department admits, "create certain adjustment problems."

By the speedy resolution of these adjustment problems, the Department could wipe out a great deal of the harm it has done. It could, as a measure of national defense, arrest the anti-Japanese, caution the Hearst newspapers, and forbid the anti-Japanese mass meetings that are springing up all over the West Coast.

It could do these things with as much justification as it did the one thing that now lends these others sanction.

It could do these things, but it won't. The matter is no longer in its hands, it says. It is now up to the people—the "white citizens"—of California, Oregon, and Washington to give to the returning Japanese-Americans (there is a touch of irony here) the "consideration to which they are entitled as loyal citizens and law-abiding" Americans.

This article is from the *Afro-American*, Jan. 6, 1945. The title is supplied by the editor.

HITLER'S END—MYSTERY OR HISTORY?

Often the news dispatches that are relegated to the back pages among the classified ads and the obituaries stimulate the most excitement and speculation; and a certain kind of news is not news at all if it does not stir the imagination.

None of the big headlines of the past eight days has had this effect upon me. In spite of the efforts of headline writers and correspondents,

I've simply found it impossible to give more than a grunt of satisfaction to news of the shelling of Hokkaido, to the fact that the Cruiser Augusta arrived safely at Antwerp and that President Truman disembarked from it looking "tanned and fit and trim."

How else was President Truman to look after the sun and the sea? . . .

What did arouse me were two dispatches, neither of which rated either front-page or headlines in any of the papers I saw. The first of these items appeared on July 11, and its date line was Mar-del-Plata, Argentina.

The item said that a Nazi U-boat surfaced at Mar-del-Plata, which is an Argentine U-boat base, and surrendered to the Argentine commander there on July 10.

The U-boat, the dispatch said, had cruised "the Atlantic apparently for eight weeks." I clipped the item and filed it because it aroused my imagination.

Then on July 16, another item, also considered unworthy of headlines in the paper I saw, aroused my imagination. It was a dispatch from Montevideo, which is the capital of Uruguay and just across the Plata River from Buenos Aires, Argentina.

The reporter who wrote this item said that Hitler and Eva Braun had landed by U-boat, in Argentina and were now safe in Patagonia, which is a section of Argentina.

Two and two sometimes make a most unlikely five; but consider these items! Consider the stories—the dozens of stories we've heard about Hitler since the fall of Berlin. Consider that no reliable witness saw him die.

Consider that the Russians, who were there first and who have had weeks to conduct a painstaking investigation, have said that they have discovered no evidence of Hitler's death.

Then, finally, consider that the U-boat which landed in Argentina was thought to have been cruising for eight weeks—almost exactly the number of weeks since Hitler was last reported alive in Berlin. Then think of Argentina's internal history of the last decade!

It all fits. It makes a kind of crazy sense, and it has that audacity with which Hitler has done things before.

This article is from the *Afro-American*, July 28, 1945. The title is supplied by the editor.

POSTWAR U.S.A.

A month and a half after V-J Day it all begins to look strikingly familiar again. A citizen of the country, dead these last 12 years, resurrected into this moment, would say, "Ah! America; these United States," and take up life again exactly where he left off.

The restraints imposed by the greatest war in all history are off. Reaction has set in.

The people of the United States are at their eternal business of being disunited individuals, factions and cliques with the one homogeneous trait of doing and being and saying what they d——n well please.

We are again making a licentious cult of the liberty someone else fought and died for.

The old restlessness, the often painless seeking, the congenital itch, the rejection of all forms of control which might in any way be misconstrued as tyranny rise again.

The old intolerances are coming back to life.

Nowhere are the cohesive forces of national life—the press, the radio, the pulpit, the school—less effective and nowhere are these forces greater.

Nowhere in the world is the citadel of individual liberty so valiantly defended (and this is one of the many paradoxes) by men who will fight among themselves simply because they have met walking in opposite directions.

Nowhere is there a nation of people with so many ants in its collective pants.

Nowhere is there a people with more blind and unreasoning attachment to a set of principles of life and government, and nowhere is there a people who flout their principles more.

Nowhere in the world is there such a crazy, fickle, bullheaded, lawless, religious, violent, prejudiced, free, enslaved, sublime, ridiculous, proud, humble, justice-loving, justice-flaunting, unjust, sentimental and cynical people as those of the United States.

Nowhere is a creed so much talked about as is Americanism and nowhere is a creed so little understood. Nowhere is the hatred of violence so greatly affirmed and nowhere is it so much used as the first expedient.

No country's people respond more readily to humanitarian appeals from total strangers and nowhere is there more need for humanitarian charity.

No nation has so great an urge toward world peace and world prosperity and no nation is less ready to take up the responsibility for peace and prosperity.

No country spends more on education or has as many schools or so many great institutions of learning and no country is less educated.

Nowhere is God so revered and the Devil so followed. Nowhere is the dove so well loved and the buzzard so well fed. Nowhere is there such a strange concord of discords.

And nowhere is there so much hope for you and me, for nowhere is there more earnest striving by so many free men for the ultimate victory of man's brotherhood.

This article is from the *Afro-American*, October 13, 1945. The title is supplied by the editor.

A HUMAN PERSPECTIVE

Someone asked me the other day why I do not stick exclusively to comment on American racial problems, of which there are, he said, enough to keep any man's mind busy for several lifetimes.

I was surprised at the question because we were in the kind of social gathering in which people ordinarily try to avoid mentioning the "problem" except in the lightest and most impersonal terms.

In fact, no one gets ponderous over anything. Life is just a big red apple. And here was this fellow revealing the worm in it.

I was embarrassed because I was a stranger, a guest, and at the moment everybody had stopped talking. I gave a purely social-level answer which everyone accepted. "Must we," I asked, "go into that?"

Now, of course, the true answer is much longer, though the very core of it seems to me to be that all racial problems are first and essentially human problems.

I may comment on what's happening to a bunch of Moslem-Indians in Seringapatam, or on what's doing in China, or on something President Truman said to Mackenzie King," * or on the atom bomb.

It is not because I am any less interested in whether Jane White† puts Nonnie across the footlights, or in whether Jackie Robinson‡ will make good in white organized baseball, or in restrictive covenants that make colored neighborhoods so unsightly and crowded.

It is simply that it is salutary to see American racial problems in some sort of broad, human perspective. Otherwise there is fearful danger of becoming near-sighted.

Certainly I get quite emotional about the race business. I knew, as everyone who is colored knows, that the biggest, single, overall conditioning circumstance in my life is the fact that I am colored.

I get mad because this genetic accident has been given so much importance by whole generations of American people who have passed down to society this crazy imbalance in the scale of human values.

I get mad because I have to face it so often when it should be irrelevant but isn't. I get mad because it uses up a lot of energy merely to be colored, and I could use all my energies for something else.

It should be no more important to me or to anyone than the fact that the man I see through my study window has brown eyes or black hair or half-moons at the bases of his fingernails.

I like occasionally to push the fact of color away by might and main. There is a world full of human problems, and the world is very close.

That's why I comment on the recent elections in France, on what Russia may do with Poland, and on the Jewish-Arab-British business in Palestine.

They're all human problems too; and though I am colored, I've never quite believed that rabid fringe of fools who say that because I am, I am not human.

This article is from the *Afro-American*, Dec. 8, 1945. The title is supplied by the editor.

Editor's Notes: *William Lyon Mackenzie King (1874-1950), Canadian Liberal party statesman and prime minister, who represented Canada in post-World War II international conferences. †Jane White, Afro-American actress, who portrayed character Lonnie Anderson in Broadway dramatization of Lillian Smith's best-selling 1944 novel, *Strange Fruit*, in which Lonnie, a college graduate, is able to find employment only as a domestic in a segregated Georgia town following World War I. ‡Jackie Robinson (1919-1972), first Afro-American baseball player in major leagues.

IT'S IN THE HEART

You go along for a few days, and it's all right. You have made a resolve not to be bothered by the color question, to ignore or avoid the inconveniences of its personal ramifications, and to shy off from any arguments or discussions that touch upon it.

You meet people, and they say, "How are things?" and you answer, "Fine," even though just that day perhaps you have seen a brutal cop club a drunken colored person over the head because clubbing him into unconsciousness was easier than holding him until the patrol wagon came. You think of the cop as merely ignorant, an isolated case absolutely, and you tell yourself that this one cop would have clubbed a drunken white in the same way.

What you're doing, of course, is trying to get out of the racial frame of reference. What you're doing is trying to forget, as Gunnar Myrdal puts it, that "the American colored people's problem is a problem in the heart of the American."

For a few hours—maybe for a few days, if you're lucky, you succeed in forgetting. You go home and you read a romance, or you listen to a symphony, or you go to a dance, or you sleep without dreaming. You succeed in forgetting. You forget that pretty soon now your son, aged eight, is going to be asking questions, and that he will demand answers.

You forget that pretty soon now there will be heartbreak and lonely questing for him, as there was for you, and that unless you have built for him the strong bridges he will need, he may be swallowed up in the dark abyss between the American Creed and the American Deed. You forget all this. You luxuriate, as it were, in a Fool's Paradise.

Then one day, in spite of your resolve, the thing happens which you knew was bound to happen anyhow. The predacious devils of the color problem are back at you again. You ward them off. You say, "Get thou behind me, Devils!" You run. But the very struggle to elude them is part and parcel of the colored problem, and it is no less in its intensity and its cost in spirit than the struggle to overcome them.

The minor legions of them come on, and they annoy you with little things first—the cheap sales girl in the store who scowls as she wraps your purchase, and then, slamming it on the counter, hisses, "Here you are, boy"—the unbelievable effontery of a vulgar public official who lets you know in no uncertain terms that he was not elected to serve the interests of colored citizens too—the shameful deterioration of soul-fiber in men who once were virtuous men but who now would get money or a kind of power or a kind of notice by doing anything.

These minor devils come at you. So finally you turn to face them squarely, and in defiance you unstop your ears, and in desperation you lay hold of weapons, such weapons as your hopeless belief, beliefless hope, and unutterable aspirations will let you wield. You oppose appeasement with hate, to no avail, reason with violence, to no avail; prayer with politics, to no avail; the American Creed with the American Deed.

You can't get away from the color problem, because it is a problem in the hearts of Americans.

This article is from the *Afro-American*, Feb. 5, 1944.

AFRO-AMERICANS AND JEWS

Many colored Americans who count a facile belief in popular concepts about colored people as a crime are themselves guilty of a similar crime against people of the Jewish faith. The beliefs too many of us hold about Jews are as unjust as the beliefs too many Gentiles hold about colored peoples.

It is unfortunate that we should allow our reason to be imposed upon by the prejudices of those same people who exploit both the Jew and the Aframericans. There is no room for any sort of racial, economic, or religious prejudice in America, and by fastening upon popular conceptions of Jewish character we help perpetuate a situation against which we ourselves have struggled for nearly a half-dozen centuries.

The Jew is a cheat and a thief, a great many people say, apparently with the utmost conviction, meaning ALL people of Jewish faith are cheats and thieves. And of course this is no more true than the popular belief which holds that ALL colored people are liars and chicken stealers.

Of course there are people of Jewish faith who cheat (and of course there are colored people who lie and steal chickens), but it is a pretty safe bet that if all Jews cheated, or if a majority of them cheated, or even if a fairly large percentage of them did, some logical means would have been found to keep them out of opportunities for cheating—to keep them out of the very considerable part they play in American economic life.

The Jew never produces anything; he merely sells and distributes the products of others, is another popular conception which is as wrong as all the others.

Almost any Jewish agency of enlightenment, but especially the Jewish Welfare Society, will prove that in proportion to their numbers in the United States there are as many Jewish farmers as there are farmers of any other peculiar religious, racial, or national classification excepting only the Japanese (before their removal to relocation centers), Italians, and Mennonites.

There are also Jewish fishermen, Jewish miners, and Jewish cattlemen.

The Jew controls the wealth of America and the greatest private fortunes belong to Jews are conceptions most of us have heard all our days and have taken for gospel.

"A rich Jew," people say, putting into the expression so much venom that they might be speaking of a particularly abominable abnormality in society. And of course it is not true that Jews control the wealth of America, or that there are no poor Jews, a corrollary which many people hold.

Among the names of the great financial giants in America—the men whose proved wealth and whose control of wealth are indisputable—there are no Jews: Ford, Morgan, the DuPonts, Rockefeller. And there are poor Jews—untold thousands of them—just as there are poor colored people, for by and large Jews suffer from the same economic discrimination.

Of all the groups in America, the colored group can least afford the luxury of holding prejudices.

This article is from the *Afro-American*, July 7, 1945. The title is supplied by the editor.

INFERIOR EDUCATION

More than half a century ago, President Charles Eliot of Harvard implemented a curriculum study by starting at the college in Cambridge a system of elective courses. Shortly thereafter, colleges (and even high schools) adopted the same system. If one is to judge the influence of that Harvard report upon American education, then the recent "Harvard Report" is no whistle in a gale. *It is the gale destined, one hopes, to blow American education clean of much of its errant nonsense, many of its false and pathetic creeds and its cheap substitutes for learning and wisdom.*

The influence of this new Harvard report promises to be salutary. The exercise of this influence upon "colored education"—and one uses the term advisedly—cannot come too soon. There has been and there still is a "colored education." It is, even in its own terms, an inferior education.

Out of one temporarily valid assumption grew other assumptions of no validity at all and, worse, a straightening concept which very early determined the policies of some of the most potent agencies and philanthropies in the field. The temporarily valid assumption, wisely exploited to the hilt by Booker T. Washington, was that colored people should first be taught to make a living.

The policy-controlling desideratum that derived from this was that colored people should be restricted to particular fields of endeavor. On the basis of this came the assumption that making a living in particular fields of endeavor was all that colored people could and should be taught.

By the values they hold, by the ways in which they live their private lives, by the matters they talk about, by the interests they think good, by the things they strive for, one is hard put to distinguish the average colored college graduates from the unfortunate clodhoppers who have never seen a school.

This is much less a damnation of colored college graduates than it is of teachers and administrators in colored high schools and colleges. It is much less a damnation of these latter than of the general system—the whole of American society. Like it or not, it nonetheless remains true that, with only the doubtful exception of Howard, there is not a colored liberal arts college in the land. In an increasing progression of ever narrowing fields, we have produced specialists at many things that matter not at all, and we have done this without ever suspecting that experts are not necessarily educated men—and without guessing that if they were educated first they would be better experts afterwards.

The colored people in America, who above all people need a grounding in the humanities, in truly liberalizing knowledge, in sympathetic understanding of human society and its all too human foibles, have been taught only to make a living.

This article is from the *Afro-American*, Sept. 15, 1945. The title is supplied by the editor.

VI

TRAVELOGUE/DIALOGUE INTERNATIONAL

Redding's three-month foreign assignment as an exchange lecturer in India in 1952 for the Department of State resulted in two published documents excerpted here, *An American in India: A Personal Report on the Indian Dilemma and the Nature of her Conflicts* and "Report from India." His assessment a few years later on "The Meaning of Bandung" for the *American Scholar,* is also excerpted here.

From his 1962 lecture tour of Africa, where he visited a dozen countries and documented his travel experiences in a weekly column for the *Afro-American,* comes his final column and a condensed essay, "Home to Africa," originally published in the *American Scholar.*

His prose, vividly describes a part of the world at the dawn of its political independence, as well as his personal impressions as a foreign observer.

THE COLOR OF MY SKIN

. . . Accepting the State Department assignments was to be a test of my freedom. I was told, "Your job will be to help interpret American life to the people of India." Very well, I was prepared to give such knowledge and intelligence as I have, but in the manner of the clinician, disinterested, detached, as one in no way involved, as one with no concern in writing prescriptions or in treating disease.

"I will tell the truth," I said. And that was the extent of my commitment. What would the telling of the clinical truth do to America? No matter—I had no spiritual investment in it. The national unit called America meant nothing to me now. At last my hopeful, loving hate for her had died, and the final result of the American experience had been to force me to depersonalize myself. I was glad. I was free. As for the rest, I looked forward to a pleasant excursion halfway around the world.

But before I had gone a third of the way, my ideas as to what I might expect from this journey were subjected to sudden rearrangement.

2

At the Geneva airport one could not overlook the Americans. When I stepped out of the glittering sunlight into the glowing shade of the airport lounge, there they were—eight or ten of them, tanned, sport-clad and boldly sizing up each new arrival. In any place in America they would have been unremarkable, but here in the foreign, air-conditioned room, where people were packed like fish in ice, they were as conspicuous as billboards and almost as loud as barkers at a county fair. . . .

Everyone was looking at them, and the passengers for the flight to Marseille and Barcelona, which was being announced, made a wide circuit around them to get to the door. They were graceless and unlovely, and yet I had a sudden great urge to defend them. It was strange, I thought, even as remembered experiences stirred up a muddy residue of doubt. If our positions were reversed, would they acknowledge and defend me? There was the old, bedeviling duality—the two-in-one feeling. I had not really shed them—American, Negro; American-Negro—and the realizaion made me gloomy. This journey was to be taken clean, I thought, and I was to travel light. Now I felt like Sisyphus. . . .

3

My flight reached Bombay at five-thirty in the evening. I had no business there. Since I was several days overdue in Delhi, I thought my immediate problem was to get on to that city. But I was mistaken; my immediate problem was to gain entry into the country. Already damp with perspiration and slimy with a greasy film of dust, I was inclined to exaggerate the difficulty. Police and customs officials seemed intent on blocking me. It was easy to guess who had trained them. They spoke English like Oxonians; their civility was close to insult, their abruptness just short of command. One had the feeling of being deprived of something indefinable, abstract but good—courtesy, I think, or a sense of society's protection. What was my destination in *Inghia?* Sniffing suspiciously, they examined my medical certificates, travel orders and passport. Very well, they said at last, but I must know that I had no immunity from the ordinary regulations. There would be a flight for Delhi in the morning, and I should report to the police within twenty-four hours after my arrival there. Did I have British pounds? American dollars? Amount? They dismissed me with a curt "You may take your leave."

Beyond the official cages the huge hangar was packed with a quiet, unmoving crowd. I had read enough about India to know that these were Moslems. The men wore fezzes, long coats buttoned to the chin, and trousers that encased the legs like sheaths. So far as I could see they did not talk to one another nor to the women, many of whom were in strict purdah. The women and young girls who were not in purdah kept their heads lowered and their faces averted when strangers passed. An air of melancholy torpor hung over the crowd like a pall. People squatted on the bare ground, apparently in family groups, surrounded by mounds of portable household goods—wicker boxes and metal chests, fiber suitcases and brass vessels, bedrolls, mirrors, bundles of clothes. Though there were many children, there was no play, no laughter, no talk. Even the babies, wrapped in the folds of women's cloaks to protect them from flies, were silent and listless, as if their natural instincts were smothered in unnatural gloom. It was very hot.

I learned later that I had walked straight into one of the tragic dramas of history, into a scene that had been played before. These people were in flight, for they remembered catastrophe. Uprooted once more, populations of great density were pouring in a two-way avalanche between India and Pakistan. The Moslem state had suddenly annulled the right of unrestricted entry to India's citizens, and India had retaliated by closing her borders to Pakistanis. The reasons for this were not clearly explained; some said they could not be clearly explained. Each government, however, accused the other of malice, perfidy and dark designs. It was said that the Moslems wanted to confiscate the property of wealthy Hindus in Pakistan; it was said that the Hindus coveted the rich farming land of Moslems in northern India. Incidents had occurred. Though it was still some weeks before the new restrictions were to go into effect, despairing peoples of both sides were on the move.

These at the airport were some of them, luckier and wealthier than most. No one knew how many were fleeing in stifling third-class railroad coaches, in bullock carts, on foot, or on the backs of kinsmen. (In July a reporter for the *Times of India* was to estimate that ten thousand fled each week; others gave higher figures.) But soon enough I was to see crowds of homeless refugees wailing for alms, their stomachs drum-tight with the nauseous gas of hunger or concave from the pitiless suck of starvation. Indeed, that night, in the process of letting an unexpected circumstance have its way with me, I found myself amid the homeless and, in a moment of acute sentience, recovering again in sickened wonder the knowledge of my twisted integration.

It was Rena Mark's doing. When we were thrown together in customs check and discovered our mutual Americanism, I was prepared to ignore her. My defenses were up, for I was still feeling the effects of the Geneva encounter, and I was dangling in the void of that schism which the Geneva experience had unclosed. But Mrs. Mark seemed so glad to see another American of whatever degree of aloofness that my reserve melted quite away. We rode together from the airport to the hotel. The first glimpse of the dense Gothic-Moghal jungle of Bombay drew from her exclamations of wonder and delight. Such crowds! Such cries! Such color! Everything was "simply wonderful!" Though no longer young, Mrs. Mark was as trim as a schoolgirl, and she had that quality of eagerness and excitability, unmodified by serious thought, that Americans seem to find attractive in women. The Taj Mahal Hotel fascinated her. Oh, the spacious grandeur of it, the "wonderful" servants and, later at dinner, the exciting food! The mystery of Bombay! She must see as much of it as she could in this one night, for she might not have the chance again. From Ceylon, where she was going to join her husband, she would travel eastward back to the States.

So after dinner we hired a horse cab. It was past ten, and the hotel plaza was deserted. I thought there could not be much to see, but, settled in the slow, creaking cab, we left the plaza, crossed some car tracks into a square, where the lights of teahouses, all apparently empty, blazed in furious white splendor, passed a statue circled by an iron railing and entered a dim length of street. There were closed and boarded shops and folded stalls on each side of the street, and the measured *clop-clop* of the horse reverberated hollowly back from them. Night shadows were thick. Mrs. Mark shivered a little and pulled her gauzy stole closer about her shoulders. I dropped my head against the moldy cushion, for there was nothing to see, and I was tired. I closed my eyes.

When I opened them again, Rena Mark was sitting on the edge of the seat staring about her. She clutched my arm. "Look!" she whispered.

At first I saw nothing. Then, straining, I saw what looked to be inert bundles lying in serried rows. The pavement on each side of the narrow roadway was covered with them.

"What is it?"

"People!" Mrs. Mark said. "People sleeping in the street—men, women, children."

They were lying four and five pressed together, then a space, then two or three more and another space. Some were lying on the bare ground, some on bits of rags; some were covered, some were not. We kept passing them, seeing distinctly those who lay in the murky glimmer of an occasional street light. Debris lay scattered in the gutters and on the road. Now, too, I detected an odor, fetid and inescapable, compacted of all the smells that poverty, sickness and death give off.

As we approached a street light we saw a figure rise to a sitting position, pause, detach itself from the shadows on the ground and step into the road. He stood for a moment waiting, giving us a good look as we came into the light; then he trotted out and came abreast of us. He stared at us—at me first, then past me at Rena Mark. His face seemed quite expressionless.

The hackman said something to him, and the man answered, but without taking his eyes off us. His body was thin, fibrous and quite black. Mrs. Mark tightened and shrank against me. "Tell him to go faster," she whispered tensely. "Faster," she said aloud to the driver, who understood no English.

"No dacoit, memsahib," the man said quietly in English.

To hear him speak English relieved my tension somewhat, but to have him walking beside us staring at us still seemed a threat. Leaning forward, I touched the driver and gestured him to go faster. The horse broke into a labored trot. The naked figure trotted with us.

"Give him money," Mrs. Mark whispered, feeling for her purse which lay wedged between us. But I restrained her. I reasoned that the last thing in the world to do was to show money. My imagination got to work on all those sleeping forms that seemed to stretch endlessly ahead on both sides of us. What would happen if this man should arouse them?

Suddenly the man touched my knee. "By you 'frika?" I did not understand him. "By you 'frika?" he repeated slowly. Then I understood him and shook my head.

"Not Africa. America," I said, pointing to myself. I saw his expression change. "America. America," I said again, indicating Mrs. Mark.

"By you America?" he questioned doubtfully, tapping my knee. I nodded. Keeping his eyes on me, he raised his voice and said something to the driver, and I caught the word "America" again.

"*A-cha*," the driver said, jerking his head.

Then the man reached in, took my hand, pulled back the sleeve to expose my forearm and placed his own naked arm beside it. A slow smile of recognition and wonder trembled like a light on his dark face. "Same like me," he said then, looking at me. "Like by you." For a moment longer, trotting there beside us, he held my hand.

All at once I knew I was closer to this nameless man than I could ever be to Rena Mark, who pressed against my side in fear. The feeling and the knowledge came spontaneously, unbidden, without the intercession of my will, and I tried to deny it, ignore it, stamp it out. It seemed a second, final betrayal of my new dispassionate curiosity, of which the Geneva incident had been the first. The barriers of language, culture and national birth dissolved before it, and I stood face to face with an indestructible truth: the color of my skin was still the touchstone. I did not like it. For thirty years I had consciously struggled to destroy the truth's hold on me, and for a year and a half I had been free of it. But where was my freedom now? Where was the impersonal curiosity of the clinician? Even here in a foreign country among a foreign people was experience to be tested by the color of my skin?

Apparently the significance of the by-play had been lost on Mrs. Mark, for she still cowered against me. "There's nothing to worry about," I told her a little impatiently.

"By Kangra," the man said, touching himself. I nodded. He was from a place called Kangra. "Soon time go Kangra." I nodded again. "Soon time no food," he said, pressing his hand to his naked stomach. "Go Kangra."

The row of sleepers had thinned. Looking ahead, I could see that we were coming to a place where the street gave onto a brightly lighted square. There was some kind of monument in the center of the square, and a rank of cars was parked on one side of it.

"A rupee, huzoor?" the man supplicated gently, nodding and smiling.

We were very near the square now, and I could see that the ranked cars were taxis, and as we moved into it I handed the man a rupee. Instantly he stopped, brought his hands together with the rupee folded between them and bowed his head. He was still standing on the edge of the square when Rena Mark and I transferred to a taxi, and when our car rounded the monument and shot past him, he again bowed his head over his pressed hands.

Though Mrs. Mark relaxed, we did not talk much going back to the hotel. She seemed a complete stranger to me. Once, when we were speeding along a wide, well-lighted boulevard that ran by the sea, Mrs. Mark said that she was reminded of Chicago, but I saw no point in responding to that. And another time, because of my silence, I suppose, she asked whether something was wrong, but I did not want to go into that. What was wrong, even had I the words to express it, would probably have been incomprehensible to her, and most certainly would have shocked her. So mostly we were silent. When we got back to the hotel and stopped at the desk for our keys, I saw a sign I had not noticed before. It was propped on an easel behind the desk, and it said: NO WHITE SOUTH AFRICANS ALLOWED. . . .

This selection is from *An American in India: A Personal Report on the Indian Dilemma and the Nature of Her Conflicts* (Indianapolis: Bobbs-Merrill, 1954), 11-20. The title is supplied by the editor.

FROM "REPORT FROM INDIA"

Let me grant at the start that three months in India is time enough for only limited observation and that judgments based on limited observation are open to question. But I do not pretend to know or write of all India or all Indians. Also, there are several factors which may somewhat offset the limitations of time.

First, the trip was an unusually extensive one. I made the circuit of India from Bombay on the west coast down to Trivandrum and up the east coast to Calcutta. Inland, I visited Poona, Hyderabad, Mysore, Bangalore, Guntur, Cuttack, Patna, dozens of university centers, and a considerable number of villages.

Second, my assignment put me in touch with a restricted segment of India's population—the university people and other professional intellectuals, especially writers and journalists. I also talked with a good many assorted political officeholders, from mayors and municipal councilors to chief ministers and chief secretaries of state. I had the opportunity for close observation in these groups, and because of their relative homogeneity, it was not necessary for me to make constant changes in my frame of reference. It is of these groups only that I report.

Third, I think it should be said that dozens of Indians told me that I was "one of them," that (obviously because of my color) I looked like a "Madrassi" or "Bengali," that they felt "at home" with me. I was taken into dozens of Indian homes, some of them the most orthodox Hindu and Moslem homes, and treated with an intimacy that I have been told is most unusual for a Westerner. I think the significance of this is that my Indian hosts met me with their guards consciously lowered and free of the reticences with which they meet most Westerners. I think that in general my Indian friends and acquaintances spoke candidly and freely.

What follows is the truth as they see it.

The Indian people believe that the United States is imperialistic and that American designs in India are imperialistic. They are afraid of American "influence" and suspicious that America's various technical and other aid programs in India are methods of buying influence. "Why does America insist on sending experts to us?" was one of the questions I got from professional intellectuals and politicians time and again. "We have our own technical experts, trained in the West and some of them in America itself." The ex-Secretary General of the Congress Party said, "Why can't America give us aid and equipment and leave her advisors at home? The Indian people are suspicious of American advisors. . . ."

The Indian people believe that American policy is opposed to the "liberation and rise" of the colored people of the world, and that the treatment of Negroes in America is a home demonstration of this. The color question is linked with imperialism. No matter what the original subject of a conversation, my Indian acquaintances always managed to bring in the color question either on a political or a personal level.

"Why doesn't the United States recognize Red China?" This question came unexpectedly, and I had no ready answer. But I needed none, for the questioner gave his own answer: "Because the United States does not want to admit that nation of colored people into national equality with her." It did no good to cite the instances of India herself, the Philippines, Haiti, Liberia and Japan; for excepting India, these were all "satellites" of America, and America was trying "to bring India into the same position."

The belief is that America is prejudiced against non-whites and that the prejudice, long documented in the disabilities under which Negroes suffer in the United States, is now expressed in American world policy. My Indian acquaintances contrasted the American billions given or loaned to Europe with the few millions disbursed in the East. They showed a great ignorance of the actual facts of race relations in the United States, and there was a strong resistance to being set right on the facts. . . .

The Indians believe that eventually they can take the best from communism, the best from socialism and the best from democracy and create something better for themselves. They point to England as an example of a country where such an amalgram is (or was until recently) having success. They point particularly to Yugoslavia. The "social welfare state" plus "nationalization" plus "free enterprise" they believe to be a workable combination. . . .

Once I came to realize what was facing me in my contacts with professional intellectuals, I saw my job as an effort to sow seeds of doubt as to the validity of the false and distorted information they were getting about America and American democracy. The only way I saw to do this was to tell the absolute truth. I had to admit that democracy is sometimes tragically slow. I had to admit that race relations in America are bad, but I also pointed out that they are increasingly bettering. (Fortunately I had considerable documented information with me.) I pointed out that the right to petition for redress of grievances and that the right of minorities to sue and protest and work for reform were not abridged in the United States. I had to admit that the mammoth American news agencies tended to monopolies and that their power was a potential danger to freedom of opinion and expression. I had to admit that many American movies and books exported to India are cheap and vulgar, but I pointed out that they were not representative of

American life, and that if there were no market in India for these cheap and vulgar misrepresentations, then they would not be exported for the consumption of the Indian people. (Radio Peiping got hold of this and spent two minutes blasting me for *insulting* the Indian people.)

The truth—and where possible, the truth backed with facts and figures—is not always immediately effective, as the Communist "big lie" has proved; but I have a hunch that in time—and surely there is still time?—the truth eventually wins.

I think what is needed is a concentration on two groups: the professional groups that should be sought out, encouraged, helped in a spirit of complete equality and friendship by visiting American writers, teachers and journalists; and the indecisive mass who, through our Information Service should be shown more and more representative films, illustrated books and magazines and the like. We must bombard them with the truth, for in general even a bitter truth is more effective than apologies for it, and has greater impact than professions of abject shame.

For sincerity is another word. The insincere can lose us the friendship of India and of the whole Near East, and we sorely need that friendship, which cannot be bought. Those who do not believe in the equality of man and who are not themselves examples of it can lose us a struggle which, even for all our best technical and financial efforts, will remain for some time in doubt. The Indian people are not going to be fooled by any play-acting by Americans.

Until I went out to India, I had no idea that there was in me so great an urge to defend America or that there were so many dangerous untruths to defend her against. Until I went to India, communism simply made interesting reading in the newspapers. Though I am still unmoved by the foghorn rantings of certain American legislators, now I know that communism abroad offers more than a blow to American pride.

Everywhere I went in India, American Foreign Service personnel treated me with consideration and kindness far beyond the needs of official duty. There were no exceptions to this. The Indians too (and especially those who were my officially designated hosts and companions) were kind to me— perhaps too kind, for if they sometimes awakened me at 5:00 A.M. (and they did) to ask whether a change in the American administration would mean a change in American foreign policy, they also sometimes kept me up until the same hour listening to the sublime music and poetry of Tagore.

This excerpt is from the *American Scholar,* Autumn 1953.

FROM "THE MEANING OF BANDUNG"

When the present century was just two years old, a young scholar, brooding over the problem that was to occupy him the rest of his long life, wrote "The problem of the twentieth century is the problem of the color line." No doubt many who read that sentence thought that it referred generally to America and specifically to the South. But W.E.B. DuBois' mind, well stocked with knowledge and sharpened by insight, moved in a much wider compass. In two years of foreign study and travel he had talked with South African and Indian colonials in England, and with African tribal chiefs in France and Belgium; and while he was a student in Germany one of his warmest acquaintances was an Asiatic "refugee" from the Straits Settlements. Already, too, DuBois was dreaming of an organization that would unite all the colored peoples of the world. Such an organization came into being in April, 1955, in an Indonesian city named Bandung, of which few people of the West were aware until then.

But there was another matter of which most Westerners were and even now are not aware, or—even more disturbing—pretend not to be aware. The delegates to the conference at Bandung were there because of a conviction that *the problem of the twentieth century is the problem of the color line.* Although the American press alone sent seventy reporters (jocosely described as "the largest delegation to Bandung") and the British press, including Canada and Australia, sent thirty, no American and no British newspaper easily available on this continent gave this conviction the preponderant weight it had in the thinking at Bandung. The *Christian Science Monitor* did remark that "the West is excluded. Emphasis is on the colored nations of the world." But this is not quite the same as saying, as it might in truth have done, that emphasis is on the color problem in the world, and that it was this that made the Asian-African Conference "perhaps the greatest historic event of our century." Of the half-dozen or so book-length essays about the Bandung Conference, only the one by Richard Wright* gave due weight to the central truth—and that book has been largely ignored.

What Western newspapers did not neglect to emphasize was the diversity of those gathered. And, indeed, there were great and basic differences. The twenty-eight nations nominally comprised four orientation blocs—neutralism, communism, socialism and democracy—and if the great divisive factor in the world is differences in ideology, as the West claims, then the Bandung Conference should not have been held at all. Surely, too, the jingo nationalism plangent in all the countries arching over the Indian Ocean from the Tasman Sea to the South Atlantic increased the divisive potential.

And as great as were the differences of a political kind, the diversities of a cultural and historical kind were greater. They ran the scale from animal worship to ancestor worship; from polygamy to polyandry; from practical classlessness to theoretically rigid caste; from industrial competence to agrarian stagnation. Indonesia has nearly the highest illiteracy rate in the world; Japan, the lowest. The people of Africa speak a hundred different dialects. The people of India speak a dozen different mother tongues and passionately resist the idea that Hindi should be the tongue of all. The language problem was so pervasive at Bandung that English, which is not the language of any of them, was made the official language. In India there is a militant resurgence of orthodox Hinduism. Egypt, Iran, Iraq, Saudi Arabia and Syria are Muslim, and Pakistan was established as an Islamic theocracy. In Nkrumah, the Gold Coast had a leader who relies heavily on the methods of fascism. There were two Vietnams at Bandung, represented by the same ethnic strain, but one is Communist and the other is not. In short, the Asian-African nations that met at Bandung seemed to be, as the London *Times* said, an assemblage of "self-irritants."

The London *Times* spoke the West's conscience, the West's fear, the West's hope. It is a conscience made painfully tender by the recognition of the jinni that six hundred years of cant and incantation have at last conjured up. It is a fear aroused by the reflected knowledge of that jinni's potential for evil. "The first international conference of colored peoples in the history of mankind," President Sukarno† called it—and so it was, representing more than half the population of the earth, an awesome thing to contemplate. In *Cry, the Beloved Country,*‡ Msimangu, a native, says, the "great fear is that when they are turned to loving we shall be turned to hating." It is a fear that is hard to live with, and it was therefore quite in the nature of things that the Western press should reflect less of the truth that aroused that fear and more of the delusions that sustained hope. Certain Western spokesmen reacted quite normally by pumping out propaganda designed to make the Asian-African Conference appear something other than it was—the organization of a new bloc, perhaps a new power bloc, that had been forming in the world for a quarter of a century.

Even before the delegates could assemble, their intentions were variously misconceived and misinterpreted. The New York *Times* said that the mission of the Conference was "to see that peace would prevail in the world." Like other sober-minded people, the delegates doubtless did want peace to prevail, but as a matter of cold fact this was the least and last of the intentions set forth in the official invitation. The first intention was "to promote goodwill and cooperation *among the nations of Asia and Africa;* to explore and advance *their* mutual as well as common interests." The second was "to consider social, economic and cultural problems and relations of the *countries represented.*" The third intention was "to consider problems of *special interest to Asian and African peoples,* for example, problems . . . *of racialism and colonialism.*" The fourth was "to view the position of Asia and Africa and *their peoples* in the world today." And finally, almost an appendix not really necessary to complete the text, was the intention "to view the contribution they can make to the promotion of world peace and cooperation."

Although the New York *Times* thought that world peace was the mission of the Conference, its chief on-the-spot correspondent, Tillman Durdin, took care to remark, "Rivalries, cross-currents and animosities abound . . . at Bandung," and, inferentially because of them, "Bandung seems to promise very limited achievements." Many influential metropolitan dailies—the St. Louis *Post-Dispatch,* the Louisville *Courier-Journal,* the Norfolk *Virginian-Pilot*—suspected some ulterior Communist motive cooked up by Chou En-lai[§] and naïvely abetted by Nehru,[#] who was suddenly—in the pages of the American press—"peevish" and "unpredictable," and altogether something less than the "friendly, decisive and pro-Western" figure he had been before. While there was much talk to the effect that Nehru and Chou would influence the Conference to promote their Five Principles of Peaceful Coexistence—principles, it was widely hinted, which were somehow Machiavellian—there was on the other hand a rainfall of predictions that the Conference would resolve into a struggle between Nehru and Chou for dominance among the colored peoples of the world: *Time* took this view, and so did *U.S. News and World Report.*

On April 20, the New York *Times* printed excerpts from the Conference's opening speeches, and the next day various sectors of the American press followed its lead. The excerpts were carefully selected for their anti-Communist slant, and the *Times* commented editorially: "The Bandung conference . . . attended by some of the major participants for the purpose of indicting the West for its *alleged* 'colonialism, racism and imperialism,' has started with a dramatic turnabout which dispels any notion that Asia and Africa speak with one voice." The exculpating "alleged" is a Swiftian stroke that deserves remarking, but it is more important in the present context to point out that the excerpted speeches plainly misrepresent the truth, while the editorial itself is just as plainly a misinterpretation of fact. Reading in full those opening speeches, one is thunderously impressed that all of them laid primary emotional and intellectual emphasis upon the West's racism and colonialism. And why not? This and their hatch of attendant evils—poverty, ignorance, personal indignity—had brought the delegates together in the first place. . . .

Editor's Notes: *Richard Wright, *Bandoeng, 1.5000.000.000 hommes.* Trans. Hélène Claireau. Paris: Calmann-Lévy, 1955. Book published in the U.S. as *The Color Curtain.* Cleveland: World, 1956.   †Akhmed Sukarno (1901-1970). Indonesian independence leader and first president of the Republic of Indonesia (1949-1966).   ‡*Cry, the Beloved Country.* Novel (1948) by South African author and humanitarian Alan Paton.   §Chou En-Lai (1898-1976). Chinese Communist head of delegation from People's Republic of China to the Bandung Conference. Premier and foreign minister (1949-1976).   #Jawaharlal Nehru (1889-1964). Indian nationalist leader, lawyer, author, and prime minister (held office 1947-1964).

"MISLED ABOUT AFRICA"

Sunday, July 15, [1962] I left Africa after a stay just ten days short of half a year.

I have seen many places and talked to many people, and I know now something; but by no means all, of what I do not know.

I brought certain misconceptions with me.

Some were merely stupid, funny, but some I will pass over in shamed silence for a while.

Considering that I had never been south of the Sahara, and considering the insidious kind of popular learning about black Africa that still prevailed in the States and elsewhere in the western world forty years ago, the misconceptions were inevitable.

I do not say this to excuse them.

They cannot be justified.

They can only be explained.

Although when I was a boy colonialism was even then dying its protracted death, you wouldn't have thought so from the moving pictures, which showed colonialism triumphant in all those parts of the world where non-white peoples made their homes.

The moving pictures were designed to promote the notion of the unconquerable European's dedicated bearing of the "white man's burden," which was Africa.

And Africa was symbolized when cameras focused in on rivers filled with crocodiles, or on a savage dance to the beat of juju drums, or on a flight of deadly, poisoned spears.

Who of my generation, for instance, does not remember "Sanders of the River" which starred Paul Robeson and Nina Mae McKinney?

When it was cut and edited for theatre production cameras, it was so unlike the picture Robeson thought he had made to the greater glory of Africa that he threatened to sue the producers for deceiving him.

Or who does not remember "Zanzibar," which billed a famous pair of movie stars who could not have cared less whether it maligned and villified every black man ever born.

In those days, the books, too, about Africa were generally the products of colonial minds and no one questioned them.

Some books still are—and I've no doubt others will be—but now many question them.

One such book was being read in Kenya, or at least in Nairobi, last month. I do not wish to dignify it, nor to incite curiosity about it, so I will not mention its name: the fewer people who read it, the better, and the sooner it's forgotten.

But it was written by a swaggering and careless white American who claims to know and to love Africa especially east of Lake Victoria.

Bad as the book makes Africans appear to non-Africans who credit it, the book makes its author (and by inevitable association, other white Americans) appear worse.

When independence comes to Kenya, he will not be welcomed there.

His book and one called *The Reluctant African*, by a black American, compound all the misconceptions and prove the dangerous folly of irresponsibility.

I hope I have got rid of the grosser misconceptions that popular learning fostered.

This is not to say, "Now I know Africa."

As of this moment, nobody knows Africa.

Nor is this to say that I can put true meanings to all I have seen, and infallibly interpret all that I have heard.

Whatever political sophistication I have is not enough to cope with the sophisticated politics of Africa.

It is not enough to cope with and to judge the future shape of what is still unfixed, still shapeless, still in process of becoming.

All I mean to say is that I no longer make the equations that many people—I among them—of my generation were abominally taught to make.

"Strange" no longer equals "savage."

"Pagan" no longer means "unbridled sin."

I no longer think that the African's (or the Hindu's, or the Samoan's or Maori's) idea of beauty is less commendable than mine because it is different.

I do not believe that all his customs are to be deplored because I cannot follow them.

I submit that witch doctors are not devils incarnate; and so far as I'm concerned, the "white man's grave" is where he digs it.

It surely is not Africa.

In short, I no longer believe in the Africa I was taught to believe in.

I no longer believe in it for the very best of reasons—there is no such Africa.

Perhaps there never was.

Perhaps that Africa was always a dark continent of the mind.

This article is from *Afro Magazine*, Aug. 18, 1962.

FROM "HOME TO AFRICA"

In this excerpt, Redding shares his view of the continent before his visit, plus a personal recollection of the African Writers Conference, which he attended in Uganda in 1962.

. . . Africa had been a vague, troubling presence in my imagination for nearly as long as I can remember. Like most Americans of my generation, I had the wrong learning about Africa, and, like most Negro Americans, had never felt any pride in what I had been uncritically taught to believe. Indeed, the opposite—which I think was probably intended. I was ashamed that Africans were rated the "lowest of the human species"; that once captured and sold into bondage, often by other Africans, "they took happily to slavery, as if it was their natural condition"; that they lived in mud huts, went naked and ate human flesh; and that Africa was the "white man's graveyard." So wasn't I glad that my ancestors had been brought from that "benighted land"—that "dark continent"—and I could enjoy the "blessings of civilization"? I could not then (say forty years ago), but I could now counter that question with another: what blessings? . . .

Since a cultural history is proclaimed everywhere to be the unassailable testimonial to the dignity and worth of a people, and since by definition I was excluded from the cultural heritage that should have been mine by right of birth, Pan-Africa was the door through which fulfillment gleamed.

Yet so frustrating and divisive was the learning of my youth and so charismatic the projection of the American dream, when that door was opened at the All-African Writers Conference in Uganda last spring [1962], I could not enter through it.

Of the black African writers most likely to be known to the West, only Leopold Senghor, Peter Abrahams and the ailing and aging Amos Tutuola were missing. Chinua Achebe, Ezekiel Mphahlele, Gabriel Okara, Wole Soyinka, Amadou Samb, Bloke Modisane—thirty-two in all, representing the finest writing talent in Africa, were there. There were four Americans, and of the several British at least four were publishers or publishers' representatives. Including the poet Langston Hughes, who is Negro, and the novelist Robie Macauley, who is the editor of the *Kenyon Review,* we Americans were guests, and our participation in the conference was appropriately low-keyed. The British had a somewhat different status, difficult to explain but supported by the fact that they were there on business. They were scouting the conference for publishable manuscripts, and they were prepared to announce that a group of publishers—British and American— would sponsor a competition for the best novel by a black African on an African theme.

Knowledge of this, however, was a well-kept secret. It was to be the *pièce de résistance* of the cultural feast, to come as a surprise in next to the last plenary session. Having been let in on it in strict confidence, I had three or four days in tingling expectation of a joyous reaction, almost as if the competition was a project devised of my own thoughtful generosity. Many of the sessions had been taken up with questions—more complex and more passionately discussed than I make them seem now—of the African writer's audience, which is limited, and the cold indifference of the non-African world to Africa's literary aspirations. The announcement, I thought happily, would be the satisfaction of a real complaint. I rather expected a spontaneous cheer.

But I was mistaken in supposing that the silence that followed was the speechlessness of ecstasy. The dark, sensitive, intelligent faces, over which I had watched animation play for nearly a week, were immobile and impassive. The silence was a challenge to a code I had learned so thoroughly that I had ceased to think of it. I did not know the depth and substance of my African friends' pride. I had been taught that at the very least one should look thankful for even gestures of small favors from an all too casual and perfunctory white world. I looked toward Langston Hughes, but he was far down the table, and opposite me Robie Macauley's head was lowered, and I could not see his face. Plainly, though, the publishers were puzzled, and I guessed hurt, by this indifference to their charitable intentions.

It was not quite indifference. Someone asked a question: When did the competition open? Close? There were other questions—neutral, routine products of politeness. Gradually, however, I could sense a subterranean flow of thought and feeling I could not guess. Then:

"Who will judge this competition?" The answer was that since they, the publishers, were primarily interested in a non-African audience, the judges would be non-African. Suddenly all the writers were talking at once. I will not try to relate all that was said, for, indeed, I cannot; but the gist was this:

It is all very well for European publishers to establish a rich prize for us Africans to compete for—and we thank them—but what are these publishers' expectations? Essentially non-African. Perhaps they do not understand the insidiousness of this. Our standards, reflecting our own values and ideals, are different from theirs, and until they accept our standards we can have no pride in our accomplishments as Africans and no hope that the dignity of black men is recognized. Although colonial despotism has forced us to use their language, our standards of expressiveness are different from theirs. Our imaginations work differently from theirs, and are not inspired by the same realities. They make certain assumptions about experience that we do not make, nor ever will make. They would have us disregard the new political sanctions that have come with independence and that encourage black artists and writers to be creative according to the standards and tastes of our own people. Will competing for this prize assure our cultural rebirth? Indeed, will it not have the opposite effect? And if this is not a hazard, who are the Europeans to judge us by our own standards and expectations? If it is their mind to favor us, then let it be on our own terms. Let them know that African nationalism, the African personality and *négritude* are adequate to inspire black writers and artists with themes and to creative works justified by the authority of a black audience. Let us define our own genius!

Stated with a blunt eloquence of passion that I have completely failed to convey, this was the argument. This was Pan-Africa both in spirit and in word. There was no discourtesy in it—no fleer of sarcasm, no intentional, sharp anger of reproof. It was simply triumphant, and it moved its dark-skinned audience to triumphant cries of "Hear! Hear!" and to surges of spontaneous applause that were not meant to be a reproach to an American Negro guest's pallid conception of his Negro-ness. I felt small, gutted, wretched. I was locked out of the brotherhood of blacks by the terms used to define the black brotherhood. Confronted by this palpable African presence, I was neither American nor black: I was no one. America had not made me real in the sense that Africa had made real the men my elbows touched on either side. They were substance. I was shadow. The African Personality and *négritude* were no longer a myth compounded by a mystique.

Again my eyes stole toward Langston Hughes, but I still could not see his face. Across from me Robie Macauley looked withdrawn and remote.

This excerpt is from the *American Scholar,* Spring 1963.

CRITICISM

Redding wrote a weekly "Book Review" column for the Baltimore-based *Afro-American* newspapers from 1946 to 1966. During those twenty years, he produced nearly 1,000 reviews, many of which were of first books by then unknown authors whose talent he immediately recognized. Among them were James Baldwin, Gwendolyn Brooks, Ralph Ellison, Ernest J. Gaines, Ann Petry, Paule Marshall, and John O. Killens.

At a time when "Negro" critics were invited by the white American media only to review works by or about persons of African descent, Redding integrated his book review column. He included novelists such as John Dos Passos, William Faulkner, Ernest Hemingway, along with black writers. He likewise examined important works by eminent white historians such as Herbert Aptheker, Eleanor Flexner, and C. Vann Woodward, as well as pioneering histories by notable black scholars, such as Carter G. Woodson, John Hope Franklin, Rayford Logan, and Benjamin Quarles. He covered titles on the arts, humanities, and social sciences, including civil rights and race relations. Due to space constraints, only his reviews on literary topics from the *Afro-American* are represented here, although his byline as book critic often appeared in the *New York Times*, *New York Herald Tribune*, and *Saturday Review*.

Together with his book reviews, Part VII comprises a cross-section of Redding's essays and speeches written for various sources over a period of three decades.

BOOK REVIEWS, ESSAYS, LECTURES: A MISCELLANY

The Negro Author: His Publisher, His Public and His Purse

The careful checking of a bibliography of Negro literature reveals four general facts, each of which seems significant.

Prior to 1865, of every ten books known to be of Negro authorship, only three carry the imprints of commercial houses. The other seven of every ten were printed privately (and generally at the expense of some anti-slavery group) and offered for sale at anti-slavery meetings or other gatherings of folk who might be interested.

Between 1865 and 1905 several works, such as those by Douglass, Chesnutt, and Dunbar, were issued by regular commercial publishers, but in this same period, of some sixty titles examined, forty-six, including the first two of Dunbar's, were printed at the author's expense.

Between 1905 and the First World War, the commercial publication of books by Negroes was practically monopolized by houses with a pro-Negro tradition to maintain—mostly Boston companies such as Small, Maynard and Houghton Mifflin, and H.B. Turner. In this same period, however, Negroes had an increasingly difficult time bringing their work to the attention of the public, and we find them resorting to dummy publishers bearing such names as Nixon-Jones, St. Louis; Trachlenburg Co., N.Y.; The Metaphysical Publishing Co., N.Y.; The American Negro Academy, Washington, and dozens of others, some of which, in fact, did not exist.

Since the First World War many of the books by Negroes have been issued through old-line houses in Boston, New York, and Philadelphia, but most have been issued by houses specializing in vanity publications; and books by Negroes published since the World War come to less than one-half the total of Negro books published during the period from 1890 to 1915.

Do these facts speak for themselves? Perhaps not. But if I may be permitted to speak for them, they seem to say first that until comparatively recently Negroes have had few relationships with publishers. In the days down to 1918 or thereabouts, publishers simply had nothing to do with works by Negroes unless they were specially championed by such patrons as William Dean Howells, who championed the work of Paul Dunbar; Walter Hines Page, who championed the work of Chestnutt; and Richard Watson Gilder and Brander Matthews, who championed the work of James Weldon Johnson.

An examination of the early works of these three men reveals another curious fact: in the days when they had champions, the work of none of them had any quality that stamped it as the work of a Negro. Indeed, both Page and Gilder were reluctant to reveal that their literary finds were Negroes. Page rejected Chesnutt's novel, *The House Behind the Cedars*, on the grounds that such a work, bearing the unmistakable stamp of Negro authorship, simply would not go. He accepted the book called *The Conjure Woman*, which had no better writing than the other, but which might just as well have been written by a white author.

Illuminating this whole topic is something Chesnutt has to say in "Breaking Into Print," a compendium of the publishing experiences of many American writers. Following the rejection of *The House Behind the Cedars*, Page suggested that "Perhaps a collection of the conjure stories [which had been appearing in the *Atlantic Monthly* without any indication that the author was Negro] might be undertaken by the firm with a better prospect of success. I was in the hands of my friends," Chesnutt goes on, "and I submitted the collection. After some omissions and additions, all at the advice of Mr. Page, the book was accepted and announced"—And more pertinently still, he goes on to say that "at that time a literary work by an American of acknowledged color was a doubtful experiment, both for the writer and the publisher, enirely apart from its intrinsic merit. Indeed, my race was never mentioned by the publishers in announcing or advertising the book"—And this because Mr. Page considered that it would be harmful to the book's success.

In these words, I think, is the heart of a matter many of us are so altruistic as to overlook. Publishers earn their living by publishing and selling books. They usually have two criteria: Will a book sell? If it will not sell, will it add to our publishing prestige to issue it? So far, relatively few books by Negroes have met either of these tests. Really good publishing houses do not discriminate against talent because it happens to be Negro talent. Some of them (and I merely throw this in), some of them, like Knopf, have gone out of their way to foster it; and even now Doubleday, Doran is sponsoring a contest for the best book written by a Negro.

But what I'm trying to get at is this: The publisher is the public's representative. He is this, if he is to survive at all commercially, whether he likes it or not. Here and there and now and then, some publisher may be independent enough or careless enough of the public's taste to defy it, or to make a serious effort to change it. But, by and large, published books are commercial ventures, and they must be salable. It is the publisher who must gauge the reading taste of the public and respond most sensitively to it; and it is through him that the reading public exerts a powerful influence on the methods and materials of writing. (I speak here only of popular literature, and not of the great and important technical and special works, or even of the classics.) Through the exertion of this control, whether conscious or unconscious, the reading public has had a tremendous effect upon books by and about Negroes.

This leads naturally to inquiries regarding the reading public. What is its attitude? What are the concepts it holds about Negroes? Where have these concepts come from? And how have they affected books by and about Negroes?

In the first place, grounded in the historical fact of slavery is the notion of Negro inferiority. This notion is basic. Its validity need not concern us.

Even for a great many of the highly intelligent who have been convinced to the contrary by the arguments of science, there is an emotional strength in this notion. At first, in the full sweep of the romantic tide of the late 18th century, there were a great many people in the Colonies, and later in the early States, who damned the idea of racial superiority. The idea tended to give moral validity to slavery, and there were many people opposed to slavery. Curiously enough, it was the very strength of the notion that worked to the personal advantage of early Negro writers like Phillis Wheatley and Jupiter Hammon, for these could be held up as proof positive that the Negro was not inferior. In only one or two cases did the personal advantage thus gained work to the ultimate advantage of the Negro race, for we have examples of the shoddiest doggerel and the most clumsy prose offered as proof of the race's intelligence. The equalitarians' zeal often outran their discrimination. But in any case, Jupiter Hammon was as good a poet as the authors of the "Bay Psalm Booke" and Phillis Wheatley was a better poet than Anne Bradstreet.

Nothing that could be called a general public ever saw the output of the earliest American Negro writers; and the public, in spite of them, went on believing that racial inferiority was proved by the fact of slavery. When, later, the artistically worthwhile work of George Horton, Wm. Wells Brown, and Frederick Douglass came along, it was not taken as proof that the Negro had a mind and a spirit, but rather as exceptions that proved the rule. These men, the general opinion ran, were some sort of freaks, a superior type of an inferior breed—not unlike monkeys who learn to eat with knives and forks at table—and whatever interest attached to them was derived from this fact.

Moreover the pro-slavery South evolved an ideology to buttress its professions. When slavery was being attacked, "Southern authors gave forth with the contented slave; when cruelties were mentioned, they gave forth with the amusing, happy Negro"; when equality was talked about, they found the picture of the Negro as brute. The Negro was insensitive, he had no soul. He was quaint and with a peculiar endowment. He was cursed of God. It was all comfortably metaphysical thinking, but it was measured in such practical terms as to lead to the legal definition of a Negro as five-eighths of a human being, and it was sicklied o'er with the humanitarianism that led J.P. Kennedy and others like him to justify slavery because the Negro was "essentially parasitical, dependent upon guidance for his most indispensable necessaries, without foresight or thrift of any kind. No tribe of people has been better supplied with mild and beneficent guardianship better adapted to the actual state of their intellectual feebleness."

The general tradition was easily established with two extremes, but no middle-ground whatever. And so, as Sterling Brown points out, we have this on the one hand: "The old plantation; a great mansion; exquisitely-gowned ladies and courtly gentlemen moving with easy grace upon the broad veranda behind stalwart columns; surrounding the yard an almost illimitable stretch of white cotton, darkies singingly at work in the fields, Negro quarters off on one side, around which little pickaninnies tumbled in gay frolic"; and this on the other: "A brutish race, devoid of both sense and sensibilities, incestuous except under the eye of a strict master, incorrigible in his physical lusts, moaning curses and blasphemies and instantly ready to kill the white man the moment vigilance is relaxed."

Following the Civil War these concepts of the Negro became graphic and solid. I need not review all the names that helped in this process of fixation, but the belated answers to *Uncle Tom's Cabin* ranged from Caroline Rush's *North and South, or Slavry and Its Contrasts*, to Mrs. Henry School-craft's *The Black Gauntlet*, with many men getting in their words edgewise. The image of the Negro as chicken-thief, melon-stealer, incorrigible liar; befouler of his own nest; ravisher of women; irresponsible, lazy, errant, and yet withal laughable grew. It grew until it came about that only within the pattern of this concept was the Negro acceptable and credible to a large portion of the white reading public. These were the extremes, and these extremes remained valid until the basic notion of racial inferiority found more congenial expression in the pseudo folk-tale of local color as practiced by Mary Murfree, Joel Harris, and Sherwood Bonner.

These at least were nearer truth in manner and material than the earlier work had been, and they prepared the way for George Cable and Mark Twain, both of whom wrote of the South and of the Negro with a startling approximation of the truth and with a more startling sympathy.

But even this closer truth was not wholly acceptable to Negro writers. But look at the fix they were in! What they themselves were and what their characters should be was already determined for them. They were not free. They had to cling to the established concept if they wanted to save their professional skins. Literature must be based upon more or less well-established conventions, upon ideas that have some roots in the general consciousness, upon ideas that are at least somewhat familiar to the public mind. White America had—and still has—some pretty fixed opinions as to what the Negro was, and consequently some firm ideas as to what should be written about him. What those opinions were we have already seen. Publishers wanted characters and situations in prose and images and ideas in poetry that did no violence to those opinions. Publishers were not concerned with a Negro public, for there was none; and so as not to do violence to the concept, Dunbar, writing his autobiography, had to portray himself as a white youth because what had happened to him could not, in the limits of the pattern and the view of the general public—what had happened to him could not have happened to a Negro.

But within a few years of Dunbar's death in 1906, a wholly new problem was beginning to face the Negro author. That problem was the one of writing for two audiences.

The late James Weldon Johnson has called this the Negro author's dilemma. Even in Dunbar's day Negroes were beginning to read books about themselves. Having intelligence enough for this intellectual pastime, and being, by the very nature of things, sensitive, they could not find themselves mirrored in the books they read—that is, in the books that were published. The exaggerations which they did see offended them. They resented dialect, which, being lettered, they did not speak; they resented the picture of the Negro as a funny man and brute; they resented the notion of Negro inferiority. The burden of this resentment—since they could not get at the white men and women who were the principal offenders—fell upon the writers of their own race. Dunbar knew some of this because of his dialect. Langston Hughes even now will not read certain of his folk and racial-rhythm pieces to Negro audiences; and after the publication of Richard Wright's *Native Son*, the Negro press and platform were stormy with denunciations of the author as a traducer of his race.

The problem posed the Negro author writing for two audiences is almost insurmountable. The barriers to honest work in writing for either the one or the other are high enough. Influencing the author who writes for a Negro audience (as many of them do in newspapers and magazines) is the clamor to glorify the race, to increase the race's pride in itself, to speak only honor of it. And the exertion of this influence within certain limits, I should say, is legitimate.

Writing recently in the *Saturday Review of Literature*, Professor Harry A. Overstreet said: "The Negro writer of fiction is inevitably a spokesman for his people. He is not free to write what he pleases. Such freedom is reserved for the Whites. It is of little moment if a white novelist depicts white characters who are wholly despicable. Every white reader knows that such characters are in a minority and that the white race as a whole will go on quite safely in spite of them. Not so if the Negro writer depicts Negroes who are despicable. The white reader will be likely to shake his head and say, 'nigger blood. Bad business.' The Negro writer, therefore, has a double obligation: to truth, and to the effect upon his readers of the particular truth he selects. He dare not take the position that since all that is human is his novelist's province, he has a perfect right to describe scoundrel

Negroes if he so prefers. He does so at peril to his people. For every scoundrel Negro he describes gets magnified out of all proportion into a person supposedly typical of all Negroes."

On the other hand, as Professor Overstreet did not point out, the Negro author who writes primarily for a white audience is up against many long-standing artistic conceptions about the Negro; against numerous conventions and traditions which are more or less binding; against a whole set of stereotypes which are not easily destroyed.

It is a terrifying, and, I suspect in too many cases, an atrophying dilemma. Occasionally a Negro author extricates himself by saying, in effect, the devil with a white audience, but he runs a great risk of publishing the book himself and peddling it from door to door. Others have extricated themselves by saying the devil with a Negro audience, and have thereby given themselves the freedom—a rather specious and spurious kind of freedom, I should say—to produce the empty, banal, psuedo-exotic tripe that is sometimes mistaken as the substance of Negro life in America. A lot of these fellows flourished in the 1920s, but, thank heaven, they have largely passed. Some of them, like Wallace Thurman and Claude McKay (when he wrote *Banana Bottom*) made what seemed fabulous sums to some of their honest fellow craftsmen.

But there is a third means of escape from the dilemma, and here at the close I should like to suggest it, for the Negro writer of integrity, it seems to me, must come to this or be lost. He must make a common audience out of white and black America. He must believe that this can be done. He must write American books for American audiences. Richard Wright is already doing this. He did it in *Native Son*, where his purpose was to make of Bigger Thomas "a symbolic figure of American life, a figure who would hold within him the prophecy of the American future."

Standing on his racial foundation, the Negro author of skill and depth, working in the material he knows best, "can make his appeal to the whole American audience." He must do this if he is to remain true to his best creative instincts; he must do this if he is to survive as an artist. And America, both the white and black portions of it, must grant him the freedom for it. It is only in freedom that the creative man can grow. It is only when this freedom has long been established that he begins to produce his best work.

This article is from *Publishers Weekly*, Mar. 24, 1945.

Homage to Countee Cullen

Countee Cullen is dead.

Of that small, indomitable band of highly talented young men and women who did so much to give authenticity to the voice of colored America in the Twenties, he is the second to go.

Rudolph Fisher was the first.* Fisher's eye saw all the pathos behind the high facades of Striver's Row. † His ear heard all the troubled undertones beneath the boisterous bluff of Lenox Avenue. His pen recorded what he saw and heard in numerous lusty tales and stories. And now, cut off like him before his time, Cullen.

His was a delicate, more bitter-sweet fragile talent than Fisher's. It was almost dainty in its expression. He had no truck with the cult of primitivism.

Back in the Twenties, some white observers were mistaking the sophisticated rhythms of Langston Hughes, the clean naturalness of Florence Mills, and the studied abandon of the steps of the Charleston for pure Africa.

They were saying that primitivism was the essential attribute of colored writers and artists. It was not that there was anything wrong in primitivism. What was wrong—and what all these new young men and women understood—was the assumption of the white people that the colored man was not quite civilized.

What white people assumed did not bother some of them. They went on to make the assumption look silly against the evidence of highly finished work—Hughes and Bontemps and Fisher and Brown in writing, Aaron Douglas and Hale Woodruff in painting, and Roland Hayes on the concert stage.

Cullen made it look silly too, but the assumption bothered him. Of all the things that cut and bruised him most, it was probably this that left the deepest wound. And it was from that wound that some of his finest lyrics came.

> Lord, being dark, forewilled to that despair/
> My color shrouds me. . . .‡

Once in 1931, when he visited my room at Brown University and autographed two of his books for me, he started idly turning the pages of *The Black Christ*, and then suddenly he was reading aloud:

> . . . God knows I would be kind, let live, speak
>   fair,
>   Requite an honest debt with more than just,
> And love for Christ's dear sake these shapes
>   that wear
> A pride that had its genesis in dust,—
> The meek are promised much in a book I
>   know
> But one grows weary turning cheek to blow.§

I feel certain that at the end he felt pretty much as he had felt earlier.

> . . . I hide no hate, I am not even wroth
> Who found earth's breath so keen and cold;
> I have wrapped my dreams in a silken cloth,
> And laid them away in a box of gold.#

This selection is from the *Afro-American*, Jan. 19, 1946. The title is supplied by the editor.

Editor's Notes: *Rudolph Fisher was actually the *second* of the Harlem Renaissance authors of the Twenties to die; his death by cancer on December 22, 1934, followed by four days of the death of novelist Wallace Thurman.   †An exclusive row of Harlem brownstone houses designed by architect Stanford White in the late nineteenth century; located on West 138th-139th Streets and originally built for white owners, the residences were called "Striver's Row" when purchased by affluent Afro-Americans during the Twenties.   ‡From poem, "The Shroud of Color," by Countee Cullen.   §Excerpt of "Mood" from *The Black Christ* by Countee Cullen.   #Excerpt of "For a Poet" from *On These I Stand* by Countee Cullen.

Black Art, White Audience

It is strange, when you stop to consider it, how much more interested white people are in the literature and art of colored people than we are ourselves. It is as if colored people were saying, "Oh, well—so what?," in regards to those fields of creative endeavor to which a few have contributed so much.

Only in music have colored people themselves shown any abiding interest, and even in this particular only after its beauty and importance was pointed out to them by others. Moreover, there still operates, especially among the last dozen college generations, a certain resistance to the appeal of the Spirituals.

It is uncommon to see in Marian Anderson's (or Dorothy Maynor's, or Todd Duncan's) Northern concert audiences more than a sprinkling of colored people.

I can not document this city by city, but a few years ago, when a collection of Negro art was sent on exhibition through the East and Midwest, in one city, where it hung for a week, exactly forty-three colored people (in a population of roughly 12,000) saw it as compared to 18,000 whites.

The names of Barthe, Savage, Lawrence, Woodruff, Douglas and even Tanner are much less known among their own people than among whites.

The work of Chesnutt, the non-dialect pieces of Dunbar, the poetry of Anne Spencer, Myron O'Higgins, Robert Hayden, Gwendolyn Brooks and M. Carl Holman, winning praises and prizes from whites, is scarcely known to colored people at all.

For the most part, colored Americans just do not buy books, or visit art exhibits, or go to concerts.

And this is bad for them and bad for their artists. Art is a solidifying, unifying force. It is the one level upon which, in America, peoples can meet on a plane of absolute equality.

Or, to change the figure a little, it is the one avenue down which peoples can march abreast to the fulfillment of a perhaps diverse but commonly embraced cultural destiny.

When colored people fail to take this avenue, they are failing to do the one thing which indisputably leads somewhere.

This failure effects the artists in ways that are incalculably bad and real as death. What encouragement is there to the artist who, springing from a people and that people's compacted experiences, can find no following among them?

What sense, the artist asks himself, in drawing upon the ethnic and cultural life for the materials of expression when the very people my art expresses deny or ignore me?

Is it any wonder that colored writers and artists are turning more and more toward sources of inspiration outside the race?

Should it surprise anyone that Barthe has not done a colored figure in a long, long time?

That Yerby, Motley and Ann Petry concentrate on white characters?

That Maynor and Anderson put more and more German lieder and French airs in their programs?

That the poets Hayden and Holman and O'Higgins turn first to white magazines as publishing media?

All this was brought forcibly to mind not long ago when I went down to Yale for the formal opening of the James Weldon Johnson Collection of Negro Art and Letters.

Though just as a matter of courteous recognition, invitations were sent out to some, the exercises were announced open to the public.

Muriel Rahn sang beautifully, and Fisk President Charles S. Johnson spoke intelligently, and President Seymour of Yale commented warmly on the importance of the occasion. But there were only a handful of colored people to several hundred whites.

This selection is from *Afro Magazine*, Feb. 25, 1950. The title is supplied by the editor.

Ralph Ellison's *Invisible Man:* Eleven Years Afterward

When a contemporary and still living writer's reputation is sustained over a period of a dozen years on the strength of a single book, and particularly if it is also an only book, then some extraordinary force of genius, or some phenomenal concatenation of circumstances is at work.

If it happens, further, that the book which sustains the reputation is a work of fiction, the matter becomes awesome indeed, and in almost the same class of wonders as Haley's comet.

Average works of fiction—and only one such work in several thousand transcend the average—languish in the space of a few months, and die an almost certain death within a year, irrespective, generally, of what sales records they have broken.

And if the authors of these works died themselves forthwith, only their immediate families would remember their names for longer than a year.

Without looking it up (as I just did), who can name the author of *Raintree County*, which in 1950 had the greatest sale since *Gone With the Wind?*

Or who can repeat the title of the book, or the name of the author who won the National Book Award for fiction in 1956?

Yet here is *Invisible Man*, which as of this moment is still an only novel, and it was published eleven years ago.

If its author has published any book of any kind since, the fact of it is the best kept secret since the Manhattan Project.

Yet lights still go on and bells clang and whistles toot when that author's name is mentioned.

Ralph Ellison owns one of the brightest reputations in the world of modern writing. It has not dimmed since he won the National Book Award in 1952.

But we cannot account for this uncommon circumstance by saying, as has been said above, that some strange power of genius or some fortuitous linkage of events has brought it about.

It was not either one thing or the other: it was both.

Now it must not be supposed that I am repudiating some of the things I said in my first review of *Invisible Man* a decade ago.

I still think that the book contains a good deal of inarticulate chatter, and that the style is often a mixture of styles, and that the method sometimes allowed to dictate the substance.

Nevertheless *Invisible Man* is a resounding accomplishment, especially in terms of dramatic action, character and theme.

The drama builds, the characters live, and the theme drives inexorably home.

One can pick the spots and the people: the college and Dr. Bledsoe; Jim Trueblood and the one room cabin; the Golden Day and Halley; Ras the Exhorter and the streets of Harlem; Sybil and the Chthonian; Brother Clifton.

After ten years I remember most of it with great clarity; for the genius of *Invisible Man* is that it is more vivid than life.

And as for the phenomenal concatenation of circumstances, they are an epic of colored life which imitates in striking ways the fictional epic that is *Invisible Man*.

Or perhaps there are those who, beguiled by the living immediacy of both, would forget the fiction came before the fact, and put it the other way around.

Either way, by a process of almost mystical union of fiction with fact, Ralph Ellison's reputation is kept wonderfully alive.

This review is from *Afro Magazine*, Jan. 28, 1964.

Review of *Notes of a Native Son*
by James Baldwin

A few years ago James Baldwin gave us *Go Tell It on the Mountain*. It was a good first novel—autobiographical, as most good first novels are, and with an integrity and truth in it that can come only from the courage of youth or the discouragement of unfulfilled age. (Mr. Baldwin is young.) The style, too, was minted—tensive, perhaps, but firm and controlled and clean. Here was a new, good talent, one said. Here was heart. Here was instinctive knowledge of human nature. Here was a nice discernment of truth, and splendid honesty.

Now James Baldwin gives us his second book, *Notes of a Native Son*. If there is a "sophomore jinx," it rides this book—hard. The courage has become a kind of boasting. The knowledge of human nature has become an absorption with—but not in—Freudian psychology. The "splendid honesty" is something much less—something traumatic, ill, diseased.

The style is mere pyrotechnics, making a momentary brilliant display, but kindling no fires of thought or admiration. False! false! and unfelt, unfelt! One gets an unhappy sense that James Baldwin has been playing around too much and too long with Montmartre, the Left Bank crowd, and all the intellectual and spiritual eunuchs that spawn in and—when they can (and sometimes they do)—spoil that rich soil.

I am being consciously harsh. I believe that James Baldwin has a fine talent. I think I am appreciative of talent, and it sickens me to see talent sicken. It hurts to face the possibility that one is mistaken, and that Baldwin is a dilettante manipulating knowledge that is not truly his; a braggart ass who plays with the lightning that because it does not strike twice, can be caught only once and must then be cherished forever, though it burns, though it blinds.

It is the lightning of honesty, of integrity, of truth—of personal honesty, integrity, and truth which run out on the writer who does not truly love them. There is no evidence in *Notes of a Native Son* that Baldwin loves them.

Can Baldwin believe that the American Negro is unqualified (not merely disqualified!) in the very nature of him and in experience to find his identity in America? Can Baldwin really believe that all of life is a search for identity and that only American Negroes search in vain?

Such notions are a kind of inversion of existentialism. Of course each man exists as an individual in—if you will—a purposeless world; but he does not exist without identity!

But, as I've said, Baldwin has been listening too hard on the Left Bank. He has been reading too much in the three *sou* pamphlets written by the anemic 10th echelon disciples of Jean-Paul Sartre and Sigmund Freud.

The style of *Notes of a Native Son* is also false. It is false not only because it is forced, but because it is used to display a knowledge and a reaction to experience that are not really Baldwin's.

It is false because it attempts an appeal to the cognitive—to which it is unsuited—at the same time that it pretends to appeal to the connotative and affective.

But it is very pretty. That's the thing, really, about *Notes of a Native Son:* it is pretty. Even when one finds a pretty in the street, one cannot completely turn his back on it until the pretty proves a whore. *Notes of a Native Son* proves.

This review is from *Afro Magazine*, Mar. 17, 1956.

Review of *White Man, Listen!*
by Richard Wright

White Man, Listen! is anything but as hysterical as the title makes it sound. Indeed, the book is a sober and thoughtful analysis of the meaning of today.

There is, of course, passion in it, though Wright disclaims passion as inappropriate to his subject and as out of character for him.

"I'm a rootless man," he avers, . . . I do not hanker after, and seem not to need, as many emotional attachments . . . as most people."

But this is a self-deception. He has very strong emotional attachments. He emotionalizes ideas. He did in *The Color Curtain;* he did in *Black Power.* He does in *White Man, Listen!* which, though it flashes with intellectual brilliance, is shot through with passionate polemic.

The emotion is warranted. The concept with which Wright principally deals—the unity of man—is itself emotional rather than intellectual.

As an intellectual concept, thanks to science, all but the least intelligent accept it: as a social notion, even many of the most intelligent reject it.

A trite question represents this rejection in the crudest, simplest terms. "Would you want your daughter to marry. . . . ?"

The unity—the oneness—of man as a social concept is fraught with emotion.

It is this emotion that *White Man, Listen!* aims at dissipating. The means Wright employs is as direct as it can be. He slices off hunks of emotion and examines them in the strong light of social history.

He examines particularly the consequences of the rejection of the unity of man as a social idea.

He shows what this rejection has done to the Western World—the rejectors, and to the colored world—the rejected.

It has made psychological cripples of both worlds.

"Generations of emotionally impoverished colonial European whites wallowed in quick gratification of greed, reveled in the cheap superiority of racial domination. . . ."; became, in short, anti-human.

And as for the colored world—"There lies exposed to view a procession of shattered cultures, disintegrated societies, and a writhing sweep of more aggressive irrational (ity) . . . than the world has known for centuries."

In both worlds the social failure of the concept has created anti-human attitudes and practices which are "not worthy of man as we dream of him and want him to be."

Between the psychological premise and the sociological conclusion of *White Man, Listen!* there are brilliant analyses of historical and political facts that go back to the 16th Century—the beginnings of European domination of the colored world, the influence of Christianity and of the Age of Enlightenment, the impact of industrialization, and the meaning of democracy and communism—and come forward to the recent establishment of the African state of Ghana.

These are all considered within the established frame of reference, the unity of man.

The last two of the four essays—"The Literature of the Negro in the United States" and "The Miracle of Nationalism in the African Gold Coast"—serve as graphic illustrations of Wright's theme, which is, broadly speaking, that the unity of man must be achieved; that the two worlds must become one world, else there will be no world at all.

Wright has never written either more poignantly or more brilliantly, but he has not written to catch only the ear of the white man: he wants the colored man to listen too.

This review is from *Afro Magazine*, Oct. 26, 1957.

Richard Wright: An Evaluation

When Richard Wright died in Paris recently his reputation stood very high with Europeans, and especially with the French, among whom he had lived for a decade. Translated into the major European languages, three of his first four books had assured him large audiences for his lectures in Italy, Holland, Germany, the Scandinavian countries and, of course, in France. Europeans ranked him with the great moderns of fiction, but they—and again especially the French—admired him for qualities quite different from those for which they admired some other modern novelists. He was, however, a writer of great raw power with a genius for direct communication. It was this power and this genius, sometimes crude and never cunning, that the Europeans admired.

Because of these same qualities he was much less admired in his native land, where he was too frequently charged with sensationalism, which in America, and only in America, is almost exclusively associated with the emotionally cheap, the tawdry, and the pornographic. But Wright's work was none of these, and the charge was made as an easement to the conscience; for that was his power here at home—to smite the conscience, and to smite the conscience of black as well as white. For Negroes made the charge of sensationalism too, and for the same reason as the whites. They read Wright's imaginative works and quaked, "Is this us?" As Wright said, Negroes "possessed deep-seated resistances against the Negro problem being presented, even verbally, in all its hideous fullness, in all the totality of its meaning." They did not want to believe what other Negro writers had been telling them in academic terms, or by implication, and also sometimes by imaginative inversion (Chesnutt was the man for that!) for years. They did not want to believe that they were as helpless, as outraged, as despairing, as violent and as hate-ridden as Wright said. But they were. They did not want to believe that the America that they loved had bred these things into the fibers of their lives, their being. But it had. "Is this us? And is this our America?" It was.

Deliverance and redemption lay in revolution. So Dick Wright was a Communist. And this, too, was charged against him. He proved the charge at about the time of *Native Son:* he was, he said, a "card-bearing Communist." He gave his reasons. American democracy isolated him because he was a Negro: communism, the Party, offered "the first sustained relationships of my life." He was amazed and immensely gratified to learn "that there did exist in this world an organized search for the truth of the lives of the oppressed and the isolated." In communism's revolutionary expression he thought Negro experience could find "a home, a functioning value and a role." He joined the search; he was a member of the revolution. "If you possess enough courage to speak out what you are, you will find that you are not alone." He had enough courage, and he spoke out. It was the only literary creed—and it was certainly no aesthetic theory—he ever went by; and, like his mother's face when she stared at a particularly lurid communist cartoon, America's face reflected what it saw through the windows of Wright's soul—disgust and anger, shame and fear. This was Dick Wright's intention, if anything so compulsively created of experience, the organic functioning of the mind and the unwilled beat of the heart can be said to be intentional. Anger, fear and shame combined with innate honesty to form the main elements of Wright's literary power.

He struck with that power in the books for which he will be remembered, *Uncle Tom's Children, Native Son* and *Black Boy.* The first is a collection of four novellas, and three of them are about lynching, and one, "Fire and Cloud," is about revolution and deliverance, and it ends, "Freedom belongs to the strong!" Each is a violent and brutal and brutally communicated comment, not on life, but on a way of having to live and on the ways of being forced to live in ignorance, fear and shame. In his first book, Wright is already preoccupied with "the disinherited, the dispossessed," and he has already created the prototype of all his heroes. Like Big Boy in the lead story, Wright's heroes were ever to be angry, bitter, vengeful, violently hurling themselves against the walls that barred them from a life that they knew vaguely was a better life than theirs belonging to people no better than themselves. They know this from the movies they had seen, the picture magazines they had read, and from the screaming headlines in the daily press. White people were no better, but they were different—so different as to seem to Wright's heroes not people at all, but "a sort of great natural force, like a stormy sky looming overhead, or like a deep swirling river stretching suddenly at one's feet in the dark" threatening a death to which one could react "only in fear and shame."

These were Richard Wright's own emotions. He did not have to create them for his fictional purposes. They were the staple food of his childhood, youth and manhood, until he moved abroad. He tells us in *Black Boy,* his autobiography, that he learned at an early age "the reality—a Negro's reality—of the white world. . . . I was tense each moment . . . and I did not suspect that *the* tension I had begun to feel would lift itself into the passion of my life. . . . I was always to be conscious of it, brood over it, carry it in my heart, live with it, sleep with it, fight with it." In a way more direct than with most important modern authors, Wright's heroes were in naked honesty himself, and not creations that served merely to express his complicated personality. This is not to say that their adventures, and their characterizing quirks and habits, and their whims of thought, or the violence of their behavior were his. Not by any means. These were the fancied and observed externalizations of what such hero-personalities would do and say and outwardly be; personalities which, unlike Wright's, had no direction from a moral intelligence, an active social sense, or ethical thought. The tragedy of Wright's heroes is that they lack this direction, and that the American society denies them the opportunity to acquire it. This is the substance of the Communist lawyer's defense of Bigger Thomas in the novel *Native Son;* and this is the theme of Wright's most powerful work.

The externalizations, then, are the measure of Wright's imagination, but the structure of his heroes' personalities, the patterns of their emotions, and the types of their dreams are the measure of Wright's honesty and of his self-knowledge as a Negro. It is inconceivable that Wright's essay, "How Bigger Was Born," is true in fact. It is true only—and the "only" implies no derogation—in spirit. Though the essay declares it, it is hardly to be taken literally or credited that Wright conceived of Bigger Thomas as sometimes Negro and sometimes white. This is an elastic rationalization to cover what Wright himself then embraced as a saving *modus vivendi:* the brotherhood of the oppressed, the people's movement, the united front of the Communist line. Bigger Thomas was Negro all the time. And so, of course, was Richard Wright. He made this clear, after he left the Party, in what is probably his most brilliant essay, where he speaks of the "inevitable race consciousness which three hundred years of Jim Crow living has burned into the Negro's heart."

But this neglected essay—the introduction to a book entitled *Black Metropolis*[1] is of far greater importance than this one citation indicates, for it reveals all the major influences on Wright's thinking, though certainly not on his techniques. These influences in addition to William James certainly included the men who taught the authors of the book which the essay introduces—W. Lloyd Warner and Allison Davis—both of whom stand among the great social scientists of the present day. Though it was not meant to be, the essay is an annotation to Wright's entire development. It takes us to the fountainhead of his being both as man and writer, to the source of his thought and feeling, into the matrix of his creative conceptions. He read William James early, at fifteen or sixteen. He got to read him by a subterfuge which involved a denial of his *self,* and while this was certainly a part of the matter, the greater part was that experience had already taught him that "the lives of the dispossessed are not real to white people." More than once he had had the experience of being treated as if he did not exist as a sensate being. As a hotel bellboy in a Southern town, he had been summoned to rooms to find naked white women lolling about unmoved by any sense of shame at his presence, "for blacks were not considered human beings anyway. . . . I was a non-man, something that knew vaguely that it was human but felt that it was not. . . . I felt doubly cast out." Then he read James, and James was later confirmed by the professional social scientists named earlier. It is revealing to quote the passage that Wright quotes.

"No more fiendish punishment could be devised . . . than that one should be turned loose in society and remain absolutely unnoticed by all the members thereof. If no one turned around when we entered, answered when we spoke, or minded what we did, but if every person we met 'cut us dead,' and acted as if we were non-existent things, a kind of rage and impotent despair would ere long well up in us, from which the cruelest bodily tortures would be a relief; for these would make us feel that, however bad might be our plight, we had not sunk to such a depth as to be unworthy of attention at all."

This is the ground of all Wright's works, fiction and nonfiction. It is the thought, the theme, and the thematic design. The passage revealed, as it were, him to himself. It is scarcely to be doubted that from the moment he read it, groping through it toward the knowledge of its truth for him and listening to its mournful echoes in the still locked chambers of his soul, Wright became a man with a message and a mission. Long before he wrote *White Man, Listen!*, the message was addressed to white folks, and the mission was to somehow bring awareness to their world and thereby save it.

Both the message and the mission were particularized by Wright's conception of a world where men still "cling to the emotional basis of life, that the [old] feudal order gave them," and by his supraconsciousness of being Negro in that world. Translated into creative terms, this necessitated the rendering up of Negro life with greater circumstantiality than had ever before been attempted. Oh! what psychological details, what analysis of external influences, what precise attention to physical minutia. He was in the naturalistic tradition, but without the naturalistic writer's aesthetic controls. He put everything in for an audience which he hoped would be white, as principally it was. Only rarely did he write for Negroes, and only then when he was pressed, and then only on political subjects. He reasoned that Negroes knew the particulars of what it was like to have "uncertainty as a way of life" and "of living within the vivid, present moment and letting the meaning of that moment suffice as a rationale for life and death. But whites did not know, so he had to tell them—in the rage of Silas[2], in the weakness of Mann[3], in the despair of Bigger, and in the words of the white Communist lawyer at Bigger's trial:

" . . . I plead with you to see a mode of *life* in our midst, a mode of life stunted and distorted, but possessing its own laws and claims, an existence of men growing out of the soil prepared by the collective but blind will of a hundred million people. I beg you to recognize human life draped in a form and guise alien to ours, but springing from a soil plowed and sown by our own hands. I ask you to recognize the laws and process flowing from such a condition, understand them, seek to change them. If we do none of these, then we should not pretend horror or surprise when thwarted life expresses itself in fear and hate and crime.

"This is life, new and strange. . . . We have kept our eyes turned from it. This is life lived in cramped limits and expressing itself not in terms of our good and bad, but in terms of its own fulfillment. Men are men and life is life, and we must deal with them as they are; and if we want to change them, we must deal with them in the form in whch they exist and have their being. . . .

Listen, white folks!

Wright's books sold more than a million copies here at home, so there were those who listened, and many of them must have felt, as Dorothy Canfield Fisher felt, that what they heard was "honest, dreadful, heart-breaking." It changed little except among the literate. What Wright had seen as a possible agent of change—the American Communist Party—disappointed him. He held on for a while, and he was glad that he had written those stories in which he had "assigned a role of honor and glory" to the Party, but his commitment of faith was beginning to crumble. His rejection of the Party early in the war years was only a gesture, for the Party had already rejected him. After the war, when change still did not come, he rejected America. This, however, was more than a gesture: it was an action of the greatest consequences. Life in France, in Paris, where he went to live, in some ways completed him as a person. The freedom was good. The "strangeness" was good. The reputation his books had earned him with the French and Europeans generally was good to savor. He and his family could live where they wished and go where they wanted without the old uncertainties, the fears. It was all good. "I do not expect ever again to live in the States," he told me in the spring of '59.

But what was good for him as a social being was bad for his work. He had taken his Negroness with him, but he could not take with him the America that bred and fed his consciousness of Negroness. Perhaps he thought to nourish that consciousness by a kind of forced feeding. Naturally he read the American press. He made friends with French Africans—Negroes—and especially those who projected, edited and largely wrote the quarterly publication *Présence Africaine* and with them helped to found the Société Africaine de Culture, and was instrumental in establishing an American branch of that Society. He went to the Gold Coast (now Ghana) and wrote a book (*Black Power*) in which he said he felt an "odd kind of at-homeness" there. But if he did, it does not appear in the book. He went to Spain, and he read the Falangist catechism, and wrote another book, in which he declared that what he "felt most keenly in Spain was the needless, unnatural, and utterly barbarous nature of the psychological suffering. . . . For that exquisite suffering and emotional torture, I have a spontaneous and profound sympathy. I am an American Negro. . . ." But Spain fed his consciousness only the thinnest of gruels. In France, existentialism attracted him and, trying to make that philosophy pertinent to Negro life in America, he wrote a very poor "existentialist" novel, which has much more of Celine than Sartre in it.

When *The Long Dream* was published in 1958, what was happening to Richard Wright, what, indeed, had already happened, seemed obvious to some of his critics in the States. The Fishbelly of that book was Big Boy of "Big Boy Leaves Home," and was the preacher's son of "Fire and Cloud," and was Bigger Thomas of *Native Son,* except that now he was an anachronism. In going to live abroad, Dick Wright had cut the roots that once sustained him; the tight-wound emotional core had come unravelled; the creative center had dissolved; his memory of what Negro life in America was had lost its relevance to what Negro life in America is—or is becoming. This is not to say that the imagined events in *The Long Dream* have no relation to some aspect of the present reality of America. It is to say, though, that the people who move in and through these imagined events are so emotionally unrelated to the present reality as to seem lifeless, as stiff and dead as old tintypes, as false as roorbacks. And in some subconscious, unadmitted and inadmissable way, perhaps Dick Wright knew this. The writing is as direct but less honest. It insists too much. It is overdone. It sometimes flushes purple, especially toward the end, when Fishbelly, renouncing America, is airborne for France.

"He peered out of his window and saw vast, wheeling populations of ruled stars swarming in the convened congresses of the skies anchored amidst nations of space and he prayed wordlessly that a bright, bursting tyrant of living sun would soon lay down its golden laws to loosen the locked regions of his heart and cast the shadow of his dream athwart the stretches of time."

The Long Dream was the first volume of a projected trilogy that now never will be completed, although the second volume may be done, or nearly done—since Dick was working on it when I visited him in the spring that I have mentioned. I know that "ifs" are no good, but if he had lived to complete the planned work, my guess is that the final volumes would have found him again at the top of his form. My guess is that his hero in France would have made quite a book. The guess cannot be proved, but this much is indisputable: Dick has earned the right to be judged finally by his best, and that best is very, very good indeed. He must have gone in pride and peace wherever good men and good writers go.

This selection is from the American Society of African Culture, *AMSAC Supplements* 18 (Dec. 30, 1960).
Author's Notes: 1. By St. Clair Drake and Horace Cayton, N.Y., 1945.   2. In "Long Black Song," from *Uncle Tom's Children*.   3. In "Down by the Riverside," from *Uncle Tom's Children*.

The Task of the Negro Writer as Artist

The Negro writer in America has a dual commitment: to his people and to his art. It is a commitment that is too often violated at the expense of honesty and honor, but it is a commitment that can never be completely resigned. If the problems created by this commitment cannot be resolved by a resort to logic, they can be transcended. And not only by the vaulting genius of, say, a Ralph Ellison, or the comic brilliance of a Langston Hughes, or the sheer emotional power of a Richard Wright— all of whom, incidentally, embrace the obligation to their people as a source of creative strength and moral sustenance. They can be transcended by the dedicated exercise of an order of talent and skill such as Ann Petry's, or Julian Mayfield's. Transcendence begins where Wright's begins, negatively, with the rejection of those "fundamental assumptions" that have so long dominated writing *about* Negroes that they have come to permeate writing *by* Negroes. Or transcendence begins positively, where Ellison's and Petry's and Gloria Oden's begins, with a recognition of the fact that Negro behavior—character, sensation, thought— is dredged from the same deep mine of potentials that is the source of all human behavior. Or, finally, transcendence begins with the Negro writer's conviction that, as Ellison has said, "it is important to explore the full range of American Negro humanity and to affirm those qualities which are of value beyond any question of segregation, economics or previous condition of servitude. The obligation was always there and there is much to affirm."

This selection is from the *Negro Digest*, Apr. 1965.

Review of *No Longer at Ease* by Chinua Achebe

On the narrative level this good novel, *No Longer at Ease,* is deceptively simple. It relates the story of Obi Okonkwo, the brightest boy in his village. Sent to England to complete his education with money lent him by his village union, his expectation is to return to Nigeria, take a job in senior civil service, and thus become one more in a small but growing cadre of new Nigerian leaders.

Four years of England, even without the formal learning at the university, taught Obi much, and although there were times when "his longing to return home took on the sharpness of physical pain," he became Europeanized, or, more strictly, Britainized. Four years of England taught him much, as I have said, but it did not teach him enough.

Returning to Nigeria as "a young man of brilliant promise" he gets his job in the senior civil service in Lagos. He also gets Clara, a Europeanized girl: he gets a car, an apartment, and a few friends perhaps more worldly and sophisticated but less scrupulous than he.

The careful discipline of Obi's Christian upbringing enables him to control the exercise of the western tastes he had acquired in England. Self-willed, intelligent, honest, he decries the incompetence of some of his colleagues, maintains his dignity in the face of insults and his honesty in the face of great temptations. Unlike many high-placed civil servants, Obi refuses to be bribed.

But a series of circumstances conspire against him. His preacher father retires, and Obi must send money to help support his parents. The quarterly insurance premium on his car unexpectedly falls due. His mother is stricken with an expensive illness. Income taxes—he had given them no thought, never having had an income before—fall due. The loan from the village union must be repaid.

And finally to complete the sorry score, Clara becomes pregnant at about the same time Obi learns that her great-great grandfather had dedicated himself to a tribal god, and she is therefore "osu"—a pariah with whom marriage is forbidden, and who, anyway, for reasons of her own, refuses to marry him. So added to his innumerable debt is another for an abortion: and in the end, Obi supplements his salary by accepting bribes. He is caught.

The story line in *No Longer at Ease* is clear, fast-moving, simple but *No Longer at Ease* is not a simple novel. Mr. Achebe has more than a story to tell, and he had more to say than what he says of one man's conflicts. The story is a parable, and it is summed up in some lines from T.S. Eliot:

> We returned to our places, these Kingdoms,
> But no longer at ease here, in the old dispensation,
> With an alien people clutching their gods. . . .*

In these terms, the principle conflicts are not Obi's: they are universal man's. They are conflicts between the old and the new; between sterility and change; between instinct and thought; and between a generation that is passing and one just attaining adulthood.

But these complicating conflicts should not frighten the reader, for Mr. Achebe presents them with a sharp sense of their dramatic values. His scenes come alive; his characters have vitality. Thoughtful, provocative and sometimes a little pedantic, Chinua Achebe is first of all a talented novelist, and *No Longer at Ease* proves it.

This review is from *Afro Magazine*, Aug. 26, 1961.
Editor's Note: *Lines (40-42) from Eliot's poem "Journey of the Magi."

Review of *The Third Rose: Gertrude Stein and Her World* by John Malcolm Brinnin

Dylan Thomas in America caused many things—all of them without substance—to be said about its author: John Malcolm Brinnin had abused friendships, betrayed confidences, assassinated characters, and thrown dirt at a saint.

What these insubstantial charges proved of course was that Brinnin had been objective and painfully honest in reporting what he knew of the life in America of a Welch poet who had been held in almost idolatrous regard.

Brinnin did not dispute Dylan Thomas' genius as a poet—indeed, the opposite—but he did show him unworthy of idolatry as a man.

Now Mr. Brinnin brings the same objective honesty to his giant biography of Gertrude Stein; but this time even the most rabid of his subject's fans (if any of the most rabid are still alive) cannot accuse the author of throwing dirt at a saint.

Whatever dirt is thrown is thrown by Gertrude Stein's own friends and most intimate contemporaries, and thrown in the full knowledge that their target was no saint.

Unbeautifully obese, and with a penchant for ridiculous off-beat clothes, Gertrude Stein was monstrously self-centered, deplorably naive and inept in many of her critical judgments of both literary and graphic art, savagely forthright, troublemaking, and all but intolerably arrogant.

How she managed to live with her brother, Leo, for so long is a mystery of personal adjustment that Brinnin helps to solve. Leo, too, was wholly self-involved and arrogant.

Gertrude Stein's character and the work she produced became the stuff of legend.

It is not to be doubted that some of her works will endure: *Three Lives, The Making of Americans*, and perhaps *Geography and Plays*.

But much of the rest is worthless, full—as Gertrude Stein's friend, Edith Sitwell, put it—"of an almost unsuperable amount of silliness, an irritating ceaseless rattle. . . ."

She was after dissociating words from history and knowledge and philosophic content—a task clearly impossible (since words—though not necessarily as speech sounds—become language and communication only when tied tight to meanings), but in pursuing her impossible aim, Gertrude Stein met with some happy accidents: flashes of beauty and insight, and instances of inexpressibly poignant communication.

As for the rest, as a writer she was a hoax, who claimed Henry James and the Cubist painters—especially Picasso, Cézanne and Matisse—as the greatest influences upon her, but who actually (though Brinnin does not say so, and neither did Miss Stein) cribbed a good deal, both in character and writing, from the now forgotten Amy Lowell.

John Malcolm Brinnin has done what must have been a remarkably difficult job remarkably well.

He has converted a very complicated legend to graspable reality, and this is a service to modern literary history.

But also, though collaterally, he has done another service: he has brilliantly analyzed and explained the meaning of the "modern spirit" (there is no other term) in art and life, and this is a considerable service to social history.

This review is from *Afro Magazine*, Dec. 26, 1959.

Review of *Thomas Wolfe: A Biography* by Elizabeth Nowell

This is the biography of an adolescent prodigy who was still an adolescent though no longer a prodigy when he died in Baltimore of tuberculosis of the brain at the age of thirty-eight.

Thomas Wolfe was a playwright who never wrote a professional play, a poet who never intentionally wrote a poem, a novelist who never really learned the tough craft of the novel, and in general a literary artist who lacked the first requisite of all artistic expression—restraint, control.

He was nevertheless a great writer, as one may be a great talker without ever becoming a conversationalist.

He poured out in torrential spasms millions of words, sometimes at the rate of ten thousand a day, filling boxes and crates with manuscript of what he conceived to be a single book ("the book")—a book about himself.

Others, performing the miracles of labor which Wolfe himself should have performed, hacked and pieced and organized out of this milliary prodigality of words a half dozen books.

Look Homeward, Angel was the first; then followed *Of Time and The River, You Can't Go Home Again, The Web and the Rock,* a volume of stories, *The Hills Beyond,* and a book of "poems" "selected and arranged in verse" by someone else.

The last four of these were principally edited and published after Wolfe's death.

All the same and in spite of the work he did not do, Tom Wolfe was a great writer.

He was also an adolescent. His published works make the fact clear enough.

They depict an adolescent's reaction to every experience he ever had:

to train rides, to the landscape of home, to college, to love, sex, the lure of great cities, to America and the "manswarm."

They are full of the dark brooding, the lyrical passions, the naive prurience, the innocent great wonder, the compulsive seeking and the disillusionments of discovery that adolescents know.

In his books he never succeeds in untangling the awful skein of his youth.

In his books he is Eugene Gant and George Webber and George Spangler and Joe Doaks, and everything that happened to them had happened to Tom Wolfe. His (auto) biography was finished twenty years ago.

But for all that, Miss Nowell's new biography is no work of supererogation.

There is a wealth of new details covering the dangerous bigness of Tom Wolfe's heart, the sometimes cramping meanness of his mind; his mistrust of Scott Fitzgerald and of the "literary set" in general; his murderous jealousy of Aline Bernstein—a woman "old enough to be his mother" and who had grown children when Wolfe fell in love with her; his ingratitude to this same woman and to almost everyone who gave him help.

The whole story of Wolfe's break with Maxwell Perkins and the publishing firm (Scribner's) of which Perkins was senior editor has never been told before.

Wolfe's final and fatal trip to the West is here too.

This new material and the exploration of the old material make Miss Nowell's book important to all those thousands who remember with what rare excitement they first met the works of Tom Wolfe and absolutely indispensable to the lovers of that period of great literary wealth which brought forth, along with Wolfe, Sherwood Anderson, John Dos Passos, Scott Fitzgerald and the early Hemingway and Faulkner.

This review is from *Afro Magazine*, July 23, 1960.

The Death of Ernest Hemingway

There have been and there will be many encomiums on Ernest Hemingway, and there is no need for me to write one.

I will say simply that from the late 1920s until the '50s he was the most influential writer of his time.

I do not mean that he made people's careers and reputations by saying good things about them and their work.

He was not much given to praising other writers.

Indeed, one of his earliest books, *The Torrents of Spring*, was a slashing, cruel and wholly unwarranted attack on Sherwood Anderson, a man to whom he had cause to be grateful.

In one of his books—I think it was *Death in the Afternoon**—he did say kind things about Gertrude Stein, but not about her as a writer, and later, when so many people seemed to think that she had done so much for him that she seemed to have created him, he resented her.

The only career and the only reputation Hemingway made was his own.

Nor do I mean that his influence was of the kind that a writer like, say, T.S. Eliot has (or had), or C.P. Snow, or Sartre and Camus.

Hemingway was not an intellectual, and he changed nobody's thinking.

His own thinking was adolescent, and the things he thought never developed into idea-concepts about anything.

And they—his thoughts—had only to do with notions about strength and courage, glory and death, out of which notions he fashioned—not a philosophy, certainly, but an attitude toward life little different from the attitude of a teen-age boy who wishes he could be at one and the same time a soldier who fights bravely, a sailor who saves his ship, a marine who subdues rebellious natives, and a matador whose grace and skill win the hearts of beautiful women.

Hemingway thought with his muscles.

But for a quarter of a century the world could offer no greater praise to a writer than to say, "He writes like Hemingway."

No one except Hemingway ever did write like Hemingway, but thousands tried.

That was his influence.

And for twenty-five years, only the truest writers bucked it; only those who studied to know themselves, and who believed in themselves, and who wrote out of themselves withstood it.

And only they shared Hemingway's secret, which was to work at knowing what you experience, to work at trying to understand it, to work at expressing it in terms of oneself and to work, work, and work.

Doing what Hemingway did, and given the artist's equipment, no creative writer can completely fail, without doing it, no creative writer can even approach success.

This Hemingway knew.

He did not know or need to know much else. He was not a man of wide experience.

He had experience in depth—all of it physical, muscular, visceral, sensational rather than intellectual.

This is nothing against him.

Passion comes simultaneous with physical action, or with the image, anticipation or thought of physical action, and cannot ever be divorced from it, and increases as the action proceeds.

Try it.

Or try reading part two "Big Two-Hearted River," or the best bullfight scenes in *Death in the Afternoon*, or even the prurient episodes in the only really cheap novel Hemingway ever wrote, *To Have and Have Not*, and you will see what I mean.

Earthy, elemental, primitive? Certainly. And what's wrong with that?

Hemingway was a primitive, like Whitman. And like Whitman, he was a great one: "One of the greatest known to the modern world."

This selection is from *Afro Magazine*, July 22, 1961. The title is supplied by the editor.

Editor's Note: *Death in the Afternoon*, Hemingway's classic work on the art of bull-fighting, does not mention Gertrude Stein; she is discussed at length in Heming-way's posthumously published *A Moveable Feast*, his memoir of Paris during the years 1921-1926 in which he includes a chapter "Miss Stein Instructs."

Review of *Soul Clap Hands and Sing* by Paule Marshall

Soul Clap Hands and Sing is a book of four novella-length stories that present different aspects of a single subject and striking variations on a single theme.

It is a fine book, and such a tremendous advance over the same author's novel *Brown Girl, Brownstones*—which, let it be said, was a good first novel—as to astonish even the most dubious reviewer.

Yet *Soul Clap Hands and Sing* is no spot of a literary accomplishment—
no flash in the pan, no freak, no lucky strike.

It is clearly in the line of Mrs. Marshall's development as a writer.

The subject of these linked stories cannot be stated in a single word or
phrase, and the theme is not merely the tragedy of love.

They are stories about men and women.

But no: that is wrong.

They are stories about man and woman, and about the impoverish-
ment of the flesh and of the decay of the spirit as well as of the flesh, and of
the withering away of identity which, at best, is never fully realized, and of
love.

There is little dramatic action in the sense of violence and physical
conflict.

In this corrupt sense—except for the last story—indeed there is no
action at all.

What happens happens on the deepest level, below the consciousness
of the characters themselves, until, in a final revelation of self-knowledge
they become aware of what life might have been but for a fatal, tragic
flaw—of sham, of fear, or pride or indifference—that barred them from
life.

On the purely narrative level the stories are quite simple and similar.

In the first, an old man, already decaying in his pride, is finally
destroyed by his love of a young girl.

In the second, an aging professor tries to renew himself through
immersion in the fresh vigor of a young woman's awakening.

In the third, a middle-aged "bastard spawned of the world's commin-
gling" finds in drink and cynical perversion a sorry refuge from the love his
prejudice has blighted.

And in the last and longest—and some will say the best—a famous
actor known as Caliban tries and fails to recover his true identity.

All these parable-like tales shine with the purity of truth—and truth is
seldom pure.

What gives them their astonishing quality is Paule Marshall's great
sensibility and sense.

These, I think, above all—and these marked by the power to "expand
and contract perception" (the phrase is E.M. Forster's), and to create an
extraordinary variety of experience within the limits of a single episode.

But Mrs. Marshall has other powers and more explicable skills.

Her language does not fuzz out. It is clean and strong—of exactly
measured tensibility—in all the right places.

I nearly said her style is jewel-like, but of course gem-like is what I mean.

As a descriptive writer no young author surpasses her, I think, for no other young author sees so well and so truly.

And this brings me back to the first assertion about sensibility and sense and perception.

Paule Marshall perceives more than scenes and people. She perceives and enters into the secret hearts of men.

This review is from *Afro Magazine*, Oct. 28, 1961.

Review of *Selected Poems*
by Gwendolyn Brooks

When *A Street in Bronzeville*, a first volume of poems, appeared, this reviewer said of its author, Miss Gwendolyn Brooks, that she "comes bringing valid and valuable gifts. Here is a poet whose subjects are so pertinent, whose sense of beauty is so true, and whose expressiveness is so felicitous that she must be ranked with the very best of her contemporaries.

This opinion, fully justified by her first work, was confirmed by her second—and a distinguished panel of critics must have thought so too, for that second work, *Annie Allen*, was awarded the Pulitzer Prize for poetry in 1950. Since then Miss Brooks has produced nothing that can be judged as a falling off. Her gifts are still valid and valuable.

Indeed they are more so. Even her short novel, *Maud Martha*, seemed to underscore the talents that make her a poet with very special qualities. But "special qualities" is not quite the proper phrase, for good poets all have some special qualities in common.

What I suppose I really mean is that Miss Brooks's special qualities as a poet are so linked with her particular and special experiences as a human being as to produce poetry that is quite new; poetry that provides unexpected insights; poetry that is full of both intellectual and emotional surprises; poetry that comments upon experience truthfully and precisely, and not in private and obscure ways.

You follow her lines with bated breath. There is in Miss Brooks's best pieces a fullness of communication of some of the most subtle emotions, the most delicate shadings of thought, the most intricate images. One has only to read such a poem as "The Chicago Defender Sends a Man to Little Rock"—or any of a dozen others to see what I mean.

And having read it, one is drawn on to read, and read—with inevitably sharpened perceptions and with increasing pleasure and poignancy. As in that painfully beautiful sonnet sequence, "The Children of the Poor":

> What shall I give my children? who are poor,
> Who are adjudged the least wise of the land,
> Who are my sweetest lepers, who demand
> No velvet and velvety velour;
> But who have begged me for a brisk contour,
> Crying that they are quasi,
>   contraband
> Because unfinished, graven by a hand
> Less than angelic, admirable or sure.
> My hand is stuffed with mode, design, device.
> But I lack access to my
>   proper stone.
> And plenitude of plan shall
>   not suffice
> Nor grief nor love shall be
>   enough alone
> To ratify my little halves
>   who bear
> Across an autumn freezing
>   everywhere.

Although *Selected Poems* is a generous culling of her earlier volumes, Miss Brooks has added a dozen new poems, including one that is a tribute to Langston Hughes. However, it is what Miss Brooks says of Robert Frost that I would say of her:

> Some glowing in the common blood.
> Some specialness within.

This review is from *Afro Magazine*, Nov. 2, 1963.

Review of *Simple's Uncle Sam*
by Langston Hughes

Some years ago—I think it was in the '50s*—when Langston Hughes was inspired to create the character Jesse B. Semple, otherwise known as "simple," I remarked that the day would come when Simple would take his place among the great folk hero-gods in the American pantheon.

I did not expect that day to come so soon, but it is already here, and my impulsive judgment (for that is what it was) seems less impulsive in the light of its confirmation by the opinions of such critics and observers as Brooks Atkinson and Max Lerner.

As a folk figure Simple stands on the same plateau with Paul Bunyan, Davy Crockett, Calamity Jane, and Johnny Appleseed. And yet how different from them he is. And it is not an ethnic difference only—though that is certainly a part of it.

Bunyan, Crockett and the rest are folk heroes of the frontier. In spite of the fact that some of them had corporeal being, figments of the frontier imagination which, in tall tale and anecdote, notoriously stretched the boundaries of experienced reality to accommodate the incredible, the fantastic and marvelous.

These frontier folk heroes were always more than ten feet tall, could subdue grizzly bears, kick over mountains and cross the widest river in one stride. Measured against their physical capacities, Simple "ain't nothing but a natural man." Bunyan and his kind represented the expansive optimism, the limitless horizons, the unbridled strength, and the pure exuberant idealism of an America still committed to rugged individualism, still bucolic and environed by prairie, forest and rushing waters.

The only waters Simple has seen since he left Virginia as a ("passed-around") child are the East and Harlem Rivers and the gray and equally polluted Hudson; and the nearest to a forest he has seen are the woods in Central Park.

The frontier folk-heroes are romantics; Simple is a realist. They were without sophistication; Simple is urbane, cerebral, and utterly sophistical. While they were devoted to action, Simple is devoted to thought—and always to thought about everyday experience in a real, often funny and always pathetic world:

"Now they come talking about a cooling off period. Were I any cooler, I would be dead. How long must I wait? Like the blues says, 'Can I get it now, or must I hesitate' . . .†

Did not a soul tell that man who shot Medgar Evers in the back with a bullet to be cool. Did not a soul say to them hoodlums what slayed them three whites and colored boys in Mississippi to cool it . . . They burnt down fourteen colored churches in Mississippi in one summer, yet I'm supposed to be cool! Well, I am my own leader, and I am not cool!" ‡

"I have lived in so many empty houses full of peoples, I do not want to live in a crowded empty house no more." § "If white Americans can learn how to fly past Venus, go into orbit and make telestars, it look like to me white barbers in Ohio could learn how to cut colored hair."

To quote Simple out of context is unfair. Like Ellison's "invisible man," Hughes's Simple (though on another level) represents, or sums up nearly all that is seminal, and that is, finally, projective in the contemporary colored man's life.

This review is from *Afro Magazine,* Feb. 12, 1966.

Editor's Notes: *Langston Hughes created Jesse B. Semple for a newspaper column in the *Chicago Defender,* Feb. 13, 1943, although the character first appeared in book form in 1950.   †Quote from sketch entitled "For President" in *Simple's Uncle Sam.*   ‡Quotes from sketch entitled "Wigs for Freedom" in *Simple Uncle Sam.*
§Quote from sketch entitled "Empty Houses" in *Simple's Uncle Sam.*

Review of *Black Man's Burden*
by John Oliver Killens

It is possible to read John Oliver Killens' new book at one sitting and within an hour—and what an hour!—but I wouldn't advise it.

For unless you go back and read it again, you will miss some of the points of an argument constructed on the premise that it is the black man who carries the white man as a burden, and, Rudyard Kipling to the contrary, not the other way around.

It is not that the points are ever-subtle, or trickily intellectualized (Killens is not that kind of writer), if *Black Man's Burden* is not read again, or more slowly in the first place, the surface dazzle will fool you.

It flashes and slashes, shimmers and grins, and one might think that's all there is (as is so frequently the case—begging your pardon humbly—with Baldwin). And perhaps for some, that will be plenty.

But—again with apologies—all I can say is, Killens did not write for them. He wrote for the many others, including me. And what he wrote in these half dozen essays is his personal reaction to various aspects of the present situation in race relations.

Take non-violence, which Killens calls (mistakenly I think) a myth. For all his respect for Martin Luther King, Killens sees non-violence—which is no longer a "tactic," but a way of life—as emasculation, as self-castration, as furthering the process of unmanning the black man.

And since this is what white America has wanted, all along "to" "waive the colored man's right of self-defense;" since it has wanted all along "to grind down black men bit by bit and turn them into eunuchs," is it any wonder that white people are happy to have colored people do it to themselves?

Does not this non-violent way of life, this negation of the first law of human nature, which is self-preservation, prove once again what whites have always said about colored men that they are less than human?

Or take the myth—and thank heavens this one at least is beginning to erode—that "to write out of the frame of reference of a colored American is ipso facto anti-universal"; that to enter the so-called mainstream (Oh, much abused phrase!) of American letters requires colored writers to deny their colorness.

Who, then, will tell the real story of America? Not the literary "nit-pickers" like Updike and Salinger, who "write page after page of precious prose about absolutely nothing." And not the "awant gardy" the "beatnik", the "new wave" writers, black as well as white, who are not really anti-bourgeois, nor anti-white supremacy, but only anti-people.

American colored writers, then, have the profoundest obligation, the solemnest duty it has ever been the privilege of any group of writers to bear.

They have to "un-brainwash" the rest of the Western World.

They have to make it very clear that the history of Western (white) man is not "the history of the entire human race."

For all its surface dazzle, and for all the wry smiles it will evoke, *Black Man's Burden* is a serious, deeply sincere and provocative book.

I am glad and grateful that *John Oliver Killens wrote it.*

This review is from *Afro Magazine*, Mar. 5, 1966.

Of Men and the Writing of Books

Please let me say at once that I shall not speak to you in any tone of authority. Writing is so deeply private and personal a business in the practice of it that only those who do not write can speak of writing with magesterial warrant. Of all the exercises of sophisticated expression, only writing seems commonly to demand the strictest privacy. In biographical legends we get glimpses of workers in other areas of expression calmly going about their work surrounded by crowds of varying degrees of density. We are told, for instance, that the composer of "Clair de Lune" worked best in the presence of others, and Rodin, the sculptor, frequently had a mad party going at one end of his studio while he chipped away on "The Thinker" at the other. Pictures of painters daubing at canvasses set up in the streets and hemmed in by groups of the curious are a part of this folklore. Workers in purely interpretive arts—actors, singers, dancers, and the like—not only need but crave audiences for their performances, and this craving is a part of their built-in equipment. The case of the writer at work is quite contrary to this.

Another thing that I should like to say at once, principally to put your minds at ease, is that I will not talk about my own writing, because, indeed, I cannot. About the work of others, I can talk a blue streak—and this seems to be a psychological quirk congenital in most writers, the other and darker side of which is that when writers talk about the work of other writers, they usually have nothing good to say.

I remember reading some time ago a novelist's review of someone else's novel, and what the novelist-reviewer had to say almost literally froze my blood. Now I had read the novel in question, and with my indiscriminate and vulgar taste, had found it stimulating, enjoyable and artfully crafted. But according to the novelist-reviewer, the book possessed none of these qualities. As a matter of fact, he found it dull, stupid and esthetically objectionable to the point of nausea; and therefore anyone who read it— who had such low, unlettered and perverted tastes as to enjoy it—was himself dull, stupid and objectionable.

This was a blow to me as a somewhat naive reader, but this was not the last. A week or so later, I saw a magazine interview of which the novelist-reviewer was the subject. He was at that time being much spoken of because a book of his had just been awarded a literary prize, and he had been requested to say something about his book. "But that is impossible," he is reported to have answered, hanging his head with the burden of his modesty. "It's a poor, poor thing, written really for my own pleasure. But it did win a prize, didn't it? But, no, no—I can't talk about it." After which laudably modest declaration, he proceeded to give the interviewer three full pages of talk about the book's conception, its characters, its symbolism, its language and its style, occasionally throwing in chit-chat about his writing habits, his peculiar friends, his preferences in food, and the quality of his whiskey, his women and his tobacco.

Now I cite this for two reasons: first, becuse it is an exception proving the rule, and second, because I wish to emphasize the obvious untruth of the novelist's assertion that he wrote his prize-winning book solely for his own pleasure. No writer gives himself to the enervating labor of writing solely for his own pleasure. Every writer writes in the enduring hope that he will be read.

In another instance, a minor poet was not so much untruthful as mistaken when, brazenly aping Emily Dickinson, he wrote:

> I lock the door, I draw the shade,
> And out of darkness vision comes;
> And God and I collaborate, and Lo!
> The poem is made.

Now it was considerate of him to give some credit to God, but he neglected to give credit to one other collaborator—and that is the psychological agency which created the compulsion to write in the first place; an agency and an urge which actually is a condition of life itself. I speak of the urge to communicate.

One writes in the hope of communicating, and those writers who say that they have no wish to be published, and who affect arrant disdain of response from their fellowmen are either liars, or fools, or both. Of course, one may write for money too, or in the desire to attain prominence or preferment, but these are incidental; for always at the center of the writer's mind and instinct in every beat of his pulse is the need to communicate and the hope to generate some kind of response, and I might add, the attendant fear that he will fail to do so.

But what is it that the writer wishes to communicate? I think the answer is that the writer wishes to communicate his vision of the world; whatever basic concepts he has of his world and his relation to it; whatever there is of meaning for him in the general and the specifics of life and humanity and of the relations of man to man. If he pretends to honesty, he wishes to communicate those values which he holds to be good, and if he is an artistan he wishes to communicate them in a preconceived pattern of beauty.

These values may not be specific; they may not have total definition;

they may not be susceptible to statement in a word. Indeed, in truly great writers, they seldom are. Socialism in Tolstoi, for instance, is not socialism alone; nor pessimism in Hardy; nor Anglo-Catholicism in Eliot; nor humanism in Donne. These terms are mere conveniences. To speak of the socialism of Tolstoi is to neglect the light for an examination of the source of the light—and, of course, to get nowhere, for the source is hidden in a private philosophy, in beliefs and values that are not always strictly known in perceptual terms to the writer himself, and which he certainly cannot proclaim in a few well-chosen maxims.

Indeed, it may be this very thing that distinguishes the greatness of the creative literary mind from the greatness of other minds. Benjamin Franklin and Mohandus K. Gandhi and Henry Thoreau were great minds too, but their beliefs and values can be pinned down, catalogued and neatly exhibited and logically explained. Tolstoi's cannot. His beliefs and the values he held supreme are mystical and rationalistic, radical and extremely conservative, pietistic and agnostic, and even he could not build them into a structure of logical thought—as anyone who reads Tolstoi's *The Kingdom Of God Is Within You* can discover for himself—but they are nonetheless values and beliefs. And what I wish to point out is that the writer's conviction of *something* is what he wishes to communicate.

Nor does it greatly matter what he lends his conviction to. It may be as shallow and empirically untenable as the beatniks corrupt modification of existentialism, or hedonism, or absolute pessimism, but if his conviction is honest and if he is serious and sincere, his writing has vitality. We may shake disapproving heads over Sartre and Silone, Dreiser and Jeffers, but we read them, and light shines from their beliefs and illuminates at least a bit of the world, and reveals at least some aspect of the relations of man to man.

On a lower level of creativity, to which I consign most of the literature of travel, it might be said that the values which the writer wishes to communicate are often too particular, too special, too local and ephemeral. And it seems to me that the pursuit of specialized social, or political, or ideological aims in writing poses a question as to the relation between art and action; and another as to the relations between the creative writer and his audience; and a third having to do with literature as didacticism and literature as affirmation. Certainly there seems to be a great difference between literature as didacticism and literature as affirmation, and I think the difference is nowhere more clearly seen than in the writing that is consciously aimed at some social or political end.

It is not that such writing cannot also make an affirmation of life, of the broad and enveloping moral and ethical principles that are thought to be and believed by most of us to be the struts and stays of man's life on earth.

There is, for instance, that famous and nearly final passage—weaker than some other passages—in *The Grapes of Wrath*, when Rose of Sharon, pregnant and deserted by her husband, gives suck to the starving man. Get the setting and the symbolism. The place is a barn, and the sick man lay on straw. "Rose of Sharon," Steinbeck writes, "moved slowly to the corner and stood looking down at the wasted face, into the wise, frightened eyes. Then slowly she lay down beside him. He shook his head slowly from side to side. Rose of Sharon loosened one side of the blanket and bared her breast. 'You got to', she said. She squirmed closer and pulled his head close. 'There,' she said. 'There.' Her hand moved behind his head and supported it. Her fingers moved gently in his hair. She looked up and across the barn, and her lips came together and smiled mysteriously."

As we come to the end of that passage, we have no doubt that Rose of Sharon's smile—her mysterious smile—was an acknowledgement and an affirmation of something beyond the didactic purposes of the book, and far, far beyond Rose of Sharon; of something that she could not grasp, and that yet affirmed her oneness with all the men and women on earth.

Now I think it need not be argued that, except for the effete and fantastic among them, writers live in society and are conditioned by society. They are attached emotionally and intellectually to society, even when, like Byron, they are not in alliance with it. The writer is affected by the knowledge common to his time, by the attitudes, by the kind of government he lives under. Ideally, though he is affected by society and has his being in it, he is not overly class-conscious, or race-conscious, or kind-conscious. Ideally he is only culture-conscious, and this consciousness embraces all that he has learned of the world. This consciousness is the matrix out of which emerge the ideas, the values and the convictions that he wishes to communicate. The power of his communication is in almost direct proportion to his ability either to confirm and illumine or to extend and reveal experience.

I take it that those who read Jane Austen, say, or May Sarton, or Willa Cather, or Virginia Woolf do so for the satisfaction that confirmation and illumination gives them. They read a work by such a one with the indescribable feeling that *this is it:* that the emotional experiences delineated in it are their own experiences marvelously confirmed and illuminated by the author's observation and insight. I think it can be said that women writers in general deal with what Sir Leslie Stephen called "transfigured experience," and Ellen Glasgow may have been speaking for all women writers when she said that she had "endeavored . . . to heighten what I prefer to call illumination, to increase understanding of that truth of life which has not ever become completely reconciled to the truth of fiction." I think that this is what many writers—and particularly women writers—are after communicating. Women almost never, for instance, deal with abstract good and evil, nor abstract love and hate; but almost always with the concrete truth of the experience of these things, knowing in their consummate womancraft, as someone has said, and taking warning from the example of George Eliot, that wisdom in woman sometimes grows pompous and that philosophy is no real substitute for the creative instinct. But so as not to seem to confine this to women, let me mention in this connection Samuel Richardson, Anton Chekhov, Glenway Wescott—indeed, the list of men, too, is inexhaustible.

Writers of another sort seek to extend and reveal experience. Sometimes, of course, they confirm and illumine, but this is as it were by accident. Take that superb episode in *Darkness At Noon*, when Rubashov, his mind engaged in speculating on the question of whether one must pay for righteous acts that have resulted in evil as well as unrighteous acts, and whether there is another measure for human conduct besides that of Divine Reason, is suddenly assailed by a long-forgotten, detrusive and inappropriate memory, and though he is alone and is, indeed, the only living person who could have had the memory, he whistles to relieve his embarrassment. Or take that fascinatingly horrible scene in *Native Son*, when Bigger Thomas, having committed one murder, determines to commit another, but before he does he is so overcome by desire that he must perform the act of love with the girl he is about to kill.

Now only those truly blinded by squeamishness can fail to find confirmation and illumination of their own emotional experiences in the details of these two episodes. But in neither instance did the authors have this in mind. They were concerned with the breaking up of the surface of confirmable experience and with a fearless bloodletting in the labyrinths of the mind and heart. Writers of this sort are not content to imitate and record and embroider the standard patterns of consciousness. They frighten us. They fill us with a sense of nameless terror and exhilaration at the revelation of what the human soul is capable of in the way of goodness and evil, love and hate, sublimity and degradation, weakness and strength, sacrifice and selfishness. We cannot achieve confirmation from many of the experiences they give us, sometimes because the geography and the physiology is against it, as in *Paradise Lost* and *The Divine Comedy* and *Moby Dick* and *The Tempest;* but more often because the psychology, the intricate windings of mind, which we recognize as our own minds wonderfully revealed, is against it. There is no confirmation in the sense that *this is it* in Stephen Dedalus, Joe Christmas, and Iago, Ahab and Hamlet, Wiligis and Sibylla. They loom gargantuan, beyond confirmation and proof. But we accept them because they are truly communicated to us; they broaden our sympathies, enlarge our souls. They extend and fulfill us. If those writers who confirm and illumine transfigure experience, then those who extend and reveal transmogrify it, and both communicate to us values and convictions which we may or may not accept, but which we recognize and respond to because, for good or ill, they quicken for us the quality of our living.

And, finally, how does the writer elicit response from his reader? But perhaps the question of why he wishes to do this comes first, and I think the answer to this is relatively simple, though perhaps not so simple and bald as I make it now. He wishes to create response because he must. It is response alone that makes us, writer and non-writers alike, know we live. It seems not altogether facetious to say that any writer would rather have a bad review than no review at all, although invariably he thinks that a bad review is proof of a jealous conspiracy against the creative and intellectual life in general and against him in particular.

But to go back to the question. How does the writer create the desired responses? Is it through the strength of his convictions alone, or because of the intrinsic value of his values? I think not. We know, for instance, that nihilism is actually the repudiation of conventional and intrinsic values, and yet this is the moral flavor of Hemingway, and thousands of people who are not nihilists have read him and praised him. Nihilism is also more than a little of the moral matter in the works of Dostoevski, and when one reads *Crime and Punishment* one becomes so involved with this moral matter that he forgets that *Crime and Punishment* is in its simplest terms a murder story, a detective story.

But the fact that it is a detective story has a great deal to do with the creation of the desired response. It is a more sophisticated application of the device the 19th century English schoolboy used when his teacher of rhetoric and composition told him that he must try to catch immediately the attention and interest of the reader, so he began his next composition, "Damn me,' said the drunken duchess as she lit her black cigar."

Devices is the word—technique, craft. Now I am not so cynically inclined as to belittle an art over which I have been trying assiduously to establish some command for more years than I care to remember; and I think I speak only the truth when I say that, although the writer certainly uses the very essence of him—his emotions, his experiences, his spirit— he promotes the desired reactions and the appropriate response by employing the tricks of his craft, by setting traps with his technique.

Those who have done editorial work, or read first year college essays, or some of the sermons from the period of the Wesleyan revival, are well aware of how unresponsive one can be to the outpourings of the most fervent emotions, the most indisputable knowledge and the most unassailable truths. And whether we have had this experience or not, we have all had the experience of reading fascinated, almost against our wills, the substantively quite worthless works of certain popular novelists and the arrant nonsense of some of those writers who appear rather regularly in the more esoteric of the so-called "little" avant garde magazines. What fascinates us of course—though we do not stop to think about it unless we are practicing writers—is less the matter than the manner—the technique, the craft.

The greatest writers, and especially those who are novelists, have always been also great magicians. They have had to learn magic because they have dealt in the greatest of mysteries—causality. They are not content with the uncomplicated, untricked-out narrative of events which E.M. Forster exemplifies in the sentence, "The king died and then the queen died." There must be complication: "The king died and then the queen died of grief." The elaboration and the delineation of complications require the magic, the tricks of craft I have referred to. No writer is born with a knowledge of them. They can be learned, and indeed, they must be learned. It is not true that only the slick and popular writers bother to learn them. What happens is that for slick writers craft becomes the end. But it is only a means and it never becomes the end for the serious and honest writer, any more than the use of the knife becomes the end for the surgeon who is humane.

And the word "humane" strikes the note I wish to close on.

This speech was first presented publicly in April 1963; it was delivered in slightly different form on several other occasions and reprinted for National Library Week in April 1969.

The Black Revolution in American Studies

The concept "Black Studies," conceived in frustration and bitterness by an articulate and highly emotional minority, is of questionable validity as a scholarly discipline. It encompasses too much. It presumes no less than the universal social, cultural, and literary history of blacks from pre-Islamic times to the present and the biological and anthropological linkage of all black people. It presumes, too, a genetic constant, although the theory of a genetic constant has been repudiated by the best scientific minds for a hundred years. The Black Studies concept is action-oriented, and to the extent that it is so oriented it is anti-intellectual. Represented in a mystique called "Négritude," it embraces a heavy, indeed, overriding emotional component that is referred to as "soul force," which force conditions ways of acting, feeling, and thinking that are distinctly racial and that characterize black people wherever they are and under whatever conditions they exist. All black men, therefore, are brothers both in the genetic and spiritual sense.

The advocates of this way of thinking have no corpus of cognitive knowledge to fall back on. They adduce the works of Marcus Garvey (whose recently discovered "lost papers" they cannot wait to get into), the romantic appeal of the Back-to-Africa movement, the position—which is grossly misunderstood—that Franz Fanon takes in *The Wretched of the Earth*, and various statements put forth by the self-exiled Stokely Carmichael. Fortunately few of the advocates of this way of thinking are professional academicians; they lack the authority to dilute the demanding intellectual endeavor that a mastery of black studies requires. This is not to say that they totally lack influence. They are of the Black Revolution, leaders and spokesmen for activist groups and political programs. They speak their views from respectable platforms, and they publish them in the Black Muslim newspaper *Mohammed Speaks, Black World* (formerly *Negro Digest*), and *Ramparts*.

Many, and perhaps most, black scholars, who are also of the Revolution, neither condemn nor exculpate the non-academic revolutionaries. They say, truthfully enough, that there are emotional components and biases in all humanistic thought and learning, and, having defined them, the job of the academician is to modify or correct them by disseminating true knowledge. They say that Western learning begins from a bias that can be summarized as "Rah, rah, Whites!" and that, proceeding from this, white scholars generally have distorted facts, knowledge, and the truth by excluding blacks from, or by defaming the role of blacks in the history and culture of the Western world, and particularly the history and culture of America. Black scholars submit that this is likely due to the whites' conscience-stricken realization that the ideals—social, political, and religious: in short, humanitarian—which were and are set forth as the basis for human action and interaction, have been ignored; and the way to ease the abraded conscience is to write American history and to examine American civilization so as to exclude from consideration the victims of this falling away. White scholars have found justification for this exclusion in question-able theories, obsessively rationalized by some of the most eminent American minds from Thomas Jefferson to George F. Kennan, and dubious psychological and social data and "proof" of black people's inherent inferiority.

This way of thinking has produced several interlocking complementary reactions and results, and black scholars and intellectuals have documented them in recent works that no honest student of American civilization should ignore. The scholarly caliber of John Hope Franklin's *From Slavery to Freedom* (now updated), of Benjamin Quarles' *The Negro in the Making of America*, and of Kenneth Clark's *Dark Ghetto* is very high. Less scholarly, but important to an understanding of the reactions and results mentioned above is Austin, Fenderson, and Nelson's *The Black Man and the Promise of America*. Then there are certain personal books and an official report: *Manchild in the Promised Land*, by Claude Brown; *Soul on Ice*, by Eldridge Cleaver; *The Autobiography of Malcolm X*; and the *Report of the National Advisory Commission on Civil Disorders*.

The results and the reactions that these books explore and document are social. They document the development and the operation of race prejudice. They present evidence of the American whites' calculated avoidance of knowledge and learning about American blacks. They give information about the operation of this willful ignorance in the day-to-day rounds of American life, and about the efforts of blacks as individuals and as communities to accommodate and to moderate the ignorance of whites, which is commonly called "racism."

A second result of the exclusion of black people from a role in the drama of American civilization and a place in Amerian history is—or rather, was; for this is not new—the institution of courses in Negro history and literature in Negro high schools and colleges, where white supervision of curricula is minimal and careless. The tradition of studying Negro history and literature is more than a half centry old. It goes back to W.E.B. DuBois, the black social historian who, believing that the solution to the "Negro problem was a matter of systematic investigation," tried to induce white institutions (notably the University of Pennsylvania and Harvard) to adopt black courses. He did not succeed, but he did inaugurate (in 1904) the Atlanta University Studies program, which focused on Negro material, and which annually published scholarly monographs and papers on the Negro. DuBois inspired Carter G. Woodson, also a Harvard Ph.D., who founded the Association for the Study of Negro Life and History in 1915, set up a company to publish books about blacks, edited and issued the quarterly *Journal of Negro History* (which the Association still issues), and himself wrote the texts—*The Negro in Our History* and *Negro Makers of History*—most widely used down to the Second World War.

A third result of the neglect of the black experience in American Studies is the Black Student Revolution—a social as well as an intellectual rebellion against the "irrelevance" of so much that passes for education in American institutions of higher learning. The social phase of the Black Student Revolution, like the instruction in black courses in Negro schools, goes back a long way—a fact which Harry Edwards' book, *Black Students*, an excellent account of contemporary temper and attitudes, fails to report on. It goes back to the 1920s. At Lincoln University, at Hampton Institute, and at Shaw University, private black colleges administered and faculty-staffed principally by whites, students rebelled against the patronizing "missionary" attitudes of their white instructors and against the rigid "etiquette of race" that characterized all their relations with them. White administrators and instructors were said to feel that blacks were not capable of really mastering the more demanding subjects, and that, perhaps excepting the manual arts, the subjects they were taught by the few black teachers— physical education, music, and a "folk variety of Negro history"—were not worth learning anyway. In short, the rebellion was against the inferior black status per se. The students demanded and gradually got more black administrators and teachers, a modification (at Hampton and Shaw) of the social rules that stigmatized them as irresponsible, sexually irrepressible "children," and increased respect as maturing human beings.

Not until the 1950s, when court decisions and steadily mounting pressures at home and abroad challenged the American status quo, and, among other things, made for a substantial increase in the enrollment of black students in predominantly white colleges—not until then did the intellectual phase of the Black Student Revolution begin to acquire definition. Even now, though, the definition is blurred by social factors and an emotional cloud cover and is rendered imprecise by the rhetoric of revolution. "Soul," "Black nationalism," "Black separatism," and "Black power" have been taken to mean what they seem to mean in the formation of Black Student Unions and Alliances and in the demand—bitterly ironic and cynical—on predominantly white campuses for autonomous Black Studies programs to be directed and taught by blacks for black students only. In "The Role of Afro-American Education," one of the essays in *Basic Black: A Look at the Black Presence on Campus*, it is argued that "Black studies must be taught from a black perspective. The spirit of blackness must pervade . . . Black education must be based on both ideological and pedagogical blackness." The fact that one trained and practicing as a scholar can make such an argument is a measure of the extent to which emotionalism blurs, and, if not checked, will dilute the content that Black Studies must have if it is to attain respectability as a scholarly discipline.

Black Studies can attain that respectability. There are both black and white scholars—at Berkeley, Brown, Harvard, Michigan, Texas, and Yale—who believe this and are working toward that end. They seem agreed that "Black Studies" is a misnomer. They prefer Afro-American Studies, a title designating a body of potentially manageable knowledge focusing upon the experience of black people in America, in, specifically, what is now the United States. Afro-American Studies is not African Studies, which, thanks to the British universities and Berkeley, Boston University and predominantly black Howard University, has been deemed academically respectable for a decade. Afro-American Studies is not conceived as structurally dependent on other area studies, like Latin American Studies, for instance, which is also an independent discipline; or Caribbean Studies, which scholars at the University of the West Indies and the University of Puerto Rico are making distinct and independent.

All this is to say that Afro-American Studies is basically American Studies, an interdisciplinary major that must draw upon relevant knowledge and experience outside the United States. I have suggested elsewhere that a line of historical continuity and development peculiar to what is now the United States has generated a new breed of black man with a new "Americanized" orientation to life, with, demonstrably, a special culture and, one strongly suspects, a different psychological and emotional structure from that of his "brothers" in Africa, in South America, and in the Caribbean. Until scholars conscientiously pursue this line of development, American Studies will remain diminished and of questionable validity. Until this development is pursued, Americans will remain poorly equipped to deal with the problems that confront them. An intellectual pursuit—any intellectual pursuit—serves a social function too. That, of course, is what education is all about. And when American students black and white complain about lack of "relevance," they are saying that education in America is not preparing them to serve an important social function, and they are saying this no matter what their definition of importance is.

Although the integration of Afro-American Studies with American Studies will probably require a new methodology for the measurable attainment of respectable scholarly performance and achievement, much of the material to be integrated is already at hand. Some of it was produced before the intellectual phase of the black student revolution got under way. The scholars who produced it were aiming at a revision of the American past; they were intent on correcting the errors of fact and the faults of interpretation of other American historians. C. Vann Woodward certainly had this in mind when he wrote *Reunion and Reaction, The Strange Career of Jim Crow,* and *The Burden of Southern History.* So did Leon Litwack in preparing *North of Freedom,* and Kenneth Stampp when he wrote *The Peculiar Institution.* Though all of these works, appearing in the late 1950s and early 1960s, draw upon sources that have been neglected by writers of "standard" American history, none of them begins to fill what American blacks feel to be the most urgent need—that is, the recreation of the American blacks' history as separate from (but not independent of) the history of American Whites.

There have been efforts along this line, and they continue at a quick-ened pace. Scholars and intellectuals of both races have turned out more histories of black Americans in the past decade than in the preceding half century. Although Herbert Aptheker's *A Documentary History of the Negro People in the United States* is good, the editor too often assumes that the collected documents can stand alone and independent of the historical background which produced them. Blaustein and Zangrando do not make this mistake in their more particularized *Civil Rights and the American Negro,* a compendium of legislative acts, court decisions, Executive Orders, and official public policy speeches documenting and illustrating the Negro's struggle for civil rights. The materials in *The Black American,* edited by Leslie H. Fishel, Jr. and Benjamin Quarles, are more discrete; some of them were chosen on the basis of non-historical criteria; but all relate directly or indirectly to the major themes of the book—"the primary role of the Negro in American history and the importance of the Negro's own history in America."

A different class of historical works—many of them first published years ago and now reprinted—were written, as Charles H. Wesley, who co-authored one of them, says, "to create a sense of pride on the one hand and appreciation on the other." In other words, they were written for black Americans. Only rarely do these books avoid the distortions that some of them purposely employ to counterbalance the distortions of white history. Only the very best of them is free of the intellectual and emotional parochialism that characterizes the race chauvinist. The best is Benjamin Brawley's *A Social History of the American Negro,* which is now reprinted after fifty years. Were it updated by a scholar as highly qualified as the original author was, *A Social History* would be all but indispensable. Markedly lesser achievements than Brawley's are Arnold Schuster's *White Power: Black Freedom,* and recent collections of historical writings edited by Dwight Hoover *(Understanding Negro History),* by Ross Baker *(The Afro-American),* by Bracey, Meier, and Rudwick *(Black Nationalism in America),* and by Charles E.

Wynes *(The Negro in the South Since 1865)*. Whether or not St. Clair Drake, a very perceptive black social scientist, is right in describing the "ultimate purpose" of historical works written specifically for the black American audience as "defining ourselves for ourselves" and "getting ourselves together—necessary conditions for an intelligent participation in a democratic society," one thing is certain: these works challenge contemporary scholarship in American Studies with the facts of black Americans' stolen past and contested future.

Upwards of thirty anthologies of literary writings by blacks have been issued in the last twelve months. Many of these are quickies, collections of contemporary writings published in the hope of riding the wave of the fad for anything black. Others are intended as textbooks in black literature courses, and the selections are representative of the development of Negro writing as art. Their editors establish both a critical and historical context. *On Being Black*, edited by Charles T. David and Daniel Walden has a brilliant critical introduction touching upon the "black aesthetic," and Addison Gayle's anthology, *Black Expression*, has an equally brilliant historical introduction. *Black Voices*, which was edited by Abraham Chapman, and *From the Ashes*, edited by Budd Schulberg, are important because they present work of a whole new crop of black writers heretofore unpublished.

Finally, there are current books that deal with the black American experience from the point of view of traditional scholarly disciplines. Using the methods and tools and providing the insights of psychology, sociology, economics, political science, and cultural anthropology, these books are responsive to the notion of the black American's "difference," and how that difference came to be. The books are "studies," but not all of them deserve the definition. The "black perspective" intrudes, as in Floyd McKissick's *3/5 of a Man*, which Justice William Douglas declares "a must," not because of its scholarly and objective examination of American jurisprudence as it affects the Negro, but because of its "mood . . . which reveals the depth of the anguish and anger in the black community." In Grier and Cobbs's *Black Rage*, a study of the psychology of black youth, mood is restricted to the authors' introduction. And except for the somewhat sensational title, *The Forty Billion Dollar Negro*, the black perspective is entirely absent from Vivian Henderson's study of the black experience in the American economy.

Taken altogether, the books mentioned in this essay—and dozens not mentioned—are a measure of the deficiencies of most American Studies programs; of the extent to which American scholars have been either oblivious to or inexcusably mistaken about black Americans and the materials and substantive issues involving black Americans. These books suggest, too, the dimensions of the educational revolution that must take place in American Studies and that, hopefully, is now gathering momentum. Adversaries of the revolution have already surfaced, but they will scarcely prevail against the persistent work of even a small handful of dedicated scholars of both races who are rediscovering old, neglected historical facts, publishing and testing new theories in the social sciences, and devising new instruments of scholarly humanistic endeavor. The adversaries of the revolution in American Studies will scarcely prevail, either, against the demands for "relevance" by a great and growing number of students.

This selection was first published in *American Studies: An International Newsletter,* Autumn 1970, and reprinted the summer of 1979 in the renamed periodical *American Studies International.*

Some Remarks: On Humanism, the Humanities and Human Beings

I would like to begin with a statement that present experience seems to support: the humanities are at a crossroads. Which fork they take will affect their place in the educational scheme and, more importantly, their effectiveness in society.

When the National Endowment for the Humanities was created in 1965, it was declared in the national interest that the humanities flourish as a national resource, not simply to embellish American life, but to form it, and to make it more meaningful. In short, the postulate of the declaration was that the humanities are—or certainly should be—meaningful to all. But the humanities were defined as that rather obvious collection of academic fields—literature, art, philosophy, religion, and so forth. It is in this academic context that the problem exists and from which the crossroads lead.

Humanism as we currently know it was formed in the Renaissance, but it was not really new. It was a redirection of man's thinking and his aspirations from the Christian belief that man's activities must be shaped toward his relations with the Divinity and his life in the hereafter. The early Renaissance emphasized attention to the Greek and Roman classics, though the study of the classics had not been lacking in the Middle Ages.

The Greco-Roman classics, of course, came into being without any Christian preconceptions or preoccupations. They relate to man's activities on earth. They have etiological components, it is true, but when they involve a divinity, it is another divinity than the Christian. And the classics, therefore, became associated with the "this-worldly" orientation of the Renaissance, and humanism became a study of the classics, and acquired them—and since has kept—much of its very academic orientation. It is today primarily scholarship in literature, in art, in religion and philosophy, rather than an *interest* in literature, philosophy, art and so forth, as a part of man's daily activities. This is the problem.

The substance of the humanities is the creative work of men and women, their speculations about their condition, their nature, their relations to each other, their place in the universe, their aspirations. Much scholarship in the general field of the humanities ignores the substance of the humanities, and even the best scholarship is likely to underplay its relevance. . . . Humanistic scholarship and our present efforts and work are disassociated, and there should be no disassociation. If we can force ourselves to take time to think—time stolen from the work and play that so effecively prevent us from thinking, and from the procedures and the machinery that we create so that thought will be unnecessary, we may well shape a new future. We may even develop educational institutions that will inspire students to continue to investigate and learn things that are related to larger concerns rather than simply to the work that they are at the moment doing. Hopefully, we may remember in time that it is thought and understanding and belief—whether assumed or reasoned—that give life its meaning, and we may save ourselves from tragic mistakes by embracing the proposition that the records of man's activities in the past can serve as roadsigns to the future.

We face many problems today, and because some of the most obvious of these are amenable to technological and/or scientific solutions and because others appear to have been solved by these means, we have come to put our faith in such solutions. We know, for example, how to prevent air pollution, and how to cleanse the water of our rivers, but we have not been able to bring ourselves to look for and apply those social and political devices that reduce our tensions as individuals, as a country, and as a world. We have the wealth with which to eliminate material poverty. We have the educational resources to educate and train people so that no one need, because of ignorance, be poor, but we have not found the way to remove the greatest poverty of all—the poverty that results from lack of aspiration. And the record of human aspiration is the very substance of the humanities.

We have a systematic body of beliefs, which we frequently profess, and we have an unstated set of assumptions which underlie those beliefs. Accepted beliefs and assumptions are generally thought to control behavior, but in our society they do not, for even while we state our beliefs, we behave quite contrary to them, and we have not yet been willing to account to ourselves for this disparity. There is, for instance, the popular American belief that most human and social problems will respond to money and "expertise." We speak easily and quickly of "management" and "technical competence" as the principal factors in social restoration and stability.

It has been said—and is widely believed—that "If industry can produce such miracles as smokeless combustion engines and pocket-size digital computers year after year, it is wholly reasonable to expect that the *same* intellect, energy, and technology can be brought to bear on the problems threatening our civilization."

There are few constraints on such optimistic nonsense. Problems as difficult and global as population control are looked at almost strictly in terms of economics and technology and science, and looked at in this way we fail to see the tension between the individual and society, between practice and belief, between conservatism and radicalism—which tensions, it might be said, are the real problem, just as they are the real problem in the ethical controversy raging around the technological success of organ transplants, and just as they will be the real problem when science breaks the genetic code. The inescapable conclusion—the complete refutation of the belief that science and technology can alone solve our problems is that overriding ambiguities in social values and goals make it practically impossible to define with clarity the humane changes that should be striven for. . . .

And this brings us back to the humanities, to humanistic learning, and the purposes of it which have been either neglected or forgotten. We have neglected to consider or we have altogether forgotten that humanistic training was not given in a vacuum. The classical authors who were the principal objects of study were Socrates and Plato, Cicero and Virgil, and on the Hebraic side, Solomon and Moses and Leviticus; and they were principally studied because they tried to define the duties of man in society, man responsible for his society, man guiding the destinies of his society. Until well after the start of the nineteenth century—with certain minor or at least temporary lapses—the center of gravity of the humanistic tradition and humanistic learning was political, using that term in its broadest sense. . . . Political was the public side of moral; moral was the personal side of political."

Modern scholars in the humanities tend to stress everything but the moral-political. They stress the language and the literature, the elements of formal beauty, the esthetics, and the retrospective aspects of the humanities. The humanistic scholar's sense of identity is not sufficiently based in the observable fact that man is consciously making history today. Humanists are very poorly adjusted to reality. Part of the reason for this is that fields once belonging to the humanities—like history, for instance—are now occupied by the social sciences, and the social sciences are trying, with increasing success, to be more scientific and quantitative, and, with increasing effectiveness, to produce changes on the basis of quantitative data alone. Witness the deliberations of that body of Presidential advisors who influenced the President's new policies on poor relief. Contemplate for a moment the power position of a Daniel Moynihan. The thoughts which these men offer on social and political life and on the moral-political aspect tend to be uninformed and uninspired by real humanistic knowledge. I can think of no great change that has been brought about as the result of the application of humanistic knowledge and research in the last half century. Changes there are, of course, and some of them are good. Think of the changes that penicillin has made, that atomic energy has made, that "the pill" will make. But also think of the dearth of value judgments that accompanied these changes.

No matter how important objectivity is to the scientist and the technologist, it should be anathema to the humanist. As a professional scholar, he must work to restore the concept of the humanities that once prevailed, and to provide the contexts within which humanistic learning is again seen to be relevant to our social and political life. He must not shun value judgments. While he is providing knowledge and understanding of what is past, he must realize that his target is the active citizen in the present, and that that citizen, who may be a future leader, must be value-oriented; must achieve greater perspective, must be inspired to develop wisdom, and, ultimately to master himself and his environment, including that part of the environment that the scientists and technologists have created. Perspective, judgments of value, wisdom, mastery of self—these are the goals of the humanities. They should be involved in all important decisions, public and private. It is up to the community of humanistic scholars to drive this lesson home.

This speech, condensed for this volume, was first presented publicly in September 1970, and in slightly different form on several subsequent occasions.

W.E.B. Du Bois:
A Mind Matched with Spirit

The following piece, previously unpublished, is condensed from a lecture delivered by J. Saunders Redding at the University of Iowa, June 25, 1972, for the opening of the University's W.E.B. Du Bois Institute. The title, supplied by the editor, is adapted from a line in the text.

. . . I recall the first time I saw W.E.B. Du Bois. It was on an occasion when he spoke in Philadelphia, back in the 1920s. My father had anticipated the event for days, for he had not then heard Du Bois either. But he had read him with great avidity and sometimes aloud, when we gathered around the dining room table after dinner, we children to do our school work and our mother to mend the clothes which we incorrigibly ripped and tore. Gathering there, under the chandelier of many colored glass, instead of scattering all over the house, saved electricity which was definitely a consideration. At any rate, assuming the grand oratorical tone and manner in which he coached us for speaking contests at school, my father read editorials from the *Crisis* and Du Bois' commentaries on all sorts of matters about which we had not the faintest intellectual comprehension. We children were more interested in our reading of Effie Lee Newsome's "Children's Corner" which the *Crisis* carried monthly, and in looking at the pictures of black high school and college graduates which were published two or three times a year.

But at the time of the occasion referred to, I was in my teens and Dr. Du Bois had begun to mean something, though I do not claim that I thoroughly understood the meaning of such earlier works of his as I was beginning to read on my own: *The Souls of Black Folk, The Quest of the Silver Fleece*. Although I reacted to it emotionally, I lacked the knowledge to understand what Du Bois meant when he wrote [in *The Souls of Black Folk*]: "I sit with Shakespeare and he winces not; Across the color line I move arm and arm with Balzac and Dumas where smiling men and welcoming women glide in gilded halls . . . I summon Aristotle and Aurelius and what soul I will, and they come all graciously with no scorn nor condescension. So, wed with Truth, I dwell above the Veil. Is this the life you grudge us, O knightly America?"

When the opportunity came to see and hear the man who had written those words nearly a quarter of a century earlier, I was quite as eager as my father, partly, I suspect now, because going to Philadelphia from Wilmington, Delaware by steamer, as my father planned it, meant a two-hour boat ride up the Delaware River, a kind of excursion. . . .

Shortly after we entered the gym of the colored Y.M.C.A. on Philadelphia's Christian Street, the audience was hushed by someone who brought a pitcher and a glass to the lectern. Then the moment came when the chairman, a Professor Lambert, if memory serves, emerged followed by another much smaller man, Dr. Du Bois. I was disappointed. I had seen pictures of him, but I had somehow expected a man of giant stature, and not the delicately structured man he turned out to be; and when he spoke, I expected a voice of thunder, and an apostolic storm of words—for that was the way my father read him—and not the quiet, calm, deliberate speech that Dr. Du Bois gave us. I expected fire and brimstone, ringing iron. And not tempered steel. But Dr. Du Bois of course was tempered steel, forged in the crucible of parlous times and cast in a mold that was forthwith destroyed.

Both mind and character were distinctively his own. So far as the record shows—and it is voluminous—he never experienced a crisis of identity. Oh, I know some will argue otherwise, as does an esteemed historian who is also a personal friend. They will cite that famous passage from the first essay in *The Souls of Black Folk* ["Of Our Spiritual Strivings"] that reads:

. . . One ever feels his two-ness—an American, a Negro; two souls, two thoughts; two unreconciled strivings; two warring ideals in one dark body, whose dogged strength alone keeps it from being torn asunder.

The history of the American Negro is the history of this strife—this longing to attain self-conscious manhood, to merge his double self into a better and truer self. In this merging he wishes neither of the older selves to be lost. He would not Africanize America, for America has too much to teach the world and Africa. He would not bleach his Negro soul in a flood of white Americanism, for he knows that Negro blood has a message for the world. He simply wishes to make it possible for a man to be both a Negro and an American. . . .

And I will say to those who argue thus that this very passage was an affirmation of his identity.

And much, much, later, when he went to Ghana and became a citizen of that country at age 93, it can scarcely be said, as William Buckley implied, that Dr. Du Bois suffered an identity crisis. It was simply a question of where he wanted to be. Choosing an identity: It is a matter of identification—and the difference, which may seem merely semantic, is substantial. Dr. Du Bois always knew who he was. In a symbolic poem entitled "The Song of the Smoke," published in 1907 he had declared,

. . . I am black . . .
I will be as black as blackness can,
The blacker the mantle the mightier the man.

Choosing to live in an African country in 1963 had nothing to do with identity. It was a consequence of his disillusionment with his identification as an American and his bitter disappointment with the total kinematic failure of the notional formulations that supposedly inhere in the American structure of values.

Perhaps earlier on he was too sanguine about the American notional formulations. He was born and largely brought up in an age of great technological and material expectations (in spite of the Panic of 1873) and in a family that, though poor, was never poverty-shocked. There were no complexities in the personalities that formed the family circle, and until he entered Harvard, there were none in Du Bois. Small farmers, laborers, servants, his family was proud and self-contained. They danced around the same totems as most of the rest of Americans. They held the same beliefs. They believed that history was a progression toward perfection; and until he went to Germany and studied under Gustav von Schmoller* and Rudolf Virchow,† Du Bois believed this too. His family believed that equality could be attained and that in the long run justice triumphed. As a boy and a very young man, the last of the Du Boises assumed what his family assumed—I quote—"That all who are willing to work could easily earn a living; that those who had property had earned it and deserved it and could use it as they wished; that poverty was a shadow of crime and connoted lack of thrift and shiftlessness." Not until he became a graduate student in history and the social sciences did young Du Bois begin to chuck these assumptions and, I quote, "Begin to see clearly the connection of economics and politics; the fundamental influence of man's efforts to earn a living on all his other efforts."

But the perception and the sharpness of mind that produced these insights were already developing while he was still a boy in his small New England hometown. In Great Barrington, Massachusetts, the very mildness of the color problem made it possible for him to cultivate the sensitivity that an upbringing in a typical small southern town, with its overriding component of emotionalism, would forbid. In the valley of the Berkshires, the tides of race ran calm, and the young Du Bois could brest them with arrogant disdain. He did not have the beaten-in feeling of combating an emotional force too wild and unreasonable to comprehend. This is not at all to say that he viewed race as of no importance. He realized even then, he tells us, that "color had become an abiding and unchangeable fact," and whenever he went to Bedford to visit his paternal grandfather or to Albany as a guest of his half-brother, he got "swift glimpses of the colored world and had veritable seizures of awareness of the Negro world's peculiar isolation, its tensions, and its precarious place in the economy of the surrounding white world." But he saw it objectively, and in impersonal terms, as a matter of social condition . . .

Only when he went south to Fisk and saw and experienced large numbers of black people in their daily struggle against the self-conscious instincts that were a function of racial prejudice did the emotionalism of the color problem hit him with telling impact. Only then did he begin to overcome his New England bred emotional constraint and the taciturnity that was a part of his Dutch heritage. Only then did he begin to lose his reserve and to sacrifice something of his inner life. But he never lost all of his reserve, his privacy. The habit of it was impossible to break completely. Though a handful of intimates of later years often found him magnetic, warm, and gay, from most people he kept a measured distance. He was considered aloof. Only among friends did his personality light up. His presence in a room full of people generally went unnoticed, except for those who appreciated the fine cast of his features and his beautiful head.

At Harvard, where he took a second baccalaureate in 1890 and a master's degree the spring of 1892, and at the University of Berlin, he was attracted to the relatively new discipline of sociology. This was especially true in Berlin, where the discipline, weaned from anthropology, psychology, philosophy, and history, but combining some elements of all these— since all knowledge is interrelated—had already obtained the academic respectability that William Graham Sumner would give it at Yale.

At Berlin, also, somewhat in defiance of the rigid protocol that characterized the relations between education and government and between student and professor, the strength of reform ideology had influenced some scholars to question, and to encourage their students to question, if not effectively attack, the whole existing conservative order and the imperialistic hold that Germany and other European countries, following England's lead, were establishing on what the exulting Rudyard Kipling called the "dark places" of the globe and, again to use a Kipling term, the "backward peoples of the earth."

In Germany, Du Bois, soon to be the first black man to earn a Ph.D. at Harvard, began to get it all together. Like Tennyson's Ulysses, he followed "knowledge like a sinking star." Not knowledge simply for its own sake, which is an indulgence of his practical idealism, and his concerned awareness of the worldwide color problem scorned, but knowledge purposeful, knowledge working. If he returned from Germany something of a fancy dan, sporting a Vandyke beard, wearing spats, and carrying a cane, as some of his would-be detractors gloatingly remarked, he also returned with knowledge that would make him "strong in will to strive, to find, and not to yield"; knowledge that would also animate an already indomitable spirit, and stock one of the most catholic minds of the century.

Yet, it is not a difficult mind for us to know. It lies exposed in more than a dozen major books, hundreds of editorials, articles, and lectures, and a scattering of poems. Dr. Du Bois' prose writings have the clarity and sharpness of anatomical drawings, showing the progressive stages in the development of an organism. In this case, the organism is truth. Du Bois used truth—the concrete truth of facts as well as the abstract truth of a humanistic philosophy—as a tool in the performance of the task "of probing and assaying the scope of chance and irrationality in human action." That he applied it only to the area of race relations was partly due to the traditional specialization of modern scholarship and partly to the personal need to maintain a careful balance between intellectual curiosity and emotional involvement. He thought of himself as the scientist . . .

After the *Suppression of the African Slave Trade*, his doctoral dissertation, which was described as the first scientific historical work produced by a Negro, and was the first volume published in the Harvard Historical Studies Series, and after the publication of *The Philadelphia Negro*, and in the midst of preparing his Atlanta University Studies on the Negro, he published *The Souls of Black Folk*, which, for all its erudition and lucid reasoning, is perhaps as subjective and passionate a book as any written in the first decade of this century. Discounting some editorials and again the poetry, several times in a long career devoted principally to investigation and research in material that generates passion—in material to which he was the first to apply the scientific method—he had to give himself a thorough emotional housecleaning. *Darkwater: Voices from Within the Veil* is a book like *The Souls of Black Folk; The Gift of Black Folk* is another; and the novels in a different way, are others, even when they read like history, and/or sociology.

What strikes me as remarkable is not that he indulged in these introspective sprees, but that he indulged in them so seldom and that they did not promote habits of thought and a manner of speech characterized by an incoherent and echoic jumble of invective and condemnation, exhortation and jubilation, apology and defense, such as we are being treated to by some of the current crop of black militants whose chaotic passions are matched only by their benighted ignorance of the historical situation and of the social circumstances that have made so-called Black Studies a necessary addition to the curriculum of American institutions of higher learning. As teacher-scholar, Dr. Du Bois would have known a sense of fulfillment from the best of what is happening along this line in higher education. Believing as he did that the solution to the race problem was "a matter of systematic investigation," as a teacher-scholar his professional commitment was to— and again I quote—the "scientific investigation into social conditions," primarily for humanitarian ends.

For a quarter of a century, almost alone among black spokesmen, Dr. Du Bois declared and believed that the basis for racial change for the better and toward interracial brotherhood was a knowledge of the facts and the broader truths they documented. His choice of subject for his doctoral dissertation and, subsequently, thirteen years of work at Atlanta University were posited upon this belief; and this belief was at the heart of much that appeared in the *Crisis* and, later, in *Phylon* under his editorship. He was the intellectual father of E. Franklin Frazier, of John Hope Franklin, of Benjamin Quarles, and a host of black—and some white—scholars. One who reads his chief works is bound to be convinced that whatever emotional overcast they have is inherent in the material and is not a quality of the treatment.

But Dr. Du Bois' scientific concerns—for that is the way he described them—were complicated in a way unknown to most professional scholars until the Second World War. When a group of outstanding scientists came to realize that the consequences of the application of their research and knowledge was the atomic bomb, they could no longer contain themselves as theoretical mathematicians, physicists, chemists, and metallurgists, and they could not see the atomic bomb as merely a great scientific and technological achievement. It presented them with a moral and social problem of universal proportions—and they were social beings. Thus it was with Dr. Du Bois. He was a socially responsible factor in the universal problem of race; he was concerned with the practical application of his discovered knowledge to the solution. This accounts in part for his controversy with Booker T. Washington; his insistence on programs of higher education for blacks; for his espousal of the Talented Tenth; for his founding the Niagara Movement and his later connection with the N.A.A.C.P.; and for his active involvement with Pan-Africanism.

These interests and activities were the function of a mind perfectly matched with spirit, the function of a vital awareness of the real combined with an equally vital commitment to the ideal. The reality forced him to embrace the idea of the Talented Tenth; but the ideal was advancement of all black people and he exhorted the Negro intelligentsia which, Truman Nelson tells us, Du Bois created, to lead the advance, to fight for equality with, I quote, "The weapons of truth, with the sword of the intrepid, uncompromising spirit." The reality of the Negro's status as second-class citizen, which Booker T. Washington seemed to accept as the stable state of American society, led Dr. Du Bois into political action, though it was often far from diplomatic, was somehow always the right action. It was rebellious, but not revolutionary.

He believed in the principles of democracy, and for a long time he believed that the machinery of American democracy could be made to work, and he tried to make it work. But in the 1940s, when he was already into his seventies, he grew somewhat discouraged, and this was signified in his advocacy of racial separation, which he viewed as a tactic. Negroes, he declared in the 1940s, "are now segregated largely without reason. Let us put reason and power beneath the segregation." And in another place he said: "Negroes could not only furnish pupils for their own schools and colleges, but could control their teaching force and policies, their textbooks and ideals. By concentrating their demands, by group-buying, and by their own plans, they could get Negro literature issued without censorship upon expression and they could evolve Negro art for its own sake and for its own beauty and not simply for the entertainment of white folks. Rail, if you will against the race segregation here involved but take advantage of it by painting secure centers of Negro cooperative effort and particularly of economic power." This he called "non-discriminatory desegregation" and it got him into trouble with the N.A.A.C.P. from which he resigned in 1934; but forcing him to resign was no more to be justified than his Federal indictment as an unregistered foreign agent seventeen years later, when he was in his eighties. Is it criminal to work as Dr. Du Bois did, for the realization of the principles of democracy? Is it criminal to advocate and work for Dr. Du Bois' ultimate commitment—the breakdown of all segregation based on color?

His joining the Communist Party in 1961 was not really inconsistent with this commitment. It meant simply that the halting, rattling machinery of democracy had at last broken down and Dr. Du Bois, as it were, merely changed vehicles so, hopefully, to reach the same destination faster. Nor was his going to Ghana, also in 1961, inconsistent either. He went to Ghana in the first place in order to work unimpeded by the need to scurry for funds on the long projected encyclopedia of the Negro which would supply—and now I quote—"The scientifically attested truth concerning Negroes" and this truth would ensure—and again I quote—"The survival of the Negro race not for itself alone but for the emancipation of mankind, the realization of democracy and the progress of civilization."

Langston Hughes and I visited Dr. Du Bois in Ghana in 1962. He was ninety-four then. Though he was shrunken and stooped with age and too much talk tired him, he listened to others with unwavering attention, and his eyes sparkled briefly whenever the sentiments expressed agreed with his own.

The mind does not always perfectly reflect the man or the personality. In spite of the tremendous respect which his accomplishments earned him, Dr. Du Bois was not generally liked. Many of the stories about him set him forth as a crusty, mordant-witted intellectual and social snob. He was, many stories say, a little too proud and full of himself. In the days when he still smoked, many thought his preference for a certain brand of expensive cigarette an affectation. Just below average in height, he was meticulous about his clothes, giving many an impression of dandyism which contradicted the popular image of the scholar and of the dynamic leader.

Yet it is the highest tribute, it seems to me, that even those who grumbled about the Du Bois personality acknowledge him as *the* Negro world leader from 1910 almost until his death in 1963. He did not seek the role of leader. His intellectual honesty in the search for truth, his prophetic vision, his all-embracing humanitarian spirit, and the fundamental integrity of his personality destined him to it. Everything you will learn about him . . . will support the fact that he lived in the faith that one day truth will make men free. And will support also the claims I have made for him. . . .

Editor's Notes: *Gustav von Schmoller (1838-1917), conservative German economist and professor who advocated an alliance between Prussian imperial monarchy and the working class as a means to prevent revolution.   †Rudolf Virchow (1821-1902), German pathologist and professor; a founder of cellular pathology, who also taught anthropology.

Paul Laurence Dunbar: A Reminiscence

I refuse to call this a lecture. Certainly in the formal academic sense it is not, nor was it my intention for it to be. I shall not lay out a series of assumptions and critical postulates or explore literary theories and scholarly resolutions to the various problems a close examination of Dunbar's work discovers—problems that are both narrowly aesthetic and broadly cultural, sociological and historical, psychological and metaphysical. One does sometimes get tired of both the means and the ends of academic scholarship and one gets tired of manipulating scholarly apparatus. I am chuck-

ing all that now. What I have to say in the next few minutes is in the nature
of a memoir, the recapturing of a memory, a reminiscence, if you will. It is
highly subjective, as of course all literary studies eventually boil down to
being. If I say flatly I like Dunbar and his work, or most of it at any rate, I
am making a subjective judgment which I straightaway qualify. I did not
say, remember, that I have nothing but admiration for the poet and the
writer. There are certainly components in his character and items in his
canon that are admirable, but there are also things from which one turns
with feelings of embarrassment. But let me get on with my reminiscence.

When I was a child a signed photograph of Dunbar hung over the
mantel in what was called "the back parlor." This room was separated by an
arched and curtained doorway from the front parlor, which was reserved for
the entertainment of rather special company, like a visiting clergyman or
other dignitary, and on one occasion, Charles Gilpin. He had come to
Wilmington, Delaware, to play the title role in *The Emperor Jones* in the
segregated and only legitimate theatre in the town. The hotels, too, were
for whites only, and for three nights and two days Gilpin was a welcomed
guest in our family's home.

I mention him particularly because after he had gone I learned in a
dinner table conversation between my parents that Mr. Gilpin had known
Paul Dunbar many years before, in the first half of the first decade of this
century. He had known him in New York, where black artists, writers,
singers, entertainers and figures in the sports world used to gather in
Marshall's Hotel in the San Juan Hill section of what is now mid-Manhattan
between Fifty-first and Fifty-seventh Streets west of Fifth Avenue. I
estimate now that the time of Gilpin's acquaintance with Dunbar was about
nineteenth hundred and two, or three, and Dunbar was no longer at the
zenith of his fame. The poet's best work in both poetry and fiction was
behind him and he was only three or four years from the close of his life.

And it was quite a life. In the operation of the vaunted American
system of values, his choices were severely limited, as indeed they were for
all of his black contemporaries. He could not really choose a career or a
profession. Indeed, he had yearned to be a lawyer. Nor could he either
accept or reject the hazards and the rewards of the career he was persuaded
to follow. And this matter went even deeper. His search for identity was
never completely successful because society never acknowledged him as
the person he thought he was. He could not choose to be wholly himself.
He had to make his life conform to one or another stereotype and to live up
to the white man's models.

This was not easy for him. It is difficult for any man to achieve a
definition of self in American society. You must find a slot to fill and a

category that represents what you feel to be the essence of yourself that you can take to heart and be a part of. If no category is available, you have to make one. To accomplish this on a personal level is difficult enough, but to correlate the view that others have of you with your image of yourself is far more difficult. Coming to early manhood in a time when Booker T. Washington's accommodationist philosophy seemed to give validity not only to the prevailing paternalistic concept of race relations, but also to the dominant stereotypes of the black man that supported the concept, the difficulty was compounded for Dunbar. Chief among the stereotypes he had to contend with or reconcile himself to was that of the Negro as an irresponsible child, completely dependent upon the largess, the good will, and the loving kindness of white people, and eternally happy with this state of affairs and in this situation.

Paul Dunbar knew that this was not the way things really were. He sensed something sinister beneath the prevailing attitude and he saw behind the interchangeable mask of degradation, self-abasement, and clownishness his people wore another people altogether. This generated in him a certain ambivalence, a kind of double consciousness he found it difficult to deal with:

> We wear the mask that grins and lies,
> It hides our cheeks and shades our eyes—
> This debt we pay to human guile;
> With torn and bleeding hearts we smile,
> And mouth with myriad subtleties.
>
> Why should the world be over-wise,
> In counting all our tears and sighs?
> Nay, let them only see us, while
>   We wear the mask.
>
> We smile, O great Christ, our cries
> To thee from tortured souls arise.
> We sing, but oh the clay is vile
> Beneath our feet, and long the mile;
> But let the world dream otherwise,
>   We wear the mask!

Forgive him if he gave some substance to that false dream in at least a hundred poems and a score of stories. The easiest way for the black man to survive in white society is to go with the flow. This passive attitude cannot be simultaneously held with an individual concept of existence based on individual pride and goals. A black man could not follow the dictates of white society and remain at peace with himself. A new, different, and personally established identity had to be created. Forgive him if in the days when he read his poetry to select audiences he made the dream seem real with mimetic performances and by dancing to the rhythm of his dialect jingles.

After one such literary concert in Newport, Rhode Island, a staid and imperiously aristocratic white lady rose while the all white audience was still applauding, waited for silence and said, "Paul"—she had never seen him before much less met him—"Paul," she said, in a most complimentary and gratified tone, "I shall never again wax impatient and cross at the childish antics of my servants, members of your race. Tonight, you have made me understand and love them." Following this remark, the applause was resumed more enthusiastically than before, and Paul Dunbar fled through a side door to an anteroom where his wife waited. There he dropped to his knees before her, buried his head in her lap, and wept convulsively.

Though there are many apocryphal Dunbar anecdotes, I can assure you this one is not apocryphal. I heard it from Paul Dunbar's widow, who besides being my high school English teacher, was also a family friend. She lived just around the corner and was occasionally in our home. She was Mrs. Alice Dunbar-Nelson then, having married sometime before a widower with two children who were my friends. "There was much bitterness in Paul which he had to suppress," Mrs. Nelson said more than once. If you play the game to survive, will the knowledge of your spiritual position keep you from being dominated? Hardly. Read *The Uncalled*, which, his widow said, was Dunbar's spiritual autobiography, in which, for the sake of credibility, he represents himself as a white youth. And in both *Along This Way* and *Black Manhattan* James Weldon Johnson suggests the same sense of suppressed bitterness and frustration.

But one does not have to go to these sources. Dunbar himself was very explicit. From London he wrote to a friend in 1897, "I see now very clearly that Mr. Howells has done me irrevocable harm in the dictum he laid down regarding my dialect verse." William Dean Howells was then the most outstanding and the most highly respected American literary critic. And what was the dictum he laid down? Here is what he wrote in the Introduction to Dunbar's first regularly published volume of poems, *Lyrics of Lowly Life*. He wrote,

Yet it appeared to me then, and it appears to me now, that there is a precious difference of temperament between the races which it would be a great pity ever to lose, and this is best preserved and most charmingly *suggested* by Mr. Dunbar in those pieces of his where he studies the moods and traits of his race in its own accent of our English. We call such pieces dialect pieces for want of some closer phrase, but they are really not dialect so much as delightful personal attempts and failures for the written and spoken language. In nothing is his essentially refined and delicate art so well shown as in these pieces, which, as I ventured to say, *describe the range between appetite and emotion*, with certain lifts far beyond and above it, *which is the range of the race. He reveals in these a finely ironical perception of the Negro's limitations*, with a tenderness for them which I think so very rare as to be almost quite new. I should say, perhaps, that it was this humorous quality which Mr. Dunbar had added to our literature, and it would be this which would most distinguish him, now and hereafter. (Italics mine)

Years later, Dunbar's bitterness found explicit expression in "The Poet":

> He sang of love when earth was young,
>   And Love itself was in his lays.
> But ah, the world, it turned to praise
>   A jingle in a broken tongue.

Do not think that the poet was repudiating all of his poetry in a "broken tongue." His righteous complaint was that his poems in standard English were slighted or completely ignored by an audience that seemed to think it ludicrous for a black poet to express in pure English the nice sentiments, the laudable attitudes, and the higher passions the blacks were assumed not to think, feel, and experience. But if we accept the testimony of his widow and the evidence of the poems themselves, Dunbar labored harder on and put more of himself into his standard English poems than those in dialect. In such pieces as "Black Samson of Brandywine" and "The Conquerors" he tried to establish his people's rightful claim to their humanity and their share in the American heritage. In other works in standard English, and especially in his lyrics—for his was essentially a lyric gift—he proclaimed his own share in the Western heritage of ideas and ideals, of wonder and glory, of moral victory, and the ever-present hazard of moral defeat.

So, what is Paul Dunbar's place? for certainly he has a place in the corpus of American literature. But as I did not do some years back, I would now demur at trying to establish that place on objective grounds. Subjectively, he inspired in me a sense of wonder for the richness and complexity of the real, though unseen world of the heart and mind, and he inspired in me an overwhelming sorrow for the fragility of the human spirit yearning toward the ideal. And that, I submit, is enough. And that, I hold, is sufficient reason for the honor this celebration bestows upon him.

This selection is from *A Singer in the Dawn: Reinterpretations of Paul Laurence Dunbar*, edited by Jay Martin (New York: Dodd, Mead, 1975), 39-44. The title is supplied by the editor.

James Weldon Johnson
and the Pastoral Tradition

In a book entitled *Some Versions Of Pastoral,* published in 1935,[1] the
English critic and poet William Empson set forth a definition of the
pastoral that differed from both the ancient classical and the later Eliz-
abethan concept, both of which comprehended poetry only. Empson's
definition more or less ignored the elements of form, of meter, and of
subject matter in order to emphasize technique and intent. He conceived of the pastoral as a "device for literary inversion," a method for
"putting the complex into the simple," and of expressing, in whatever
literary genre, "complex ideas through simple personages" and dramatiz-
ing these ideas through the imitation of actuality and the representation
of the concrete and the real: "Any work in any genre which sets forth the
simple against the complicated, especially to the advantage of the simple,
is a pastoral."

If one accepts this definition—and in view of the topic of our discussion one must accept it—it is scarcely to be argued that much if not all of
the fiction and a good deal of the poetry of the South is pastoral. Applied to
the one novel and practically all of the verses of James Weldon Johnson, this
critical proposition should not need to be documented. But unfortunately it
does, and for the reason that Johnson's use of Negro dialect has struck some
critics as the only defining characteristic of his verse, while other, kindlier
critics, hoping to redeem Johnson from the pejorative designation "dialect
poet" which so embittered one of his well-known contemporaries, have
ignored Johnson's work in dialect and focused upon such pieces as "Lift
Every Voice and Sing," "My City," "Fifty Years," "The Glory of the Day
Was On Her Face," and the seven Negro sermons in verse in *God's
Trombones.*

In the beginning Johnson did not seem to want to be redeemed. He
deliberately set out to write dialect verse, with, as he tells us in his
autobiography, "an eye on Broadway." If he judged these pieces to be
somewhat trite and trivial, he nevertheless declared himself "fully satisfied" with the recognition they brought him. And he wrote many "coon
songs" and pastoral lyrics in dialect, some of which his brother Rosamond
set to music for the stage, and some of which he included in a section
entitled "Croons and Jingles" in his first volume of poetry, *Fifty Years and
Other Poems,* published in 1917. In his own estimation the best of these was
"Sence You Went Away":

Seems lak to me de stars don't shine so bright,
Seems lak to me de sun done loss his light,
Seems lak to me der's nothin' goin' right,
    Sence you went away.

Seems lak to me de sky ain't half so blue,
Seems lak to me dat ev'ything wants you,
Seems lak to me I don't know what to do,
    Sence you went away.

Seems lak to me dat ev'ything is wrong,
Seems lak to me de day's jes twice as long,
Seems lak to me de bird's forgot his song,
    Sence you went away.

Seems lak to me I jes can't he'p but sigh,
Seems lak to me ma th'oat keeps gittin' dry,
Seems lak to me a tear stays in my eye,
    Sence you went away.

But by 1915 he had come to the realization of a vexing problem, and that was the problem of trying to depict Negro life and the Negro character in a language taken to be distinctly expressve of the Negro, but which at the same time communicated the wide range of human experiences and values. Dialect was limited and, as Dunbar had discovered, could not do this. Dialect was expressive of the pastoral component in Southern Negro life, but it had also been employed to reflect the cultural abasement of Negro life in the city; and wherever Negro life was lived, the acceptable mythology represented it as basically simple, irresponsible, mimetic, and, even in moments of pathos, amusing. The mythology was not created by the Negroes themselves. It was created largely, but, considering Washington Irving and J.F. Cooper, not exclusively, by Southern whites, among them J.P. Kennedy, Edgar Allan Poe, William Gilmore Simms, and Thomas Nelson Page; and it had been kept current by a host of lesser writers who, like those already named, used the mythology to justify an amused contempt for the Negro people. In short, the myths projected a life and life styles that encouraged the concept of the Negro as a lower species of the human animal. And this posed a problem for certain black writers which Johnson called "the author's dilemma," and which he defined in terms of the duty of the black writer to appeal to and to promote the receptive disposition of two audiences, one white and the other black. Dialect had been used primarily to appeal to the white audience, and it was not altogether a failure in appealing to the black, which had the heaven-sent capacity for recognizing and finding amusing the limitations dialect suggested. This audience's amusement derived from its knowledge that whites were incapable of perceiving the essence and the spirit which underlay the dialect. It was in-house amusement, coterie humor, nurtured by an ironic perception. But Johnson, who by this time—circa 1910—had passed the point of apprehending literature merely as entertainment, wanted to get at the white audience with the deeper truths of Negro life while avoiding giving direct offense to that audience's preconceptions.

But how was this to be done? His friend and early contemporary, Paul Dunbar, had tried to do it with dialect and to a degree had succeeded, but his approach was on the level of sentimentality, of humor and pathos, and when, pitching his appeal to higher levels of emotional and intellectual perception, he employed standard English to this end, he was rebuffed.

> He sang of life, serenely sweet,
>   With, now and then, a deeper note.
>   From some high peak, nigh yet remote,
> He voiced the world's absorbing beat. . . .

Johnson, too, had tried as a novelist in *The Autobiography of an Ex-Colored Man,* his only work of fiction, and he smashed into a stone wall of white indifference and even resistance to the recognition of the Negro as a complicated human being, all of whose problems could not be solved by the emotional and moral equivalent of a stick of peppermint candy. *The Autobiography* was the story of the development of a Negro youth from pastoral simplicity to complex sophistication through his experiences in some of the great cities of the world. Published in 1912, it sold fewer than 500 copies. And when his volume of poetry, *Fifty Years and Other Poems,* was published five years later, the few white critics who commented on it fixed their attention on the "Croons and Jingles" section and virtually ignored all the rest. Johnson wrote:

What the colored poet in the United States needs to do is something like what Synge did for the Irish; he needs to find a form that will express the racial spirit by symbols from within rather than by symbols from without, such as the mere mutilation of English spelling and pronunciation. He needs a form that is freer and larger than dialect . . . and which will . . . be capable of voicing the deepest and highest emotions and aspirations [of the Negro] and allow of the widest range of subjects and the widest scope of treatment. Negro dialect is at present a medium that is not capable of giving expression to the varied conditions of Negro life in America, and much less is it capable of giving the fullest interpretation of Negro character and psychology. This is no indictment against the dialect as dialect, but against the mold of convention in which Negro dialect in the United States has been set.[2]

By 1926 Johnson thought he had found what he sought—a form or language that held the racial flavor but which was also capable of "voicing the deepest and highest emotions and aspirations" and allowing for the treatment of Negro life and experience in all of its great variety. He thought he had found it in the Southern Negro idiom, with its syntactical and metaphorical peculiarities. He was laboring under this illusory discovery when he wrote "The Seven Negro Sermons in Verse" already referred to, which do indeed voice deep emotions and high aspirations, but which do not define the character of nor encompass the experience of Negroness in America. In this regard the Negro idiom is nearly as limited as Negro dialect. And the irony is that Johnson the poet's use of the idiom was a contradiction of all that Johnson the social and political being believed and fought to establish practically all of his life: the validity of the concept of the Negro as man, motivated by the same forces and responding to life's circumstances and experiences like any other man. The Negro is not different from other Americans except in the color of his skin, Johnson declared in his book, *Negro Americans, What Now?*, and in another place, "the sooner they write American poetry, the better."

Finally, Johnson both as poet and sociopolitical man would have been appalled by what is happening now in Negro writing and in the mind of the Negro community. The concept and the current use of so-called Black English would have dismayed him, although he was the unwitting god-father of the concept, and although it in great part succeeds in doing what he failed to make dialect and idiom do: it holds the racial spirit by symbols from within; and it is more flexible, versatile and truer than both dialect and idiom. Johnson would have decried it, and the more especially because it is the instrument of communication between Negro and Negro; because it is employed as a kind of thieves' jargon to express the delusory dif-ferences of perception and response between Negro and white, and be-cause it is a reflection of the contemporary Negro masses' conscious wish to keep the white man at arm's length and to reject so-called white values.

Johnson was all for promoting the receptive disposition of whites, for promoting understanding between the races; in short, he was for integra-tion. . . .

This selection is from the *Mississippi Quarterly*, Fall 1975.

Author's Notes: 1. (Norfolk, Conn.: New Directions Books).   2. "Preface," *The Book of American Negro Poetry* (New York: Harcourt, Brace, 1922).

American Foreign Policy and
the Third World

Redding—as Ernest I. White Professor of American Studies and Humane Letters
Emeritus, Cornell University—made this speech before the U. S. Senate Foreign
Relations Committee, April 12, 1976. The title is supplied by the editor.

Mr. Chairman and distinguished though absent members of the Committee, I am highly honored by the invitation to appear before you, but I think
I should begin by saying, first, that the time limit, which you justifiably
impose, makes over-simplification inevitable; and, second, that I do not
presume to speak for the more than twenty million Negroes in the United
States, whose deep sense of racial unity is not—contrary to the opinion of
certain amateur sociologists and the wishes of some politicians—a reflection of a monolithic structure of thought on the subject under discussion
here, or indeed, on any other subject.

But although I do not speak for Negroes, I think I can speak about
them with the authority that derives from being one of them.

Until relatively recently Negroes, I dare say like the vast majority of
Americans, had no interest in their country's foreign policy per se. (Few
Negroes, for instance, back in 1945 made any connection between foreign
policy and the State Department's designation of Ralph Bunche as an
official U.S. delegate to the first meeting of the United Nations Organization.) Until at least the 1950s our exclusive concern was with domestic
policy and how its fulfillment—or the failure to fulfill—affected us. What
we had minds for and eyes to were local, state and national laws, court
decisions, what the Secretaries of Labor, Commerce and Interior said, or
failed to say. We did not care a damn who was Secretary of State and what
his politics were vis-à-vis Europe, Asia and Africa—although we had some
faint sense that America's foreign policy in regards to Africa might be a
reflection of our country's domestic policy and practice as affected America's Negroes.

Not by any means as suddenly as a statement of the fact may make it
seem, but gradually in response to a series of circumstances and events, the
history of which need not be recounted here, this faint sense became a
perception that color and race, which are inherently meaningless, are not
only the focuses of passionate sentiments throughout the Western World,
but the symbolic means of distinguishing between those countries and
people who deserve the attention of the U.S. (in terms of preferential
consideration) and those who do not. (Let me say parenthetically—and I

think no observant person can disagree—that these symbolic bases for determining foreign policy have given the U.S. trouble as between Dacca and Delhi, Taiwan and Peking, China and Japan, in Guyana, and in the Islamic world).

By the beginning of the middle years of this century, this perception on the part of American Negroes had contributed to—if, indeed, it was not the primary cause of—a sense of oneness with all the non-white people in the world, but especially a sense of oneness with the uni-racial (though multi-cultural) people of Africa. I hope you will accept my apology for a personal reference. (When I was in India in the early 1950's, more than a handful of quote "radical" Indian intellectuals, politicians and civil servants asked me in passionate seriousness whether my people—meaning American Negroes—would join the rest of the colored world in a war (a "race war") against the West—a war which they predicted would come before the end of the century. The question shocked me then. It would not now.)

The perception I have been talking about helped to inspire the new cultural chauvinism of American Negroes and the separation of their culture from white American culture. This perception inspired the concept of négritude and the concept of black power; it brought about the proud use of the once-insulting racial designation Black (instead of Negro); and the adoption of the Afro hairstyle, and bubas and dashikis as modes of dress. This perception led to the discard of American "slave heritage" names, and Cassius Clay becomes Muhammad Ali; the political activist Amiri Baraka replaces LeRoi Jones. And this perception, supported by the stated policies and the public activities of the Congressional Black Caucus, the old line organizations like the NAACP and the National Urban League, by congregations of black officials on local and state levels and of non-professional groups, has created a deep and abiding interest in American foreign policy as it pertains to the non-white world: Asia, parts of South America, and particularly as it pertains to countries in Africa. American Negroes couldn't care less about America's European foreign policy, so long as it does not get us involved in war.

Still speaking only for myself, several things about policy toward the non-white world bother me. First, it is improvised, extemporized, ad hoc. It is a reactive *response*, but not to given African countries themselves: rather to what it is believed other non-African nationals are doing in Africa. There is nothing in American foreign policy that can be identified as even suggesting that we look upon the countries of Africa as viable members of the international community and as potential contributors to the progress and survival of the brotherhood of nations. Our recent response to Angola was not a response to Angola and its people, but a reactive response to the presence of Cuba and Russia; just as our response to Tanzania is a response to the Chinese presence in that country.

Second, this kind of response represents the differences of color and race that symbolize the differences between wealth and poverty, power and weakness, conquest and alien rule. It is a non-humanist response and it evinces no regard for the national independence, the freedom and the equality that the natives of African countries want and more and more strive after.

Finally I would say that the wave of the future is rolling left, and the sooner American foreign policy rolls with it, the less likely it is that the United States of America will be swamped.

Absorption with Blackness Recalls Movement of '20s

It is unhappily true that three of every seven books by and/or about Negroes now pouring into print can (and perhaps should) be ignored by all except the most conscientious social and cultural anthropologists and those department heads at our institutions of learning who have yet to be convinced that the field of "Black Studies" is now being overworked by well-meaning but misguided blunderers, "instant" experts, and self-seeking quacks.

What has been happening for the last several years, and will probably continue to happen for a good many more, is not unlike what happened in the 1920s. The context is different and so (if one plumbs it carefully) is the level. But then, too, there was a wave of popular interest in the black man, who was called the "new Negro."

Back then, too—and specifically in the "red summer" of 1919—white America was shook up when Negroes, in a "spirit of defiance born of desperation," declared themselves no longer willing to accept the status they had been forced into, and when in proof of this resolve they mustered a determined and violent resistance to aggressive white racism in Chicago, in Chester, Pa., in several cities in the South, and in the Nation's Capital. It was suddenly quite apparent—as indeed it should have been all along— that the boast of knowing the Negro (Mr. Chairman, I know the nig-gra), mouthed with arrogant relish by most Southern congressmen, was not only inane but false. The South did not know "the Negro" for the simplest of reasons: There was no such thing. There never had been "the Negro," though certain congressmen and novelists, preachers and teachers had persuaded much of the world to believe otherwise.

Facing something of a crisis of ignorance, which few cared to admit, a scholarly segment of white America turned to the business of learning about "the Negro," and sociologists at Chicago, anthropologists at Yale, and cultural historians at the University of North Carolina soon discovered that "the Negro" was a myth. But the general public did not, and has not, even now. Its interest, though widespread, was superficial and, as it turned out, temporary. The general public had neither the resources nor the will really to learn. It turned to its usual sources of knowledge: to the fourth estate, which reflected the public's own structure of artless biases; to the theater; to bookstores. It turned, in short, to news editors, novelists, playwrights, and essayists (and even to composers and performers!) who were as various in breadth of knowledge, level of talent, and depth of sympathy as Sherwood Anderson and Gilmore Millen, Claude McKay and Julia Peterkin, Eugene O'Neill and Al Jolson, Walter Lippmann and Arthur Brisbane— and on and on and on.

Black writers of the time knew that there was no such thing as "the Negro," but some of them (here unnamed) after a first honest work were overwhelmed, corrupted, and made cynical—in just that order of development—by the extent of interest and attention given such works as "Sweet Man," "Prancing Nigger," "The Blacker the Berry," "Lulu Belle," "Cabin in the Sky," and "The Jazz Singer." They went and did likewise. They catered to the popular interest in that misbegotten black stereotype—male and female—which was simultaneously irrepressibly comic, savage, apathetic, lecherous, sullen, and "a creature of instinct and nature . . . bursting with an animal zest for life." Some of the black writers of the time simply withdrew their talents from the service of telling as much of the truth as they knew the painful truth to be. And their excuse was pure cynicism: They were putting something over on Mr. Whitey by making him believe that things were the way they weren't. And, damn it, they were getting paid for it!

Most of the white writers on the other hand didn't know any better than what the myth taught them. Moreover, they had a socio-psychic heritage of contemptuous ignorance and fictional distortion to draw upon. They didn't want to know any better, or to have any other heritage. Certain scholars were making their disinterested assessments of the life and life styles of black people, and of how these life styles came to be, and of their relatedness to other life styles in America, but they were ignored. The creative writers were all for the familiar whimsies, the traditional humor, and the conventional horrors, and they pursued them in the conventional ways.

So, as I have said, a part of the past is being repeated in the present. The popular interest in black people is certainly there, and it developed out of a real crisis of ignorance that, this time, did not have to be. For there were all those philosophical analyses and scholarly works of 30 and 40 years ago that, had they got the attention they should have, would have served as sufficient forewarning of this present "Black Revolution." But some of these works, reprinted now, are as relevant and informative as they were back then. The revolutionary thrust toward black separatism and the mystique of Négritude—a spiritual return to Africa—became less difficult to understand when one reads "Philosophy and Opinions of Marcus Garvey," which puts the one in historical context and gives the other a philosophic perspective. Black revolutions are nothing new, and the present one would have come as no surprise to anyone who had read Herbert Aptheker's *Documentary History of the Negro People in the United States*, or John Hope Franklin's *From Slavery to Freedom*, or Benjamin Quarles' *The Negro in the Making of America*, when they were first published several years ago. These are first-rate studies which complement each other, and which, incidentally, silently indict the dangerous stupidity of those historians—some of America's most respected among them—who have left Negroes out of history. Respectful of the academic amenities, for they are themselves distinguished scholars, Aptheker, Franklin, and Quarles are no stodgy pedants. They do not pontificate. Their individual insights still hold up, and they let the historical facts speak for themselves.

This selection is from the *Washington Star,* May 25, 1969, and was condensed by the editor for this volume.

The Black Arts Movement: A Modest Dissent

Let me begin this essay, which I conceive as an argument against the Black Arts Movement in general and against that movement in literature in particular, with a statement of certain propositions that seem as demonstrably valid as they are necessary to a critical appraisal of Negro American writing.

The first proposition is that Negro Americans do not have a separate culture. Although ostensibly communal, their culture derives from and is in great part defined by their experience as black people in a predominantly white America. This is not to say that the cultural consciousness and the cultural activities and artifacts of Negro Americans do not have distinctive qualities, which may derive from their African heritage, but these distinctive qualities are not "racial" in the commonly accepted meaning of the term.

The second proposition—a corollary to the first—is that the literature created by Negroes in America is American literature, and that to segregate it from the corpus of literature created by other Americans—Bellow, Jewish-American; Theodore Dreiser, German-American; James T. Farrell, Irish-American; Lawrence Ferlinghetti, Italian-American; Scott Momaday, American Indian; etc.—is to do grave harm to the whole corpus of American literature as a resource for social and historical diagnosis.

The third and final proposition is that until relatively recently the literature produced by Americans of all ethnic backgrounds had little to do with *aesthetics* either as philosophy or in practice. Until recently, American literature—not excluding poetry—was created to appeal as much to the cognitive as to the connotative and affective side of man's being. Until recently, American literature self-consciously synthesized the "is" and the "ought to be," the "real" and the "ideal." Until recently, there has been no reason to modify the judgment expressed by John Adams and seconded by George Washington back in the Eighteenth Century: American literature has the practical aim of elevation and instruction, "to advance the interest of private and political virtues . . . and to polish the manners and habits of society." But putting literature aside for the moment and acknowledging that this judgment is no longer valid, there can be no denying that black and white Americans together are (and have always have been) the creators of the structural characteristics of our society and of the socio-cultural changes that modify those characteristics from time to time.

And now, returning to the main topic of this discourse, consider the fact that the categories into which American literature is traditionally divided are not descriptive of aesthetic concerns. We speak of the "Literature of the Colonies and the Revolution," and under this category include the journals of Captain John Smith, the chronicles of William Bradford, the diary of William Byrd, the sermons of Cotton Mather, the political tracts of Thomas

Jefferson and Tom Paine, the pamphlets and the autobiography of Ben Franklin and the poetry of Anne Bradstreet, Edward Taylor and Phillis Wheatley. We establish a chronology of Negro American writing and the chronogram is inscribed "Part One: 1760-1808," "Part Two: 1809-1863," or we denominate Negro American writers and writing as "The Pioneers," "Black Abolitionists" and "Renaissance and Rebellion." We refer to the "Beat Novelists," the "New York School"—designations that connote and conjur up social types, political ideologies and historical events and periods. And even when we do think of American literature as esthetics, generally we think only in terms of genre—fiction, poetry, drama, essay—modified by exegetical words and phrases like "proletarian," "realistic," "romantic," "revolutionary," "the novel of manners," "didactic poetry"—terms that tell us nothing about the esthetics of the novel or the poem. Until recently, when the native critic of American literature set out to examine that literature, he soon discovered that what a highly respected literary scholar and critic wrote specifically about the novels of James Fenimore Cooper and the poetry of Walt Whitman applied generally to the whole corpus of American literature. Willard Thorpe wrote, "The novels of Cooper are exercises in national definition. . . . Cooper [like Whitman in his poetry] sets out to tell his countrymen what it should be to think and act like an American."

And this is exactly the case with most of the literature written by Negro Americans. Either explicitly, as in the novels of Sutton Griggs, Langston Hughes, Richard Wright, et al, or implicitly, as in the poetry of Gwendolyn Brooks, Margaret Walker, Nikki Giovanni, and Etheridge Knight, Negro American writers tell Negro Americans "what it should be to think and act like an American" who is Negro. If one were asked to define the work of these writers in terms of esthetics, he would be hard put to say who are symbolist, imagist, or euphonist poets, and who write novels that can be defined as Gothic romances, picaresque tales, or fabliaux. Contradicting the opinion expressed by such critics as Addison Gayle, Imamu Amiri Baraka (christened LeRoi Jones) and Haki R. Madhubuti (christened Don L. Lee) and others, whatever distinctions there are between writing by black Americans on the one hand and white Americans on the other are the function of American socio-cultural history and not of race. It is pitifully ironic that quite contrary to Gayle, Baraka and Madhubuti's wishes as blacks, and to their disingenuous body of doctrine propagated to support the definition, the works of the most talented and representative Negro literary artists—poets, novelists, essayists—supply significant insights into what it means to be American.

The Black Arts Movement is predicated on the assumption that black people are *inherently* different from people of other races and that the difference, quite apart from the influence of learning and experience, embraces emotional, spiritual and intellectual incitement and response. The assumption is a snare and a delusion, but those who accept it are not either phony or mendacious. Harold Cruse was absolutely sincere in setting forth *(Crisis of the Negro Intellectual)* the metaphysical argument that being black confers a special grace under the dispensation of which American Negroes can and should disclaim and reject their history in America and be born again as "pure blacks . . . nationalistic in terms of the ethnic and cultural attributes of art expression."

Whatever this may mean to one who is not caught up in the social hazards, the intellectual dilemmas and the emotional complexities of the American racial experience, it quite evidently means to Gayle, Baraka, Madhubuti, Cruse and other spokesmen for the Black Arts Movement what Larry Neal, one of these spokesmen, defines as "a radical reordering of the western cultural aesthetic." Neal calls upon the "black artists" and writers in America "to create a separate symbolism, mythology, critique, and iconology." Lifted out of context, the admonition could be attributed to ignorance; but Larry Neal is not ignorant. He knows that symbolism and iconology are practically one and the same; he knows that iconology is symbolic representation in which the components are pictographs, and that pictography represents ideas and conveys information in pictures—such "pictures" as one sees on traffic signs and in places of public accommodation in most of the world; and he knows that mythology, which all cultures create to explain natural, preternatural and supernatural phenomena, is universal, and that the only differences between the myths of Africa, America, Asia and Europe are in the "persona" and the nomenclature, and not in thematic substance, and only rarely in dramatic structure. That these universals are not perceived and responded to by a universal consciousness is the result of group and/or communal learning and experience; and in the United States (until recently—and even now in great part) group learning and experience are dictated by race. But this is not to say—and, indeed, it is a long way from saying—that communal/group learning and experience are exclusively racial. History offers supporting evidence.

The literature of Negroes in America, like the literature of all peoples everywhere, derives from and more often than not reflects their experience. Since slavery time, the literature written by Negroes in America has its source in and is reflective of the Negro people's need to accommodate and adapt to a social environment in an emotional climate that, until recently, was as inconstant and whimsical as the moods of the gods. The felt need to adjust generated in many Negroes an impulse to reconcile and even—in extreme cases—to accept those opinions and attitudes about themselves that seemed to a great majority of whites justified by the visible evidence of Negro lives and Negro living.

When William Dean Howells (1837-1920), the most respected literary critic of his time, praised Paul Laurence Dunbar as "the only man of African blood and of American civilization to feel the Negro life aesthetically and express it lyrically," he was praising Dunbar's dialect pieces for what they seemed to suggest as the intrinsic attributes that white Americans ascribed to black: humility and patience, a talent for mimicry, amusing ignorance of the simple virtues, gross sensuality. In short, any and all characteristics that supposedly marked the black person inferior to the white. Before his untimely death, Dunbar deeply regretted accommodating his white audience's assumptions; but those poems of his that—by the very fact that a Negro composed them—refuted those assumptions were either harshly criticized as "imitations" (of white poetry) or completely ignored. Toward the end of his brief career, Dunbar wrote bitterly:

> He sang of love when earth was young,
>   And Love itself was in his lays.
> But ah, the world, it turned to praise
>   A jingle in a broken tongue.

Within a little more than a decade of Dunbar's death in 1906, interracial dynamics and the Negro American consciousness, operating in unprecedented ways, had produced the "New Negro," who aroused great and wary interest among whites. Negroes were no longer humbly submissive to overt prejudice and rank discrimination. White Americans wanted to know what had happened to the "carefree," "irresponsible," but "hardworking," "subservient" black Americans Booker T. Washington had promised them. White scholars sought answers. Robert Park of the University of Chicago, Jerome Dowd of the University of Oklahoma, and Howard Odum and Guy B. Johnson of the University of North Carolina published "studies" of Negro life that, by and large—and whether intended or not—were supportive of the opinions and findings of Negro scholars, thinkers and editors such as W.E.B. Du Bois, Charles S. Johnson, Roscoe Dunjee and Hockley Smiley.

Quite suddenly in the months immediately following the First World War, the Negro was the focus of attention. Whites went to Harlem, often as guests of prominent Negroes. They went to Harlem's theatres and night clubs, where they heard Bessie Smith and Ma Rainey singing the blues, and where they saw Florence Mills, Valaida Snow and the very young Josephine Baker beating out the "Black Bottom" and the first steps of the "Charleston." Things Negro were in vogue. By the early 1920s a white musician named Whiteman (Paul) was hailed as the "King of Jazz," and white Sophie Tucker, Helen Morgan and Ruth Etting, calling themselves "torch singers" and "red hot mamas" and the songs they sang—without even a nod in the direction of the Negroes who composed them—"torch songs," were belting out blues and ballads downtown in Texas Guinan's night club, and Delmonico's, and on the stage of the Palace Theatre; and soon thereafter a Texas blond was winning public acclaim as the "Queen of the Charleston"—a dance that all but Negroes credited her with creating.

Afro-Americans' reaction to this usurpation was an unequally proportioned mixture of pride, amusement and contempt. They were amused and contemptuous because Tucker, Morgan and Etting could not match the individual talents and sensibilities—to say nothing of the special American Negro consciousness—of Rainey, Smith and other Negro artists and entertainers. But Negroes were more proud than they were scornfully amused. They were proud because jazz, the blues ballads and the dances they had created were being accepted as genuine and authentic expressions of American national culture. As Alain Locke said in 1925, this usurpation meant "that the creative talents of the Negro race have been taken up into the general artistic agencies" and have become "a significant segment of the general American scene."

This was the first step toward the attainment of what was then heralded as the ideal. And the ideal was integration. Throughout the first half of this century, Negroes in the U.S. did not think of themselves in any except the American context. Though they defined themselves as Negroes or Afro-Americans, and although they knew they were set apart as Negroes, they did not think of themselves as developing a separate and distinct culture. Nor did they wish to. They knew, perhaps instinctively, that culture is the product of a people in a given environment; that culture-building and culture-possession are continuing processes, and that these processes are vitalized and set in motion by social circumstances and historical experiences commonly shared. And whether they knew it or not, the iron work that graces a few ante-bellum houses in Charleston and New Orleans, the spirituals, blues and jazz that give expression to a consciousness of what it is to think and act like an American who is Negro; the dialect poetry of Dunbar, a book entitled *Cane*, and a play, "Goat Alley," and much, much more were the cultural and artistic manifestations of a particular environment that can be defined only as American. To have thought and believed otherwise would have been to support those theoreticians at home and abroad who categorically affirm that Negroes are born inferior, and that no quality or quantity of education and learning can alter the fact and make them equal to whites; those theoreticians whose breed is presently perpetuated and represented in Richard Herrnstein of Harvard, and Arthur Jensen of the University of California (Berkeley) and William Shockley of Stanford. The leaders and spokesmen of the Black Arts Movement, the Black Aesthetic—call it what you will—give aid and comfort to such as these.

This selection is from the *Crisis*, Feb. 1977.

Selected Bibliography of
J. SAUNDERS REDDING

This bibliography is confined to published writings by J. Saunders Redding. It does not list reviews of his books, periodical interviews, critical evaluations, or unprinted speeches.

The writings are arranged categorically and chronologically by publication date. They begin with fiction, the genre in which he began and ended his career. His first short stories were published in literary periodicals at Brown University while he was an undergraduate. Three of those early stories are in this bibliography.[1]

After his retirement from Cornell, he was at work on a "novel in progress"—tentatively titled *No Score of Wrongs*, and later changed to *At Eventide*. His request was honored not to excerpt it for this anthology.[2] *At Eventide* was unfinished at Redding's death.

Fiction

"Delaware Coon." *Brown University Quarterly* (17 Dec. 1928): 3-4, 14-16. Reprint in *transition: An International Quarterly for Creative Experiment* (June 1930): 311-20.

"Osceola John and Peace." *Brown University Quarterly* (Nov. 1929): 5-9.

"A Gift of Beads." *Folio* [Brown University] (Dec. 1931): n.p.

Stranger and Alone. New York: Harper, [1950], 1969. Reprint. Boston: Northeastern Univ. Press, 1989.

"A Battle Behind the Lines." *Reporter,* 9 Jan. 1958, 29-31.

Nonfiction

Books

To Make A Poet Black. Chapel Hill: Univ. of North Carolina Press, 1939. Reprint. Ithaca: Cornell Univ. Press, 1988.

No Day of Triumph. New York: Harper, [1942], 1968.

They Came in Chains: Americans from Africa. Philadelphia: Lippincott, [1950], 1973.

On Being Negro in America. Indianapolis: Bobbs-Merrill, 1951. Reprint. Indianapolis: Charter Books, 1962; New York: Harper & Row, 1969.

An American in India: A Personal Report of the Indian Dilemma and the Nature of Her Conflicts. Indianapolis: Bobbs-Merrill, 1954.

The Lonesome Road: The Story of the Negro's Part in America. Garden City, N.Y.:
    Doubleday, 1958. Reprint. *The Lonesome Road: A Narrative History of the
    Black American Experience.* Garden City, N.Y.: Anchor/Doubleday, 1973.
The Negro. Washington, D.C.: Potomac Books, 1967.

Books Co-Edited by J. Saunders Redding

Reading for Writing (with Ivan Taylor). New York: Ronald Press, 1952.
Cavalcade: Negro American Writing from 1760 to the Present (with Arthur P. Davis).
    Boston: Houghton Mifflin, 1971.

Articles, Essays, and Book Reviews

Note: J. Saunders Redding wrote a weekly column of social commentary titled
"A Second Look" for the Norfolk *Journal and Guide* from April 10, 1943, until
December 25, 1943. Because of a disagreement with the *Journal and Guide*
publisher, he switched his column to the editorial page of the Baltimore-based
Afro-American newspapers on January 29, 1944. He continued writing there
weekly on various topics until June 29, 1946—when his column changed to
"Book Reviews." He was appointed the newspaper chain's book review editor,
a position he held for twenty years until June 4, 1966. During that period, a book
review or literary piece could be found beneath his by-line in the newspaper or
its *Afro Magazine* every week; he rarely missed a column, except while on
foreign assignment in India and Africa. His total columns from 1943 to 1966
number over 1,000 and are not listed here individually because of space restrictions. The titles of some of these columns were supplied by the editor for this
bibliography. Only a limited number of Redding's other publications could be
represented in this collection. Thus the literary and historical value of his
prolific canon is not confined to the works included below.

"Playing the Numbers." *North American Review* (Dec. 1934): 533-42.
"Mobbing." *Harper's,* July 1942, 189-98.
"Rosalie." Excerpt from *No Day of Triumph. Negro Quarterly* (Fall 1942): 255-76.
"A Negro Looks at this War." *American Mercury* (Nov. 1942): 585-92.
"I Believe in this War." Condensed from "A Negro Looks at this War" *American
    Mercury* (Nov. 1942). *Negro Digest* (Dec. 1942): 3-8.
"A Negro Speaks for his People." *Atlantic Monthly,* Mar. 1943; 58-63.
"Negroes in the North." *Journal & Guide* (18 Sept. 1943): 8.
"The Black Man's Burden." *The Antioch Review* (Dec. 1943): 587-95.
"A Case for Semantics." Condensed from 26 June 1943 *Journal and Guide. Negro
    Digest* (Dec. 1943): 4-7. [Round Table: "Do Negroes Want Social Equal-
    ity?"]
"What the Negro Believes." Condensed from 27 Nov. 1943 *Journal and Guide.
    Negro Digest* (Jan. 1944): 4-6.
"Is the Negro Problem Primarily a Southern Problem?" Condensed from 18
    Dec. 1943 *Journal and Guide. Negro Digest* (Jan. 1944): 4-5. [Round Table].
"It's in the Heart." *Afro-American,* 5 Feb. 1944, 4.
"Langston Hughes." *Afro-American,* 4 Mar. 1944, 4.
"Van Vechten's Gifts." *Afro-American,* 11 Mar. 1944, 4.

"Du Bois, Superior Man." *Afro-American*, 3 June 1944, 4.

"Honor in Politics." *Afro-American*, 8 July 1944, 4.

"Southern Defensive." *Common Ground* 4.3 (1944): 36-42.

"Here's A New Thing Altogether." *Survey Graphic* (Aug. 1944): 358-59 + .

"Snookie's Saloon Was Never Like This." Condensed from Aug. 1944 *Survey Graphic*. *Negro Digest* (Nov. 1944): 81-84.

"The Blindness of War." *Afro-American*, 4 Nov. 1944, 4.

"My Most Humilitating Jim Crow Experience." *Negro Digest* (Dec. 1944): 43-44.

"Justice to Japanese Americans." *Afro-American*, 6 Jan. 1945, 4.

"The Negro Author: His Publisher, His Public, and His Purse." *Publisher's Weekly*, 24 Mar. 1945, 1284-88. [Paper presented at Pembroke College, Friends of the Library, Brown University, 1944].

"On Universal Values: Richard Wright's Thesis." *Afro-American*, 21 April 1945, 4.

"Afro-Americans and Jews." *Afro-American*, 7 July 1945, 4.

"Hitler's End—Mystery or History?" *Afro-American*, 28 July 1945, 4.

"Postwar U.S.A." *Afro-American*, 13 Oct. 1945, 4.

"On Colonial Revolt." *Afro-American*, 3 Nov. 1945, 4.

"A Human Perspective." *Afro-American*, 8 Dec. 1945, 4.

"Homage to Countee Cullen." *Afro-American*, 19 Jan. 1946, 4.

"U.S.-Russian Relations." *Afro-American*, 23 Mar. 1946, 4.

Review of *All the King's Men* by Robert Penn Warren. *Afro-American*, 11 Jan. 1947, 4.

Review of *Africa and the World* by W.E.B. Du Bois. *Afro Magazine*, 1 Feb. 1947, M3.

"What I Think of Richard Wright." *Afro Magazine*, 1 Mar. 1947, M2.

Review of *Fields of Wonder* by Langston Hughes. *Afro-American*, 12 Apr. 1947, 4.

Review of *Slave and Citizen: The Negro in the Americas* by Frank Tannenbaum. *Afro-American*, 17 May 1947, 4.

Review of *Kingsblood Royal* by Sinclair Lewis. *Afro-American*, 28 June 1947, 4.

Review of *Masters of the Dew* by Jacques Roumain. Translated by Mercer Cook and Langston Hughes. *Afro-American*, 2 Aug. 1947, 4.

Review of *Knock on Any Door* by Willard Motley. *Afro-American*, 9 Aug. 1947, 4.

Review of *Up from Slavery* by John Hope Franklin. *Afro-American*, 11 Oct. 1947, 4.

Review of *Country Place* by Ann Petry. *Afro-American*, 1 Nov. 1947, 4.

Review of *The Negro in the American Theatre* by Edith Isaacs. *Afro-American*, 8 Nov. 1947, 4.

Review of an *Appeal to the World*, ed. by W.E.B. Du Bois. *Afro-American*, 21 Feb. 1948, 4.

Review of *Frederick Douglass* by Benjamin Quarles. *Afro-American*, 5 June 1948, 4.

Review of *The Story of the Negro* by Arna Bontemps. *Afro Magazine*, 17 July 1948, 10.

Review of *The Living is Easy* by Dorothy West. *Afro Magazine*, 24 July 1948, 4.

Review of *Seraph on the Suwanee* by Zora Neale Hurston. *Afro-American*, 6 Nov. 1948, 4.

"Portrait: W.E. Burghardt Du Bois." *American Scholar* (Winter 1948-49): 93-96. Reprint in *Afro Magazine*, 15 Jan. 1949, 9.

Review of *One Way Ticket* by Langston Hughes. *Afro Magazine*, 15 Jan. 1949, 2; and as "Old Form, Old Rhythms, New Words" in *Saturday Review of Literature* (22 Jan. 1949): 24.

Review of *North from Mexico* by Carey McWilliams. *Afro Magazine*, 5 March 1949, 4.

Review of *The Autobiography of an Ex-Coloured Man* by James Weldon Johnson. *Afro Magazine*, 12 Mar. 1949, 2.

"American Negro Literature." *American Scholar* (Spring 1949): 137-48. Reprint in *Black Expression*, ed. by Addison Gayle, Jr. New York: Weybright and Talley, 1969: 229-39.

"The Fall and Rise of Negro Literature." Condensed from *American Scholar* (Spring 1949). *Negro Digest* (Sept. 1949): 43-44.

Review of *Black Liberator* by Stephen Alexis. Translateed by William Stirling. *Afro Magazine*, 6 Aug. 1949, 4.

Review of *Annie Allen* by Gwendolyn Brooks. *Afro Magazine*, 27 Aug. 1949, 3.

Review of *The Story of Phillis Wheatley* by Shirley Graham. *Afro Magazine*, 8 Oct. 1949, 4.

Review of *Knight's Gambit* by William Faulkner. *Afro Magazine*, 26 Nov. 1949, 5.

"The Half-Century in Literature." *Afro Magazine*, 21 Jan. 1950, 4.

"Black Art, White Audience." *Afro Magazine*, 25 Feb. 1950, 6.

"The Significance of Carter Woodson." *Afro Magazine*, 6 May 1950, 3.

Review of *Simple Speaks His Mind* by Langston Hughes. *Afro Magazine*, 13 May 1950, 4; and as "What It Means to be Colored" in *New York Herald Tribune Book Review*, 11 June 1950, 13.

"The Negro Writer—Shadow and Substance." In *The Negro in Literature: The Current Scene. Phylon* [Special Issue]. (Fourth Quarter 1950): 371-73.

Review of *Montage of a Dream Deferred* by Langston Hughes. *Afro Magazine*, 24 Feb. 1951, 3; and as "Langston Hughes in an Old Vein with New Rhythms" in *New York Herald Tribume Book Review*, 11 Mar. 1951, 5.

Review of *Boy at the Window* by Owen Dodson. *Afro Magazine*, 10 Feb. 1951, 6.

Review of *Deep is the Hunger: Meditations* by Howard Thurman. *Afro Magazine*, 28 Apr. 1951, 4.

Review of *The Negro and the Communist Party* by Wilson Record. *Afro Magazine*, 14 Apr. 1951, 4; and in *New York Times Book Review*, 29 Apr. 1951, 6.

Review of *Introduction to Haiti: Selections and Commentaries* by Mercer Cook. *Afro Magazine*, 8 Sept. 1951, 4.

Review of *A Documentary History of the Negro People in the United States* by Herbert Aptheker. *Afro Magazine*, 1 Dec. 1951, 6.

Review of *Invisible Man* by Ralph Ellison. *Afro Magazine*, 10 May 1952, 10.

Review of *The Mark of Oppression: A Psychological Study of the American Negro* by Abraham Kardiner and Lionel Ovesey. *New York Herald Tribune Book Review*, 10 June 1951, 7. Also in *Afro Magazine*, 30 June 1951, 2.

Review of *The Far Side of Paradise: A Biography of F. Scott Fitzgerald* by Arthur Mizener. *Afro Magazine*, 28 July 1951, 4.

Review of *Spartacus* by Howard Fast. *Afro Magazine*, 15 Mar. 1952, 10.

Review of *Origins of the New South* by C. Vann Woodward. *Afro Magazine*, 29 Mar. 1952, 10.

Review of *The Life and Writings of Frederick Douglass* by Philip S. Foner. *Afro Magazine*, 14 June 1952, 2.

Review of *The Selected Poems of Claude McKay*. *Afro Magazine*, 14 Mar. 1953, 2.

"The Wonder and the Fear" [Editorial]. *American Scholar* (Spring 1953): 137-39.

Review of *The Outsider* by Richard Wright. *Afro Magazine*, 9 May 1953, 2.

Review of *Go Tell It On the Mountain* by James Baldwin. *Afro Magazine*, 16 May 1953, 2; and as "Sensitive Portrait of a Lonely Boy" in *New York Herald Tribune Book Review*, 17 May 1953, 5.

Review of *Simple Takes a Wife* by Langston Hughes. *Afro Magazine*, 13 June 1953, 9.

Review of *The Narrows* by Ann Petry. *Afro Magazine*, 12 Sept. 1953, 2.

Review of *Southern Renascence* by Louis D. Rubin, Jr. *Afro Magazine*, 10 Oct. 1953, 2.

Review of *In the Castle of My Skin* by George Lamming. *Afro Magazine*, 31 Oct. 1953, 2.

Review of *Maud Martha* by Gwendolyn Brooks. *Afro Magazine*, 14 Nov. 1953, 2.

"Report from India." *American Scholar* (Autumn 1953): 441-49.

Review of *The Souls of Black Folk* by W.E.B. Du Bois. [50th anniversary publication of book]. *Afro Magazine*, 28 Nov. 1953, 11.

Review of *Libretto for the Republic of Liberia* by Melvin B. Tolson. *Afro Magazine*, 23 Jan. 1954, 2.

Review of *The Negro in American Life and Thought: The Nadir 1877-1901* by Rayford W. Logan; and of *Breakthrough on the Line* by Lee Nichols. *Nation*, 14 Sept. 1954, 194-95.

"Alain Locke is Dead . . ." *Afro Magazine*, 17 Jan. 1954, 2.

"No Envy—No Handicap." [Review of *It's Good to be Black* by Ruby Berkley Goodwin.] *Saturday Review*, 13 Feb. 1954, 23, 40.

Review of *Black Power* by Richard Wright. *Afro Magazine*, 23 Oct. 1954, 2; and as "Two Quests for Ancestors" in: *Saturday Review of Literature* (23 Oct. 1954): 19.

"Hemingway's Nobel Prize:" *Afro Magazine*, 4 Dec. 1954, 2.

Review of *Eyewitness in Indo-China* by Joseph R. Starobin. *Afro Magazine*, 11 Dec. 1954, 2.

Review of *Black Moses: The Story of Marcus Garvey and the Universal Negro Improvement Association* by Edmund D. Cronon. *Afro Magazine*, 12 Mar. 1955, 3, 10.

Review of *The Strange Career of Jim Crow* by C. Vann Woodward. *Afro Magazine*, 6 Aug. 1955, 2.

Review of *The Mind of the South* by W.J. Cash. *Afro Magazine*, 13 Aug. 1955, 2.

Review of *A Good Man is Hard to Find* by Flannery O'Connor. *Afro Magazine*, 17 Sept. 1955, 2.

Review of *Sweet Flypaper of Life* by Langston Hughes. *Afro Magazine*, 24 Dec. 1955, 2.

"James Baldwin Miscellany." *New York Herald Tribune Book Review*, 26 Feb., 1956, 4.

Review of *Notes of a Native Son* by James Baldwin. *Afro Magazine*, 17 Mar. 1956, 2.

Review of *The Color Curtain* by Richard Wright. *Afro Magazine*, 26 May 1956, 2.

Review of *The Negro in American Culture* by Margaret Just Butcher. *Afro Magazine*, 6 Oct. 1956, 2.

Review of *The Peculiar Institution* by Kenneth Stamp. *Afro Magazine*, 10 Nov. 1956, 2.

"Meaning of Bandung." *American Scholar* (Autumn 1956): 411-20.

Review of *Giovanni's Room* by James Baldwin. *Afro Magazine*, 17 Nov. 1956, 2. Reprint in *Afro Magazine*, 8 Dec. 1956, 2.

Review of *Dylan Thomas in America* by John Malcolm Brinnan. *Afro Magazine*, 22 Sept. 1956, 2.

Review of *The Pictorial History of the Negro in America* by Langston Hughes and Milton Meltzer. *Afro Magazine*, 22 Dec. 1956, 2.

Review of *I Wonder as I Wander* by Langston Hughes. *New York Herald Tribune Book Review*, 23 Dec. 1956, 6; and in: *Afro Magazine*, 12 Jan. 1957, 2.

Review of *The One and The Many* by Naomi Long Madgett. *Afro Magazine*, 29 Dec. 1956, 2.

Review of *Pagan Spain* by Richard Wright. *Afro Magazine*, 9 Mar. 1957, 2.

Review of *Lady Sings the Blues* by Billie Holiday. *Afro Magazine*, 16 Mar. 1957, 2.

Review of *The Negro in the United States* and *The Black Bourgeoisie* by E. Franklin Frazier. *Afro Magazine*, 4 May 1957, 2.

Review of *The UnAmericans* by Alvah Bessie. *Afro Magazine*, 18 May 1957, 2.

Review of *The Ordeal of Mansart* by W.E.B. Du Bois. *Afro Magazine*, 1 June 1957, 2.

Review of *Simple Stakes a Claim* by Langston Hughes. *Afro Magazine*, 19 Oct. 1957, 2.

Review of *White Man, Listen!* by Richard Wright. *Afro Magazine*, 6 Oct. 1957, 2.

Review of *The Hit* by Julian Mayfield. *Afro Magazine*, 2 Nov. 1957, 2.

"A Plea for the Buying and Reading of Books." *Afro Magazine*, 18 Jan. 1958, 2.

Review of *Captain of the Planter: The Story of Robert Smalls* by Dorothy Sterling. *Afro Magazine*, 8 Feb. 1958, 2.

Review of *Here I Stand* by Paul Robeson. *Afro Magazine*, 15 Mar. 1958, 2.

Review of *The Langston Hughes Reader* by Langston Hughes. *Afro Magazine*, 19 Apr. 1958, 2.

"Tonight for Freedom." (Excerpt from *The Lonesome Road*, on Col. R.G. Shaw.) *American Heritage* (June 1958): 52-55 +.

Review of *The End of the Road* by John Barth. *Afro Magazine*, 4 Oct. 1958, 2.

Review of *The Long Dream* by Richard Wright. *New York Times Book Review*, 26 Oct. 1958, 4, 38; and in *Afro Magazine*, 15 Nov. 1958, 2.

Review of *Tambourines to Glory* by Langston Hughes. *Afro Magazine*, 27 Dec. 1958, 2.

"Advice to Writers." *Afro-American*, 18 July 1959, 2.

Review of *Henderson the Rain King* by Saul Bellow. *Afro-American*, 12 Sept. 1959, 2.

Review of *Brown Girl, Brownstones* by Paule Marshall. *Afro-American*, 3 Oct. 1959, 2.

Review of *Century of Struggle: The Women's Rights Movement in the United States* by Eleanor Flexner. *Afro-American*, 10 Oct. 1959, 2.

Review of *The Third Rose: Gertrude Stein and Her World* by John Malcolm Brinnin. *Afro-American*, 26 Dec. 1959, 2.

"Contradiction de la littérature négro-américaine." *Présence Africaine* Tome II, no. 27-28 (1959): 11-15.

Review of *Mansart Builds a School* by W.E.B. Du Bois. *Afro-American*, 6 Feb. 1960, 2.

Review of *The Story of the Negro Retold* by Carter G. Woodson and Charles Wesley. *Afro-American*, 13 Feb. 1960, 2.

Review of *The Bean Eaters* by Gwendolyn Brooks. *Afro-American*, 7 May 1960, 2.

"Negro Writing in America." *New Leader,* 16 May 1960: 8-10.

Review of *Thomas Wolfe: A Biography* by Elizabeth Nowell. *Afro-American*, 23 July 1960, 2.

Review of *An African Treasury* by Langston Hughes. *Afro-American*, 6 Aug. 1960, 2.

Review of *Cuba: The Anatomy of a Revolution* by Leo Huberman and Paul M. Sweezy. *Afro-American*, 27 Aug. 1960, 2.

Review of *African Voices* ed. by Peggy Rutherford. *New Leader,* 26 Sept. 1960, 16-17.

The Genius of Dick Wright" [Eulogy]. *Afro-American*, 24 Dec. 1960, 2.

"Richard Wright: An Evaluation." *AMSAC Supplements*, 30 Dec. 1960, 3-6.

Review of *Eight Men* by Richard Wright. [Short story collection prepared by Wright in 1960; published posthumously 1961.] *New York Herald Tribune*, 22 Jan. 1961, 33; and in *Afro-American*, Feb. 18 1961, 2.

Review of *The Chateau* by William Maxwell. *Afro-American*, 22 Apr. 1961, 2.

Review of *The Black Muslims in America* by C. Eric Lincoln. *Afro-American*, 17 June 1961, 2.

"In His Native Land" [on James Baldwin]. *New York Herald Tribune Lively Arts and Books Review,* 25 June 1961, 36.

"The Death of Ernest Hemingway." *Afro-American*, 7 July 1961, 2.

"In the Vanguard of Civil Rights." [Review of *One Hundred Years of Negro Freedom* by Arna Bontemps.] *Saturday Review of Literature* (12 Aug. 1961): 34.

Review of *Muntu* by Jahnheinz Jahn. *Afro-American*, 12 Aug. 1961, 2.

Review of *No Longer at Ease* Chinua Achebe. *Afro-American*, 26 Aug. 1961, 2.

Review of *Soul Clap Hands and Sing* by Paule Marshall. *Afro-American*, 28 Oct. 1961, 2.

Review of *Ask Your Mama: 12 Moods for Jazz* and *The Best of Simple* by Langston Hughes. *Afro-American*, 28 Nov. 1961, 2.

Review of *Reconstruction: After the Civil War* by John Hope Franklin. *Afro-American*, 5 Dec. 1961, 2.

"J.S. Redding Talks about African Literature." *AMSAC Newsletter* 5:1 (Sept. 1962): 4-6.

Review of *Fight for Feedom: The Story of the NAACP* by Langston Hughes. *Afro-American*, 10 Nov. 1962, 2.

Review of *Black Cargoes: A History of the Atlantic Slave Trade* by Daniel P. Mannix and Malcolm Cowley. *Afro-American*, 15 Dec. 1962, 2; and as "Sound of Their Masters' Voices" in *Saturday Review of Literature* (29 June 1963): 26.

Review of *And Then We Heard the Thunder* by John O. Killens. *Afro-American*, 26 Jan. 1963, 2.

Review of *Congo, My Country* by Patrice Lumumba. *Afro-American*, 9 Feb. 1963, 2.

Review of *Negroes with Guns* By Robert F. Williams. *Afro-American*, 16 Feb. 1963, 2.

"Home to Africa: A Journey of the Heart." *American Scholar* (Spring 1963): 183-191. Reprint in *Negro Digest* (May 1963): 80-87.

Review of *Something in Common & Other Stories* by Langston Hughes; *Five Plays by Langston Hughes;* and *Poems from Black Africa* ed. by Langston Hughes. *Afro-American*, 28 May 1963, 2.

Review of *Selected Poems* by Gwendolyn Brooks. *Afro-American*, 2 Nov. 1963, 2.

Review of *Freedom and After* by Tom Mboya. *New York Herald and Tribune Lively Arts and Book Review,* 3 Nov. 1963, 4.

Review of *The Stone Face* by William Gardner Smith. *Afro-American*, 23 Nov. 1963, 2.

"The Alien Land of Richard Wright." In *Soon, One Morning: New Writing by American Negroes, 1940-1962*, edited by Herbert Hill. New York: Knopf, 1963, 50-59.

"Invisible Man Over a Decade Afterward" [paperback edition of *Invisible Man*, by Ralph Ellison]. *Afro-American*, 1 Feb. 1964, 2.

"Modern African Literature." *CLA Journal* (Mar. 1964): 191-201.

Review of *Many Thousands Gone* by Charles Nichols. *Afro-American*, 14 Mar. 1964, 2.

Review of *Saint Genet: Actor and Martyr* by Jean-Paul Sarte. *Afro-American*, 4 Apr. 1964, 2.

Review of *Resistance, Rebellion and Death* by Albert Camus. *Afro-American*, 11 Apr. 1964, 2.

"Man Against Myth and Malice." [Review of *Mr. Kennedy and the Negroes* by Harry Golden.] *Saturday Review of Literature*, 9 May 1964, 48-49; and in *Afro-American*, 16 May 1964, 2.

Review of *Keepers of the House* by Shirley Ann Grau. *New York Herald Tribune Books*, 22 Mar. 1964, 4; and in *Afro-American*, 9 May 1964, 2.

Review of *A Moveable Feast* by Ernest Hemingway. *Afro-American*, 18 July 1964, 2.

"The Problems of the Negro Writer." *Massachusetts Review* (Autumn/Winter 1964-65): 57-70. Reprint as "Problems of the Negro Writer" in *Black and White in American Culture: An Anthology from the Massachusetts Review*, edited by Jules Chametzky and Sidney Kaplan. Amherst: Univ. of Massachusetts Press, 1969, 360-371.

Review of *Catherine Carmier* by Ernest J. Gaines. *Afro-American*, 19 Dec. 1964, 2.

Review of *Selected Poems* by Leopold Sedar Senghor. Translated with introduction by John Reed and Clive Wake. *Afro-American*, 23, Jan. 1965, 2.

Review of *Arrow of God* by Chinua Achebe. *Afro-American*, 3 Apr. 1965, 2.

"Tasks of the Negro Writer as Artist: A Symposium." *Negro Digest* (Apr. 1965): 66, 74.

Review of *Dark Ghetto* by Kenneth Clark. *Afro-American*, 12 June 1965, 2.

Review of *The Catacombs* by William Demby. *Afro-American*, 3 July 1965, 2.

Review of *American Negro Art* by Cedric Dover. *Afro-American*, 31 July 1965, A2.

Review of *Manchild in the Promised Land* by Claude Brown. *Afro-American*, 25 Sept. 1965, 2.

Review of *Betrayal of the Negro* by Rayford W. Logan. *Afro-American*, 9 Oct. 1965, 2.

Review of *Who Speaks for the Negro?* by Robert Penn Warren. *Afro-American*, 6 Nov. 1965, 2.

Review of *The Political Economy of Slavery: Studies in the Economy and Society of the Slave South* by Eugene D. Genovese. *Afro-American*, 18 Dec. 1965, 2.

Review of *Malcolm X Speaks*, edited by George Breitman. *Afro-American*, 22 Jan. 1966, 2.

Review of *Simple's Uncle Sam* by Langston Hughes. *Afro-American*, 12 Feb. 1966.

Review of *Harlem: The Making of a Ghetto* by Gilbert Osofsky. *Afro-American*, 12 Mar. 1966, 2.

Review of *Black Man's Burden* by John O. Killens. *Afro-American*, 5 Mar. 1966, 2.

Review of *In Cold Blood* by Truman Capote. *Afro-American*, 26 Mar. 1966, 2.

"In Search of Reality." [Review of *The Sign in Sidney Brustein's Window* by Lorraine Hansberry.] *Crisis* (Mar. 1966): 175.

"The Negro Writer in the United States." In *Anger, and Beyond: The Negro Writer in the United States*, edited by Herbert Hill. New York: Harper & Row, 1966, 1-19.

"Reflections on Richard Wright: A Symposium on an Exiled Native Son." [With Horace Cayton, Arna Bontemps, Saunders Redding, and Moderator, Herbert Hill]. In *Anger and Beyond*, 196-212.

Review of *Anger and Beyond: The Negro Writer in the United States*, edited by Herbert Hill. *Afro-American*, 30 Apr. 1966, 2.

"Since Richard Wright." *African Forum* (Spring 1966): 21-31.

Review of *The Proud Tower: Portrait of the World Before The War, 1890-1924* by Barbara W. Tuchman. *Afro-American*, 28 May 1966, 2.

Review of *A Choice of Weapons* by Gordon Parks. *New York Times Book Review*, 13 Feb. 1966, 26.

"A Fateful Lightning in the Southern Sky." [Review of *The Confessions of Nat Turner* by William Styron.] *The Providence Sunday Journal*, 29 Oct. 1967, W18.

"A Survey: Black Writers' Views on Literary Lions and Values." *Negro Digest* (Jan. 1968): 12.

"Literature and the Negro." *Contemporary Literature* (Winter 1968): 130-35.

"Black, Male and American." Review of *Richard Wright: A Biography* by Constance Webb. *New Leader*, 26 Aug. 1968, 22.

"Ends and Means in the Struggle for Equality." In *Prejudice U.S.A.*, edited by
    Charles Y. Glock and Ellen Siegelman. New York: Praeger, 1969, 3-16.
"Absorption with Blackness Recalls Movement of the 20s." *The [Washington]
    Sunday Star,* 25 May 1969, E3.
Review of *The Omni-Americans: New Perspectives on Black Experience and American
    Culture* by Albert Murray. *New York Times Book Review,* 3 May 1970, 6, 34.
"The Black Youth Movement." *American Scholar* (Autumn 1969): 584-87.
"A Writer's heritage." In *Many Shades of Black*, edited by Stanton L. Wormley
    and Lewis H. Fenderson. New York: Morrow, 1969, 87-91.
"One Revolutionary Impulse." [Review of four books.] *New York Times Book
    Review,* 16 Aug. 1970, 6-7.
"The Black Revolution in American Studies." *American Studies: An International
    Newsletter* (Autumn 1970): 3-9, (*American Studies International*, rpt. Summer
    1979): 8-14.
"Afro-American Studies" [Essay-review of three books]. *New York Times Book
    Review,* 20 Sept. 1970, 20, 24, 26.
Review of *Down Second Avenue* and *The Wanderers* by Ezekiel Mphalele. *Africa
    Today,* Oct. 1971, 78-79.
"Hiram Hayden" [In memoriam tribute]. *American Scholar* (Summer 1974): 381.
"Black Literature in the United States: An Historical Overview." *National Scene*
    (Oct./Nov. 1975): 9-11.
"James Weldon Johnson and the Pastoral Tradition." *Mississippi Quarterly* (Fall
    1975): 417-21.
"The Black Arts Movement: A Modest Dissent." *Crisis* (Feb. 1977): 50-52.
"Black Chauvinism and Black Culture: A Modest Dissent." *Brown [University]
    Alumni Monthly* (Sept. 1978): 12-17.

Printed Speeches

"The Negro Writer and His Relationship to His Roots." [First presented at the
    First Conference of Negro Writers, convened by AMSAC, New York City,
    Mar. 1959.] In *The American Negro Writer and His Roots*. New York: American
    Society of African Culture (AMSAC), 1960, 1-8. Reprint in *Afro-American
    Writing: An Anthology of Prose and Poetry*, edited by Eugenia W. Collier and
    Richard A. Long. University Park: Pennsylvania State Univ. Press, 1985,
    462-468; and as "The American Negro Writer and His Roots" in *Cavalcade:
    Negro American Writing from 1760 to the Present*, edited by Arthur P. Davis and
    Saunders Redding. Boston: Houghton Mifflin, 1971, 438-44.
"Equality and Excellence: The Eternal Dilemma." [First presented as Phi
    Beta Kappa Speech at William and Mary College, Dec. 1967.] *William and
    Mary Review* (Spring 1968): 5-11.
"The Negro Writer: The Road Where." [First presented at Boston University,
    1968.] *Boston University Journal* (Winter 1969): 6-10.
"Of Men and the Writing of Books." [First presented at Rockford College,
    Rockford, Ill. Apr. 1963.] Printed for National Library Week, Vail Memo-
    rial Library, Lincoln University, Lincoln Pa., 1969.
"Negro Writing and the Political Climate." [First presented at University of

Denver, May 1969.] Printed for National Library Week, Vail Memorial
Library, Lincoln University, Lincoln, Pa., 1970.
"Portrait against Background." [Presented for the Centenary Conference on
Paul Laurence Dunbar, 1972.] In *A Singer in the Dawn: Reinterpretations of
Paul Laurence Dunbar,* edited by Jay Martin. New York: Dodd, Mead, 1975,
39-44.

Introductions, Forewords to Books

Introduction to *Lincoln University Poets: Centennial Anthology 1854-1954,* edited
by Waring Cuney, Langston Hughes, and Bruce McWright. New York:
Fine Editions, 1954.
Introduction to Premier Americana Series, Fawcett World Library edition of *The
Souls of Black Folk* by W.E.B. Du Bois. New York: Fawcett, [1961]1967, v-x.
Reprint. New York: Dodd, Mead, n.d. Compiled in "The Souls of Black
Folk: Du Bois' Masterpiece Lives on." In *Black Titan: W.E.B. Du Bois, An
Anthology* by the Editors of *Freedomways,* edited by John Henrik Clark,
Esther Jackson, and J.H. O'Dell. Boston: Beacon, 1970, 47-51.
Foreword to *Good Morning Revolution: Uncollected Social Protest Writings by Lan-
gston Hughes* edited by Faith Berry. New York: Lawrence Hill, 1973, ix-x.

Posthumous Publication

Troubled in Mind: J. Saunders Redding's Early Years in Wilmington, Delaware. [Ch. 1
of *No Day of Triumph.*] Wilmington: Delaware Heritage Press, 1991.

---

1. One nonracial vignette, titled "Dancin' Monkeys Here!" was published
under the name J.*E.* Redding at Brown in March 1923—a year and a half before
J. Saunders Redding entered the University. It is not in this checklist because of
uncertain attribution. The piece appeared in a short-lived Brown literary magazine,
Casements, which advertised itself as "open to writers in colleges and universities
other than Brown, and to the younger authors." Unlike other contributors to the
issue, "J.E. Redding" was not identified; and many years later J.S. Redding did not
recollect the one-page piece as his own and acknowledged that most stories that he
wrote during his college years met with rejection slips.
2. Letter from J. Saunders Redding to Faith Berry, Jan. 31, 1982.

INDEX